A FATAL VERDICT

TIM VICARY

The second novel in the series 'The Trials of Sarah Newby'

White Owl Publications 2013

First published as an ebook by White Owl Publications Ltd 2011

Copyright Tim Vicary 2011

ISBN 13: 978-1482343786

ISBN 10: 1482343789

This is a work of pure fiction. Although most of the places in the book exist, any resemblance to real people or events is purely coincidental.

A Fatal Verdict

Tim Vicary

The second novel in the series 'The Trials of Sarah Newby'

Other books by Tim Vicary

Historical novels

Cat and Mouse
The Monmouth Summer
Nobody's Slave
The Blood Upon the Rose

Legal thrillers

A Game of Proof
A Fatal Verdict
Bold Counsel

Website: http://www.timvicary.com
Blog: http://timvicary.wordpress.com

Part One

Bloodbath

1. Minster Bells

THE MAN had been outside the door for over a minute now, just standing and listening. He could hear no sound from within; only the hum of the traffic in the street outside, and canned laughter from a TV on the floor below. But here, on the landing halfway up the steep, narrow staircase, it was quiet. His own door was directly in front of him, to his left the stairs continued to the flat above.

He bent his ear closer to the door, making a funnel for it with his hand. Still nothing. No voice, no sound of movement. He was about to straighten up when the door of the flat above opened. The man jerked upright abruptly as a young priest came down the stairs. He nodded at the flowers in the man's hand.

'Special occasion, is it?' he asked.

'What? Oh, yeah.' The man fumbled in his pocket, and held up his keys as if relieved. 'Thought I'd lost them.'

'That's good, then.' The young priest examined his neighbour coolly for a second, then let his eyes flick back to the flowers. 'Always best to make up.'

He smiled briefly and was gone, clattering away down the uncarpeted stairs two at a time. The man waited until he heard the street door open and close far below. Then he opened his own door with the key and stepped inside.

As he entered the flat the bells began. Not just any bells, but a tumultuous carillon of cathedral church bells in full voice. The tower of York Minster, the largest Gothic cathedral in England, was just across the city wall behind the flat, and the bells were a regular trial to the residents. As he entered the hall of the flat the sound came at him in waves, making thought difficult and speech at anything less than a shout impossible.

'Shelley?' he called out. 'I'm back!' But his voice was swept away like a squeak in a thunderstorm and as he expected he heard no response. He turned right into the kitchen and put the plastic bag with the flowers, the garlic and olive oil on the worktop. The vegetables - carrots, potatoes, onions - were already neatly peeled and chopped in small piles beside the cooker where he had left them. The two steaks, he remembered, were still in the fridge. Soft red meat on a bloody saucer.

He filled a saucepan with water and put the vegetables in. His fingers stayed in the water, holding one of the potatoes as though it might move. He stared at it for a moment, wondering what to do next. Then he withdrew his hand quickly. For Christ's sake get a grip, man, he told himself. Just do what you set out to do and it will be all right. But what *was* that, exactly? The vast sound of the bells made it hard to think. He looked around, confused.

The flowers! Of course - they were his masterstroke. A talisman to make everything fine. If it could ever be fine again, between the two of them.

But he had to try. Or appear to try, rather. That's what it's always been about with women, hasn't it, he told himself cynically. Appearances. Making things look right even when they aren't. Making them see things the way you want them to.

You can't change the past. But you can change what it looks like.

He found a vase, filled it with water, even remembered to tear open the little sachet of plant food and sprinkle it in before shoving the flowers in after. It didn't really matter, they were only for show, not to last. Nonetheless, do it right. Symbols make all the difference.

He carried the vase out of the kitchen, stepping casually through the disordered pile of Shelley's jeans, teeshirt, bra and panties on the living room floor, and arranged it reverentially in the centre of the small dining table by the back window.

The noise in here was tremendous. The window looked out over a first floor roof garden to the city wall with the Minster towering beyond, and the sound of bells crashed into the room like waves from a storm. His heart raced faster, his breathing came shorter.

About fifty yards away, a group of tourists were clustered on the city wall, some photographing the Minster, others covering their ears with their hands. If they looked this way they could see straight into the flat. If they had been there earlier it would have been embarrassing, he thought, but it didn't matter now; all they would see was a man arranging flowers on a table. There was frosted glass in the window of the bathroom next door, where Shelley was.

One of the tourists, a middle-aged Japanese woman, was in fact looking his way. He smiled mirthlessly, stood up, and, as though in some No theatre, called out again. 'Shelley? I'm back. Are you OK?' To the Japanese woman it would look like mime; he had to shout to make the weak chords of his voice carry even a few yards through the volume of sound produced by eight ten-ton bells. But there was no answer.

Steeling himself, he walked the two strides to the bathroom, watched all the way by the idle, innocently curious eyes of the little Japanese woman on the wall. He opened the door.

Shelley lay facing him, in a bath full of bright red water that covered most of her breasts, and dribbled into her mouth as her head lolled sideways like a broken doll. Her left wrist was out of sight, under the crimson water; the right hung limply over the side of the bath, pulsing blood onto the floor, where a kitchen knife lay in a red pool under the washbasin.

Shelley's eyes were closed, her face as white as the side of the bath. But as he stepped into the room something - perhaps the tumultuous, earsplitting racket of the bells approaching their crescendo - penetrated her brain. Her head rolled to the left, out of the water; her right wrist twitched up from the floor, smeared a red curve along the edge of the bath, and flopped down again.

It was then - even though no one, not even the Japanese woman on the walls, was watching - that he opened his mouth to scream.

As he drew breath the bells stopped, all together, so that his scream sliced into a sudden, humming silence. Then he turned to the living room, to grab the phone.

And Shelley opened her eyes, and saw him.

The ambulance was less than half a mile away. Having just delivered a pensioner with a suspected broken hip to Casualty, the crew were looking forward to a cup of tea in the canteen when the call came through. They were back in their vehicle and out of the hospital grounds in under a minute, and at this time on a Sunday evening the roads between York District Hospital and Gillygate were blessedly clear. Just two sets of red traffic lights to negotiate, the siren turning heads outside the Salvation Army Hall, and then they were there, paramedic Sally Barnes calling out the numbers on the shop doorways to her partner, Jim Swales, as he drove along Gillygate. Jim parked on the double yellow lines and Sally jumped out. Finding the street door locked, she leaned her thumb against the bell of the first floor flat labelled David Kidd, the name of the man who had phoned 999.

There was no response. Jim joined her and pressed his hand flat against all three bell buttons at once. After another wait an elderly man opened the door and peered around it cautiously. 'Yes?'

'Ambulance, emergency,' said Sally briskly. 'There's been a 999 call.'

'Oh, I don't know,' said the old man hesitantly. 'I've heard nowt about that.' He tried to close the door but Sally got her foot in just in time and the old man moved back.

'It's in the first floor flat, upstairs, sir. Please, let us through. It's an emergency.'

They hurried up the stairs and Sally would testify later in court that it was only when they had almost reached the landing that the flat door opened in front of them and a young man emerged. He looked shocked, Sally would tell the lawyers, his face pale, his eyes wide and staring. But what chiefly marked him out was the blood on his hands and his white teeshirt. There was blood on the side of his face, too, the left side, and his jeans and teeshirt were wet.

'Mr Kidd? David Kidd?'

'Yeah ... you're here already?'

'Where's the casualty?'

'In ... in the bathroom. I don't ...' He waved a bloody hand towards the flat but when Sally strode past him through the door he followed her quickly, blocking Jim's way and talking urgently.

'I just found her like this, I think she's dead, I tried to do what they said on the phone but it's no good, she's killed herself. God knows why, I did everything for her but ...'

By this time Sally had found the bathroom and was not listening, so she would agree later with the defence lawyer that she couldn't be sure exactly what David had said, only that he had found the girl in the bath and believed she had killed herself. Her attention after all was not focussed on his explanations but on the horrific scene in front of her. A girl collapsed in a bath full of bloody water. She lay slumped strangely sideways; her right arm hung over the side of the bath and was bleeding profusely onto the bloodstained, slippery floor, and her right leg hung over the side of the bath too. This had the effect of bringing her left knee, which was bent, right down to the bottom of the bath where the taps were, while her left arm was under water by her side next to the wall. Her head was turned to the left too, and her fair hair was wet and streaked with blood in a way that would later haunt Sally unpleasantly when she visited the hairdresser's and saw someone having highlights put in. But what immediately grabbed her attention was that the girl's face was underwater.

The young man was still talking. 'I tried. I mean I tried to give her the kiss of life but I've never done it before and she's so slippery and then you rang, I mean I did try but I'm no good at this and she's dead anyway, look I had this plaster ...'

He was in her way, Sally remembered that, fussing and talking while she went straight to the body and pulled the girl's face out of the water. Bloody froth dribbled from her mouth and nose and then there was a weak, spasmodic choking movement. Somehow Jim bundled the man out of the way and knelt to join her. He saw it too.

'She's not gone yet. Come on, let's get her out of this.'

There was no sign of spinal injuries, nothing to indicate other than that they should get her out of that water instantly, clear her airways to apply resuss and staunch that bleeding. The two of them knelt beside the bath and slid their hands in under the water to lift her out. It wasn't easy; she was slippery, as this man, her boyfriend or whatever the hell he was, had said, and floppy too, completely relaxed like a rag doll, or rather a doll with the weight of a tree and the consistency of a jellyfish. Sally had hurt her back the week before and this wasn't going to do it any good, she knew that as she lifted but there was no choice, it was a girl's life that was at stake here and that wretched man was no use, there was no point asking him ...

When they had the body on the floor they could see that the cut on the right wrist was much, much worse than the one on the left. The left wrist oozed blood, but this one was pumping - feebly, Sally thought, for an arterial cut but that was probably because most of the blood was gone already, out into the bath and now down the plughole, for in their struggle to lift the girl out of the bath they had dislodged the plug and that was where her life's blood was going, out into the city drains and down the river Ouse to the sea.

Most of it anyway. The rest was pumping out onto the bathroom floor, so Sally immediately jammed her thumb into the artery at the elbow while Jim fumbled in his bag for a tourniquet which he tightened just above the elbow, watching and turning until the flow was cut off. But all the while they did this it was not possible to attend to her breathing, other than to push the girl's head to one side and hope that the airway would clear. It must have been nearly a minute, maybe two, before Sally could leave Jim to attend to the bleeding while she turned her attention to the possibility that their patient was drowning as well as bleeding to death.

They didn't have to check for a pulse - the feeble pulsing of the arterial blood had shown that the heart had not yet given up. But the pink frothy blood dribbling from the mouth was a terrible sign - it was different from the bloody bathwater which came up too when Sally pressed her chest - more like froth on beer, the colour of strawberry mousse. Still, when Sally checked the airway there was no obvious blockage. Breathing was hard to detect. It was faint but still there, surely it must be? Then the girl choked and coughed up more froth and she was sure of it.

'She's killed herself, hasn't she? I don't know why. She's cut her wrists and killed herself, that's what she's done.'

'Not yet.' Sally glanced contemptuously at the man hovering uselessly in the doorway. 'You're in luck. She's still alive, so far, anyway.' Later that evening she would remember how she'd said '*You're* in luck' rather than '*She's* in luck' or '*We're* in luck' and wonder whether she had meant anything by it or if it was just a slip of the tongue. And she would decide no, it wasn't a slip of the tongue, it was exactly what she meant. Whatever had happened to the young woman this man must have caused it or been responsible in some way, and so *he* was lucky and should be grateful that she wasn't dead. Or not dead yet, anyway.

But if he was grateful he didn't seem so. He simply looked more shocked than ever and stood there in the bathroom doorway repeating himself: 'She must be dead, she's killed herself. Look at all that blood, I don't know why she did it, I wasn't here. God, she must be dead by now, surely ...'

Jim and Sally had no time to listen to this, they had urgent decisions to make. Jim stood up, put an arm on the man's shoulder to push him aside. 'I'll get the stretcher.'

While he was away Sally put a pressure bandage on the girl's left wrist, to stop the blood which was oozing everywhere, though with nothing like the force of the arterial blood which had pumped from the right. As she was doing it the boyfriend - what was he called, David something? - came back into the bathroom and bent over her. He picked up something from the floor, a wet bloodstained piece of elastoplast, and waved it at her.

'I tried to do that with this, but it wouldn't stick, she was too wet I suppose, but you've had practice, haven't you? But I did try, you see that, I did my best, it's just that I don't know how ...'

'Yeah, well, it would have helped if you'd pulled the plug, wouldn't it?'

The moment the remark had left her lips Sally regretted it, knowing how unprofessional it was, how it could easily get her into trouble before a disciplinary enquiry. She had had extensive training in dealing with people who had witnessed an accident, had been told again and again how they were often in shock, and couldn't be blamed for what they did or said in a crisis which came on them out of the blue, without warning. She also knew that they remembered things, sometimes with blinding intensity because of the horror of the moment, and an unguarded remark imputing blame to an innocent bystander could plunge some people into an abyss of post-traumatic guilt from which they would emerge, if at all, only with psychiatric help. The fact that she had taken an instant dislike to this young man was her problem, something she, as a professional, was trained to deal with and to ignore. The disciplinary panel would confront her with all this, and more, if she ever had to face it.

So as soon as the remark had left her she tried, as quickly as she could, to retract it. 'Anyway that doesn't matter now. She's still breathing, see? If she hasn't lost too much blood and we get her in quick she has a chance, at least. You may have phoned just in time.'

But her first remark must have gone deeper than she thought, for this only elicited silence. She finished the pressure bandage, checked the girl's airway again and felt for the faint but still discernible pulse in her neck, then glanced over her shoulder at the boyfriend. He was watching her with a look of - what? Terror, she thought impulsively. And something like loathing too, as though the naked girl on the bathroom floor was some sort of monster that any moment might come alive and destroy him.

'Do you mean she's not going to die?' he whispered. 'She hasn't killed herself?'

'She has a chance,' Sally answered. 'That's all I'm saying. Just a chance, if we're quick.'

'Then I want to come,' he said. 'I've got to come with her. To the hospital.'

'Not in the ambulance,' said Sally. He wasn't the sort of relative she wanted to cope with while trying to save this girl's life. 'You'll be in the way.'

'But I've got to,' the young man insisted. 'She can't talk, so I ...'

'It's not up to me,' said Sally. 'Ask them.' She pointed to the door where Jim had just come in with the stretcher. And behind Jim, two uniformed policemen.

2. Garden Party

THE INVITATION to a garden party had been on the mantlepiece for a week. The man to whom it was addressed, Detective Inspector Terry Bateman, was pleased, even excited by it. But his two daughters, Jessica, 10, and Esther, 8, were not. Basically, they didn't want to go.

'It'll be boring' Jessica said. 'Terminally dull. A lot of grown-ups yakking and patting us on the head - if they notice us at all.'

'Why can't we go to the sea with Trude?' asked Esther. 'I want to catch crabs.'

'Because Trude's going to Leeds with her boyfriend. She's been looking forward to it for weeks. Anyway, it'll be fun,' their father insisted vainly. 'You'll enjoy it when you get there.'

None of them believed this, but Terry felt he had to try. This sort of problem was one of the recurring themes of juggling his career with his life as a single parent. He was the senior detective on call that weekend so he couldn't take the children to the sea, and if anything serious did crop up he had no one to leave them with either. He had made several phone calls to parents of his daughters' friends, without luck - either they were going away to grandparents or it turned out that, unbeknown to him, the little girls had fallen out, and the mother he was speaking to was no longer the parent of Esther's best friend as she had been last week, but of the person she hated most in all the world. Terry's sister, Susan, was away in Newcastle and Trude, their Norwegian nanny, wouldn't be back from Leeds until six. So they had to go.

At first, it turned out well. Sarah Newby, the barrister who was hosting the party, had put her 17-year-old daughter Emily in charge of entertaining her youngest guests. Another barrister had brought his family as well, so Emily and her boyfriend Larry had organized an elaborate treasure hunt which took the children all over the house, garden and fields outside on the river bank searching for clues. After that there was food, and choice of croquet on the lawn, organized by Sarah's husband Bob, or a rope swing which Larry had hung from the branch of an oak tree at the end of the garden, under which he had placed a plastic paddling pool which Emily had found in the loft.

'There are plenty of towels,' Sarah said, smiling, as they watched Esther and a six-year-old little boy run shrieking across the lawn in their knickers, covered with water and grass cuttings. 'It's good to see them having fun.'

'Yes,' Terry said. 'They were dreading it, you know. Grown-up party, lots of lawyers - what could be worse, from their point of view?'

Sarah wrinkled her nose, swatting away a fly. 'Yes, well, even lawyers are human - at weekends, anyway. Maybe they're learning that.'

On the lawn, a dozen or so casually dressed middle-class adults gave every impression of politely enjoying themselves. Terry's ten-year-old, Jessica, had teamed up with Sarah's colleague, Savendra Bhose, in a fiercely competitive croquet match against his fiancée, Belinda, and Sarah's husband Bob. Emily was involved in an intense debate with two handsome young lawyers about the importance of anti-globalisation protests. And Sarah's solicitor friend, Lucy Parsons, a comfortable lady in a vast flowery summer frock, was sharing a huge bowl of strawberries and cream with a diminutive judge who seemed, like her, to be an expert on Yorkshire cricket.

'How's your son, Simon?'

A frown clouded Sarah's face, shadowing her pleasure at the afternoon's success. Idiot! Terry thought. Why bring that up? But then it was Sarah's son, Simon, who had brought them together, a year ago, when Sarah had successfully defended Simon against a murder charge, and Terry's investigations had finally proved his innocence. A traumatic time, that none of them would ever forget. But even though the boy was innocent, Terry knew, he was not an easy character.

'Oh, he's ... fine, I think. He might drop in later, he said, with his new girlfriend. But ...' Sarah shrugged apologetically. 'It's not really his scene, all this. Never has been.'

'No.' Terry wished he hadn't mentioned it. Simon was Sarah's son by a working class boy who had got her pregnant when she was fifteen. He'd been the reason she had dropped out of school, and had to work her way up to her present position through years of study at evening classes, fitting in her son, and later her daughter, Emily, where she could. Imagining the years of study that must have involved, with children clinging to her knees, Terry could only marvel at the iron determination that had enabled her to do it.

I couldn't do that, Terry thought. Not now. It's all I can do to hang on to the job I've got. He had become a single parent when his wife, Mary, was killed two years ago in a car crash. At the time he'd been a successful detective inspector every prospect of rising higher. But since then, the relentless pressure of juggling career and family, of ensuring that there was always someone available to care for his daughters, and deal with their illnesses, their traumas at school, their excessively long holidays, their pets ... it had nearly driven him out of the service. Criminals didn't work school hours, after all - quite the opposite. He had survived somehow, but he was not the detective he had once been; he knew that. So the idea of combining the care of young children with further study, as Sarah Newby had done for so many years - well, it was out of the question.

Of course she'd had Bob's help, Terry thought, watching the lanky, bearded head teacher miss his shot at a croquet hoop - but then he had a full-time job as well. Except for school holidays; that would have helped a bit. Terry tensed as the man leaned over Jessica to help her with her shot. Was that paternal jealousy, or something else? He had never liked Sarah's husband. He remembered how the wretched man had panicked last year when his daughter Emily disappeared, and even, at one stage, informed against Sarah's son to the police.

How had she stayed with him, after that? Terry had often longed to ask her but dared not. Each marriage, after all, was a mystery individual to itself. And his dislike of Bob was inversely proportional to his attraction to Sarah. More than once since last year, the thought had crossed his mind that if her marriage *were* to break down ... a familiar daydream entered his mind and was dismissed sternly. After all, even if she were interested, what sort of stepmother would she make for his daughters, really? A career woman whose own teenage daughter had run away from home screaming about parental neglect, and sent the police, including Terry, scouring the county in search of her?

Thank God she'd come back alive! Remembering that search, Terry looked across the lawn at Sarah's daughter Emily. No sign of sulks or recriminations now - just a pretty teenage girl full of youth and life and laughter. Barefoot in a rather damp summer dress, she stood, champagne glass in hand, arguing passionately with two young lawyers. Will my Jessica grow to look like that, Terry wondered. If she does, how will I react to young men like these two, who are not really interested in what the girl's saying at all, but in the way her left foot, wet and stained with grass from playing with the children in the pool, rubs unconsciously against the ankle chain on the right ...

Sarah laughed softly, following his gaze. 'Just you wait until your kids are teenagers, Terry. You've got it all coming.'

'No, please! Things are hard enough already.'

'Nonsense.' Sarah smiled as Esther let go of the rope swing and fell, screaming with delight, into the paddling pool, showering her sister with water. 'Your kids are delightful. They're at the best stage - all energy and innocence and no hormones. Enjoy it while it lasts. I wish I had, more than I did.'

Before Terry could answer, they were interrupted. Savendra Bhose, a handsome young Indian barrister in his late twenties, stood in front of them, a croquet mallet slung casually over his right shoulder. 'What are you wishing for now, old lady? More money? A more beautiful house? It's hardly possible, surely?'

Terry had crossed swords with this young man a few times in court. Like most barristers, he was bright, sharp and arrogant; an attitude difficult for older policemen to take. It was because they qualified so young, having known nothing but praise and success since school, Terry thought. They observed real life from a distance but it didn't touch them, not in the way that it touched policemen who worked the streets. That was what was different about Sarah: real life had got its claws into her from the beginning, dragging her down as she heaved her way up the ladder of success, carrying her kids on her back. She'd achieved her first chambers tenancy when she was maybe fifteen years older than this smooth public schoolboy.

Yet Sarah liked this Savendra, it seemed, and he had been jolly enough with Terry's children today. He smiled at Sarah now, sliding his left arm affectionately around the waist of a slender brunette who followed him across the lawn, the heels of her sandals making her hips sway enticingly in long white trousers.

'Belinda says if you and Bob have a house like this then she wants one too. As soon as we are married, she says.'

The girl nestled affectionately into her fiancé's shoulder, smiling up at him. 'As a wedding gift. You're a rich lawyer, Savvy, you promised.'

'Rich? At the criminal bar?' Savendra sighed. 'You're living in a dream, my dear. This woman has a highly paid husband.'

'And a friendly bank,' said Sarah. 'They own most of it. Apart from the kitchen.'

'Then you must find a nice juicy murder trial to defend,' Belinda pleaded, affecting a little girly voice that irritated Terry deeply. 'One that goes on for weeks and weeks, gets in all the papers, and earns you thousands and thousands of pounds.'

God, the girl doesn't know what she's talking about, thought Terry. If she'd seen the photos, the bodies, the relatives ...

'That would keep me up all night,' said Savendra, smiling indulgently. 'Up working, I mean. That's not what you want, is it, honey?'

Belinda blushed prettily, and a look, based on a thought similar to Terry's, passed between Sarah and Savendra. Not quite such a fool then, this young man, Terry thought. It was something he had often hated about lawyers, the casual way so many of them treated serious crime, as though were an intellectual game - *a game of proof,* as Sarah had once called it, rather than the serious, painful, bloodstained matter it was.

But this was a garden party, in a pleasant village home with beautiful lawns and willow trees, leading down to meadows where cows grazed next to a river bank. There was birdsong, friendly conversation, good food and wine, sunshine, a pleasant cooling breeze and the happy screams of children. The surface of life as it was meant to be. And this was all real, too, Terry told himself. Just as real as the grime of the streets. The young woman, Belinda, had no more conception of the reality of murder, probably, than his little daughter Esther did. Why should she have?

He smiled at Sarah. 'It's a perfect afternoon.'

Then his mobile phone rang.

3. Knife and Flowers

IT HAD not been easy for Terry to leave the party. The phone call had come just at the time when Esther had stung her arm on a nettle and decided she had had enough, so he had tears and a mini tantrum to cope with for starters. Jessica, bless her, had been very helpful and found a dock leaf for the stings, and Sarah Newby had been fine, saying of course they could stay as long as they liked and sending Emily to look for a box of choc-ices in the freezer, but she had been distracted just at that moment by the arrival of her son Simon with a new girlfriend with studs in her nose, and however jolly and friendly the other lawyers were they were a bunch of adult strangers as far as Jessica and Esther were concerned.

Trude would pick the girls up soon after six, he assured Sarah, and he sent Trude a text message to confirm where they were. But it was all a familiar, heart-wrenching mess. He left Esther sitting on Emily's lap, her face and dress covered with tears, chocolate and ice-cream. No chance now of talking about the fun they had had earlier; that was all for Trude. The girls would be in bed long before Terry got home.

But on the phone, Detective Sergeant Tracy Litherland had been emphatic. An attempted suicide, suspicious circumstances, could be attempted murder. Incidents didn't get a lot more serious than that, and Terry was the senior detective on call. He had to go.

Bill Rankin, one of the two uniformed constables who had first answered the 999 call, let him into the flat. As he came in, Tracy Litherland glanced at him apologetically.

'Sorry to call you out, sir, but it does look serious.'

'It had better be.' Whatever he did he was in the wrong place, he thought irritably - if he had stayed with his children, he would have been neglecting his job; but now he was here, he was neglecting his children.

'This is where it happened, sir, from what we can make out.' Noting the scowl on his face, Tracy Litherland adopted a quiet, businesslike approach.

She led him through the tiny hall into the living room, where they stepped over a litter of scattered female clothing to the bathroom door. 'The paramedics found her in there, sir. Wrists slashed and her face under water, they said.'

Terry and Tracy contemplated the bathroom in silence. Under normal circumstances it would have been pleasant enough; the bathroom fittings were new, the walls tiled with attractive patterns of seaweed and fish. But pools of bloody water disfigured the floor, and the bath itself had a bright red ring around it halfway up where the surface of the water had been, and a long red smear of blood leading to the plughole. There was blood on the wall tiles too, and on the outside of the bath next to the basin. Always, when confronted with a scene like this, Terry had to consciously steel himself, close down the shutters in his mind against the memory of how his wife Mary had died, crushed in the wreckage of her own car. How much blood there must have been then, too.

It was the work of a moment but Tracy noticed. The way his eyes closed, his body tensed, the deep breath that was let out slowly. She had seen it before, they all had. Some pitied him for it and thought he was over the hill, but for her own part she respected the strength that allowed him to face it and carry on. He made mistakes from time to time, they all did; but he had also been spectacularly right when almost everyone else, in particular their boss DCI Will Churchill, had been wrong. And for that reason there was a tension in the department. Churchill's supporters longed for Terry to make a mistake, others fervently hoped that he would not. Most of them knew that if his wife had not died when she did, he would have got the job that Churchill now had; Tracy for one thought the department would be a better place if he had.

On the floor underneath the basin lay a kitchen knife with a black handle. Terry picked the knife up with a plastic evidence bag folded over his hand, and sealed it in.

'She's dead then, is she?' Tracy asked the young constable.

'Not when she left here, sarge, no. Still breathing, she was. That's why her boyfriend wanted to go to the hospital with her. Nick took him in the car.'

'He was the one who dialled 999? This boyfriend?'

'Yes. Name of David Kidd. This is his flat.'

'I see.' Tracy knelt to examine the clothing on the living room floor. A girl's jeans, teeshirt, bra, white socks and trainers, scattered here and there on a green, patterned carpet. Her panties were on the arm of the sofa.

'Any blood?' Terry asked.

Tracy stood up. 'Not that I can see, no sir. It looks like she undressed here and then got into the bath.'

'Where she cut her wrists with a kitchen knife,' Terry said thoughtfully. He glanced at the window to his right. There was a dining table in front of it, with an empty wine glass next to a colourful bunch of flowers in a vase. Outside the window, at this same three story height above the ground, he could see people walking along the medieval city wall, twenty yards away across the back yard. Behind them, framed by sycamore trees, rose the magnificent tower of the 14th century cathedral, York Minster, its white stones suffused with a rosy glow in the evening sunset.

An elderly couple on the city wall paused, entranced by the sight. The wife posed with her back to the Minster, while her husband photographed her. As she stood there, smiling, her eyes met Terry's and he realized that she was watching him with the same idle curiosity that he was watching her. A thought came to him.

'These curtains,' he asked the uniformed constable. 'Were they closed when you came in?'

'No sir, don't think so. Can't have been. We haven't touched anything at all.'

'Then if she got undressed there, where you're standing,' he said to Tracy thoughtfully. 'She would have run the risk of providing a free peepshow to anyone passing outside on the wall.'

'That's true, sir, yes,' Tracy agreed. 'Although there's frosted glass and a blind in the bathroom. Fancy one too, if you like that sort of thing,' she added, looking at the pattern of sea horses and ferns on the roller blind which was pulled halfway down.

'Hm,' said Terry thoughtfully. 'Maybe if you're going to kill yourself you're past caring about modesty.'

'Maybe.' Tracy looked again into the bathroom and then wandered around the living room. There were several African masks on the wall, and framed photographs of lions and giraffes. 'Looks like she didn't care about drying herself either, sir. There's no towel.'

'Yes there is, in here.' Terry's voice came from the bedroom, on the opposite side of the living room from the bathroom. Like the rest of the flat, it was clean and neat, the furnishing new and well cared for. It contained a double bed, a wardrobe, and a chest of drawers. A green towel was flung over the end of the bed. The wardrobe and chest of drawers were both open, and on the floor at the foot of the bed there was a black holdall with clothes and books in it. Terry began unpacking it slowly.

'All female clothes,' he said, as Tracy watched. 'A nightie, underwear, tights, blouses, makeup. Two university library books about the Bronte sisters, and last week's copy of Cosmopolitan, presumably for light relief, main article 'How to give a man multiple orgasms'.' He looked up, clumsily trying to lighten the atmosphere. 'I'm taking this in for closer examination, Tracy.'

'Sir.' Tracy favoured her superior officer with a deadpan stare, then relented. Terry was handsome enough for a man of his age, but had never been a great Lothario. Always a little too shy, uncertain how to act with women. Perhaps because he'd married so young, left the sexual battlefield early, and was at a loss now he'd suddenly returned to it. Anyway his children probably took up most of his social life. The corner of her mouth twitched slightly. 'I think you need help.'

'I suppose I would.' Terry glanced at her, then sighed. 'Anyway, what does this tell us? It rather looks as though the young lady was moving out, doesn't it? In which case ...'

'Why break off and kill yourself instead?'

'Exactly.' Their eyes met again, all traces of humour gone. 'This begins to look strange, sir, doesn't it. Unless ...'

'What?'

'She might have been moving in, rather than out. Unpacking that bag, rather than packing it, if you see what I mean.'

'And then tried to kill herself because of what? Something her boyfriend said?'

'Perhaps.' Tracy gave a tiny shrug. 'Either way, it doesn't make a whole lot of sense. If you're leaving, why not just go? And if you're moving in, why start by getting in the bath to slash your wrists?'

'Why indeed?' Terry swung the knife thoughtfully in its plastic bag, as though it could give him inspiration. 'Why, in any case, do it in your boyfriend's flat? Was it a cry for help, perhaps? And if so, what was he doing, all the while?'

'He did ring 999, sir,' Bill Rankin volunteered. 'And he claims he attempted first aid.'

'The least he could do, in the circumstances,' said Terry softly. He walked back across the living room into the kitchen, where there were some carrots, onions and mushrooms ready sliced in a saucepan, with a half-finished glass of red wine next to them. On the wall was a photo of a young man standing proudly beside a Lotus sports car. There was a telephone on the wall too, its receiver smeared with blood. 'He had blood on his hands when he phoned, then.'

'Yes, sir.' Constable Rankin had followed him in. 'He was soaking wet and covered with blood when we arrived. He said he'd found her like that in the bath and tried to get her out before he phoned. Or after - he wasn't very clear. He was in a right panic, in fact. Couldn't stop talking or flustering all the time he was here.'

Terry noticed the number 1 flashing on the answerphone, and pressed the play button. A metallic voice began to speak from the tape. 'You have ... one ... message. Message one.' Then a girl's voice; somewhat hesitant, Terry thought, with long pauses between each phrase as though she wasn't quite sure what to say.

'Hi. Dave, it's me ... if you're there pick this up, will you ... Dave? ... well I'm coming over this evening but don't get your hopes up ... it's just ... well I'll see you if you're around and if not it doesn't matter ... just ... don't let there be anyone else there, all right? ... bye.' The phone clicked and began its mechanical recitation. 'Sunday, three .. twenty .. seven.. p.m. End of messages. To delete all messages, press delete.'

Terry looked thoughtfully at Tracy and Bill Rankin. 'So, what do we make of that? She's coming over, she wants him to be alone but not to get his hopes up, he starts to prepare a meal ...' He glanced around the kitchen curiously, at the sliced vegetables, the half-finished glass of wine. There were drops of what looked like bloody water here and there on the floor. 'Or at least one of them did. Was it him who did the cooking or her, do you think?'

'Hardly likely to be her in the circumstances, sir, surely,' Tracy said. 'I mean, what are you saying - she stood here chopping vegetables and then thought, sod this for a lark, I'll get in the bath and put an end to it all. Just like that?'

'Not likely, is it?' Terry agreed. 'But then if it wasn't her, it must have been him. He was standing here cooking while she was slicing her wrists in the bath. What sense does that make? Anyway, where's the knife?'

'Knife?' Tracy gazed at him bemused. 'In your hand, sir. In that evidence bag.'

'Not this one, Trace.' Terry waved an arm around the kitchen. 'I mean the one in here. The one that chopped these vegetables. Where is it?'

Tracy looked, and saw what he meant. There was no knife on the worktop, or in the sink, or on the floor. There was a knife block in a corner with three other knives in, but each, when she pulled it out, looked clean. There was one empty space in the block.

'The knife that isn't there,' Terry said. 'Now what does that tell you?'

Tracy shook her head. 'I'm not sure, sir. Either she was cutting the vegetables after all, or - what? She came in here to ask lover boy for a knife? Not very likely, is it? Can I borrow that for a moment, I'm in the bath and I need to cut my wrists? He must have known. Unless ...' Her eyes met his, widening slightly as the same thought occurred to them both.

'Unless he cut them for her,' Terry nodded grimly. 'It begins to look like that, wouldn't you say?'

'He wasn't here, sir,' the young constable interrupted.

'What?' Terry turned away, surprised.

'He wasn't here. He was out when it happened, shopping, then he came back and found her like this. That's his story, anyway. He told us, over and over again. Couldn't stop saying it. He went to the corner shop on Bootham and bought those flowers.' He indicated the vase on the table in the living room.

'Ah. I see.' Terry walked back into the living room and inspected them curiously. 'Which you wouldn't do, of course, if you were about to kill your girlfriend. Would you, constable?'

'Me, sir? No!' Bill Rankin looked shocked.

'Unless he bought them to put them on her grave, but that's too soon,' Terry murmured to himself softly. 'He came in with the flowers and found her, you say?'

'So he said, sir, yes.'

'Then he rang 999. Did he try to help her first?'

'So he said, sir, yes. He was burbling something about sticking a plaster on her wrists. As if that would stop it. The paramedics were right sick of him.'

'So at what point did he do the flower arranging, do you think, Trace?'

Terry studied the flowers curiously, then lifted them out of the vase. Water dripped from their stems. 'No sign of blood on these.'

'It's a regular domestic scene, sir, isn't it? Meal prepared, flowers on the table, glass of wine, and then this ...'

Terry gestured towards the bloody bathroom. 'Does it make sense to you?'

Tracy shook her head. 'Not as a normal suicide, sir, no. I mean, if you really mean to kill yourself, why go over to your boyfriend's flat and do it in his bath? While he stands in the kitchen cooking a meal?'

'Or goes out shopping,' murmured Bill Rankin.

'Maybe she didn't like his ideas for the menu,' Tracy suggested. 'Or they had some kind of quarrel we don't know about.'

Terry shrugged. 'So what are we looking at here? Cry for help, a serious attempt at suicide, or ...'

'Attempted murder, disguised to look like suicide,' said Tracy, completing his thought.

'Exactly. In which case, we assume, until persuaded otherwise, that a serious crime may well have been committed here and get a SOCO team over here straight away to do a full examination. I want you, Bill, to put a guard on the door, make sure no one - including the owner - comes in or out until they arrive, okay? I'll get on the phone to them right away. And then I think you and I'd best get over to the hospital and start asking a few questions, don't you, Trace? If that young woman's still alive maybe she can solve some of these mysteries for us. And if not ...' He sighed, contemplating a long night's work ahead, and the emotional strains it was likely to bring. 'Well, either way, there's going to be her family to contact, as well.'

4. Phone call

THE PHONE call came when Shelley's mother, Kathryn Walters, was on the treadmill. A bouncy, energetic woman in her late forties, she had joined the health club three years ago after a cruel comment from her husband, and had found it so compulsive that she now came three or four times a week, as often as the demands of running her home and business would allow. She valued it equally for the warm comforting afterglow of the endorphins flooding through her brain, and for the physical results whose evidence she saw every day from her mirror and weighing scales. A determined woman, she had joined battle with the forces of ageing and was convinced that, for the moment at least, she had them well and truly on the run. Life, for Kathryn, had always been a struggle for achievement, and now that one daughter was married and the other settled at university she had time and energy to expend on herself.

She had just completed ten minutes power walking and had switched the machine up to jog when her phone rang, its little extract from Don Giovanni, in her handbag on the floor in front of her. She always brought her small handbag in here with her; there had been a spate of thefts a few months back and she didn't trust the lockers. Anyway her eldest daughter Miranda sometimes rang from America on Sunday nights and she wouldn't want to miss that, wherever she was. So even though she was nicely warmed up, skin glowing and breath coming smoothly, she stopped the machine and picked up the phone, just in case.

'Hello?'

'Kath? Thank God you're there.' Kathryn recognized the voice of Jane Miller, a friend who was now a senior nurse in Accident and Emergency. The next words turned the sweat on her skin to ice. 'It's Shelley - she's here in Casualty. It's very serious, Kath, you'd better come at once.'

'Shelley? Why, what's happened?'

'I can't say for sure, but she's lost a lot of blood. They're doing all they can but it's serious, Kath. It seems she cut her wrists.'

'What? Shelley - no!' At the tone of her voice heads turned on the exercise machines, some concerned, some irritated, others blankly incurious. Kathryn snatched up her bag and began to walk towards the changing room, her phone still at her ear. 'What do you mean, cut her wrists? Has there been an accident?'

'It's hard to say, Kath. She was found in a bath. Look, where are you? Is there anyone who can drive you?'

'I'm at the gym. No, that doesn't matter, I'll be OK.' She was in the changing room as she spoke, fumbling for the key to her locker when she thought, what the hell am I doing, I don't need to change, I'll go as I am. 'I'll be there in ten minutes, Jane, I'm at the Swallow Chase. My God, Jane, how is she? How bad is it?'

'It's quite bad. She's lost a lot of blood. They're giving her a transfusion now. Her boyfriend's here, at least.'

'Christ, no! Not him!' Kathryn was in the car park as she spoke, still in her tracksuit and trainers, squeezing the button on her keys to unlock the car, opening the door with one hand and talking into the phone with the other. 'What's he doing there? She's left him!'

This question was beyond Jane Miller, so she ignored it and responded instead to the panic in her friend's voice. 'Kath, for heaven's sake drive carefully, will you? Think what you're doing - you won't help Shelley by causing another accident. Is Andrew there with you?'

'No. I'll call him.' She clicked the phone off and drove out of the car park, not even noticing the young man who had to skip for safety into a rose bed as she spun the tyres on the gravel. Shelley, in Casualty, with cut wrists - a transfusion! Thank God she was so close. The health club was in the Swallow Chase hotel by York's Knavesmire racecourse, only a couple of miles through the city centre to the hospital. It was a pleasant, sunny evening in May; as she accelerated towards the city she saw a father holding up his daughter to pat the noses of some horses under the trees, and children flying kites and playing football on the Knavesmire beyond. The sight seemed surreal to her, an insult - people casually going about their normal business while Shelley was bleeding to death. No, don't say that! This can't be happening, she thought - I'll get there and find it's all a joke, a misunderstanding.

But Jane Miller wouldn't joke about a thing like this, and the fact that

Shelley's boyfriend David was there in the hospital too added a macabre touch that terrified her as much as the news itself.. Ever since she had met that boy Kathryn had loathed him. He was rude, arrogant, idle, and apparently committed to turning Shelley not only against her own parents but also against all the habits of industry and self-reliance which she, with a little help from Andrew, had worked so hard for so many years to instill. In a few weeks, beginning last December, Shelley had changed from being a moderately confident, communicative young woman to someone they hardly recognized - anxious, withdrawn, obstinate, nervous as she had been in the worst of her teenage years, prone to increasingly wild mood swings and defiant in her defence of this new and unpleasant boyfriend.

That, at least, was how Kathryn saw it. Shelley had begun at university last October, and all had gone well until six weeks later her steady boyfriend of several years, Graham, had met another girl from Sheffield and, in the cruel modern jargon, 'dumped' her. This, of course, had sent Shelley into a depression, but instead of seeking comfort from her mother, as she would have when younger, she set out to deal with matters on her own, and, to Kathryn's horror, had somehow come up with this arrogant, manipulative, pretentious boy David Kidd. Every time she thought of him her blood boiled and her mind seethed with anger and frustration - how any daughter of hers could be duped by such a self-regarding, deceitful ... the adjectives piled up like stones she would hurl at him if only she could.

And yet he was Shelley's choice, so she had tried to respect it. And not everyone loathed him as she did. Shelley's father Andrew, whom she worshipped, had welcomed David into their house at Christmas, being charming and pleasant as he so easily could. When David had seemed rude, Andrew excused his lack of manners as mere awkwardness, telling Kathryn he hoped that Shelley's love would transform him from a toad into a prince. It was a naive hope which had failed as Kathryn had always known it would. Even though, just as in the fairy tale, Shelley had not only kissed the toad but no doubt made love to him many times as well, it hadn't transformed him at all; he remained just what he had always been: an arrogant, deceitful fraud who should have had no place whatsoever in their bright, intelligent daughter's life. If any transformation had taken place it had been the other way: his slime, his idleness and cynicism had rubbed off on her, making her a stranger to her own mother - and to her liberal father too.

Cut wrists ... suicide. Kathryn's own hands trembled as she gripped the wheel and slammed through the gears with unaccustomed violence as the lights changed in Blossom Street. Surely that was impossible. However sulky and obstreperous her youngest daughter had become she had never harmed herself before. Quite the reverse - she had always turned her anger on her parents, teachers or friends, whoever was irritating her at the time. She was more likely to cut someone else's throat than damage herself in any way, Kathryn thought. So this must be an accident; either that, or something worse. Even when her marks had gone down after Christmas she never turned things inwards to blame herself; her character wasn't like that. She blamed her parents all over again, her tutors, everyone except herself and the real villain of the piece, that ghoul who was waiting with her at the hospital. Christ! Kathryn swung the car aggressively towards the station, thinking if only I was a man, if only Andrew had been tough enough to slam the door in that flashy young man's face when he first appeared. If only I could get my daughter back again, healthy and sane ...

But then that was exactly what had happened, a week ago. Shelley had come home in a tearful rage to say that she was leaving David, he had deceived her with another woman and it was over, it had all been a dreadful mistake. Joy had leaped in Kathryn's heart and she had broken open a bottle of wine to celebrate. Shelley had embraced her mother for the first time for months. Her eyes were open now, Shelley told her, she understood how David had tried to manipulate her and draw her away from her own family while lying to her about his other girl, or girls, however many there were. He was history now, she was going to start her life again, change everything. She acknowledged the dreadful marks she had had this term but her last essay had been better and she was going to work hard from now on.

So how could she possibly be in hospital now with cut wrists, the mark of a suicide, a cry for help? It made no sense at all. It must be an accident or some stupid student prank unless ... well, what else could it be? Jane's message had frightened Kathryn so much she hardly knew where she was or what to do next, except get to the hospital as fast as possible which she couldn't do now, because she was stuck in a traffic jam on Lendal bridge. She drummed her fingers furiously on the steering wheel as people strolled by in the evening sunshine, talking, holding hands, kissing, pushing babies, leaning over the parapet of the bridge to admire the river view.

My daughter may be dying in hospital, doesn't anyone understand? She felt so alone, in a glass bubble all of her own with no one to talk to. Then remembered she had to ring Andrew. She pressed the button on her mobile which stored his office number, but it rang unanswered. In the library no doubt, she thought bitterly - among the medieval archives where he said a mobile phone would be out of place and disturb his concentration, the hypocrite! If he was there at all and not in bed with some graduate student like last time. God, where is the man when I really need him? She rang the answerphone at home and left him a message, it was all she could do for the present. By the time she had finished that she was moving along Gillygate where David had his wretched flat, and past the Salvation Army Hall to the hospital on the left, a vast grey city where life and death were decided, and there was a long queue outside the pay and display car park for Christ's sake, with people carrying flowers and taking their grandchildren to visit, while my daughter may be bleeding to death at this very moment ...

Grimly, to an accompaniment of horns and shouted protests, she overtook the queue and screeched into the Accident and Emergency car park where she pulled up beside a police car.

Waiting for her at the entrance was her friend, Jane Miller. As Kathryn approached she could see in her face that the news was not going to be good.

5. Accident and Emergency.

ACCIDENT AND Emergency was always essentially the same, Terry thought. Ambulances and doctor's cars outside, a receptionist asking someone to fill out a form, a collection of patients and their relatives on plastic chairs in the waiting room vacantly gazing at the television chattering mindlessly to itself between the vending machines. As usual, Terry marvelled at how many of these people seemed perfectly uninjured, malingerers apparently content to wait two hours simply to be treated for a headache or a tetanus booster injection. So trivial and mundane it seemed. And yet Terry could never walk through this place without fear. For at any time the most dreadful injuries could be wheeled though the door only few feet away, the paramedics buzzing with concentration and energy to stop their patient's life ebbing away.

But it was most painful, Terry thought, for the relatives who came in here in shock, their minds so inflamed with anxiety that they perceived everything with the sensitivity of someone who had lost two layers of skin. So it had seemed, at least, to Terry when he had come here for the death of his wife, Mary, whose body had been extracted from her car like so much butcher's meat that was still, faintly, breathing. Three years later he could still vividly recall every word the doctor had spoken, every touch of the nurse's hand, every embarrassed, sympathetic glance. He even remembered the two people arguing in the waiting room on the way out about changing the channel on the TV.

A & E had no memory of Mary, of course, but Terry had forgotten nothing. Every time he came here he trembled. And today something similar would begin, he assumed, for the relatives of this young girl, Shelley Walters.

He and Tracy were met at reception by a nurse who escorted them along a corridor with red and yellow lines to a doctor in a crumpled white coat, who was entering something on a computer. As he turned to face them Terry noticed streaks of blood on his coat, and the look of resignation and grey weariness on the absurdly young face.

'Shelley Walters, yes,' he said. 'I'm afraid we couldn't save her.'

Well, you should have tried harder, a voice buried deep in Terry's subconscious screamed. You should never give up, never! This isn't just a day's work, it's a life.

'I see.' Terry nodded slowly, glancing away from the doctor into a room full of medical technology, where a nurse was drawing the screens around a bed. 'Was it suicide?'

The doctor spread his hands apologetically. 'That'll be for the coroner to say, I suppose, after the post-mortem. But at first sight it looks like that, certainly. Wrists slit, massive loss of blood. Though she'd also nearly drowned in the process. We thought we'd recovered her from that when we lost her, unfortunately.'

'So what did she die of, exactly?'

'Heart failure, basically. Probably caused by blood loss and shock. Though the drowning couldn't have helped either.'

And so the main question. 'Could it be murder?'

The young doctor shrugged, again in a weary, off-hand way that made part of Terry want to pick him up and shake him hard. But then he'd probably been on duty for twelve hours already, seen other deaths and injuries.

'That's for you to decide, not me. It's a possibility, I suppose. But as I say we'll learn more from the post mortem ...'

They were still talking when Kathryn appeared. Jane Miller had met her at the front door but Kathryn ran ahead of her, still in her dark blue tracksuit and trainers, until she saw the doctor talking to a man and a woman whom she knew, instantly, must be police officers. She was still half-running, partly to keep ahead of Jane and avoid hearing what she feared she might say, partly because if she kept moving, doing something, however futile, she might still be in time to save Shelley from ...

She identified the doctor immediately and interrupted, cutting in on Terry's conversation.

'Excuse me, Shelley Walters? I'm her mother, I'm told she's in here.'

'Er, yes, of course. Just a minute, Inspector.' The doctor's face changed, in a way that Kathryn would remember all her life but which she didn't want to believe, not now. Not while the words had not been said. Directing a reproachful glance at the nurse, he took Kathryn by the arm, leading her towards a room across the corridor. 'If you'd just step in here for a moment.'

Kathryn pulled back. This was not the way it was supposed to go. It must not be allowed to go like this. 'I want to see her!'

'If you'd just step this way I can explain everything.' And she knew by his face and the tone in his voice, she knew almost certainly that all was lost. Numbly, she let herself to be led those few strides towards the waiting room. But then as he opened the door she saw the room was not empty, there was someone else inside. A uniformed police constable, sitting opposite a young man with short bristly hair, large muscular arms and hands that were clenched tightly together between his knees. The man she wanted to see least in all the world. The young man saw her too and stood up, the eyes in his flushed, oddly childlike hateful face bruised and red-rimmed with something that other people might take for grief.

The doctor looked surprised, as though had forgotten the man was there, but recovered swiftly. 'You'll know her boyfriend, I suppose. Mr, er, Kidd, isn't it?'

Kathryn noticed that David's white teeshirt was stained with blood. Shelley's blood, it had to be hers. She started to tremble, she couldn't help herself.

'David, what's happened? God, look at you - what the hell have you done, you little shit?'

'What d'you mean, me?' David protested. 'I haven't done anything - it's not me, I just found her!'

'You'll have had something to do with it, you must have done!'

'Look, I didn't do it, of course I didn't.' He spread his hands wide, looking away from her to the doctor and police officers behind. 'If anyone made her kill herself, it was you, not me. You pressed her too hard!'

'Kill herself?' The words burst in Kathryn's mind, excluding everything else. 'Christ, what are you saying, you monster?' She turned to the doctor desperately, appealing to him to deny something she already knew by his face, by his look of acute embarrassment and pity, that he would not. 'She's not dead?'

Before the doctor could answer David stepped forward, confronting Kathryn directly. 'Oh yes she is,' he said bitterly. 'And what's more you drove her to it, didn't you? She's killed herself because of you, that's what she's done!'

His mocking face filled her vision. She had never been so close to him, she felt unable to stand the bitter intensity of his gaze. She looked away, down at the blood on his clothes. In a faint but crystal clear voice, she said: 'That's Shelley's blood, isn't it? You killed her.'

'Did I fuck!' The accusation seemed to enrage him further. His big hands seized her shoulders, shaking her roughly. Tears flooded her eyes.

'I've told you, she did it herself. I just found her, I tried to save her. And why do you think she did it? Because of you and all your bloody nagging, trying to get her away from me, when she'd made her own choice for once! Well, you've done it now, haven't you? She's killed herself! I tried to save her but I was too late. And now you come. Well, go home. You're not wanted!'

'No ... that's not ... she's not dead!'

Kathryn tried to push him away but she was helpless in his grip; then he threw her contemptuously aside so that she stumbled, tripped and collapsed onto the floor. For a moment all of them - Terry, Tracy, the uniformed constable, the doctor, the nurse - were struck dumb with shock, unable to move or respond to the appalling drama exploding in front of them. Then, as Jane Miller bent down over Kathryn, Terry Bateson sprang to life.

'All right, son, that's enough.' He stepped forward and put his hand on David's arm, trying to guide him away from the woman. David gasped, and flailed at Terry with his other arm, but PC Newbolt caught that before it could do any harm, and the two of them frogmarched him out into the corridor, where they held him up against a wall.

'Get off me, you fascist bastards! You can't do this!'

'All right, Nick, let him go.' Terry and Nick slackened their hold but stood close enough to prevent him getting back into the room. Terry took a deep breath to keep his temper under control. 'Look, sir. If the young woman's dead we need to take a statement, and that has to be done at the station. I've got a car outside. We might as well go there now, and get it over with.'

The two police officers towered over the young man, who was surprisingly short - only five foot six, eight perhaps. For a moment it looked as though he would put up a fight; then, like an irritated turkey cock, he shrugged and strutted to the door.

'All right. There's nothing left for me here anyway.'

Nick escorted him out to the car, past nurses, patients on trolleys and those still waiting to be seen. Terry turned to Tracey who had followed them into the corridor. She looked shocked.

'He'll complain, sir, if you're not careful,' she said. 'He's just the sort who knows all his rights.'

'Oh, sure. Rights and no responsibilities,' said Terry, straightening his jacket. 'No manners either. Christ, did you hear what he said to that woman?'

Tracy nodded numbly. 'What a way to learn a thing like that.'

'There's no good way,' Terry said grimly. 'But that was the worst I've ever seen.' He walked away from the car to gather his thoughts, conscious of the ambulance drivers and an old man in a wheelchair watching him. Would nothing good ever happen in this place? He was conscious of a tide of anger surging through him - was it just because of the way the young man had behaved, or did it have something to do with Mary as well? He so wanted to avenge her, but this was not the way. If he was to do his job properly, he had to keep control.

He drew a deep breath and smiled at Tracy apologetically. 'All right, panic over. Look, Trace, go back inside and see if you can get that woman's story, will you? She needs sympathy at the very least. You're better at that than me. I'll deal with this guy. If it is murder it must have been him. After all, she was alone with him in his flat, wasn't she?'

'Just her and him,' Tracy nodded. 'All right, sir, I'll see what I can do.'

'I'm so sorry, Mrs Walters,' the young doctor said, when Kathryn had recovered. 'I thought ... since he was her boyfriend ...'

'I want to see my daughter,' said Kathryn desperately, looking away from him to the nurse, Jane Miller. 'Please, where is she? I need to know.'

'Yes, of course.' Tracy Litherland watched as the doctor led her out, across the corridor to the room with the medical machinery and the screened bed. He drew back the screens, bent over the bed, and smoothed the sheets back gently around her daughter's face, as though it could make any difference now. 'Please, Mrs Walters, stay as long as you want. Nurse Miller will see that you're not disturbed. I'm so sorry.'

'Oh God.' Kathryn bent to put her cheek across her daughter's forehead, as though to warm it with her own blood. It was already cooler than a living person's, and pale, too, when she drew back to look. Shelley's skin was white, not like the sheet exactly, but like - tripe. She shuddered as the image flashed across her mind. This was dead flesh, meat that had been bled, not her daughter at all, ever again. She reached for the girl's lifeless hand, clasped it in her own, felt the flaccid eternal inability to respond. The skin stiffening slowly.

'Oh Shelley, Shelley ...' She bent her head and wept, and the tears fell on the hand that could never feel again, that could only decay. 'Shelley, where have you gone?'

Thanks, boss, Tracy Litherland thought, watching from the door. How on earth am I going to handle this?

6. David Kidd

IN THE car David Kidd was, as Tracy had predicted, sullen and resentful. 'You're not arresting me, are you? I've got my rights!'

'So has that girl's mother,' said Terry firmly, driving the car out of the car park. 'That was an assault, what you did to her back there.'

'Get lost! I never touched her!'

'You shook her and knocked her down. I could arrest you for assault and battery, if I wanted to. Quite apart from the brutal way in which you told her her daughter was dead. What did you think you were playing at, son?'

'You don't know what she's like. You've never met her. Anyway it's my girlfriend who's died. How do you think I feel?'

'Grief, I imagine. Do you?' Terry studied him curiously in the driving mirror, wondering what the answer to this question was. He could just see the articles in the Press if a complaint was made against him for arresting an innocent boy moments after his girlfriend had committed suicide - Police Arrest Grief-stricken Boyfriend; Passed Over Inspector Takes It Out On Public. That would really improve his stock with Will Churchill. On the other hand, if this was a murder he was dealing with, the prime suspect was right there on his back seat.

'Course I feel fucking grief. What do you think?'

It looked more like rage to Terry. The surprisingly young, smooth face glared back at him in frustration and contempt. Surely if he'd really loved the girl this 'fucking grief' might be expected to manifest itself in a few tears, rather than outright fury? But then people were different, that was one thing he had learned in eighteen years as a police officer. He had seen people laugh at car accidents and fires, and met murderers who wept bitterly when told their victim had died. Sometimes he had the impression of operating in a foreign country.

'You said she drove her own daughter to suicide, David. That's a dreadful thing to say.'

'So? It's true. Why else would she do it?'

As they passed along Gillygate, Terry saw a police Landrover parked on the pavement and forensic officers in white paper suits going inside. David Kidd saw them too.

'What the hell's all this? Is that my flat they're going into? They can't just do that!'

'A young woman's just died in your flat, Mr Kidd, in circumstances which need to be explained. It may be suicide, but it's also possible a serious crime has been committed. So we have a duty to ...'

'What if I want to go home? I need to change my shirt.'

'You'll just have to wait, son, I'm afraid. Until they've finished their investigations, you'll have to keep out of their way. So you might as well come to the station and make your statement now.'

The scowl on the stocky youth's face looked oddly childish, petulant somehow. Terry drove on in silence, wondering if he had misjudged the situation. Was that performance in the hospital an attempt to divert suspicion from his own guilt? Or was the boy just behaving badly because he was in shock? Perhaps, when he calmed down, David Kidd would become a more appealing character, easier to understand.

After a while David's voice resumed from behind him. 'All right, I'll give you your sodding statement, for all the good it'll do. Christ. You heard what that woman said. She thinks I killed her, stupid bitch. She drove her to kill herself, that's what she did.'

'Mrs Walters?' Tracy said hesitantly when at last the two women came away from the bed. 'I'm a police officer. I hate to intrude at a time like this, but there are a few basic details we need to know. If you think you can manage it, that is.'

The nurse shook her head but Kathryn Walters turned to her almost with relief. 'About how that monster killed my daughter, you mean?'

'Well, yes, about their relationship and ... if we could sit down here? It won't take long.'

'He killed her, that's what you need to know.' Kathryn looked at Tracy, almost beseeching her as though she was a saviour. 'Please, tell me you'll make him pay! You will, won't you?'

'If a crime has been committed, Mrs Walters, of course ...'

To her consternation the woman began to laugh. Not a healthy laugh but a weird ironic laugh on the verge of hysteria. Or perhaps over the verge. '*If*

...' she said. 'Oh, that's wonderful, isn't it, *if* a crime has been committed! Look in there, what do you think has happened? Isn't it obvious? He murdered her!'

The tears came then and Jane Miller tried to take control. 'This really isn't the right time. I'm sorry, officer, but ...' She beckoned the doctor, who was hovering nearby.

'Yes, I understand.' Tracy sat back, shutting her notebook. 'Maybe tomorrow.'

'How will that make things any better?' Kathryn was still focussed on Tracy, ignoring her friend's ministrations. 'It'll never be better now, will it - ever? He stole our daughter away from us and now he's killed her - that's what he's done!' She put her hand on Tracy's knee, gripping it so tightly that it hurt. 'You've got to punish him, please - for Shelley's sake, for all of us! He's a monster, that man - he'll do it again if you don't! Promise me!'

'Mrs Walters, I think ...' The young doctor was with them now, frowning firmly at Tracy. 'She's in no fit state ...'

'I want him punished! I want you to lock him up and throw away the key! He killed her, I tell you! She was fine only a few days ago - she came home, she was happy, she was going to leave him, she told me! That's why he did it, don't you see? He couldn't let her get away. She would never have hurt herself, she had so much to live for!'

'I understand, Mrs Walters.' Tracy put her own hand on Kathryn's and squeezed it, trying to comfort but also, tactfully, to release the grip on her leg. It was as though the woman was drowning and her knee was a floating branch that might save her. 'I'll talk to you later, I promise, when you're feeling a little calmer. Does her father know what's happened yet?'

Kathryn shook her head bitterly. 'No. Oh God, not yet, no. I'll have to tell him, won't I?'

'I can do that for you if you like, Mrs Walters,' said Tracy grimly. 'If you'd just give me a few details, so that I can find him ...'

7. Interviews

AT THE station Nick Newbolt took David Kidd into an interview room, and Terry rang Trude's mobile.

'Hi, it's me. Have you got the children?'

'Yes, they're both fine. Tired out and finishing up Mrs Newby's picnic.' The reassuring words from the young Norwegian nanny went through him like a soothing draught. His own daughters, at least, were safe.

'Is Esther okay?' The memory of the tear-stained, ice-cream covered face came into his mind.

'She's fine, do you want to talk to her? Here, Esther, it's your Dad.'

'Hi, Daddy. Did you catch the burglars? Mrs Newby says you're the best catcher.'

'Does she? Well, she's the best lawyer too - you tell her that. I've got a burglar here now so I'll be late home, pet. Be a good girl for Trude now, won't you?'

'All right, Daddy - hey, Jess, give it here, that's my sandwich!' He heard a scuffle, then Jessica came on.

'Dad? We went for a walk by the river and saw some ducks and a kingfisher.'

'A kingfisher? Lucky you.'

'It was blue and very fast but Emily knows where it lives in a hole. Emily knows about whales too and the environment. She went on a protest, she told me about it. Dad, can I go?'

Sarah's teenage daughter, it seemed, was a hit with his girls. 'When you're bigger, Jess. You tell me about it tonight. Look after Esther for me, now.' He clicked the phone off, smiling with relief. Family life, it seemed, was going on peacefully without him.

He squared his shoulders, and opened the door of the interview room.

'Right, Mr Kidd. You're here to give a voluntary statement, that's all.' Terry switched on the tape recorder, and explained that PC Newbolt would make notes and type them up into a statement afterwards. 'Do you want a lawyer present?'

'Why would I want a lawyer? I've done nothing wrong.'

'Is that so?'

Terry studied the young man in front of him. How old was he - twenty-five, twenty-eight? Older than most students, anyway. His skin was smooth and tanned a faint honey colour, but a twist at the corners of the mouth hinted at arrogance, cruelty perhaps. Something else caught his eye. Apart from the blood, the young man's teeshirt and jeans were normal enough, but the belt in the faded jeans was of tooled, expensive leather, and his shoes were not trainers, but genuine cowboy boots, with pointed toes and raised heels. Without these heels, David wouldn't be even average height; he'd be a genuine shortie, a mighty midget trying desperately to project himself as man size. And often, in Terry's experience, such overcompensation shaped a man's character as well. Size mattered. Will Churchill, his boss, was often aggressive and sarcastic towards women, many of whom could look him in the eye; this lad might be the same.

'This afternoon, you assaulted your girlfriend's mother in the hospital.'

'I did not!'

'Oh come on, son, I saw you. You threw her to the ground. Do you deny that?'

David Kidd sighed extravagantly, as though it was a deliberately unnecessary point. 'Okay, I may have touched her, so what? Big deal - my girlfriend's just died, copper, killed herself in the bath. I was upset, okay? So what if lost my temper, you don't know what her mother's like, do you?'

'Okay then, David, why don't you tell me. What is she like?'

'A repressed middle-class bitch, that's what she is. Mother from hell. If Shelley killed herself she's the reason behind it, for sure. She never let the poor kid alone. Shelley told me. GCSEs, A levels, all that shit - write this, read that, study all day and night or you'll end up stacking shelves in Tesco. Poor kid, she never wanted to go to university, her parents forced her. Well I hope they're pleased with the result, that's all!'

Terry listened to this diatribe curiously, trying to reconcile it with his picture of the mother, the woman in the tracksuit he had met so briefly in the hospital. To him she had looked quite normal, but then he had only seen her for thirty seconds before this young man had knocked her to the floor. But had this girl really killed herself because of parental pressure, a few bad essay marks? He doubted it, somehow.

'All right, David, let's get a few facts straight, shall we? Shelley was your girlfriend, was she? How long had you been together, then?'

'Three, four months, maybe.'

'She was a lot younger than you, wasn't she? Just a student.'

'So? I liked her. She liked me too, obviously.'

Liked, Terry noticed, not loved. 'And so she came to live with you?'

'Yes.'

'Didn't she have a room at the university? I thought most students did.'

'Yeah, well, she had both, didn't she? A room at the uni and a place with me.'

'I see. But you're not a student, are you, David?'

'Hardly. I ditched that crap as soon as I could. University of life's where I studied.'

Terry groaned inwardly. It was a phrase he'd heard too often in his job. The university's graduates seldom chose the straight and narrow. 'So what do you do?'

'I work abroad now and then, as a tour guide. Activity holidays, safaris, that sort of thing. Mostly in Kenya, sometimes in Turkey. I was going to take Shelley on one, next month. Poor kid, she was looking forward to it.'

So that accounted for the soft tan on his skin, Terry thought, and maybe the boots and belt as well. He imagined rich Americans sipping sundowners in a spacious campsite in the African bush, and David Kidd regaling them with tales of the lions and snakes he'd killed or photographed, or whatever he did. Trophies of the hunt. But if he was planning to take Shelley on such a trip, her suicide seemed even stranger.

'I see. Well, tell me what happened today. From your point of view. Take all the time you need.'

Terry watched the boy keenly as he spoke, noting the way his eyes continued to rove as he gathered his thoughts, the strength with which the hands gripped his knee before he shifted position. Was that sweat glinting on his forehead, or hair oil?

'Well, I hadn't seen Shelley for a while; she had essays to do, books and shit. I was missing her, to tell you the truth. But then she left a message that she was coming over, so I thought I'd get a meal together, to cheer her up, for Christ's sake. And now this.'

Terry remembered the tape on the answerphone at the flat. What had it said? Something like 'I'm coming over, but don't get your hopes up' - the sort of thing a girl might say when she didn't want to make love; did that fit this story? He dug a little further.

'What time did she come round to your flat?'

'About ... I don't know, two, three o'clock.'

'Was she alone?'

'Alone? Yeah, alone.'

'And what sort of mood was she in? Depressed, or fairly cheerful?'

'Well, that's just it.' David paused for a moment, frowning. Trying to remember, or invent, Terry wondered. 'You could never really tell with her. It was up one minute, down the next. That's why ... I mean, if I'd thought she was going to do anything like this, I wouldn't have gone out to the shop like I did, would I?'

It was a clever answer. Terry remembered this alibi Bill Rankin had mentioned earlier. If David wasn't in the flat, he couldn't have killed her.

'Let's take this step by step, it's easier for me to understand. You say she arrived at your flat and you talked to her, right? What sort of things did you talk about?'

David sighed. 'She was moaning about her work, like I said. So I tried to calm her down, didn't I? I told her she could give it up and live with me, if she liked. Come with me to Kenya and give the uni the boot.' He leaned forward on the table, rubbing his knuckles in his eyes. When he looked up his eyes were red-rimmed, flooded with tears. 'That's what she should have done. That's what she needed. I'd have taken care of her. Christ.'

Terry watched, wondering how much of this emotion was genuine. One moment the boy seemed sullen, aggressive; the next he turned on the tears. Was this a murderer in front of him, or not? He wondered how Tracy was getting on at the hospital, with her mother. The girl's father would have to be contacted too, as soon as possible. He didn't envy Tracy that task.

'Dr Walters' room? Yes, up the stairs over there, along the corridor, turn left at the end.'

Tracy made her way along a grey functional first floor corridor with occasional notice boards featuring examination schedules, essay deadlines, and faded posters about historical excursions to Florence. Other than that the walls were largely bare. Tracy found it oddly depressing, like a school with all the life sucked out of it - no colour, no display of the students' work. But university life is supposed to take place in the mind, she told herself. This isn't a primary school.

At the end the corridor turned to a landing with a window which looked out onto a willow tree and an offshoot of the lake crossed by a wooden footbridge. There was a battered coffee table and a couple of ancient Scandinavian armchairs in front of the window, and a door on the right with the name Professor Andrew Walters. No cartoons, no tutorial schedule. Tracy knocked.

There was no answer, but she thought she heard a sound from inside. She looked down, and saw a thin line of lamplight under the door. She knocked again.

'Professor Walters? Are you there?'

'Yes, who is it?' A man's voice answered but the door, oddly, stayed shut.

'York police, professor. I need to talk to you urgently.'

'Good God. All right, just a minute.'

What was he doing in there? Tracy wondered. Please don't play the eccentric professor on me, not now; this is too serious, too painful. She had done this sort of thing several times before but it never got any easier; several times on the way here she had regretted her impulse in offering to come. But it was part of the job, it had to be done. Tracy just hoped this man wouldn't go to pieces as his wife had done. She'd considered phoning him from her car, but decided it was best to break the news in person, if possible.

The door opened and a man stood there in shirt, trousers and shoes which, oddly, were unlaced. He was quite tall, thin, with wavy grey hair which looked as though he had forgotten to brush it properly. His face was seamed and handsome in a battered sort of way, with pale blue eyes under thick bushy eyebrows which, just now, were drawn together in a line of irritation.

'Yes? What is it?'

'It's about your daughter, sir. If I could come inside ...'

'Is that necessary? What's she been up to now? Drugs?'

'It's ... a little more serious than that, sir, I'm afraid. If I could come in...'

Reluctantly, the man stood back to let her in. The room inside was large and surprisingly comfortable, furnished from floor to ceiling on two walls with rows of brightly coloured history books and on the third with a desk which looked out through a picture window onto the lake, the footbridge, and a selection of willow and silver birch trees. The room was warm, and the bright blue speckled carpet, like the desk and chair, looked new and modern. The perks of seniority, Tracy thought fleetingly. But the real surprise was on the fourth wall, which gave into a little bay where there was a comfortable lemon-coloured sofa and an armchair arranged around a coffee table spread with more papers and a bowl of fruit. Sitting with her long legs stretched out comfortably on the cushions of the sofa, was a young black woman.

Tracy hesitated, as the girl stared coolly back at her. She was in her early thirties, Tracy guessed, about her own age, with a very black, aristocratic African looking face, long delicate limbs and hands, and neatly plaited hair. She was wearing a short skirt, a pale blue man's shirt, and, so far as Tracy could see, not much else. No tights or shoes on the long legs with the elegant pink toenails. No sign, in fact, of tights or shoes on the comfortable carpet either. Having once or twice been disturbed in such situations herself, Tracy guessed they could be found, together with several other intimate items, hurriedly stuffed behind the sofa. She groaned inwardly as the girl watched her, a cool, amused expression twinkling around her eyes.

'This is, er, Carole Williams, a colleague of mine. We were working ...' At least the man had the grace to blush, Tracy thought, as she turned her attention back to him. 'Now, what's up with my daughter this time?'

'If you'd take a seat, sir.' Tracy indicated the armchair, and waited until he sat down. 'It's ... bad news, I'm afraid. Very bad news indeed. I've just come from the hospital ...'

8. Alibi

THE LONGER Terry questioned the young man, the less he believed he was telling the truth. Some facts seemed clear, and chimed with what he had found in the flat: Shelley had left a message on David's answerphone, she had come over to see him, he had let her in, they had talked, he had been preparing a meal, she had taken her clothes off and got into the bath, and he had gone out to the local shop to buy flowers and olive oil. And someone - either Shelley herself or David, surely - had cut her wrists so she bled to death in the bath.

But the order these things happened in, and the meaning behind them, was less clear. As were David's real emotions about his girlfriend's death. At times he showed tears, then anger, irritation and even boredom - how could he be bored, Terry wondered, in a situation like this? Insistently, Terry probed at the parts of the story that puzzled him.

'We found a bag in your bedroom, David, a black holdall. With women's clothes in it, and books and magazines. Was that her bag, or yours?'

'Oh yeah, I forgot.' David glared across the table. 'You've been in there snooping, haven't you, without my permission. Like a bunch of burglars, you are. Isn't that against the law?'

'Not when we're investigating a suspicious death, son. We have a duty to find out what happened. Now, tell me about this bag. Is it hers, or not?'

David turned away, staring irritably at the wall. 'Yeah, yeah, course it's hers. She always used it.'

'Did she bring that stuff with her, or was she packing it up to take it away?'

'What?' He shook his head, as if the question were irrelevant.

'You heard. Shelley's bag was full of clothes and books. So what was she planning to do? Spend the night with you, or go back to her room on campus?'

'Spend the night with me, of course. That was the whole idea. I was going to make her a meal, and we'd spend the night together. That's what we always did. Anyhow, it was a celebration.'

'A celebration? What were you celebrating?'

'Nothing much.' David scowled, as if he'd been caught out somehow. 'I hadn't seen her for a few days, that's all. I'd missed her.'

'All right, so she brought the bag with her and took it into the bedroom, then you sat and talked, and had a glass of wine while you were preparing the meal. At what point did she decide to have a bath?'

David drew a deep breath, trying to calm himself. 'Well, I said the meal would be half an hour, and she said ... she needed to relax, chill some more, so she'd have a bath while I did the cooking. That was it, really.' He glared at Terry resentfully. 'Okay?'

'And so she got undressed in the living room.'

'What?'

'Well, that's where her clothes were, anyway. On the floor by the sofa. So where were you exactly, while she was doing this?'

'In the kitchen, I suppose. I don't remember.' There was a look on his face of anxiety mixed with contempt.

'Is that all that happened?'

'What do you mean, all?' David's eyes met his, then slithered away.

'You didn't feel tempted to watch her undressing? Have sex with her, perhaps?'

'No. I was cooking a meal.'

'I see. So she just got into the bath on her own. Taking off her clothes in the living room where people could see her from the city wall?'

'What?' David smirked. 'Only a perv like you could think of that. You should get out more, copper.'

'And before you went out shopping, Shelley was in the bath, is that right?'

'Yeah, I suppose, yeah.' David flexed his right hand so that the joints cracked.

'Did you say anything to her?'

'Say anything? Like what?'

'I don't know. Did you shout at her perhaps?'

'No, of course I didn't. Why would I?'

'Well, did you tell her you were going out? Leaving her alone for a bit?'

'Oh.' He frowned. 'Yeah, well I did, yes.'

'What did you say?'

'I dunno, something like ... I'm going out for a mo, Shelley, down to the shop. Something like that.'

'And did she reply?'

'I don't remember. Yeah, I think she said 'okay', something like that. 'Don't be long', maybe. You know, if only I'd come back sooner ...' There was a sudden catch in his voice. He rubbed his wrist across his eyes, as though brushing away a tear..

'She might have lived?' Terry wondered how genuine the sentiment was, or whether it was all an act. David had glanced at the tape machine several times in the last few minutes, as if to be certain it was recording his performance. Now he nodded earnestly.

'Yeah. I might have rung earlier. Those paramedics, they might have saved her.'

'All right, so you stood outside the bathroom door and told her you were going shopping.'

'Yes.'

'You didn't go into the bathroom?'

'No. For Christ's sake, what is this?'

Terry smiled gently. If David's story was going to break down, it was likely to happen in the next few minutes. He felt the adrenalin surge in his throat.

'Where was the knife at that moment, David?'

'I believe your wife's gone home, sir,' Tracy said quietly.

'But ... what about Shelley? Shelley's body ... I want to see her.'

'She's at the hospital, sir. Your wife's already been there.'

'Yes ... yes of course. Oh my God, I'm sorry, I ... I don't know what to do.'

'I think you should phone Kathryn, Andrew. She'll need you now. More than anyone.' The young black woman, Carole, leaned forward from the sofa and took his hands. Andrew Walters gripped them fervently, looking into her eyes for comfort, then pressed one of them to his cheek. How grotesque, Tracy thought. Of course the girl was right, but to receive - to need - such advice now, at such a moment from a girl who was clearly his mistress ... how much did the man's poor wife know about what had been going on here? As if she didn't have enough to cope with already.

'Yes. Yes, you're right.' He looked up at Tracy. 'What time did she leave? Do you think she'll be at home by now?'

'I don't know where you live, sir.'

'Out towards Wetherby. Oh, of course, she's got a mobile, I'll try that first.' With an effort he dragged a phone from his pocket, switched it on, and dialled. As he sat there, shattered, staring unseeing out of the picture window at the lake and the trees and a group of students cheerfully feeding the ducks, Tracy's eyes met Carole's. The question in her mind - does his wife know you're here? - must have been written on her face, because the young woman shook her head softly and put her finger to her lips. As she did so her lover began to speak.

'Kath? There's a policewoman here, I've just heard ... it's true then, you saw her ... oh ... oh my God ... no, of course she wouldn't ... what was he doing there? She said they'd broken up, didn't she, last weekend? ... I know, I know ... you don't think he ... Jesus Christ, Kath, did you tell the police that? What did they say? ... look, there's one of them here, I'll ask.'

He turned to Tracy. 'She thinks she was murdered. By her boyfriend, David.'

'Yes, sir, I know, she told me. We're keeping an open mind at the moment.'

'But - he was the only one with her, she says!'

'Yes, sir, so it seems. We'll investigate every possibility, of course.'

'My God!' Dazed, Andrew Walters turned back to the phone. 'They say they're investigating. Yes, I know ... where are you now? ... And Jane's with you? ... yes, I'll be there. But Kath, I want to see her first. I've got to. I'll come straight home after that ... no, I was working. Just me and the policewoman. Kath, I'll be home as soon as I can.'

He put the phone down, and buried his face in his hands. After half a minute he looked up, his face white with shock. 'I've got to see my daughter at the hospital, I'll get my car.'

He got unsteadily to his feet. Tracy put a hand on his arm. 'I'll drive you, sir, if you don't mind. You're in shock.'

'What? No, I'm fine. Anyway, I've got to get home.'

Swiftly, Carole Williams got to her feet, blocking his way to the door. 'She's right, Andrew, really she is. You're in no fit state. I can drive if you like but it might be wiser to go with this police woman. Kathryn doesn't need any more distress now, does she, love?'

Andrew Walters gazed at her like a thirsty man at a mirage, shaking his head slightly as though he couldn't quite grasp what was happening. 'No ... I mean, yes, okay, you're right, of course you are.' She put her arms around him and he returned the embrace, hugging her tightly.

'I'll be in touch.'

Tracy stepped outside while they made their farewells.

'Knife? What the hell are you talking about, knife?'

'This knife.' Terry took the knife in its evidence bag from his pocket and put it on the table. 'I found it on the floor of your bathroom this afternoon. Do you recognize it?' He watched keenly for David's reaction.

'It ... I dunno, I might do, maybe.'

'It's your kitchen knife, isn't it? The one you were using to cut up the vegetables?'

'It could be, yeah. It looks like it.'

'It's also probably the knife that was used to cut Shelley's wrists, since it was found on the floor beside the bath. Does that seem likely to you, David?'

'Well, if that's where it was found, yeah.'

'But earlier, you were using it in your kitchen.'

'So?'

'So that's why I ask you where the knife was when you spoke to Shelley before going out, David, do you see? We need to know how it got from the kitchen into the bathroom.'

'Well, I don't know, do I? How should I know?'

'It wasn't in your hand when you spoke to her?'

'No. No, it was in the kitchen, of course.'

'And you didn't take it into the bathroom? You didn't leave it there, by accident?'

'No, of course not. I didn't go in the bathroom. I told you.'

Their eyes met, and Terry waited. This was a moment, Terry judged, when an innocent man might challenge him to say what he thought. David met his eyes and said nothing.

'Okay, David, that's clear. So then you went out, to this corner shop, to buy flowers and olive oil. Did you speak to anyone there?'

'Yeah, this Indian guy, the one who owns the shop.'

'He's seen you before, has he? Does he know you?'

'Yes, sure, I go in there most days.'

'Did you talk to him about anything. Something he might remember?'

'Yeah, football, I think, he's keen on that. You know, Leeds beating Arsenal yesterday. He has a season ticket for Elland Road.'

'Did you talk about anything else?'

'Yeah, well, I think he asked about the flowers. You know, why did I want them. Shit ...' He rubbed his wrist across his eyes again. 'I'm sorry, man, I ... I told him they were for a celebration, you know. Shelley coming back to me and all. Not a bloody funeral, Christ.'

'So he's likely to remember that?'

'Yeah, yeah, he liked Shelley, had a thing about her. Said I was lucky, he wished he could find a bird like her. Not now he can't.'

'How long did this conversation take?'

'I don't know. I don't wear a bloody stopwatch, do I? Couple of minutes, maybe.'

'Did you meet anyone else on the way back?'

'No. Just came straight back.'

'So you were away for how long, would you say? I know it's hard, son. I just want a rough idea.'

'Ten minutes. Quarter of an hour maybe.'

'And when you came back to the flat, what did you do then? Take me through it step by step.'

David took a deep breath, as though to steel himself for what was to come. 'I unlocked the door, came in, put the olive oil in the kitchen I think. Then I put the flowers in a vase on the table in the living room. Then - you know there was a terrible noise in the flat because of those bells ...'

'What bells?'

'In the Minster, you know, they were ringing for some service, it's hellish, you can't hear yourself think. Anyhow I called out to Shelley that I was back, but she probably didn't hear me because of the bells, so I opened the bathroom door, and there she was ...'

He paused and rubbed his eyes, and again Terry wondered, is this genuine or staged? But he, too, had to show sympathy, in case this tape was played back later in court.

'Mr Kidd, I know it's hard, but can you tell me exactly how Shelley looked when you found her?'

'Well, she looked dead, didn't she? Covered in blood. So I rang 999. And then, when I was talking to this woman, she moved, so I knew she wasn't dead, and I ...'

'She moved?' Terry hadn't known this. It shocked him.

'Yeah. That's how I knew she was still alive. I think ... I think she saw me.'

'What did you do then?'

'Well, I tried to help her, of course. It's all ...' He shook his head. 'It's hard to remember.'

'You must have been shocked.'

'Shocked? Yeah. Course I was.' David's eyes had gone blank, seeing nothing in the room, staring inwards at the vision in his mind. The performance certainly looked genuine, and yet Terry was not sure. It could also be the intensity of imagination, visualising his story for the first time. Had this boy been shocked by his discovery, as he claimed? Or had he caused it?

'Was her head under water when you first saw her?'

'Yeah, I think ... I don't remember exactly, it was all on one side, you know, floppy. Yes; one eye was under water, I remember that, so I went and lifted her head, I did that, and I tried to get her out of the bath altogether but I couldn't because she was all so slippery and heavy. It was horrible, I couldn't do it, so ... you know, there was blood all over me, there still is, I've never seen anything like that, I didn't know what to do, it makes you feel ill ...'

'So what did you do, in the end?'

'Well, the lady on the phone, she told me to try to stop the bleeding, so I went and got a plaster from the cupboard in the kitchen, but it didn't do any good, I couldn't get it to stick on and it was too small anyway and there was blood everywhere, you know it's so slippery and I felt ill ... and then the paramedics came and took over. But they couldn't save her either, could they? So it's no good blaming me. They've had all that training but they couldn't save her. It was all too late.'

He seemed genuinely moved now. But the memory of a dead body was not a thing that most people could recall with equanimity. Even murderers could weep for their victims. Terry had seen it done.

'All right, Mr Kidd, just one more question. This knife. When you went into the bathroom did you see it there on the floor?'

'What? I don't know, I can't remember. I mean, if it was there, I must have I suppose, but I was looking at Shelley, wasn't I, not the knife.'

'But did you pick it up or touch it in any way?'

'Pick it up? No, why should I?'

'You might have wanted to move it, put it somewhere else.'

'No. No, I don't think I did that. I don't remember doing anything with it.'

'You're sure?'

'Sure I'm sure. What would I want with the knife? For Christ's sake, I was trying to save Shelley, wasn't I? Not kill her.'

'Yes.' Silence fell, and Terry watched the young man wordlessly, while the tape revolved quietly in the recorder. He was lying, Terry felt sure of it. But there was no proof, and his story seemed plausible. So unless he admitted his guilt, Terry and his team would have to prove it. They would have to examine all the evidence carefully - see what fingerprints were on the knife, what could be deduced from the clothes and other items in the flat. A lot would rely on the post mortem, and the information Tracy might get from the girl's parents. And then there was the question of David's alibi. Had anyone seen him in the local shop that night? If so, how long had he been there? And had he seemed distressed, anxious, hyperactive - or quite normal and calm?

For tonight, Terry had gone far enough.

'All right, David, I understand how difficult all this has been, and I appreciate your help. What I'm going to do now, is take your fingerprints for elimination purposes. While we're doing that PC Newbolt here will write up your statement neatly and you can read it through and sign it if you agree with what he says, okay? If you don't agree with something we can change it. We'll give you a copy of the tape. That's it. Interview ended at ...' He glanced at his watch. 'Ten thirty seven. After you've signed the statement I'll ring the SOCO team to see if they've finished with your flat. If so, you can go home and get some rest and we'll take it from there.'

And I can see my children, he thought.

9. Country House

IN OTHER circumstances, Tracy would have enjoyed driving out to the country on such a pleasant evening. Andrew Walters lived ten or fifteen miles northwest of York, along the banks of the river Nidd, and as Tracy's Clio hummed along comfortably the sun fell steadily towards the horizon in front of them.

Most of her attention, though, was on Professor Walters, slumped in the seat beside her. Emerging from the hospital after having seen his daughter, the man looked close to collapse. In other circumstances, she would have suggested that his friend come along to give moral support, but the young black woman, Carole Westerham, had made it quite clear that her presence would make things worse, a point which concerned Andrew Walters too.

'I ... suppose you've guessed that my wife doesn't know about Carole. I mean, she knows we work together, that's all, nothing more. If you don't mind I'd rather you didn't say ...'

'Of course, sir, it's none of my business. Anyway there's no need.'

'I appreciate that. After all, this is bad enough as it is. Oh, God. Shelley, we let you down.' He covered his face with his hands, and Tracy drove with one eye on the road, passing him a box of tissues which she happened to have handy. His sobs were painful, coughing, almost violent, but when she suggested pulling into a layby he just waved her angrily on. 'Don't stop. Just get on, will you. The sooner we're home the better.'

Towards Wetherby they came onto a long Roman road with the sun low ahead of them, a vast golden orange ball above the misty grey and green of the fields and trees. Below them, to their right, a river meandered slowly through a valley where cows and horses grazed. In places, reflected sunlight blazed off the water like liquid fire.

'Slow down. Next turning on the right. It's just a farm track.'

They turned onto the bumpy, potholed road, and Tracy saw a house half a mile down the slope in front of them with the river beyond it. It was a traditional stone built Yorkshire farmhouse with stables and outbuildings, and horses and sheep grazing together in a paddock. 'You live in a lovely place, sir,' she ventured.

'Yes.' He sighed. 'We only came here for the girls, really. So they could have ponies and a decent country life. They loved it, once. Now look what's happened.'

'Girls?' Tracy pulled up on a gravelled area near the front door. 'You have another daughter, then, sir?'

'Yes, Miranda. Shelley's older sister. She's in America. She'll have to be told, too, won't she?'

Inside, the house had been well, even luxuriously decorated. There was thick, expensive wallpaper in the hall, recessed lights, and modern wooden floors. A woman appeared at the end of the hall, facing them. Tracy recognized her as Jane Miller, the nurse from the hospital.

'Oh, Andrew,' she said. 'I'm so sorry. So very very sorry.'

Stepping forward, she gave Andrew a hug which he endured, Tracy thought, rather awkwardly. She followed them into the farm kitchen, a spacious room with an Aga , a wooden table in the centre, and a window looking out through the garden to the paddock and the river beyond. Kathryn Walters stood beside the table, still in her blue tracksuit, unconsciously shredding a tissue with her fingers. Her face was red and blotchy, her eyes wide and empty, as though long since drained of tears.

Andrew Walters walked up to her and enfolded her in his arms. And for a while they stood like that, the bereaved parents embracing in the centre of the room. Only not quite embracing, Tracy thought; he was holding her, stroking her back, and she had her arms round him too, but not really tight, not really clinging onto him as much as might have been expected. And when he stepped back, his wife still stood there, quite pale and still as though she hadn't moved at all.

Andrew waved a hand at Tracy. 'This policewoman brought me. She said it wasn't safe for me to drive. Quite right, probably.'

Kathryn nodded, then moved, as if in a trance, towards the Aga. 'It's a long way. You'd like some tea, perhaps?'

'No, it's all right, Mrs Walters ...'

'I'll do it, Kath.' Jane Miller moved swiftly to her friend's side. 'You sit down.'

Kathryn Walters sat down, quite abruptly, in a chair by the table, and stared across it at her husband, her eyes in the pale face wide and compelling. 'He killed her, Andy. I said he would and he did.'

'But she was found in a bath, they say.' Andrew shook his head, miserably. 'With her wrists cut. She bled to death.'

'Yes, but it was his bath, wasn't it? Shelley wouldn't cut her wrists, Andy, you know that. She couldn't kill a fly.'

'No, but ...' Andrew ran his hands through his hair. 'We should have been there. If she was upset, she should have come to us.'

'You were going to see her, weren't you?' Kathryn asked with surprising bitterness. 'This evening?'

'Yes, but not till later.' Her husband darted a swift, anxious glance at Tracy. 'I was in the library most of the afternoon, working. I was going to ring her from my room, but then ... this police woman came. I was going to ask if she wanted to have a meal with me in the college. She did that sometimes.' His eyes rested on Tracy's a moment longer, defying her to contradict him; then he turned back to his wife. 'But if what you say is true, then it's murder.'

'Of course it's murder. That's what the police are investigating now, aren't you, officer? I'm sorry, I don't know your name.'

'Detective Sergeant Litherland,' Tracy said, pulling her notebook from her bag. 'Look, it would help if you could tell me as much as you can about your daughter and this young man. For example how long had she known him? Where did they first meet, and so on? If you think you're up to it now, that is.'

'I don't know,' Andrew said. 'This is all a terrible shock, you know - and my wife ...'

'I want to tell her, Andy. David's always been a danger to Shelley. I told you he was bad news the moment I saw him, didn't I? Only you had to shake his hand, suck up to him, the filthy creep!' This to her husband, bitterly.

'He seemed all right at first,' said Andrew defensively. 'And Shelley liked him too - that's why I was prepared to give him a chance. She deserved a bit of luck, after all she'd been through, poor kid!'

'Luck? For God's sake! She didn't deserve this!' Tears flooded Kathryn's eyes, so that for a moment she couldn't go on. But as she fumbled for a tissue Tracy thought the tears were as much a sign of rage as grief. This was a woman who had not just been hurt - she felt mortally wronged, as well.

Kathryn blew her nose and glared at her husband, her eyes ablaze with pain and anger. 'And now she's dead, because you were so blind! It's Shelley's fault too, of course it is. Only she was too young, too naive and stupid to see. Whereas you ...'

More heat was being generated than light, Tracy thought, remembering her old supervisor on the detective training course. Establish the facts, leave the emotion until later. Otherwise you're lost - wandering in a fog with no landmarks to show you the way.

'When was this, actually?' she asked, pencil poised over her notebook. 'When did Shelley meet this man, David - what's his name? - Kidd?'

'Last December,' Andrew Walters answered. 'At the end of her first term at university. She brought him home for Christmas. My wife's right, of course. She said he was trouble then, but I'm afraid it didn't dawn on me until later. At that time, I even thought he might be her salvation, God help me.' He shook his head slowly, meeting his wife's eyes and then looking away. 'We all make mistakes, don't we, after all.'

'Not fatal ones, Andy.'

'Kath, please. This isn't helping. Let's just give her the facts, shall we?' Andrew Walters reached across the table for his wife's hand. She hesitated, then gripped it fiercely in both her own, shaking her head bitterly.

'I know the facts. He killed her! What more do you need?'

'I need to know the background, Mrs Walters,' Tracy insisted. 'If what you say is true, it's more important than ever. Your husband's right. Please, help me to understand.'

Jane Miller put her arm round her friend, and Tracy wondered if this was all too raw, too early. But the questions had to be answered sometime. A clock chimed in the hall. Kathryn Walters let go of her husband's hand and looked up, her face pale, bitter, determined. 'Yes, all right. Of course you need to understand. Just so long as understanding doesn't lead to forgiveness. There can't be any forgiveness for him, ever, not after what he's done.'

Tracy shivered, as though a spider had crawled along the back of her neck. This was a vendetta she had walked into, it seemed. 'All right. Tell me about Shelley, will you?'

Slowly, between the two of them, elements of the story began to emerge. Shelley, it seemed, had been in her first year at York university studying English. The fact that she had got a place there at all was, both parents agreed, a significant triumph not just for the girl, but for all concerned. Unlike her sister Miranda, she had not been a natural student, and had had many problems at school. For a while she had had psychiatric treatment for depression. But her parents - the father a professor of medieval history, the mother a pharmacist with her own successful business in Harrogate - had persisted, sending her to private school, paying for extra tuition about Bleak House which she loathed, even tutoring her themselves when she would let them - and at last she had come out with the required two As and a B to scrape a place. She had chosen York, even though it was near to home, because it would keep her in touch with her long-term boyfriend, Graham, of whom both parents spoke with a combination of deep regret and bitterness.

'He was a lovely boy, he worked hard, kind, had a sense of humour ...'

'The sort of boyfriend you'd dream of for your daughter ...'

'And she loved him.'

'Yes, she really did, that was the tragedy. The start of it, anyway.' Kathryn rubbed her eyes futilely with a wet tissue. 'Everything was going well for her, at last. He took over from us, in a way. Gave her confidence to grow up. Then it all fell apart ...'

'Why? What happened?' Tracy prompted, guessing the answer even as she did so.

'Well, he dumped her didn't he? That's the ugly word they use nowadays, like a girl or boy is just what - a sack of rubbish? Anyway, that's what he did. Right at the beginning of her first year. Said he'd met someone else over the summer and they weren't right for each other after all. It destroyed her, poor girl. You know what she said to me? It's like a trapdoor has opened under my feet. I don't know how to stand up any more.' Kathryn shook her head slowly. 'She trusted that boy, we all did.'

Andrew took up the story. 'That's true, it destroyed her. I thought she was going to give up altogether. Her work went all to pot. And then, on the rebound, she met this David. She brought him out here at Christmas.' He sighed. 'My wife's right. I should have seen through him then. He wasn't right for her at all, really. I mean, you've seen him, haven't you?'

'Briefly, this afternoon, yes.' Tracy remembered the confrontation in the hospital corridor.

'Yes, well he must be nearly thirty, at least - a lot older than her. Which would be all right if he had a proper job and a career, but of course he hasn't. He buys and sells African art, he says, and talks about adventure holidays, though I'm not sure I believe him. He's full of all sorts of stories, really ...'

'Like his career in the army,' Kathryn burst in.

'Like his career in the army, exactly. He had all these stories about his time in Afghanistan, for heaven's sake. Shooting Taliban - sounds wonderful, doesn't it? Shelley lapped it up. Only we could never quite find out which regiment he was in or when he joined up and then when he finally let slip it was the Rifles, Kath phoned them to check. And what did they say?' He looked to his wife to continue the story.

'He had been one of their recruits five years ago but he failed the training course. Never went anywhere near Afghanistan. Not with the army anyway.'

'I see.' Tracy scribbled the details swiftly. 'And did you tell him you'd done this?'

'I told Shelley. She didn't believe me at first. Lost her temper and said I was spying on him behind her back. Until a week ago when she found out about the other thing.'

'What other thing?'

Kathryn drew a deep breath as though at last they'd got to the crux of the matter and she was marshalling her thoughts. 'Well, you have to understand that for most of this year she's been a virtual stranger to us. I mean, she came home every now and then with a bag of clothes to wash, that sort of thing. Or a request for money.'

'Did David come with her?'

'Sometimes, yes, unfortunately. But that only made things worse, because he'd just sit and talk - he can talk, you know, he's good at that - and even if I'd ask her a direct question he'd answer it for her. It was like she was his little slave girl, almost. It was dreadful to see. Like he'd stolen her voice.'

'She was always a bit like that, even with Graham,' said Andrew judiciously.

'Yes, but Graham didn't monopolise the conversation, did he, with all his empty boasts that came to nothing?' Kathryn shot back bitterly. 'He had that ridiculous sports car, too, that he was so proud of. Anyway, one of his boasts was that he was going to take her on a trip to Africa in the vacation. He said he'd worked as a safari guide in Kenya - another of his lies, probably, I haven't been able to check that. And she was looking forward to it, of course she was, so when she came round last week I was going to take her for her injections, and buy her the right sort of clothes. I'd taken the afternoon off to do it; I thought at last I'd have her to myself for a while, have a proper talk for once. But when she came, well, it was all off.'

'The Kenya trip, you mean?' Tracy looked up from her notebook.

'No, not just that.' There was a look of tearful triumph on Kathryn Walters' face. 'The whole thing was off - her affair, everything! She wasn't ever going to see David again!'

'She told you that?'

'Yes. First thing she said when she walked in the door. She was in floods of tears of course, but she was angry, too. Angry like I hadn't seen her in years. And it was difficult because I was disappointed for her but also pleased as well. Delighted, in fact. I thought I've got my daughter back again at last. We both did, didn't we?'

Andrew Walters nodded. 'Yes. It was quite clear that evening that her affair with David was over. That's why what's happened today...' He shook his head despairingly. '... seems so strange. Inexplicable, really.'

'Which day was this, sir?'

'It would have been Tuesday. May 16th.'

'So why had the affair come to an end? What was Shelley so angry about?'

Kathryn Walters smiled through her tears. 'Oh, that's simple, really. Banal, in fact. She'd called in to see him that morning in his flat - she had a key, you see - and found him in bed with another girl. Naturally there was a row. And as if that wasn't bad enough, it turns out this girl isn't just some casual fling, as Shelley thought at first. Oh no. God help the poor girl, she's the mother of his child!'

'So there was another girl?' Terry said. 'Is that what you're telling me?'

He was parked in the street outside his house. It was nearly eleven o'clock at night. He could see the lights were off in the girls' bedroom upstairs. A glow flickered in the front room where Trude was presumably sitting up for him, watching TV. And Tracy, it seemed, was still out in the country somewhere, parked in a layby looking up at the stars while she phoned in her report.

'That's it, sir. Another girl with a baby. And he's the father.'

Terry shook his head in silent disgust. So David Kidd didn't just break up other people's families, it seemed, he abandoned his own. The distaste he had felt for the cocky young man during this afternoon's interview broadened into contempt.

'Did they give the name of this other girl? The mother of Mr Kidd's child?'

'Lindsay, Mrs Walters said. She didn't know the surname, or where she lives.'

'Well, no doubt lover boy can tell us. If he remembers he has a family, that is.' Terry gazed at his own house. Was that a small shadow moving, behind the living room curtain? Surely the girls weren't still up? He sighed. 'But I suppose, to be fair to him, that gives Shelley Walters a reason for suicide, doesn't it? Despair at being dumped by such a promising Lothario.'

'Her parents don't believe it was suicide, sir. They insist the girl wasn't like that, at all. They're convinced that her boyfriend killed her. But there is a problem, nonetheless. The girl had some sort of psychiatric condition. She was on medication for - what do they call it? Bi-polar disorder.'

'Oh great,' Terry sighed. 'So he found out she was a nutter and dumped her. That would drive anyone to suicide.'

'Could be, sir, yes. But the parents don't believe it.'

'No. Well, they wouldn't, would they?'

For a moment, neither of them said anything. Terry looked up at the window where his own daughters were sleeping peacefully, and tried to imagine how he would feel if either of them ended up as Shelley Walters had today. It didn't bear thinking about. The rage, the fury her parents must feel - coupled with guilt, perhaps, at not protecting their vulnerable daughter enough. 'A difficult interview, then, Tracy?'

'Pretty gruesome, sir, yes. I don't know how anyone copes with a death like that. I'm afraid I did ... make them a sort of promise, sir.'

'A promise?' An alarm bell rang in Terry's head. 'What do you mean?'

'Just that we'll take their suspicions seriously, sir. I said that if it is a murder, then ... we'll make sure the bastard's locked away for good.'

'Well, obviously.' Terry relaxed. It was the sort of thing he might have said himself. 'But you're not a social worker, Trace, remember that. We just deal with the facts. The post mortem will help. See you at the morgue in the morning.'

The moment he switched off the mobile he wished he hadn't said it like that. But then, if you focussed too much on feelings you wouldn't be able to deal with scenes like they'd witnessed this afternoon, or the visit to the mortuary they would both have to make tomorrow. You had to keep your own emotions under control.

But that didn't mean he had none. As Terry parked his car in his drive and opened his front door softly, he thought, this is my home, my nest, my place of safety. But how safe is it really? What if Jessica or Esther grows up and dies in the bath of a thug like David Kidd, what would I do? I'd string him up to the nearest lamppost, that's what I'd do. Whether he killed her with his own hands or just drove her to do it herself, it's still his fault either way, that's how I'd feel. I'd want revenge - that's how her parents probably feel now.

He stood in the hall for a moment, thinking, while his professional mind censored the dreadful images and stored them away in his subconscious. Then he drew a deep breath and opened the door of the living room.

A young fair-haired woman in jeans and teeshirt smiled up at him from the end of the sofa where she sat curled up watching TV. She put a finger to her lips, then pointed down at the tousled head of eight year old Esther asleep on her lap.

'Oh dear.' Terry sat down in the armchair and Trude muted the sound with the remote. 'Was there trouble this evening?' he asked softly.

'A little. My fault. I told her a tale about trolls and she saw one in the wardrobe.'

'I should have been here.'

'Why? Can you arrest trolls?' Trude stroked the little girl's hair gently. 'She's very tired. They had a lot of fun at the party.'

'Daddy?' Esther stirred, and sat up. 'Good. You're home.' She got up off the sofa and tottered across to Terry, trailing a battered leopard in her left hand. 'Did you catch the burglars?'

'I did, sweetie. All locked up.' He lifted the soft, trusting little body onto his knee, remembering the horrors at the hospital and the tough, cocky young thug he had released an hour earlier to go back to his bloodstained flat. 'Why are you up so late?'

'There was a troll. In my wardrobe.'

'It was just a dream, honey. He's all gone now. Come on, I'll take you up.'

'All right.' The little girl was warm, with that lovely innocent smell of a sleepy child. He picked her up, and she leaned her head trustingly against his shoulder, stroking the back of his head with her free hand as if she was comforting him, not the other way round. He smiled down at Trude, who gave them both a little wave.

'Up the wooden hill,' he said, in the quaint English phrase that his grandmother had once used to him. 'To Bedfordshire.'

10. Hamster

THE CASE conference, three months later, was nearly derailed by a hamster.

Terry thought he had everything running smoothly. He had all the evidence, which he had read through carefully last night, neatly arranged in a locked briefcase just inside the front door. His car, which had refused to start twice last week, had come back from the garage with a large bill and a promise of perfect performance. Trude had Jessica and Esther up and dressed for school on time, hair brushed, homework in satchels, lunchboxes packed, socks matching, waffles toasting in the kitchen ...

And then Esther let her hamster out.

It was a new hamster, selected with great care only last week to replace Rufus, the beloved old one which had died suddenly and been buried, with tears and solemn ceremony, under the laurel bush at the end of the garden. Rufus had been old and slow and trusting but the new hamster, Rastus, was the opposite of all these things and when Esther had opened his cage, just for a second to say good morning, he had whizzed up her arm, jumped off her shoulder and vanished behind the sofa. Hence the family panic.

Esther was convinced that the cat would kill him or he would get trapped inside the sofa or run down a mousehole where some monstrous rat with slavering jaws would tear him to shreds and nothing would persuade her to eat her breakfast or even consider going to school until Rastus was caught and safely installed back in his cage. Her elder sister Jessica was equally keen on the hunt but also desperate to get to school early because her class were performing a project about the environment for the school assembly and she had a key speaking role as a dolphin. But Rastus could not be found. Terry upended the sofa and caught sight of him scurrying between Trude's legs into the kitchen, where he disappeared into the space between the kitchen cupboards and the dishwasher. And time, as Terry was only too aware, was rushing on, as swiftly as the traffic was pouring into York from all the outlying villages to clog up the route into the chambers where he was to lead a police team to present their case to a barrister for the murder trial.

Trude promised to catch the hamster when she had taken the girls to school but Esther, in floods of tears by now, would have none of it. They considered sending Jessica to walk to school on her own while Trude stayed behind with Esther, but there was a main road to cross where a child had been run over and killed by a lorry only last month; so instead Terry promised his younger daughter faithfully that if she would only go to school *NOW* so that Jessica could be a dolphin in the school assembly, he, a senior Detective Inspector leading a murder investigation but more importantly for the moment their father, would not leave the house until Rastus was safely returned to custody.

It was a promise he broke five minutes after the children left the house.

He locked all the doors and windows so that there was no way the hamster could leave, then he scribbled a note for Trude explaining what he had done, snatched up his briefcase and hurried out to his car, which God be thanked for small mercies, started first time. Then he drove carefully the long way around the estate to avoid any possibility of being seen from the school, before emerging onto the Hull Road and getting stuck in exactly the traffic jam he had planned to avoid.

It was on occasions like this that he realized, more than ever, how much he, and the children, depended on Trude. Since Mary's death she had brought sanity and stability back into their home again, almost - but not quite - like a wife. He could trust her and share crises like this hamster business with her just as he once would have done with Mary. Probably tonight when the children were tucked up in bed and Rastus - please God - was back in his cage, they would have a whisky together and laugh over it. But there would be a catch in Terry's laughter, a necessary reserve as between any widower of forty and a young nanny of twenty three. One day he knew, she would leave, to go back to Norway with her boyfriend, Odd. And how would he cope then? It was a future that Terry dreaded.

Another thing he dreaded was the appearance of his boss, Will Churchill, at the barristers' chambers this morning. There was no real need for Churchill to come to this conference at all, but he had made a point of it nonetheless. And when Terry finally arrived, hot and flustered after a frustrating search for a parking space, there was Churchill, just as he had feared, standing outside on the pavement with the rest of the team, looking ostentatiously at his watch.

'Afternoon, Terence,' the Detective Chief Inspector said, making a point of using Terry's full name, which he hated. 'Glad you managed to fit us in.' He glanced at the two others, hoping for appreciation of his joke, and was rewarded, to Terry's disgust, with an embarrassed, complicitous grin from DS Mike Carter. DS Tracy Litherland, however, met her boss's sally with a straight wooden face, as though sarcasm was something she didn't get. For all his efforts, Will Churchill had yet to win the loyalty of the team he had taken charge of a year ago; but the less successful he was, it seemed to Terry, the harder he tried. And the main focus of Churchill's efforts was to undermine Terry, who, together with Sarah Newby, the barrister they were here to meet, had undermined him so badly in the past.

Mumbling some excuse about traffic, Terry followed his younger boss into the chambers, where the clerk showed them into a conference room on the first floor. Here they were welcomed by the CPS solicitor, Mark Wrass, a tall hearty jovial pinstriped man with oversized hands and feet which, if he had had more co-ordination, might have belonged to a farmer or rugby player. As it was, Terry had several times seen him knock a glass of water all over the table or sweep the papers to the floor with gestures of earnest, clumsy enthusiasm. Terry prudently seated himself at the opposite end of the table.

As he did so the door opened and Sarah Newby came in. She looked very different here, to the relaxed hostess at her garden party. A slender woman in her mid thirties with dark shoulder length hair and hazel eyes, she wore a black trouser suit with a thin gold chain round her neck under the collar of a white embroidered blouse. The men rose politely and she went round the table, shaking hands with each in turn. For Terry her smile was warm, the pressure of her hand firm; for Churchill it was merely civil, a brief acknowledgement of ancient enmity. There was a history to this meeting. It was less than year since Will Churchill had arrested this woman's son on a charge of murder; a charge from which she had successfully defended him in court. Sarah Newby had savaged Will Churchill in the witness box, accusing him of bullying, witness intimidation and incompetence, but Churchill had stood up to her forcefully and Sarah had been convinced, until the moment when the jury came in with their verdict, that she had lost the case and this man had put her son away for life. However smooth her complexion and polite her smile today, no one in the room doubted that the wound of what had so nearly happened was still tender under her skin.

As it must be under Churchill's too, Terry, thought. For in the end, Sarah Newby had beaten him and he had been publicly humiliated in his first major case since he had joined the York force; a humiliation that ran even deeper when Terry had uncovered evidence that Churchill had been pursuing the wrong man. For an ambitious young officer like Churchill, hoping to spend three or four years at most in his present post before rising to higher things, the acquittal of Sarah's son had been a major setback, a blemish on his CV; for Sarah, it had been a dagger pointed at the heart of her family and her career.

So Terry watched with more than normal curiosity as she seated herself at the head of the table, a few feet from the man she must detest above all others.

'Gentlemen, DS Litherland,' she began coolly, nodding at Tracy on Terry's right hand. 'I've read the file which Mr Wrass gave me, and, as usual, there are a number of questions to be settled before we decide whether to proceed, which is why we are all here. As I'm due in court this afternoon, I suggest we get down to business straight away.'

11. Counsel's Opinion

SARAH NEWBY had thought long and hard about taking this case, when her clerk proposed it to her. Over the past year she had appeared mostly as defence counsel in minor cases, the staple diet of a junior criminal barrister - burglaries, muggings, drugs - the usual round of petty crime. She had hoped that the publicity she gained for the successful defence of her son Simon on a murder charge would have raised her image with commissioning solicitors, but this had not happened. A few solicitors, like her friend Lucy Parsons, sent their harder cases to her, but many others fought shy. Mostly, she found herself scrabbling around for work as before, in the mire of petty crime, no nearer the prestige of a silk Queen's Counsel gown that, despite her late entry to the bar, she craved.

So this approach from the Crown Prosecution Service to undertake a murder trial was a compliment, a step up. The CPS, after all, had its own barristers - juniors employed on a salary to prosecute the mound of cases that clogged up the courts every day of the year. Sarah saw these people in court all the time, clutching heaps of files which they had only received the night before; it was because of their enforced lack of preparation that she was so often able to run rings round them. Any of them would have given their eye teeth for a case like this; but their very lack of experience in prosecuting major cases made them less likely to be entrusted with one, and more likely for the CPS management to go outside to a self-employed barrister like Sarah.

And Sarah, being only two rungs up the slippery ladder of success, was equally eager to take it. Even if it meant prosecuting for a change, instead of defending, as she was used to.

'As I see it,' she said now, 'our first problem is with the forensic evidence. It's not clear exactly what this poor girl died of. According to your pathologist it was "heart failure caused either by major haemorrhage or partial drowning, or a combination of both". Hardly a model of clarity that, is it?'

For half an hour they went through the details – the pathologist's report, the forensic evidence that showed three of David Kidd's fingerprints – and none of Shelley's – on the knife, and the background to the fatal relationship. Terry explained it clearly, with occasional interruptions from his boss.

'What we know for certain is that this young couple, David Kidd and Shelley Walters, were having an affair of some kind - well, the obvious kind, really. She was a first year student at the uni and her parents didn't like him - thought he was a conman and a cradlesnatcher; you've all read their statements. It's also clear that the affair wasn't going well. We've got statements from her student friends saying that she meant to dump him, in fact they thought she *had* dumped him the week before ...'

'Why was that, exactly?' Churchill asked, unable to resist filling the silence left by Terry's pause. *Does he think I don't know?* Terry wondered. Churchill, to Terry's annoyance, had stepped in to supervise the investigation for ten days while Esther was ill in hospital, which was the reason for his presence now.

'Because she found him in bed with another girl,' Sarah answered smoothly.

'Yes, that's right.' Terry nodded, approvingly. At least *she* had done her homework. 'A girl called Lindsay. She's the mother of his three year old kid - though he's no loving father. Takes her to bed every now and then and bungs her a few quid to keep her quiet, that seems to be his style. Anyway, when the dead girl, Shelley, found this girl in his bed it was the last straw, according to her friend Sandy. Shelley saw the light, and brought it to an end.'

'So why did she go back to his flat?' Sarah asked thoughtfully. 'The defence are bound to ask that. Did she want to see him again?'

'According to him, yes, according to her friend Sandy, no. She'd left a few clothes and books in the flat and wanted them back, that's all. But David now claims she'd forgiven him: she came in, they talked for a while, then made love, he says. That's the big change to his story. He didn't mention it in the first interview.'

'Why not?'

'He was shy, he says. He was respecting her privacy.' Terry shrugged dismissively.

'No sign of rape, though?'

'Not according to the pathologist, no.'

'So that, presumably, is an avenue the defence will want to explore. Who is representing him, by the way?'

Mark Wrass's large hands blundered earnestly through his papers. 'Savendra Bhose.'

'There you are then.' Sarah smiled. 'Savvy knows his job all right. He'll claim the girl thought up an excuse to see her lover one last time, hoping he'd forgive her. I know it was really a question of *her* forgiving *him*, but that's how a young girl's mind might work, especially if she was as naive and lacking in self-confidence as these statements from her mother and her tutors imply. She'd dumped him, but somehow he'd made her feel guilty, and part of her wanted forgiveness, so she went there hoping that something like that might happen. And it did, didn't it? They made love, then she got in the bath. Then while he was out of the flat she was overcome by remorse and killed herself. That's what he'll say. Trust me, I can see Savendra inventing it now.'

Inventing it. This was what unsettled him about lawyers, Terry thought. He liked Sarah, but she was still in love with her own cleverness, all of them were. She hadn't had to see the girl's dismembered body on the mortuary table as he had, or confront her hysterical mother in the hospital, wrapping his arms around hers to prevent her scratching the eyes out of the boyfriend who stood there brazenly claiming that Shelley had killed herself because of the incessant pressure from her parents to succeed. Sarah hadn't witnessed that, nor had she sat in the interview room for hours as he had, carefully restraining his temper while the cocky young bastard faked his grief and changed his story by the day.

And yet it was her job to face him in court. If she could be persuaded to take up the case at all, that is.

'He may say all that, but her student friends disagree,' he responded sourly. 'The affair was over as far as she was concerned, they say. She just went back to collect her possessions.'

'What possessions?' Sarah said. 'A bag, some underwear and jeans, a couple of novels, a magazine? Couldn't she have bought new ones?'

'They were her things. Students are poor.'

'Granted. And I'll make that point of course. But we have to accept the possibility that this girl Shelley went back to her boyfriend's flat at a time that made it virtually certain she would meet him.'

'Her friend Sandy might corroborate that,' said DS Tracy Litherland, speaking for the first time. 'She'd offered to go back with Shelley several times to collect these things, but Shelley always put her off. And then she went alone.'

'There you are then.' Sarah sat back in her chair, smiling. 'First break of serve to the defence. *And*, it seems, she'd been seeing a psychiatrist. What's that all about?'

'Bi-polar disorder,' said Tracy warily. 'She'd had treatment for a couple of years, her mother said. She took lithium to keep it under control.'

'Any suicidal tendencies?'

'Not according to her mother, no. None at all.'

'The defence aren't going to believe that, are they? Given that Kidd is claiming suicide. Savendra's going to call that psychiatrist, for sure. This could get nasty, for the parents. Especially if Kidd claims they put pressure on her, as ...' she leafed through the papers in front of her '... it seems he does. Not looking so easy now, is it?'

Terry felt a little tic throbbing in his throat as it often did when he was angry. The case his team had spent a month knitting together was unravelling in front of him.

'It's your job to counter those arguments,' he said sourly. 'If they put them at all.'

'I'll do my best, of course,' said Sarah. 'If I advise the CPS to go ahead, that is. It's my duty today to evaluate whether we have a chance of winning. What I'm pointing out is that the evidence to support your story is hardly conclusive. Not yet anyway.'

'All right,' said Terry angrily. 'Okay, she had a psychiatric disorder and she was a first year undergraduate, I'll grant you that. But most undergraduates don't kill themselves. Maybe she did go back to the flat to meet him again, I don't know. But look at his response when I asked him about these things in her bag. He said she'd come to stay and brought them with her. It was only when we'd spoken to her friend Sandy that he admitted he'd lied. You can hit him with that surely?'

'Certainly,' Sarah nodded coolly.

'Just as he lied about their happy reunion. He persisted with that until we told him his neighbour - a priest - had heard a quarrel. A violent quarrel, he said. Then Kidd admitted they'd had an argument.'

Sarah made a note.

'Then in the flat we found a meal half-prepared - onions, potatoes and carrots chopped up in a pan, steak in the fridge. And Shelley's clothes strewn all over the floor where she'd taken them off before she got in the bath.'

'Or made love?' Sarah asked.

'Or made love, yes,' Terry agreed. 'That's what he admitted they did, later.'

'And after that you think he killed her?

'That's what I think happened, yes,' Terry confirmed grimly. 'Whether this love-making was consensual or not is impossible to say; there's no evidence of rape, so perhaps it was. Maybe, as you say, she was in two minds about whether to break up with him; perhaps it was a fond farewell, I don't know. But he was never going to let her go, he's not that type. You haven't met him, I have. He's a psycho, a control freak. So when she's in the bath he goes in and says something that scares her - I don't know what. Maybe he has a kitchen knife in his hand - that would freak her out. Anyway she tries to get out of the bath and there's a struggle. He thrusts her head under water - that's how she gets the bruises round her neck and her throat - and she starts to drown. She nearly did drown, remember - the pathologist found water in her lungs and the ambulance crew say she coughed up pink frothy fluid - classic drowning symptoms. But of course, from David's point of view this is no good - how can he explain away a drowned girl in his bath? He thinks he's killed her but he's got to disguise how she died, make it look like suicide. So he cuts her wrists, sees the blood seeping out in the bath, and thinks what do I do now? That's when he decides to go to the shop. If he's out of the flat long enough he can claim an alibi, say she committed suicide while he wasn't there. So he goes out, and has a conversation with the shopkeeper who knows him. He even buys flowers, remember - a bunch of flowers for his girlfriend who's come back to him. He tells the shopkeeper all about this, then he meets his neighbour, a priest, on the stairs and tells him about it too. Then when he thinks she's had enough time to die he comes home, leaves a knife by her hand to make it look like suicide, and phones 999.'

'Only the ambulance crew find she's still alive,' murmured Sarah softly.

'Exactly. Not only that but they find a young man who seems more shocked than relieved that she's still breathing.'

'Do they say that?'

'Something like that. It's in their statements somewhere.'

'I see.' Sarah studied Terry thoughtfully. 'And is this the story you want me to put before the jury?'

'Yes.'

There was a silence. Will Churchill broke in, his Essex accent harsh and intrusive. 'Before you start questioning it in your clever lawyer's way, Mrs Newby, there's something else you should know.' He passed two slim files across the table. 'Those are the trial and probation reports on David Kidd. Three years ago he was charged with the rape and kidnap of a sixteen year old schoolgirl in Nottingham. The trial collapsed when the girl changed her story in the witness box, so all they could get him for was possession of cocaine. He got six months and probation for two years. But look at the witness statements and probation reports. He's a nasty piece of work, this lad.'

Sarah put her fingertips on the files as if to push them away. 'I can't use these. You know I can't. His previous record's irrelevant.'

'I'm asking you to read them all the same,' Churchill insisted. 'You need to know what this boy is like, and why we're so keen to bang him up. Offender profiling, if you know what that means.'

Always the snide remark. Sarah hesitated, her hand still on the files. 'All right, I may look at them if we decide to go ahead, but they shouldn't influence my decision now. What we have to decide is whether with the evidence you've got *on this case* there's a reasonable chance of conviction. So let's review it, shall we?'

She thought for a moment, then continued, counting out points on her fingers.

'First, and most important, we've got conflicting causes of death. Heart failure caused either by haemorrhage from the cut wrists, or from partial drowning, or both. Not very satisfactory, especially since the defence will say she cut her wrists first and then began to drown when she lost consciousness, which contradicts your story. On our side, however, we have the suspicious nature of the cuts - I take it the girl was right-handed, was she?'

'She was,' Terry nodded. 'And David was, too.'

'Good. So I can use that, and the bruises round her neck - they'll have a hard time explaining those away. And then there are the fingerprints on the knife; another good point for us. Then, thirdly, we have all the inconsistencies in his story. Whatever version he comes up with in the witness box I can cast doubt on it.'

'He's been a liar all his life,' said Terry. 'A serial fantasist. The girl's mother saw through him from the first.'

'So it seems,' Sarah agreed. 'But sadly, her evidence won't count for much. Plenty of mothers dislike their daughters' boyfriends. It doesn't mean they're all murderers.'

'What about the evidence of her friends?' Tracy asked. 'They knew what a shit he was.'

'That will help. Particularly this girl Sandy.' Sarah paused, thinking. 'But in the end this case boils down to two possibilities. Shelley Walters died in a bath in her boyfriend's flat. No one else was involved. So either he killed her, or, as the defence are bound to claim, she committed suicide. Now, sadly, all the evidence about the boyfriend's past character can't be used in court - not unless Mr Bhose slips up somehow, and I don't anticipate that. But evidence of the *victim's* past character *is* relevant, and this girl had a psychiatric disorder, so ...' she glanced down the table at her solicitor. 'I shall try and get that excluded but I don't hold out too much hope. A lot will depend on the psychiatrist, and how he comes across to the jury. Still, most girls don't slash their wrists, even if they are breaking up with their boyfriends. And especially not like this, holding the knife in the wrong hand and leaving no fingerprints. Nor do suicides leave bruises round their own necks. So although it's a long way from being a certainty ... '

She looked around, a faint smile playing on her lips. Terry felt a surge of relief. 'Does that mean you're recommending the case should go ahead, then?'

'I think we have more than a fifty per cent chance of conviction, yes.'

Part Two

Trial

12. Mothers Meet

THE DAY of the trial began badly for Sarah. Her husband Bob, a head teacher at a primary school in York, started talking at breakfast about the possibility of selling their house and moving to Harrogate.

'What?' Sarah asked, hurriedly buttering toast and searching the fridge for some edible cheese. 'Whatever for, Bob? We're happy here, aren't we?'

'If I get this headship, I mean,' her husband explained patiently, referring to a job application he'd made recently. 'It's for a school just south of Harrogate, much larger than mine. And you'd be nearer the courts in Leeds. Lots of lawyers live in Harrogate.'

'Have you seen the price of property there?' Sarah asked, pouring herself some coffee as her seventeen year old daughter Emily shambled past and started frantically pulling clothes out of the tumble dryer. 'We could scarcely afford a shed.'

'Oh, I don't know. I've asked someone to come and value this place and...'

'You've done what? Emily, pick those things up off the floor.'

'Just a free valuation. If we're going to move we need to know ...'

'Dad! What are you talking about? We're not going to move, are we? What about all my friends?' Emily, who Sarah had thought was ambulant but still comatose, suddenly exploded in teenage hormonal fury. 'You can't do something like this without thinking about me! Don't I matter at all? I do live here too, you know! Hello?'

'It's just a possibility, Em, that's all,' Bob answered patiently. 'Nothing's decided. It's just that I thought ...'

'Well, don't think, okay! I don't want to move. I'm happy here, aren't you?'

The explosion had gone on for some time, scattering emotional shrapnel through the few moments before they all had to leave, Bob and Sarah for work, Emily on the bus to the sixth form college. Exactly what I don't need on the morning of a major trial, Sarah thought, gunning her motorbike out of the drive after Bob had left in his Volvo. What the hell is he playing at, arranging to value the house without even letting me know? That's a huge family decision, not just a matter for him. What does he think - a move to Harrogate will revive our marriage somehow? Wreck it, more like ...

She leaned the bike into a bend and twisted the throttle viciously as a half mile straight opened ahead of her. This bike, the black Kawasaki 500, was another bone of contention between them. Bob loathed the machine as much as Sarah loved it. For him it was dangerous, noisy, unsuitable for a middle-aged wife and mother; for her it was a symbol of risk and freedom. She had originally been attracted to it by the practical advantages of being able to weave her way through gridlocked traffic into the congested city centres of York and Leeds, but this had long since given way to the sheer thrill of the deep-throated environmentally hostile roar of power between her legs each morning, the blast of wind as she crouched low over the handlebars, at speeds which, though perfectly legal, seemed to her terrifying in the extreme. For a few exhilarating moments she could stop being a wife, a mother, a professional lawyer, and become a black, anonymous figure, forgetting everything, concentrating only on the speed and the road and the wind.

Most days, at least, but not today. As she slowed off the A64 into the Fulford Road, creeping discreetly past a long line of stationary cars, the memory of the family row came back to her. It wasn't the first such event. Nothing had really been the same since Simon's trial last year. Bob, who had been such a saint when her son was small, had failed the young man in his moment of greatest need. Bob had not only believed him capable of murder, but even found a witness to support the police case. Only Sarah had stood by Simon, who was after all her son, not Bob's, and the rift in their marriage had still not healed. Perhaps it never will, Sarah thought, it's a scar we'll always live with.

Since that trial they had drifted apart. Bob had become more absorbed in his work, in his new ambition to crown his career with the headship of a larger school, or perhaps to become a government inspector, a setter of targets. All very laudable, no doubt, but not goals that filled Sarah with enthusiasm. And now to think of selling their house, their beautiful home with the willow trees and lawns and views of the river, without even discussing it with her first ...

The man must be mad, she thought, he's losing it, suffering the male menopause. Well, that would explain several other things about Bob's recent behaviour. But for now, as so often in her life, those things would have to be put on hold.

Wheeling the bike into the converted outhouse at the back of her chambers in Tower Street, she paused briefly to admire the other motorbike there, a shiny red 1000 cc Honda FireStorm, the proud new possession of her colleague and opponent in today's trial, Savendra Bhose. The bike was twice as heavy and powerful as Sarah's, and Savendra had intended to take his fiancee, Belinda, on it for a weekend in the Lake District. Wondering how that had gone, Sarah ran upstairs to her room, where she changed out of her motorcycle leathers into a smart black trouser suit, stiff white collar bands, and gown. Swiftly checking her makeup in a mirror on her desk, she peered out of the window across the street at the view of the Norman castle, Clifford's Tower, beside the Crown Court.

As she did so a car passed along the street in front of the castle. The woman in the passenger seat caught Sarah's eye - a well dressed woman in a smart black suit and hat, with an intent, serious look on her face, as though she were going to a trial or a funeral. As the car turned right towards the castle car park, Sarah put away her makeup, checked that her briefcase contained all her papers and her wig in its enamelled tin box, and headed downstairs for the short walk across the road to the Crown Court.

Getting out of the car, Kathryn Walters felt her legs trembling. This was it, then, they were here at last. Six months after Shelley's death, they had finally come to get justice. She drew a deep breath and waited while her husband Andrew bought a parking ticket from the machine. She would go in with him beside her. Their marriage was no longer close but this, above all else, was still something they shared. In sickness and in health, until death ... but this was not the sort of death the preacher had meant, all those many years ago.

Andrew stuck the parking ticket inside the windscreen, locked the car doors, and took his wife's hand. They had never been a demonstrative couple, but now ... her fingers, in the smart black gloves, laced tightly between his, in a grip just this side of pain. She looked up and saw the tension in his face, the lines around the mouth that had deepened over these long, dreadful months, the hurt and anger that were liable to break out at any time and made living with him so difficult, even without his constant, humiliating betrayals. In his eyes she saw his intention to comfort her fighting with his own urgent need for comfort himself.

'Ready then?'

'As much as I'll ever be.' She raised a gloved hand to brush a wisp of hair back over his receding temples, and made a doomed, infinitesimal attempt at a smile. 'Come on, let's go.'

They walked towards the court, attracting several curious glances on their way. The strain of Shelley's death had accentuated the differences character brought to their appearance. In Kathryn, grief had turned to anger - an inextinguishable flame of rage that this could happen to her daughter, her family - and an icy determination to make someone pay. But because the police and prosecution took so much out of her hands, she had channelled her desire for revenge into physical activity. A naturally healthy woman, since her daughter's death her keep fit activities had developed into an obsessive, gruelling regime of self-punishment, lashing her body through barriers she had never passed before, so that in the recovery afterwards she could feel peace, a flood of endorphins temporarily drowning the rage in her mind.

As a result of all this exercise she had a body as firm and fit as that of a woman in her early twenties, half her real age. But it was her clothes as much as her physique that attracted attention. For while Andrew wore his normal threadbare professor's suit with a row of pens sticking out of the top pocket, Kathryn had taken care over her appearance today, dressing as formally as she had for Shelley's funeral - black suit, black shoes, coat and gloves, even the small black hat over her shoulder length blonde hair, pinned back in a neat pony tail.

Andrew had queried the outfit when she had appeared in it this morning. 'We're not on show today, you know. No one will be looking at us.' But Kathryn had brushed him aside. 'It's a matter of respect. If you don't understand that, I do.'

At least he wore a clean shirt and tie, which was something, given the dismal state of his wardrobe. For Andrew, unlike his wife, had let grief and guilt drive him to despair. The pain of Shelley's death had destroyed his ability to concentrate. For hours, he sat in the university library with his brain in neutral, his hands and eyes working their way through medieval documents whose significance he could no longer explain; his research, such as it was, carried on by Carole, the graduate student whom he spent more time with than his wife. His listlessness infuriated Kathryn, sparking a rage which scared him deeper into his shell. She guessed he had a mistress, and no longer cared; he had become so thin and haggard that she almost welcomed the idea for his sake.

But today's ordeal, at least, brought them together.

Near the circle of grass known as the Eye of York they stopped, a forlorn, formal pair, while three teachers shepherded a line of schoolchildren in front of them. Kathryn let out a little gasp of pain.

'What is it?' Andrew turned to her in concern.

'It's ... no, nothing.' But she gripped his hand tighter. 'Don't you see? That girl ...'

'Which girl? What do you mean?'

As the children passed Kathryn saw that of course it wasn't true: the lively little girl at the front was no ghost, not Shelley come back to visit, of course not. But still - it was such an uncanny resemblance. Same long, fair hair like her mother's, same smile, same bouncy, fidgety walk that Shelley had had at age ten.

'Don't you see it?' she asked, as the children went by. 'That one there!'

'Look, Kath, you've got to stop doing this.' He grasped her shoulder with a skinny left hand. 'It's nonsense.'

'But it did look like her, didn't it? You do remember?'

'Of course I do. God!' He watched the children forming a disorderly queue outside the museum. The girl punched one of the others and then hid behind a friend, laughing, her blonde hair tossing from side to side as she ducked. 'But she's gone, Kath. She'll never come back.'

'Yes, I know.' Kathryn turned away, towards the wide steps and pillared portico of the Crown Court, with the stone statue of Justice above, holding her spear and balance. A woman in a black gown, carrying a large briefcase, came round the corner from Tower Street, and stopped on the balcony outside the entrance to the court, talking to a couple of men in suits and a security guard. A prison van with blank windows drove up and parked at the foot of the steps.

'Will he have come in that, do you think?'

'Probably.' Andrew watched the security guards unlocking the rear door. 'Let's ... walk around this way slowly. We don't want to bump into him on the steps, do we?'

'No.'

They turned back towards the museum, waiting until the prison van was unloaded. As they approached the children Kathryn saw the child who had upset her again. She was no ghost; her nose was too short, her cheeks broader than Shelley's had ever been. But if Shelley ever did come back, that would be the age she'd want to see her.

She leaned her head against her husband's shoulder, remembering.

When Shelley was ten and Miranda was twelve they'd been living in Yorkshire for what - four years? They had bought the house near Wetherby, with the stables and paddock for the ponies that the girls had always wanted. She remembered how eager the girls had been at that age, how much energy they'd had! They'd got up at six in the morning to brush their ponies before she took them to shows, pulling them there in the trailer behind the old Volvo which came back cluttered with muddy jodhpurs, saddles, boots and rosettes. Shelley's problems were just a cloud on the horizon. School, music lessons, concerts, swimming, parties - Christ, she thought, where did we get the energy? But we were a family too, busy at our work, me at the pharmacy, Andrew with his lectures. And whatever he got up to with his students, the bastard, he was always there for the girls, as I was, our lives revolved around them then, they were the centre of everything ...

And now what? Our lives still revolve around Shelley, but she's just a coffin disappearing behind a curtain, a little urn of ashes in the crematorium gardens. Was it all for *that?*

'I think he's gone inside now,' Andrew said. 'The van's pulling away.'

'Did you see him?'

'I'm not sure. He had his hands over his face.'

'That won't do him any good. He can't hide now.'

'Let's hope not.' He squeezed her hand, and they walked towards the courtroom steps, where the solicitor Mark Wrass was waiting. There was a great emptiness inside Kathryn, a despair that even the horror of this trial would not help; nothing could bring Shelley back again. But inside the horror a thin flame of anger longed for the fuel of justice to make it blaze. Fifty years ago, she thought, David would have been hanged for what he did to our little girl. I wish I were living then, that's what he deserves.

At least they'll lock him up for life, if the lawyers do their job properly. And I'll be here to see it happen.

Sarah had not met the Walters before, but as she stood with Terry Bateson and Mark Wrass on the wide stone balcony outside the Crown Court she had guessed who they were by their diffident, solemn manner, the awe with which they gazed at the elegant pillared portico of the ancient stone court, and the nervous detour they made to avoid the prison van at the foot of the steps.

No doubt, she thought, in the thousand years since Lord Clifford had dispensed brutal justice from the Norman castle on its mound to her left, many similar victims' families had crossed this round grass circle seeking compensation, retribution, revenge. Some had been satisfied in full, bloody measure - the accused convicted and hanged in full public view from the gable of the women's prison directly opposite - while others had been disappointed, but the pain, the grim nervous anxiety with which supplicants approached the court at the start of each trial must have been much the same as that etched on the faces of the couple now climbing the steps towards her.

'Mr and Mrs Walters, good morning.' Mark Wrass extended his arms in greeting, his face expressing simultaneous welcome and sympathy. Like a cross between a pub landlord and an undertaker, Sarah thought, watching wryly. 'Allow me to introduce our counsel, Mrs Sarah Newby.'

Sarah held out her hand, and smiled. 'Mr and Mrs Walters? This must be a painful day for you. I hope we can get you justice.'

'I hope so too,' said Kathryn sharply. 'That's what you do here, isn't it?'

'Well yes, of course.'

'I just hope you're prepared then, that's all.'

Sarah frowned, surprised by the aggressive tone. 'Don't worry, DI Bateson here and Mr Wrass have done a good job. I've got all the statements in this briefcase here, and I read them thoroughly over the weekend.'

'The weekend?' Kathryn said incredulously. 'You read them over the *weekend?*'

'Several times, Mrs Walters,' Sarah insisted, kicking herself. What she said was true - she'd been busy with two burglaries, an affray, and a car theft the week before - but of course she'd struck the wrong tone. All that trauma with Bob and Emily this morning must have unsettled her more than she'd thought. 'I read them again, I mean - we've had several conferences already. Don't worry, I'm used to mastering details quickly. It's part of the job.'

'Nonetheless, it would have been nice if we could have met you too,' Kathryn persisted, as her husband shook his head slowly. 'You are representing us, after all.'

Embarrassed, Mark Wrass sprang to Sarah's defence. 'Technically, Mrs Walters, Mrs Newby is instructed by the Crown Prosecution Service, not yourselves. In the eyes of the law you are witnesses in the case, not the principal ...'

'Nevertheless it was your daughter who was murdered.' Seeing the reaction his words were creating, Sarah put her hand on Kathryn's arm. 'I do understand that, Mrs Walters, really. You want this case to be prosecuted properly. Well, it will be. I can assure you of that. I know the system can seem a little ... impersonal, but it doesn't need to be. Why don't we meet for lunch? Mr Wrass can arrange it, I'm sure.'

In the cell block below the court Sarah's opponent, Savendra Bhose, was about to reacquaint himself with his client. He had met David Kidd before, of course, in the bleak Victorian interview rooms at Armley Gaol, but since then he had defended two burglary cases and taken his fiancee Belinda James on a long weekend in the Lake District on the Honda FireStorm, up and down the hills on what he'd called 'Wordsworth's rollercoaster.' Although the papers from David's case had come with them, they had received rather less careful scrutiny than his client might have hoped. Several witness statements now exuded a musky Estee Lauder fragrance which reminded Savendra irresistibly of the hotel bedroom in Keswick where they had, unfortunately, been scattered all over the floor with Belinda's underwear. The touch and scent of these papers evoked clear and beguiling images of Belinda's looks and behaviour that night; but exactly what his client looked like he found somewhat harder to recall.

As Kidd was led towards him Savendra greeted him with a professional, encouraging smile. The warder released Kidd's handcuffs and left them together in the 'stable block' - a small room at the end of the cell corridor, furnished with half a dozen wooden stalls in which a lawyer could meet his client. They reminded Savendra of the carrels where junior pupils at his public school, Ampleforth, had done their homework. Each carrel was about four feet square, with a wooden seat at the back where the defendant usually sat, with a stool screwed to the floor in front of it for his lawyer to perch on. It was a primitive, humiliating system, probably dating back to the eighteenth century when the courts were built and men were smaller. If the lawyer and his client were tall, they had to sit carefully to avoid their knees banging together.

As Kidd sat down Savendra noticed that he looked nervous; but anyone would, in a cell block like this, accused of murder. He was commendably smart, though, his shirt and tie neatly pressed. The snakeskin boots struck a jarring note; but they would be invisible from the dock. He was shorter than

Savendra remembered, and there was something rather worrying about the eyes. They seemed not to open fully, as though the man were drunk or half asleep. Savendra found it unnerving. Surely the idiot wasn't stoned, was he? That would be a fine start to the trial - himself unprepared, his client weaving around in the dock, unable to plead.

But his voice was clear enough, though slightly lacking in respect. 'What happens this morning, then? What do you do?'

'Nothing much, at first,' Savendra smiled reassuringly. 'It's the prosecution who kick off. All we do is sit and watch, today.' And try to remember the details of this case, he thought. 'All you have to do is create a good impression with the jury. They'll be watching you while the prosecutor speaks, to see if you look like their idea of a murderer. Just concentrate on looking like a decent, grief-stricken boyfriend, and leave the rest to me.'

'It's all right for you,' David Kidd said. 'You're not facing life in gaol.'

'Neither are you, I hope,' Savendra assured him confidently. 'There's plenty of room in this case for reasonable doubt and that's what I intend to create.'

The young man studied him doubtfully, as though wondering if he'd made the right choice and whether he could do anything about it even at this late stage. Heaven forbid, Savendra thought. I need this case to pay off the loan on the bike. 'What's he like, this prosecutor, then? Is he any good?'

'He's a she, actually,' Savendra yawned, picking up his wig and getting to his feet. 'Mrs Sarah Newby. She's only been qualified for three or four years. Don't worry, Mr Kidd. We're in with a chance here. Truly.'

He called for the warder, who led Kidd back to his cell. Savendra ran up the stairs into the oak-panelled courtroom. He had no great hopes, but there were certainly some holes in the case and he hoped to find others. And since his fiancee's parents were coming to watch him in court later this week, he strongly hoped he could. That was the surprise she'd sprung on him in their hotel bedroom last night, as he untied the ribbons around the brief he'd brought with him. While Belinda stood beside him, tantalisingly loosening the ribbons on briefs of her own ...

He dumped those papers now on the ancient leather covered oak table in the courtroom. If only she hadn't spilt that perfume on these witness statements! Sarah Newby slid into her seat beside him.

'Hi, Savvy, ready for the fray?' She sniffed the lingering fragrance appreciatively, and smiled. 'Had a good weekend then, did you?'

13. Savendra

THE TWO barristers chatted companionably as they waited for the judge to enter. Sarah and Savendra were friends as well as colleagues; they had shared a room together in their year of pupillage, and supported each other through the tedium, disappointments, occasional triumphs, and frequent sick humour of their first year at the criminal bar. Now she listened, smiling, as he talked of his fiancee's excitement during their motorbike trip to the Lakes, and their plans for the imminent wedding.

'It's the ceremony that scares me most,' Savendra murmured ruefully. 'I dreamt last night that I dropped the ring and it rolled away down a drain.'

'Very Freudian,' said Sarah. 'It means you're afraid of responsibility. Or riding away from it rather. Like you were this weekend.'

'Over the hills and far away.' Savendra grinned happily at the memory. 'It's tremendous, the FireStorm. I'll take you for a ride sometime if you like.'

'And scare me rigid? No chance, young man.' Sarah shook her head, laughing. 'I've seen you leaning into those bends. Your Belinda's a brave girl.'

'Love me, love my bike. That's what I told her, that's what she does.'

Their banter ended as the accused entered the dock from the cells below, handcuffed to a burly security guard. Sarah turned to look at him, the smile fading from her face. It was the first time she had seen him, this man who she meant to send to prison for life. He looked smaller than she had expected, his face pale after several months on remand, with a touch of cotton wool under the chin where, perhaps, his hand had shaken while shaving this morning. The sight evoked a pain that was as sharp, as intense as Sarah had feared. The young face, scowling with a mixture of nerves, fear and bravado in a room full of hostile faces pierced her with the memory of her own son, Simon, whose demeanour in court had been surly, truculent and defiant, just as she expected this young man's to be. It was the natural reaction of the young male, cornered and at bay. Unattractive, and likely to increase the chances of his conviction.

But the pain only lasted for a moment. As David Kidd answered the clerk, pleading not guilty in a sullen, insolent voice, Sarah looked away, above his head to the watching faces of Kathryn and Andrew Walters in the public gallery. Then, very deliberately, she slid the dead girl's photograph out of the pile of papers and laid it on the table in front of her. One of the things that had surprised her about Kathryn Walters was how closely the woman's face had resembled that of her dead daughter. They could have been sisters, almost. Everything, the features, the hair, the shape of the mouth, even the pallor was the same - although the pallor in Kathryn's face was caused merely by nerves, rather than the loss of four or five litres of blood.

Concentrate, Sarah told herself firmly as she got to her feet, and remember what that young man did to this poor girl in the photograph. And to her parents, as well. They came here for justice, and now they're relying on you.

Certainly no one who listened to Sarah's opening speech would have accused her of sympathy for the defendant. Her exposition was clear, concise, and cold. This was what she was good at, this was what she had prepared for in all those long years of sacrifice and study. She had hoped this return to prosecution, with the luxury of a trial that would probably last a fortnight, would be a pleasure, and so long as she believed in the case she was presenting it would be. She began to outline the evidence that, she said, would convict David Kidd of murder.

'On the afternoon of Sunday, 21st May this year, David Kidd called an ambulance to his flat in Gillygate, York. When the ambulance crew arrived they found Shelley Walters, his girlfriend, in a bath full of bloody water, with her wrists cut and bleeding and her face under water. They took her to hospital where she died less than an hour later, of heart failure caused by a combination of two factors - extensive haemorrhage from the cuts on her wrists, and partial drowning in the bath water.'

She paused to contemplate the jurors, like a schoolmistress checking for their attention. There were seven men, five women, three in their early twenties. Of the men, two wore jackets and ties, the others were in open-necked shirts. One man wore a fleece, and a young woman had chosen a tracksuit for the occasion. We prepare with such care, Sarah thought sardonically, then we hand the most vital decision of all to idlers dragged in off the street. The girl in the tracksuit swallowed and nodded nervously as she met Sarah's eye.

'Now, ladies and gentlemen, you may think that this sounds like suicide. A young woman gets into a bath, cuts her wrists, holds them under water to help the blood flow, and then when she faints from this loss of blood her head slips under water and she begins to drown. That is the interpretation, I am sure, that Mr Bhose will present for the defence. It is what David Kidd told the police when they interviewed him. He was the person who found her, and he was alone in the flat with her before she died. So it is clear that only one of two things happened. Either Shelley Walters killed herself, or she was murdered by her boyfriend, David Kidd. There is no other possibility, is there? It is as simple as that.'

It was not only the jury who watched Sarah attentively as she spoke. Terry Bateson had found a bench to the left of the dock, where he could watch her present his case. It was a rare pleasure for him; he could see her clearly in profile, a slender straightbacked figure in the jet black suit and gown, a delicate finger smoothing an errant wisp of hair under her wig, speaking in a low, clear, persuasive voice that resonated somewhere under his ribs, so that he felt like a teenager again. He was a fool, of course, he knew that: she was a married woman with two grown-up children and a husband to care for; any friendly flirtatious phrase she might occasionally throw him was natural feminine politeness, no more. Her normal manner when they met was pleasant but brusque, sharp, businesslike - the body language of a career woman for whom efficient time management was a function as natural as breathing.

And yet ... Terry could not help himself. If Mary had been alive it would have been different, but now ... there was an exquisite pleasure in this secret pain of hoping, like pressing a pin into your palm to prove you are alive. And perhaps ... it was always possible things might change, and she feel the same about him. And then how would that be? Where would they meet, what would they do? He watched, entranced, only the surface of his mind attending to her lucid outline of the evidence he knew so well.

'So what is David Kidd's explanation? Well, he told the police several different stories. You will hear first what he told them on the day of Shelley's death. Shelley had come to visit him, he said, and while he was preparing a meal for her, she decided to have a bath. Everything was fine between them, he told the police, but she felt under pressure from her tutors and parents because her studies were not going well. They talked about these things for a while, and then she got in the bath while he went out to buy groceries for the meal. When he came back, he found her lying in a bath full of blood, and called an ambulance.'

Savendra, too, listened to Sarah intently, as the contents of the witness statements, rather than their scent, came back to him at last.

'All very good, you may think. It sounds a reasonable story, doesn't it? At first the police believed it too. But then they began to investigate further, and found a number of things that did not fit. Much later - two weeks after he was first interviewed by the police - Mr Kidd claimed they didn't just talk - he had sex with Shelley before she got into the bath. 'We made love,' he says. But how much love was there really in what happened to this young girl? You will hear from David Kidd's neighbour, a priest, who heard the sounds of a quarrel between a man and a woman a short time before Shelley died. The shouting and screaming were so loud that they could be heard through the floor of his flat. Not the sounds of love-making, he says, but of a violent quarrel. Yet this quarrel was completely missing from the story David Kidd told the police.'

Kathryn Walters listened with cold pleasure. When she and Andrew had first entered the public gallery, they had looked down at the gowned backs and bewigged heads of the two barristers at the table in the centre of the court, engaged in what looked like a light-hearted, friendly conversation. The sight had irritated Kathryn intensely, the more so since clerks, reporters and solicitors wandered in and out, chatting as though nothing important was likely to happen for hours. A journalist told a policeman a joke; the shorthand writer was reading a magazine.

'Look at them!' she had muttered bitterly to her husband. 'They don't bloody care, do they?' To all these people, she realised with horror, this was just another day at work. Perhaps a mildly interesting one, but that was all.

But now that Sarah had begun speaking the scene was transformed. Each sentence was clear, straightforward, and damning; the case against her daughter's murderer was being presented as Kathryn had always hoped it would be. Nothing Sarah said was new to Kathryn, of course; she had worried over each detail endlessly for months, sometimes with Andrew, more often alone, unable to sleep, walking restlessly around the empty house at three in the morning while he was away with his mistress. But here at last was public affirmation. These words were not being muttered darkly in her own mind, but spoken lucidly in open court; nails hammered into David's coffin one by one. Behind Sarah, a reporter was taking notes busily.

'So what was this quarrel about, you may ask? Well, you will hear from Shelley's parents, and her friends at university, that things were not fine between David and Shelley, as he claimed. On the contrary - Shelley wanted to end the relationship, because he had been unfaithful to her. The only reason she went to his flat was to collect some clothes and books that she had left there. She was going to see him for the last time.'

The wigs and gowns, the royal coat of arms, the panelled wood, ornate ceiling and marble pillars all added to the solemnity of the occasion. One hand clasped in her husband's, Kathryn Walters glared down at David Kidd, the liar she had loathed for so long.

'Then, conclusively, you may think, the police discovered further evidence. A kitchen knife - the knife which caused the fatal injuries to Shelley's wrists - was found on the floor in the bathroom. And on this knife, you will hear, were not Shelley's fingerprints, as you might expect if this was suicide, but those of David Kidd. His fingerprints on the knife that killed her!'

The girl in the tracksuit nodded solemnly. For her, already, the case seemed proved. Other jurors' faces looked equally serious. A young man glared at David with contempt.

'So, ladies and gentlemen. Other details, small but important, will come to light during the trial. But these are the main points which the prosecution ask you to consider. Firstly, that Shelley did not go to David's flat for love or sympathy, as he told the police; she went there to collect her belongings, and end their relationship for good. Secondly, that they did not just have a quiet, friendly conversation; they had a noisy, violent quarrel. Thirdly, that she was found dead, in his bath, with her wrists cut by a knife that had his fingerprints on it. That is enough, the prosecution say, to prove that Shelley Walters' death was not suicide, as David Kidd intended it to appear; it was a cruel, deliberate murder.'

Savendra realised gloomily that his colleague was doing a good job. But then what else had he expected? Theirs was a curious relationship, in which each to some extent envied the other. Sarah was older than he was, and had seen more of life's down side than he could easily imagine. Leaving school at fifteen, after all, to bring up your baby on one of Leeds' worst council estates, is not a course recommended in careers guidance pamphlets for aspiring barristers. The more Savendra learned about Sarah's background, the more he regarded her tenacity, diligence and bloody-minded perseverance in the face of overwhelming odds as astonishing, miraculous even. In comparison, his own smooth progress from Ampleforth to Merton College, Oxford, and thence to the Bar, so celebrated by his fond admiring parents, now seemed to him merely routine, an inheritance rather than an achievement.

And yet Sarah, to his surprise, admired him too. He had, or so she told him, a certain grace and charm, a patina of effortless good manners even under pressure which gave him, like many men of his background, a steely resilient confidence which she envied. Under pressure herself she became sharp, spiky, aggressive, sometimes saying things which antagonized juries and she regretted later. And then, perhaps because of this self-confidence, he dared to take risks and shortcuts in the belief that he would get away with it as, all too often, he did. While for Sarah, the idea of going into court unprepared, without having written out each question and read each witness statement many times, set butterflies hatching in her stomach until she was ill.

It was Savendra, however, who felt ill today. As she stood beside him, calmly outlining her case for the jury, his mind was racing like a rat through the maze of ill-lit corridors which were all the details he remembered from his hasty reading this weekend. But he was used to operating like this. He could think as fast as a rat could run. And the more clearly Sarah outlined her case, the brighter the light her words shone into the corners of the maze.

There were holes in this case, he remembered now. Loopholes which he would have to gnaw at and enlarge, bit by bit, to smuggle his client out to safety. And she, like a lady with a lamp, had made them more obvious to him. But then that was all part of the game.

As Sarah turned to summon her first witness, he caught her eye, smiled, and slowly shook his head.

14. Pathologist

SARAH'S FIRST witness, Terry Bateson, described how he and DS Litherland had examined David's flat, finding Shelley's clothes strewn all over the living room floor, and, in the bloodstained bathroom, a kitchen knife covered in Shelley's blood. He was followed by the pathologist, Arnold Tuchman, who limped briskly to the witness stand and repeated the oath from memory, without glancing at the card the usher held up for him. A skinny, white-haired man, he gripped the stand with both hands and turned his attention to Sarah, who stood waiting. The wire-rimmed spectacles magnified the size of his eyes as they focussed on her, and she had a brief, unsettling sense of what it must be like to be a worm spotted by a thrush.

'Would you give the court your name and qualifications, please?'

'My name is Dr Arnold Tuchman. I am a consultant forensic pathologist.'

'And you have been practising forensic pathology for how long?'

'Thirty nine years, young lady.'

Sarah smiled gently, accepting the words as a compliment rather than the put down the crusty old man probably intended. Age was relative, after all; this man had begun practising pathology a year before she was born.

'So you are highly experienced, doctor. And you performed a post mortem examination on Shelley Walters, I understand. Could you summarize your findings for this court?'

'Certainly. The deceased was a young healthy woman about twenty years old. She had suffered severe loss of blood due to cuts on her wrists, particularly the right wrist, where the ulnar artery was pierced. Her lungs contained traces of bloody water, and there were the residues of pink froth in her mouth and throat, which is common in cases of drowning. In addition I noticed a number of subcutaneous bruises around her head and neck, as well as a circular bruise, presumably the mark of a tourniquet, around her right arm.'

'Thank you, doctor. So what, precisely, was the cause of her death?'

'She died of heart failure, caused by the severe blood loss from the ulnar artery in her right wrist, combined with the trauma caused by partial drowning.'

'You cannot say which of these factors was the principal cause?'

'Not really. As I understand it, she was still alive when the ambulance crew arrived and applied a tourniquet to stop the bleeding. At the hospital, every attempt was made to revive her, including blood transfusions and electrotherapy. Unfortunately these failed. The trauma was too great. Her heart simply stopped.'

'So, to be quite clear, you cannot say whether she died from drowning or blood loss?'

'No. She died from both.'

'Very well, let us examine the cuts to her wrists. If the jury would look at photographs one and two.' The usher distributed booklets of photographs to the jury, whose faces paled at the pictures inside. 'Could you describe these injuries for us, Dr Tuchman?'

'Certainly. The cuts to the left wrist, as you see, are relatively superficial. Several flexor tendons and veins have been severed, but there is no damage to any major blood vessel. The wrist was probably bent backwards as the cuts were made, which would cause the radial artery - the artery that is normally injured by attempted suicides - to slip into the shelter of the radius. This is a common difficulty which people encounter when trying to kill themselves, or indeed others, in this way.'

Sarah watched the jury, who had never faced photographs like this before. Several jurors were peering so intently at their booklet that she wondered if they heard a word the old man said.

'The injuries to the right wrist, however, are much more severe. In particular the ulnar artery - not the radial - has been pierced. This injury would have led to immediate and severe haemorrhage which, as I say, was one of the main causes of death. It would certainly have killed her had the bleeding not been checked by the tourniquet.'

'Are you able to say how much blood she had lost before that happened, doctor?'

'I'm afraid not, no. She received blood transfusions at the hospital, you see. So it's impossible to say how much of the blood in the body was hers.'

'What can you tell us about the state of her lungs?'

'Well, both lungs contained water. In addition to this there were traces of a pink bloody froth in her airways and around her mouth. This is a classic indicator of drowning.'

'So why is it not possible to say whether she drowned or bled to death?'

'Because both injuries occurred at more or less the same time, and both were unsuccessfully treated by the hospital.' The elderly pathologist glared at Sarah as if she were a persistent but not very intelligent pupil. 'One of the things I have learned over the past forty years, young lady, is that the cause of death isn't always as clear cut as lawyers might like it to be. In this case, both factors obviously contributed, that's as much as I can say. The young woman was already in a near terminal state when the ambulance came; it was probably too late to revive her.'

'Very well.' Sarah was amused by his manner. It didn't worry her; what he said suited her case quite well. 'As you may be aware, Dr Tuchman, Mr Kidd claims that this is suicide. Shelley Walters inflicted these injuries upon herself, he says, while he was out of the flat. In your expert opinion, are these injuries consistent with that explanation?'

'They are more consistent with murder, in my view. But suicide is not completely impossible.' The big eyes behind the wire rimmed spectacles met Sarah's unflinchingly, a faint smile flickering across his lined old face. 'Although I regret to say that I cannot be absolutely certain. The longer you work in my field, the more you find that is true. But in order to maintain that this was suicide, you would have to find a convincing explanation for a number of factors which do not fit in with that theory.'

He's enjoying this, the patronizing old coot! Sarah thought. Beside her, Savendra was scribbling down the last answer industriously.

'And those factors are?'

'Well, for one thing, the fatal cut was to the victim's right wrist, not the left. A right-handed person would naturally cut her left wrist first, and more effectively, than the right.'

'Could you explain that please, doctor?'

'Certainly.' The elderly pathologist fished in the breast pocket of his jacket and, to a murmur of interest from the jury, drew out a pocket scalpel, its blade shining clear in the lamplight. He laid his left hand on the hand on the witness stand in front of him, palm upwards. 'A right-handed person would take the knife in his right hand, like this, and cut from the outside of his left wrist, near the base of the thumb, across to the inside, like so. But the wrist has many tendons, so you would have to dig the knife in deep, and drag it across with some force. Not a pleasant business, which is why many suicides who kill themselves in this way are drunk, by the way. To deaden the pain.'

'Was this girl drunk?'

'Not really. A little alcohol in her blood - a small glass of wine or beer, that's all. But think of the results of such a cut. You decide to kill yourself, you're right handed, as this girl was, so you cut your left wrist, like so. Then to complete the job, you pick up the knife in your left hand, which is already damaged and bleeding, and try to slit the right wrist. You're using the hand you don't normally use, remember. Which cut do you think is going to be the deeper?'

By now the doctor was facing the jury, as though delivering a lecture. Sarah saw several heads nodding earnestly as they took it in. Before a juror felt drawn to raise a hand to answer, like a student, Sarah said: 'I take it you mean the cut on the left wrist will be deeper, Dr Tuchman?'

'Obviously,' he said, looking at her as though she were a halfwit. 'Whereas if someone else cut her wrist, the opposite is more likely to be case, don't you see? Come here, young woman, let me demonstrate.'

This way of being ordered around by a witness wasn't one she recalled being covered at the Inns of Court School, but Sarah was in favour of livening up court proceedings whereever possible. With a quick glance at the judge to ensure he did not disapprove, she left the table in the well of the court and advanced towards the witness stand. The pathologist, to her amusement, handed her the scalpel. It was a deadly little instrument, she saw; quite enough to cause instant death if misused. She held it in her right hand.

'Right, now, imagine I'm sitting in a bath facing you when you come in.' The pathologist held out his two hands, wrists upwards, in front of him. 'Now, catch hold of one of my wrists, young woman, and pretend to cut it, if you would. Gently, without drawing too much blood.'

There was a murmur of appreciative laughter from the jurors. Reaching forward with her left hand, Sarah grabbed the old man's bony right wrist, bending the palm back slightly to expose the network of veins and tendons, and drew the wicked little blade through the air above it, from the base of the thumb inwards. The pathologist chuckled appreciatively.

'Very good. You notice how you naturally chose my right wrist to cut, not the left. Now, do the same with the other one.'

Sarah reached across his body to seize his left wrist. The action was a little more awkward, felt less natural. When she drew the scalpel through the air above it, she hesitated, before moving it from the outside inwards, as before.

'You weren't sure which way to cut then, were you?' said the doctor. 'You could just as well have cut from the inside out. But I think the jurors could see another thing. You are right-handed, so you felt more confident cutting my right wrist than my left. So the damage you were likely to inflict would be deeper, more potentially fatal, on the right than the left.'

Sarah handed back the scalpel and walked back to her table. 'And how does that relate to the wounds suffered by Shelley Walters, Dr Tuchman?'

'Very closely. Both wrists were cut from the outside to the inside of the arm, but the cut to the right wrist is deeper - the knife has gone in much further and pierced the ulnar artery - the one nearer the little finger - whereas on the left wrist both arteries remained undamaged. On the left only veins were cut; if she had made a fist or applied pressure the bleeding would have stopped. Whereas on the right the bleeding was far more serious. It was the cut to her right wrist which killed her, not the left.'

The crotchety old pathologist, Sarah thought gratefully, was proving a star witness - one whose evidence the jury would not easily forget.

'And what would have been the result if she had cut her own wrists?'

'Then, presuming she was right handed, I would expect the opposite to be true. The left wrist would be badly damaged, the right wrist much less so, if at all.'

'Very well, is there any further evidence which leads you to suspect that this is murder, rather than suicide?'

'Yes. There is the lack of tentative cuts.'

'Tentative cuts?' Sarah frowned. 'Perhaps you could explain these to the jury, as well.'

'Well, when a person cuts their own wrists, they don't usually know exactly how to do it. It hurts, it's difficult to succeed the first time. So in many suicides we see a number of shallow, experimental or tentative cuts, next to the final cut which does all the damage. Whereas in a murder, such tentative cuts are much less common.'

'Did you find any such tentative cuts in this case?'

'None at all.' The pathologist gave a thin, triumphant smile.

'Very well. Let's move on to the bruising, if we may. Subcutaneous bruising around the head and the neck, you say in your report. Would you explain that to the jury, please.'

'It means that the bruising was less obvious on the surface of the skin than on the layers beneath. When I peeled back the skin from her skull, I found places where it had been gripped tightly against the bones. You can see this in photographs four and five.'

Several jurors turned away from their booklets in disgust. Sarah understood their reaction, but felt more concern for Shelley's parents. Pathologists, particularly those who had been working for nearly forty years, were not renowned for the sensitivity of their explanations. But there was nothing Sarah could do to minimize their pain. The Walters could leave, of course; but if she had been in their position, she imagined, the obsessive need to know every dreadful detail would overcome her disgust.

'What do these injuries suggest to you?'

'This sort of bruising is common in situations where a person has been held down against their will, particularly in drowning incidents, when the desire to escape is overwhelming and the assailant has to exert great force to subdue the victim. So it looks to me as though someone held her head underwater.'

'So in your view these bruises are further evidence of a violent assault?'

'That is the most probable explanation, yes.'

'Very well.' Sarah studied the jury quietly before asking her next question. Most of them were staring at the photographs or the pathologist, mesmerized by horror and disgust. 'But we have still not established whether this poor young woman was half drowned first, before someone cut her wrists, or whether it was the other way around. Can you help us with that, Dr Tuchman?'

'On balance it seems to me more likely that the murderer attempted to drown her first, and then cut her wrists afterwards.'

'Why do you say that?'

'Well, it would be very difficult to cut this girl's wrists in the way we have seen if she was still conscious and actively resisting. There would be quite a fight. So I would expect to find other cuts, particularly on her arms where she tried to defend herself. But I found no such cuts, so it seems more likely that he held her underwater first until she lost consciousness. Then it would be easier to cut her wrists.'

Sarah frowned, feigning confusion. 'But if he thought she had drowned, why would he think it necessary to cut her wrists as well?'

'To disguise the cause of death, I suppose. To make a murder look like a suicide.'

As Sarah had half expected, Savendra rose to his feet to protest. 'My Lord, I understood Dr Tuchman to be a pathologist, not a psychologist. He is an expert witness about the state of the victim's body, not of the assailant's mind - if indeed there was an assailant at all.'

The judge smiled patiently. 'True, Mr Bhose. But Mrs Newby is asking the learned doctor to deduce from those injuries whether this was a murder or not, and if so, how it took place. You may proceed, Mrs Newby.'

Sarah suppressed a little grin as Savendra sat down. 'So, in your expert opinion, Dr Tuchman, the murderer held his victim underwater until she lost consciousness and he believed he had drowned her, is that right? Then he cut her wrists in order to make it look like suicide.'

'That seems the most likely explanation to me, yes.'

'Very well.' Sarah glanced smugly at Savendra before proceeding to her final point. The timing of David Kidd's alibi.

'Another suggestion the defence may raise, is that the defendant claims to have been out of the flat for ten minutes before he found her. If that is true he cannot have cut her wrists before he went out, he says, because she would have bled to death before he returned. Perhaps you can help us with this point, Dr Tuchman. With a pierced artery in her wrist, how long would it take for a person to bleed to death?'

'I'm afraid that's impossible to say with any accuracy. It depends on a number of factors - the victim's age, body weight, the severity of the injury, and so on. Unfortunately, no one has carried out precise experiments to measure this sort of thing. It's not quite ethical, you know.'

To Sarah's horror, the pathologist attempted a thin-lipped, ironic smile. She frowned at him warningly. No death camp science, please. In her calmest voice she continued.

'In your opinion, then, Miss Walters could still have been alive - as she was when the ambulance crew arrived - fifteen or twenty minutes after her ulnar artery was pierced?'

'That would be possible, yes. Particularly in a case like this, where the artery was only pierced, rather than severed. It's not like severing an artery in your neck, for example - people die almost instantaneously from that. But pressure on her wrist, or the earlier application of a tourniquet, might have stemmed the flow altogether. Unfortunately in this case, it seems, that came too late.'

'So what is the maximum time a person might hope to survive a pierced ulnar artery in the wrist?'

The pathologist shrugged. 'In exceptional circumstances, people have survived such injuries for half an hour. Though most of them die at that point, it has to be said.'

'Half an hour. Thank you.' Another vital avenue of Savendra's defence closed off. 'So it is possible, then, for Mr Kidd to have cut her wrists in the way we have described, left his flat for ten minutes or so to give himself an alibi, and then returned to find Shelley Walters still faintly alive?'

'I believe so, yes.'

'Thank you, Dr Tuchman.' Sarah smiled at the wiry old man gratefully. 'If you would wait there, please. Mr Bhose may have some questions for you, perhaps.'

She folded her gown around her, smiled at Savendra quizzically, and sat down.

15. Miranda

AS THE plane began to lose height, the white towers of cloud came closer. The radiant pinnacles that had gleamed like arctic snow under the brilliant sunlight of the upper atmosphere gradually became more shadowed, disparate and wispy as the plane descended to their level. Then, quite suddenly, they were in the cloud itself, surrounded by grey, swirling mist, and the illusion of clarity and beauty was gone for good.

Passengers began to stir, folding their tables into the seat backs in front of them, handing last drinks to the stewardess, checking passports in wallets and handbags. As the plane swayed slightly in a crosswind the chime sounded and the instruction to fasten seatbelts came on. Nervous flyers braced themselves for the landing, others smiled at the acquaintances they had made on the trip. A murmur of anticipation filled the cabin.

None of this seemed to affect the young woman in window seat 5c. Her table had been folded for some time now, and she sat staring out of the window at the fields and roads appearing through the mist with the same fixed, unseeing attention that she had bestowed on the blue sky earlier. She seemed, the stewards had concluded, sunk in some inner world of her own, a glass bubble outside which things were scarcely noticed.

The plane landed and rolled to a stop, the passengers rose to their feet, stretching into the overhead lockers for their hand luggage and queuing to disembark when the doors opened. Still the young woman didn't move. The businessman who had travelled beside her failed to catch her eye for a parting remark, shrugged, and shuffled away down the aisle. Only when the cabin was nearly empty did she bother to rise, heft a green shoulder bag from the locker, and follow the other passengers out, ignoring the trained farewell of the stewardess by the door.

The stewardess, who had noted the girl's behaviour throughout the flight, raised a knowing eyebrow at her colleague. 'Private tragedy,' she suggested. 'Divorce, perhaps. It gets you like that, they say.'

But it was not divorce that was haunting Miranda Ward. Her marriage to Bruce, indeed, was the best thing about her life right now. That and little Sophie, whom she had left behind for the second time in a year.

She collected her suitcase from the carousel and wheeled it through customs to the concourse where her father stood in the sea of faces awaiting arrivals. He looked tired, more drawn than last time, she thought; and the love in his eyes was mixed with the pain, the hungry desperation that had come with the death of her sister earlier this year. Miranda was the only daughter Andrew Walters had left now, his anxious gaze said; and people can die in all sorts of horrible, unforeseen ways, including on aeroplanes.

Not this time, though. She embraced him wordlessly, each hugging longer and tighter than they had ever done in her long-ago, undemonstrative childhood. Marrying an American meant that they met only rarely on carefully planned holidays, and most recently, at Shelley's funeral. Everything had changed since then, in Miranda's life as in her parents'. A grey mist shrouded her emotions, from which there seemed no escape. It was like being trapped in a maze with no exit, only further tests of endurance.

Like this one: leaving your husband and daughter on the far side of the ocean, to sit with your parents at the trial of your sister's murderer.

Before Savendra stood up to cross examine, the judge adjourned court for lunch. Mark Wrass had booked a table for four in a quiet restaurant overlooking the river, but only Kathryn Walters met him and Sarah outside the court. Her husband had left half an hour ago, she explained, to meet a plane at Manchester airport.

The atmosphere on the way to the restaurant, crossing a busy road and dodging between parked cars, was awkward. Sarah did not know what to say to Kathryn, nor she to her, and both were grateful for the breezy avuncular charm of the solicitor, talking banalities and ushering the two women courteously to the upstairs room in which, mercifully, only one other table was occupied.

Once there, the menu was to be negotiated. Sarah, energized by her successful examination of the pathologist, was hungry, but saw immediately that to Kathryn the idea of food was an irrelevance. She temporized by ordering a Spanish omelette, and then, when the waiter had gone, leaned forward earnestly.

'This must be very painful for you. I do understand that, truly.'

'Do you?' Kathryn looked away out of the window, her eyes brimming with tears. 'I saw you having a good laugh about things with your colleague. Or am I wrong?'

Sarah was stunned. At first she couldn't think who the woman meant. Then the penny dropped. She had been teasing Savendra about his weekend away with Belinda and the new bike. 'Who? Sav ... Mr Bhose, you mean? Counsel for the defence?'

'If that's what you call him. The Indian in fancy dress. Having a fine laugh, you were. I thought he was on the other side.'

'Well, he is, of course. But we're still professional colleagues. We know each other quite well.'

'So it's all stitched up, is it?' Kathryn persisted bitterly. 'You've agreed tactics between you, before the trial's even started. I wish I hadn't come.'

'No! Good heavens, Mrs Walters, is that what you think? Certainly not. I haven't even discussed the case with him, as a matter of fact.'

'Then what were you talking about down there, so cheerfully?'

Kathryn's hands, Sarah noticed, were nervously ripping a bread roll into tiny pieces. She looked bitter, hurt, vulnerable. Sarah wondered how to answer the question. The flippant truth would only make matters worse. She chose a white lie instead.

'His fiancee, as it happens. He's getting married next month.'

'Oh.' Kathryn looked down at the mess her hands had made of the roll, then fumbled for a tissue in her bag. 'I see. I'm sorry.'

'I know it must look strange to people, but barristers work in a small and rather incestuous world, so we see each other all the time. But that doesn't mean we collude with each other in court; we don't. If I can send this man to prison, I will.'

'Is there any chance that you will fail?' Kathryn asked slowly.

Sarah drew a deep breath. 'There's always a chance of that, of course. I'd be lying if I said there wasn't. But the police have assembled a pretty strong case, and I shall lay every bit of that evidence before the jury, just as I did this morning.' Sarah paused while the waiter brought their food. A small, ignoble part of her wondered if Kathryn might praise her for the way she had handled the pathologist's evidence, but a look at her lined, pale face made her dismiss such vanity immediately. The trial was a matter of deadly seriousness for this woman, of course it was. That was why she was so edgy and nervous; and why, probably, most barristers chose to avoid encounters like this. Too much emotion can cloud your perception of the facts, her pupil master had once told her. There was truth in that, of course, but he was a typical middle-aged man who had learned to bury his emotions long ago at boarding school. Sarah's background and instincts were utterly different to that.

'What was Shelley like?' she asked softly.

Miranda was the elder of the two sisters, dark where Shelley was fair, and the brighter too, by some incalculable throw in the genetic lottery which their parents deplored but could do nothing about. Miranda had always found schoolwork easy where Shelley frequently found difficulties; she had the perseverance to finish a task where her younger sister would scrumple it up and run outside to play; and as they became teenagers, Miranda had the ability to define a goal for herself and work steadily towards it, while Shelley fluttered from one idea to another, bewildering her family with endless new enthusiasms which blossomed and died in a day.

But these things troubled her parents more than they did Miranda. To her, Shelley was an archetypal younger sister - by turns irritating, noisy, selfish, stealing her clothes and CDs without a second's qualm of conscience, and also funny, scatter-brained and amusingly rebellious against the rigid demands of parents and school. Sometimes she did things - like throwing custard in her father's face or squirting superglue onto the science laboratory stools just before class - that Miranda wished she had dared to do herself. For Shelley, for all her faults, was brave - no one could deny that. Perhaps the bravery came from a certain nerveless lack of imagination, a failure to imagine the probable disastrous consequences, but it was a fine quality for all that, and one that Miranda not only envied but was indebted to for her life.

One afternoon in the long summer of their childhood, when Miranda was not yet thirteen and Shelley ten, they had gone out for a ride on their ponies together with their dog, Tess. Miranda had a spirited pony with a tendency to shy at things it took a sudden inexplicable dislike to, like a bird rustling in a hedge or a perfectly innocuous stick on a track. But both girls were good riders who treated this more as a joke than a problem. They had a picnic with them and were exploring the extensive woods near their home, a nature reserve with a disused airfield in the middle of it. They were trotting down a grassy track when, without warning, two roe deer burst out of the woods beside them, closely pursued by Tess, her tongue hanging out in excitement. Miranda's pony panicked. It reared, throwing her violently forwards onto its neck, then spun round and took off at a flat gallop in the opposite direction, stretching its legs long and low as though all the hounds of hell were at its heels. Miranda clung on for dear life, feeling herself slipping sideways all the time because she had lost her stirrups. After a hundred yards the track divided, and the pony sped down a track they did not know. It was a mistake. Almost immediately the track led to a sunken concrete reservoir, some relic of the airfield long ago. Seeing the water in front of it, the pony tried to stop, failed, skidded sideways on the ancient concrete, and flung Miranda headfirst into the water, cracking her head against a rusty iron post as she fell.

She remembered very little after that, and was only able to construct a picture from what people told her. The reservoir - part of the drainage system of the airfield - was the size of a small swimming pool with concrete sides two feet above the dirty water. She was unconscious when Shelley found her, floating face downwards in water as black and slimy as oil. The pony was in the water too, swimming round frantically with wide eyes and feet threshing. They were at least a mile from the nearest farm, possibly more. But Shelley didn't hesitate. She dismounted, dived in, and managed to turn Miranda over, swimming on her back behind her and holding her chin up as they had practised at school. But there was no way out of the water. On all sides the concrete walls rose two feet above their heads, and though Shelley twice managed to reach up and grasp the edge there was no way she could haul herself up without letting go of Miranda, who was still moaning and semi-conscious.

Time passed. Shelley shouted for help but no one came. She grew wetter and colder and found it harder to keep herself and her sister afloat. The terrified pony swam round and round, bumping into them and shoving them out of its way. Their dog, Tess, barked and whined beside the reservoir, but no one seemed to hear her either. 'I thought we were going to drown,' Shelley told her sister later, as they stared into the black, lonely water. 'No one would come for days, and then they'd find two girls and a pony in the mud at the bottom, like Anglo-Saxon remains.'

Even though it could easily have happened she seemed to find it partly amusing. But it wasn't in Shelley's nature to dwell on disaster, or indeed on anything for long. The story haunted Miranda more than it ever seemed to trouble her sister. Perhaps that was because it was so hard for her to disentangle what she remembered from what she had been told. She remembered, or seemed to remember, lying on her back in the water looking up at the trees but feeling too weak to swim or even try. Shelley had talked to her, or so she said, but the answers she got made little sense. But nevertheless Miranda had a vague idea of what happened next, made up of her own disconnected memories and things Shelley told her later.

The pony's frantic efforts began to exhaust it so that it became more docile, and swam towards the girls hoping, perhaps, that humans would help it as they had done all its life. It was then that Shelley had her idea. Grabbing the bridle with one hand, she shoved Miranda towards the saddle with the other. 'Go on, climb up!' she yelled. 'Get on his back!' How long it took, Miranda had no idea. Time after time her feeble rubbery arms lost their grip, and the pony panicked, dragging them both away into the middle of the water, but Shelley clung on to them both and finally Miranda got her foot into the stirrup and hauled herself into the saddle. After that there was another age of splashing and floundering before Shelley managed to coax the pony to the side of the reservoir and persuade it to turn so that Miranda, with a wild desperate leap, dragged herself on shore.

She had a shameful memory of lying there, stunned and exhausted, not knowing or caring what had become of Shelley. There was a vision of pebbles in front of her face which had imprinted itself on her mind; she could see each stone clearly even today. And the dog was whining and licking her ear. But if Miranda's mind was wandering then, Shelley's was not. She still had hold of the pony's bridle and eventually managed to attract her sister's attention enough to pass her the reins and tell her to hold the animal's head close to the side. Then Shelley, too, climbed onto the pony's back and clambered ashore.

The nearest farm was more like two miles away than one. But Shelley caught her own pony and rode there while Miranda sat, cold and shivering, watching the pony in the lethal black water paddle ever more feebly around. Eventually the farmer arrived and, much later, the fire brigade who winched the drowning animal out. They still had the cuttings about it from the Yorkshire Post in a frame on their parents' wall, and Shelley had a medal from the Royal Humane Society.

The memory would stay with Miranda for life. If it hadn't been for her sister's courage and resourcefulness that day, she would have died. Shelley could so easily have panicked and run for help. Instead she had risked her own life and saved them both.

And now she was dead. Miranda had known for a year that Shelley was unhappy but she hadn't come back to help her - how could she? Her life was in Wisconsin now, the other side of the ocean. The sisters had talked on the phone of course but ... she should have done more, she knew it. No one had been there for Shelley when she needed them most. Miranda had failed her, and their parents had failed her too. And so she was dead, and all they had left was revenge.

16. Retribution

SARAH'S QUESTION was the right one - it unlocked the floodgates to what Kathryn Walters really wanted to say. She wanted to talk about her real daughter, not the corpse, the collection of cuts and subcutaneous bruises which the pathologist had so drily presented this morning. And as she talked, Sarah learned; not about the abstract victim in the brief she had read over the weekend, but about a little girl who for twenty years had been the delight and despair of the tense, angry mother opposite her. A child as real as her own daughter Emily.

Mark Wrass tactfully left them to make a call from his office, and Kathryn told Sarah about Shelley's difficulties at birth, her worries when the child developed so differently from her elder sister: scatter-brained, harum-scarum, brave and loving but unable to concentrate on anything that bored her for more than a few minutes at a time. Over the years Shelley had suffered from lack of confidence, difficulties in learning, emotional dependency, mental instability, and periods of hyper-activity conflicting with periods of depression. But she could be amazingly rewarding too, making up for the bad times with striking displays of loyalty and love. Occasionally she could show flashes of real brilliance at school too, which astonished her teachers and delighted her mother, though they were seldom sustained for long.

So when Shelley finally succeeded in getting to university Kathryn felt at once proud and anxious, relieved that her difficult, mercurial daughter had achieved so much, but sad that she as a mother would be deprived of the demands on her love which had occupied her for so long. She had been worried when Shelley's relationship with her first boyfriend, Graham, ended abruptly in the first term, but it was when she described David Kidd that the real bitterness leaked into Kathryn's voice.

'It was if he had stolen her from me. He brainwashed her, turned her into an alien almost.' She turned away, staring sadly out of the restaurant window. 'I'd given her so much love, so much time. With all her difficulties I was proud of what she'd achieved, and I thought at least she'd be grateful. She was, too, before she met him. But then she just turned. She looked at me like I was ... I don't know, a stranger almost. All because of him. He's evil, you know. I could see him laughing at me, he knew what he'd done. He'd stolen her mind, she just parroted what he said. Rubbish about how I was ruining her life, forcing her to be a success. Can you imagine how that feels?'

Sarah nodded quietly. 'Exquisitely painful, I should think.'

'It was. Sometimes when I spoke to her on the phone I could hear him in the background, whispering and muttering about me, even kissing her once to distract her because he knew I was on the line, he knew I could hear. He wanted me to know he'd taken her away from me, she didn't rely on me, didn't belong to me any more. That's what he wanted. He wanted to control her like a little sex slave, a puppet almost. And it was easy for him, because she was so loving, so trusting, so innocent. She believed everything he said. But I found out about him, all his lies. His claims to have been in the army, when he hadn't. And his convictions for beating his former girlfriend. The police told you about those. You've read about them, haven't you?'

'They're in the brief, yes.' Sarah noted the way the look of distrust had returned. 'Really, Mrs Walters, I have done my homework, believe me. But it's useful hearing these things from you, all the same.'

'You'll tell the jury, then? Make it all count?'

'I will if I can.' Sarah sighed. 'There are rules of evidence, legal niceties that can make some things difficult when it comes to character. But anyway, the basic facts of the case should be enough to get a conviction, even without that. Unless Mr Bhose comes up with something totally unexpected, which I doubt. This young man belongs in prison.'

'I think I could sleep at night, then.'

'You don't sleep?' Sarah studied the woman in front of her thoughtfully. There were lines around the eyes and cheeks, certainly, but she had dressed with care, her make-up was good, the skin of her neck and arms healthy and firm.

Kathryn noticed the look and smiled faintly. 'Oh, don't worry, I'm not wasting away. But sleep - no. Three or four hours at a time before I wake. I cherish those moments, you know. Sometimes when I wake there are times - I don't know, a minute or two, maybe longer - when I forget what's happened. I'm drowsy, half-awake, and all of it's gone. And then it comes back; it's so painful. I just think, when he's in jail, locked away, maybe those times will be longer. There'll be nothing to do, it'll be over. At the moment I feel I have to carry it with me all the time, even at night. If I forget for a moment, I'll have betrayed her, he'll go free.' She shook her head ruefully. 'That's just how it feels.'

'You don't need to feel responsible,' Sarah said carefully. 'You've got the police after all. And now me.'

'I know.' Their eyes met across the table, searching, cautious. 'But forgive me, that makes it worse, somehow.'

'Worse, how? You don't trust us?'

'No, it's not that. I'm sure you'll do your best, I saw you in court this morning. But ... you see, it doesn't belong to you. However well you do your job, that's what it is, a job - and Shelley was my daughter. Sometimes at night I wish we lived in a more primitive society. You know, an eye for an eye. So I could kill him myself. Strap him to an electric chair and pull the lever.' Tears came to her eyes and she stared away, out of the window again. 'I know it sounds awful but that's what I think.'

'It would be awful though.' Sarah chose her words carefully before continuing. 'You might find you couldn't do it and even if you could, you'd have that memory to keep you awake at night as well.'

'Maybe.' Kathryn turned back, her eyes still glistening with tears. 'Or maybe not. He killed my daughter, after all. Maybe if I killed him, that would help me sleep.'

Silence fell between them. We've come a long way from the evidence now, Sarah thought. But this is the power of what we're dealing with, in court. 'I expect if the truth were told, a lot of people think like that. But that's why we have the system that we do, to protect you from the need to commit such a crime. I represent the Queen, you know, the state. You've suffered a wrong and it's my job to put it right, if I can. It's justice, not revenge. We're there to protect you from yourself.'

'Just make sure you do it properly then. Lock him up and throw away the key. I'm sorry, Mrs Newby, I know it sounds bad. But I've tried to believe in Christian forgiveness, and I can't.'

17. Professional Doubts

As SARAH entered the robing room after lunch, Savendra was adjusting his wig in the mirror. He scowled at her with mock ferocity. 'Ah, the wicked witch of Endor! Where did your pathologist learn his trade? Treblinka was it, or Auschwitz?'

Sarah took her gown from a hanger and shrugged it on. Reluctantly, she turned her mind from the picture Kathryn Walters had painted of the young Shelley, to the pathologist's unfortunate comments about her dead body. 'When he talked about experiments on people dying from pierced arteries, you mean? He was referring to atrocities he *hadn't* committed, not to ones he had. Unlike your client, I might add.'

'My client says it's suicide.'

'You look at his record. Lies, assaults on women - this isn't Christopher Robin you're representing.' She took her wig out of its black and gold tin and picked a piece of fluff from it with her fingers.

'Nonetheless, he says he didn't kill her.' There was a thoughtful look on his face which Sarah, knowing him well, recognised as a prelude to negotiation. 'Look, what strikes me is the possibility that we're missing something here. Both of us. You say it's murder, we say it's suicide. Both of us can explain how it might have happened, but neither can really explain why. You're prosecuting, but do you have a motive? Why would he murder her?'

'Because he's a nasty inadequate male chauvinist control freak who couldn't bear the idea that his poor little sex slave had a mind of her own, that's why.' Sarah opened her handbag to search for a lipstick.

'Well maybe, maybe ...'

'There are lots of men like that, Savvy. I should know. I married one, for Christ's sake.'

Savendra stared, nonplussed. 'Not Bob, Sarah, surely ...'

'No, of course not. Kevin - Simon's father. Beat me black and blue, the little thug. Didn't you know?' She watched him coolly in the mirror before pursing her lips for the gloss. 'Bob rescued me from all that. The civilized older man.'

She raised an eyebrow ironically at her reflection in the mirror, thinking how far she'd come since then. At sixteen she'd been a tearful teenage divorcee, struggling to restart her GCSEs in night school. She'd been doped out on valium to ease the depression caused by the demands of her mother and the social services to give up her baby, Simon, for adoption. Bob, ten years older, a gentle, bearded young English teacher, had not only befriended her but offered to bring up the child himself, if only she'd do him the honour of marrying him. He'd got down on his knees to propose, like a lanky romantic poet, beside a greasy formica-topped table in the college canteen. And so he'd saved her - from losing her child and failing to learn, both at once.

Their marriage, begun in such desperate circumstances, had every appearance of success, at least to Savendra, soon to take a similar step himself. Sarah and Bob had busy, thriving careers and a luxurious house in the country. They had more or less successfully brought up two children - Simon, admittedly only an apprentice bricklayer but more settled now since the trauma of last year, and his seventeen-year-old half-sister Emily, who was studying A levels and planning to save the planet with the help of her boyfriend Larry. And they had stayed together when many couples of their acquaintance, marrying later in more promising circumstances, had divorced.

So far, Sarah thought, so good. All through her long uphill battle from the slums of Seacroft to the glory of being called to the 'utter Bar' in the ancient Elizabethan hall of the Middle Temple, she had drawn strength and support from Bob. He was not, perhaps, the greatest lover in the world, but after her exhilarating, catastrophic initiation to sexual love with Kevin, the randy, cruel, faithless little gamecock who was Simon's father, Sarah had come to distrust passion; she valued Bob's qualities of gentleness, reliability, and loyalty far higher.

Or at least she had done, until recently. His announcement this morning that he had had the house valued without even consulting her first was symptomatic of the distance that was opening up between them. Touching her lips with the lipstick, she breathed in and felt a sharp familiar ache somewhere below her breastbone. It was a pain so real she had even consulted the doctor about it once, but he'd found nothing; it was not her body that was wounded, but her heart. Her marriage was not one to be envied, not any more. Not since Bob had let her down over Simon. Kevin's fist might have bruised her face, but Bob's cruel words had frozen her heart. She doubted if it would ever recover.

She watched Savendra in the mirror as he casually proposed his deal. 'So you wouldn't be interested in a plea of manslaughter?'

'I doubt it, no. What are you saying - he cut her wrists by accident? Do me a favour, Savvy.'

'No, *she* cut her wrists, then drowned because her head fell under water. The question is why.'

'Okay then, why?' She dropped the lipstick in her bag and took out an eyelash brush, smiling indulgently. 'Go on, you tell me.'

'Look, I'm not speaking under instruction now, right. Just exploring a possibility, in the interests of ...'

'Getting your client off.'

'No, justice, Sarah. That's what we do here, isn't it? Make justice.'

Sarah finished her lashes and hunted for a eyebrow pencil, aware that something, either her words or the makeup business or both, was getting under her colleague's skin. 'All right, go on then. Surprise me.'

'Well, look, suppose we admit my client's not the great Lothario he thinks he is. Far from it, in fact. But on the other hand his victim, this poor girl Shelley, had all sorts of problems with self esteem and depression which I can and will prove, giving her a tendency to commit suicide under extreme pressure ...'

'You mean her mother disliking her boyfriend? A few bad essay marks? Is that cause for suicide?' Sarah finished her makeup and snapped her bag shut.

'Well, maybe. Such things happen. Not everyone's tough like you, you know. But what if my client admits that some pressure came from him? On the one side there's her mum, telling her to give him up, and on the other there's him, only the second real boyfriend she's had. It's tearing her apart. Then she gets this shock, finding him in bed with the other girl, and she decides to dump him. But then when she goes back to his flat something happens; they have a blazing row and then he seduces her ...'

'Rapes her, Savvy.'

'Seduces her, Sarah. There is a difference. He sweet talks her into doing what she'd told herself she wouldn't do any more. It doesn't have to be rape.'

'You mean he won't admit to it.'

'No. Well as you can see he's a cocky little bastard who thinks a quick fuck makes everything fine. So she gets in the bath and he goes whistling out to buy her some flowers, trying to be nice for once, and comes back to find she's so appalled by what she's done that she's killed herself. Well, what does the court make of that? It's not murder is it? She cut her own wrists, he wasn't even there at the time. But he has some sort of responsibility, he might manage to admit that.'

'And will he say this in court?'

'He might, if you'd go for manslaughter instead of murder.'

Savendra was in earnest now, Sarah could see that; and he had a point, of course. Sarah thought back to the lunch she had just had, and the confidence the dead girl's mother had placed in her. 'I might go for it, Savvy, if the victim was left-handed. But she isn't. I've checked with her mother, friends, everyone. She held her pen in her right hand, she cut bread with her right hand. If she'd wanted to kill herself she'd have picked up the knife in her right hand first and slashed her *left* wrist, where she would have done the most damage. But that's not what happened. The artery was pierced in her *right* wrist, not her left. And that means someone cut it for her, Savvy, clear as day. She didn't do it herself. All the rest is detail.'

'I see,' Savendra sighed, disappointed but not particularly surprised. She had never been an easy woman to convince. 'And that's what you're going to tell the jury?'

'That's it, Savvy.' Sarah smiled, as they made their way to the door. 'Nice try, but this is a murder. And your client did it.'

18. Tentative Cuts

IT WAS clear to Savendra, as it was to Sarah, that the pathologist's evidence was crucial in this case. If he couldn't cast doubt on it, he might as well pack up and go home now. So he began by challenging the time Dr Tuchman had claimed Shelley could have survived with a bleeding artery.

'Is it usual for people to survive for half an hour with a pierced artery?'

'Not usual, no. As I said, half an hour is probably a maximum time.'

'So what would be a minimum time?'

Dr Tuchman shrugged. 'Five or ten minutes, maybe.'

'Five or ten minutes?' Sarah grimaced, and Savendra glanced down at her triumphantly. This was better than he had hoped. 'That's a big difference, Dr Tuchman, isn't it? This morning you told my learned friend that she could have been lying in that bath for up to half an hour, but now you say she could have been there for only five or ten minutes. Which is right?'

'I didn't say that she was likely to have to have been there for five or ten minutes,' the pathologist protested irritably. 'I said that was a minimum time. Miss Walters clearly survived longer than that because she was still alive when the ambulance team arrived.'

'So which is more normal? Five minutes, or half an hour?'

To Savendra's satisfaction, the pathologist looked annoyed, even flustered. A quick glance at the jury confirmed that they were following the exchange with interest.

'Somewhere in between, of course. The half hour figure would typically be for a large fat person with a slow heartbeat and a lot of blood.'

'But Shelley Walters was a slim young woman. So presumably it would take less time for her to bleed to death. What would be the maximum time, for a girl of her age and condition?'

Dr Tuchman scowled at his young tormentor. 'Fifteen, twenty minutes, perhaps. Unless of course the artery healed itself.'

'Is that possible?' Savendra looked stunned.

'Certainly it's possible, particularly when a small artery like the ulnar is pierced rather than severed, and where the blood flow is not aided by water.'

'But ... that didn't happen in this case, did it?'

'The artery didn't heal itself, no.'

'Very well then.' Savendra drew a deep sigh of relief, coupled with annoyance at this deliberate red herring. 'Then since the artery did not heal itself, Dr Tuchman, this young woman would have bled to death in fifteen or twenty minutes. That's your best guess, is it?'

'That, young man, is my educated opinion.'

So far, so good, Savendra thought. For the next ten minutes he worked away at this point, dragging further damaging admissions from the elderly pathologist. The ambulance had arrived after seven minutes, so if Shelley could have died from blood loss fifteen minutes after David Kidd had cut her wrists, he would have had to leave the flat, walk to the shop, discuss football with the shopkeeper, buy olive oil and flowers, return from the shop, and ring 999 - all in under 8 minutes. Surely that was impossible?

'I know nothing of that,' Dr Tuchman answered stiffly. 'As I said, she may well have survived longer. It is impossible to be sure.'

'Quite.' Savendra paused, to let the jury take this point in. He glanced down at Sarah, a faint smile playing round his lips as he anticipated her reaction to his next question.

'Then let us turn to another issue, shall we? The tentative cuts. You told Mrs Newby that you found no tentative cuts on the victim's wrists, which inclined you to regard this death as murder. But perhaps I could suggest another way of interpreting this evidence, Dr Tuchman. You also claim, do you not, that if this was suicide the wound to the left wrist would have been inflicted before the one to the right?'

'Since this girl was right handed, yes.'

'So isn't it possible, doctor, that the wound to the left wrist - a much shallower, less fatal wound than the one to the right - is in itself the tentative cut you are looking for? Miss Walters had never cut herself before, so she cut her left wrist first, as you say, but didn't really cut deep enough. It was only on her second attempt, to cut her right wrist, that she nerved herself to press hard enough to do lethal damage.'

Sarah groaned inwardly. It was a typical Savendra point - smart, unexpected, appearing to completely turn the tables on the expert witness - and therefore highly likely to delight any smart alecks and wise guys there might be among the younger jurors.

The pathologist sighed, making a conscious effort to balance his irritation with objectivity. 'It is a remote possibility, I suppose. Very remote, in my view.'

Nonetheless, Sarah thought ruefully, the damage is done, another doubt lodged safely in the jurors' minds. With Savendra on this sort of form, this trial may not be so easy after all.

Savendra moved on smoothly to his third point, the subcutaneous bruises on Shelley's head and neck, which the pathologist had claimed were typical of someone being forcibly drowned. 'These bruises to her head and neck which you mention. You cannot say that they were necessarily caused in the bath, can you?'

Dr Tuchman stared at him, surprised. 'Not if you look at the bruises on their own. But ...'

'Isn't possible that they were caused before she entered the bath, doctor? In a previous argument of some kind?'

Dr Tuchman sighed, his commitment to objectivity fighting with his increasing dislike of this supercilious young barrister. 'Possible, yes, if you consider them on their own. They could have been caused by an incident up to an hour before her death.'

'Very well, so it's also possible, isn't it, that Mr Kidd may have taken a firm grip on her head and neck to restrain her during an argument which took place some time before she entered the bath. An argument which he admits did take place. If she resisted, his hands would have caused these subcutaneous bruises then, wouldn't they?'

'That's a possible explanation, yes.'

Savendra paused, surveying the jury to make sure he had their full attention before his next, key question which, he hoped, would radically transform their view of what had happened in the flat and begin his client's rehabilitation. The picture he was painting was ugly, but not as ugly as the one Sarah had offered.

'So it's perfectly possible, is it not, that the bruising was inflicted upon Ms Walters long before she entered the bath? And if that was the case, these bruises wouldn't be evidence of a murder, would they?'

'Not in that scenario, no.'

'No.' Savendra glanced at the jury, and was gratified to see they were following with rapt attention. 'In your experience, Dr Tuchman, does it occasionally happen that a person commits suicide as a result of a bitter, perhaps violent argument with their lover? A person is so upset by the way they have been treated that they decide life is simply not worth living, and decide to kill themselves instead?'

'As you yourself pointed out before, I am a pathologist, not a psychologist. I can tell you about the state of a person's brain, but not the state of their mind.'

'Very well, Dr Tuchman. Unlike Mrs Newby, I won't ask you to extend your opinions beyond your proper sphere. But as I recall, you did tell Mrs Newby that ... ah, here it is ... suicide is not completely impossible. Is that still your opinion?'

'I believe I did say that, yes. But taking all facts into account, the balance of probability suggests that it was murder. I also said that, young man.'

'You did, Doctor, yes. And you said one other thing, Dr Tuchman, which I would like to ask you about. Here it is. "I regret that I cannot absolutely be certain. The longer you work in my field, the more you find that is true." Do you recall saying that?'

'I do, yes.'

'Thank you. That is all.'

19. Priest

As THE priest nervously took the oath, both lawyers saw that this witness had to be handled much more gently than the previous one. Dr Tuchman was a professional, used to speaking in open court, confident of his own opinion. Canon Rowlands, by contrast, was a church mouse. His speech was low and hesitant; his hands fluttered and frequently clutched the testament which the court clerk had thoughtfully left on the witness stand. Sarah led him kindly through his evidence about the quarrel he had heard in the flat below his on the day of Shelley's death - a violent quarrel in which he had feared a woman was being hurt. But he had done nothing about it, and shortly afterwards, leaving for evensong in the Minster, he had met David Kidd on the stairs outside his flat.

'If only I'd done something,' he muttered repeatedly, glancing anxiously around the court as though in search of forgiveness, 'that poor girl might still be alive today.'

His fluttering ineffectualness served Sarah's case quite well. No juror, watching the priest give evidence, could fail to be convinced that the man was telling the truth as he saw it, or that he was seriously upset by his failure to prevent the crime which he had overheard. When Sarah sat down Savendra got to his feet thoughtfully. To appear to bully or intimidate this man, as he had done with the previous two witnesses, would be a disaster. Nonetheless, somehow he had to mitigate the damage his evidence had done.

'Canon Rowlands, you are a man of God, and one of your trials, perhaps, is to live amongst sinners. You were David Kidd's neighbour for over a year, you said - did you find that relationship difficult?'

'With David? Yes, well, he was a very different person to me, certainly.' A faint charitable smile accompanied the answer.

'Yes. How did these differences show themselves?'

'Well, he liked to play loud music sometimes, which I found trying. And then he had a lot of friends in, for parties and so on. Girls, often.'

'And these people made a noise that you could hear through the floor, did they?'

'Yes, that's right. It could be quite disturbing.' The priest nodded, grateful to see his difficulties understood.

'Did he ever invite you to these parties?'

'No.' The priest smiled. 'I wouldn't ... it's not my thing.'

'I understand. But you could hear people talking and shouting through the floor and you imagined - you couldn't help it after all - you often imagined what was going on?'

'Yes, of course. The floor's not very thick, unfortunately.'

'Quite. But you'd never been in to his flat with his friends so you didn't know for certain what they were doing, did you? You just had to guess.'

The priest's hands fluttered uneasily, as he began to see where this was leading. 'Well, yes I suppose that's true, but I had a general idea.'

'A general idea, perhaps. But it's fair to say, isn't it, that David Kidd and his friends lead very different lives to you? They have very different attitudes, different ways of behaving?'

'Well yes, certainly.'

'You wouldn't shout at a woman, would you, Canon Rowlands?'

'Oh no.' The little man fluttered his hands in horror. 'No, of course not. I never have. The whole idea, it's ... awful. I detest violence.'

'Yes, exactly.' Savendra smiled in sympathy. 'So when you heard these very distressing sounds which you have described to the court - a man and woman shouting at each other - you naturally imagined there was violence involved, didn't you?'

'Well, yes. It sounded like he was hitting her.'

'So you say. Although in fact no bruises were found on her body, apart from those on her neck. None of the forensic evidence suggests that she had been hit. So do you accept that maybe you were wrong about that? You *imagined* he was hitting her, but in fact he wasn't.'

'Well, I ... I don't know, do I? It sounded like that.'

'Exactly. You don't know. You couldn't know, how could you? You heard something, and you used your imagination as anyone would in your position. Nothing wrong with that, Canon Rowlands. It's all you could do, really.'

'I could have gone in to help her,' the priest insisted earnestly. 'If I had she might still be alive today.'

'Well, perhaps, yes,' Savendra agreed patiently, wishing he had avoided that. 'But we can't really be sure of that, because we don't know yet when or how she met her death. We are here to decide whether David Kidd killed her, or whether, as the defence say, she killed herself.'

Savendra paused, considering how wise it was to ask the next question he had jotted down on his pad. It might turn some people against him, but he felt he was already doing well with the younger men in the jury, and anything which might consolidate that position further was worth a try. 'Now you told Mrs Newby that you heard one more sound from the flat, a little while after the quarrel ended. Could you describe that sound?'

'Well, yes. I couldn't be sure, but I thought it sounded like a laugh, perhaps. God forgive me. A strange laugh, but ... I couldn't be sure.'

'A laugh, or something different, I think you told my learned friend. Not like someone in pain.'

'Yes. I think I said that.'

'Could that *something different* have been the sound of a woman having a orgasm, perhaps, Canon Rowlands? The sound of pleasure, rather than pain?'

The little priest blushed bright red, and fumbled with the testament. 'Well, I don't know, it's hard to say. I suppose it might have been that, yes.'

Savendra noted a few flickers of amusement on the lips of the younger jurors. 'Did you continue to listen?'

'Well, yes, but ... I mean, there was no more noise, so I hoped everything was all right, and began to get ready for evensong.'

'How long did that take you?'

'About ten, fifteen minutes, I suppose.'

'And you didn't hear any more noise in that time?'

'Nothing unusual, no.'

'Very well. Then when you left your flat you met Mr Kidd outside his flat with a bunch of flowers in his hand, didn't you? How did he look at that time?'

'I don't know; a little nervous, perhaps. I think he was surprised to see me.'

'But he wasn't covered in blood, was he? You would have noticed that.'

'No.' The priest shook his head, surprised. 'His clothes were quite clean.'

'And they weren't wet? He wasn't wet with bath water?'

'No. His clothes were clean and dry.'

Savendra paused, choosing his words carefully. This was his key point.

'So when you saw him there was nothing to suggest to you that Mr Kidd had cut her wrists, as the prosecution allege, or drowned her before he went out? You didn't imagine that had happened, did you? The idea never entered your mind?'

'No. No, of course not.'

'Was Mr Kidd sweating or shaking? Did he look upset, frightened or panic-stricken in any way? Like a man who has just committed a murder?'

'No. He just looked a little nervous, that's all. Because I'd seen him listening at the door.'

'All right. So what you saw was a man in clean dry clothes, looking a little nervous, as any man might do, perhaps, if he'd just had a shouting match with his girlfriend, and carrying a bunch of flowers in his hand. Is that right?'

'Yes. Yes, that's what I saw.'

'So is it fair to say that you imagined, from what you saw, that Shelley Walters was still alive inside the flat, and that David Kidd had bought the flowers in the hope of making things up with her, after the quarrel that you had overheard?'

'Yes, I ... I suppose that *is* what I thought, yes. And so I went out to evensong. But if only I'd known ...'

'But you couldn't know what went on in the flat, could you, Canon Rowlands? You weren't there. All you can tell us is what you actually saw and heard. And you've done that very fairly and well. Thank you.'

Savendra smiled politely, and sat down. As the priest left the witness stand Savendra thought he looked grateful, as though a burden had been lifted from his shoulders, and something was becoming clear to him at last.

Sarah's next witness was Sandy Murphy, Shelley's closest friend at university. She and her boyfriend knew David Kidd well - the couples had been on several dates together. Shelley, she said, had been besotted with David - hanging on his every word in a way that she, Sandy, had never liked. So she had been delighted when, a few days before her death, Shelley had come into Sandy's room, distraught, saying David had deceived her and everything was over between them. She had found David in bed with a young woman called Lindsay. Not only were the pair naked in bed together - the bed she normally shared with David - but they had set up a camera on a tripod to record what they were doing. It was a porno film, David had explained, a new business venture Lindsay had thought of. In fact, it would be a brilliant idea if she, Shelley, joined in.

But Shelley hadn't seen it like that, Sandy said. Instead of joining in, she had smashed the camera on the floor. A tremendous screaming row had then ensued, during which Shelley discovered that not only had this Lindsay lived with David until he had dumped her a year ago, but she had even had his child, for Christ's sake! She lived in Liverpool, but had come over this afternoon with this idea of combining a reunion for old times' sake with something she could sell on the internet.

The court listened to this tale, riveted, much as Sandy and Richard had in the university bedsit all those months ago. From time to time the jurors stole appalled glances at David, who sat back lounging in the dock with a faint smirk on his face like some yob from Big Brother who was proud of the whole episode.

After this, Sandy confirmed, Shelley saw her relationship with David as completely, definitely over. During the rest of that week she'd had a flurry of phone calls from David but her decision hadn't changed; she'd even gone home for a night to her mother and confirmed that she was dumping him. The only reason she had gone round to the flat that Sunday was to return her key, collect her things, and bring it all to a final conclusion.

Savendra tried hard to challenge this story. Crucially, he established that Sandy knew about the psychiatric treatment Shelley had been having, although Sandy insisted that Shelley seemed perfectly normal and took her medication regularly. Sandy admitted that she and Richard had offered to accompany Shelley to the flat that Sunday to collect her things, but she had turned them down. She wanted to go on her own, she said.

So why was that? Savendra asked. If Shelley had really had no intention of staying, why not take her friends along for moral support? And anyway, what was the real value of these 'things' she had gone to collect?

One by one, Savendra held up the contents of Shelley's bag for the jury. A blue satin nightie, a lacy bra and thong, three pairs of tights, a teeshirt, and a box of make-up containing a used lipstick, a powder puff and some eye liner. There were two novels by the Bronte sisters, and a copy of Cosmopolitan. The total cost, according to him, was £68.50. Surely, he suggested, she had no real need to go back for such items; they were just an excuse for her to see David on her own, one last time, to give the relationship one last try.

'And then, when something went wrong, perhaps she had a further argument with him,' he suggested. 'A violent, emotional argument perhaps. And maybe she decided that this was all too much, and she simply didn't want to live any more. She was so upset that she decided to take her own life. Isn't that possible, Sandy?'

Firmly, Shelley's friend Sandy denied it. 'No,' she said. 'It's not possible, Shelley wasn't like that. She never spoke of suicide, and she didn't love him any more, she hated him, that's what she told me. Maybe those clothes weren't worth much, but they were hers, and she wanted them back. That's why she went there: to get her stuff back and show him she wasn't afraid. And that's why he killed her, I think. Because he couldn't stand it when she told him what a scumbag he really was. That's what I think happened. He killed her because she told him to get lost!'

Savendra sat down, having no further questions. As he did so, to his horror, he heard something like applause from the public gallery. Not for him, it seemed, but for the witness, Sandy. He twisted round in his seat, and saw Shelley's mother and sister Miranda clapping their hands - softly, but loud enough to encourage Sandy, who smiled back at them through her tears. He turned back, to find Sarah Newby grinning at him in cruel sympathy.

'Good try, Savvy,' she murmured softly. 'But I don't think they buy it, do you?'

20. Silent Mother

ON FRIDAY evening, Sarah Newby rode out into the countryside towards Wetherby. There had been a storm that morning, and the newly washed trees and fields glistened in the sparkling evening sunlight. Through her polarized helmet visor the clouds were so beautiful that it was difficult to keep her attention on the road. But at last she found the gate and turned down a track towards the river, the wheels of her bike splashing through puddles as she approached the Walters' house.

A small black and white collie ran out barking hysterically as she pulled up outside the front door, and Miranda Walters came hurrying after it. 'Down, Tess, down! Come here, you wretched dog! I'm sorry, she's not used to motorbikes, you see.'

'Don't worry.' Sarah took off her helmet and bent down to make friends with the suspicious animal, which crept forwards with its belly low on the ground to lick her hand. It was an old, grey-muzzled dog, but still quite fit. 'There. I'm not a burglar after all.' She smiled up at Miranda, whom she had only met briefly in court. 'This is a fine place.'

'Yes. We grew up here, Shelley and I.' Beyond the old stone farmhouse was a paddock, where two old ponies stood nose to tail in the shade of a horsechestnut tree, swishing their tails against the flies. Beyond the paddock was the river, meandering through a valley of low hills and isolated farmhouses.

'It looks idyllic.'

'Yes, well. It was a great place to grow up, but now ...' The wind blew a strand of Miranda's long brown hair across her face, and she tossed her head impatiently. 'I shall be glad to get back to the States. It's painful coming back, with all these memories of what we did.'

'Were you very close, you and your sister?'

'Pretty close, yes.'

Sarah studied the young woman carefully for the first time. She was about five foot eight, with brown eyes and a face bronzed and slightly freckled by the sun. She wore jeans, an old teeshirt and a pair of black trainers which looked like she had lived in them for years. She had a trim, healthy figure very like her mother's but, Sarah thought ruefully, probably bursting with twice as much energy.

'You don't look much like her.'

'Oh no. Shelley was the beauty. Not that it's much good to her now.'

Kathryn came out of the house, still in the black dress which she had been wearing earlier. 'Welcome. I didn't really believe it when you said you'd come on a motorbike, but that's certainly the real thing, isn't it?'

'Yes.' Sarah glanced at the Kawasaki, resting on its stand behind her. 'Is there somewhere I could change, perhaps? Slip out of these leathers?'

'Sure. In here.' Miranda showed her into a utility room, where a washing machine, dryer and freezer rubbed shoulders with racks of coats, boots, and a dog basket. She left her motorcycle gear on the freezer and emerged in a slightly rumpled black trouser suit.

'Tea?' Kathryn asked, as Miranda had disappeared, leaving them alone together.

'Please. I'd love one.'

While Kathryn put the kettle on Sarah took in the large farm kitchen. It had low wooden beams, a red tiled floor, and a large window over the sink which looked out across a paddock to the river. There were oak cupboards around the walls, and a nondescript armchair in an alcove near the Aga, with a pile of newspapers and magazines beside it.

'This is our main room, really. We mostly eat and read in here, especially in the winter. Andrew's even taken to falling asleep in that chair since Shelley died, like an old man.'

'Yes.' Sarah sat at the table, folding her hands gratefully around a mug of tea. 'He's taken her death very hard, you said.'

'We've both taken it hard, Mrs Newby. Miranda as well, of course, they were very close. But it's had a dreadful effect on Andrew. He seems to have given up, almost. That's why I think I should give evidence, not him.'

'Hm.' Sarah sipped her tea thoughtfully before answering. 'Well, that's why I'm here, as you know. To run through what that's likely to mean.'

'It's my chance to tell the world exactly what sort of a swine that bastard Kidd really is. Someone's got to stand up and do that. So it had better be me.'

This was why Sarah had come. Since their lunch together on the first day, Kathryn had assumed that she would be giving evidence. But the more Sarah had considered this idea, the less she had come to like it. She was taking a risk coming here; there were strict rules against coaching a witness. But her intention was the opposite of that - to keep Kathryn Walters out of the witness box. So long as she succeeded in that, there was no problem. She spoke softly.

'Yes, well, that's just it, really. What counts in this trial - any trial - are the facts.'

'Such as that he murdered my daughter,' Kathryn said sharply.

'Exactly. That's what we have to prove. And to do that I have to focus the jury's minds exclusively on the key facts, which are ...' She counted the points off on her fingers. '... that he was alone with her in the flat; his fingerprints were on the knife; there were bruises on her neck; the artery was severed in her right wrist not her left - all these terrible, distressing things.'

'But they need to know what a swine he was too - the way he lied and boasted from the moment he met Shelley, the way he took over her whole life, kept her under his thumb like a little slave, away from her friends and family and all the people who'd ever wished her well. That's what I can tell them.'

'Yes, perhaps,' Sarah nodded cautiously, worried at the tide of emotion she might unleash, yet determined to do it if necessary. At least Kathryn was safe here, in her own home. 'But before we decide that, listen to me. You're her mother, and I'm a mother too. My daughter's not dead, thank God, but I thought she was once. I can't imagine anything worse. And I've had to defend my own son in court, so I know what that's like. The problem is, everyone knows that a mother's on the side of her children; we don't really have a choice. And so people can use that against us. Even when we're telling the truth, they don't always hear what we say.'

'You mean, the jury won't believe me?' Kathryn looked dazed, as though the thought had not occurred to her. Sarah tried again.

'No, not exactly; it's subtler than that. They'll believe what you say, but turn your words against you. Look at it this way; we, the prosecution, have to prove this case beyond reasonable doubt. Savendra - Mr Bhose, the defence counsel - he doesn't have to prove David Kidd is innocent. He just has to create that reasonable doubt in the minds of the jury. And in this case his tactics are obvious: to stop them thinking about the incriminating facts like the fingerprints and the knife and the cuts, and make them speculate about the possibility of suicide instead. Now he's going to call her psychiatrist. I can't stop that ...'

Kathryn shook her head miserably. 'Why? Shelley hadn't seen the man for months. What can he possibly know about what happened?'

'That's just it. Nothing, if she was murdered. Nothing at all. But if, as the defence say, Shelley committed suicide, then he can shed light on her state of mind, and get the jury interested in that. She had bi-polar disorder, did you say?'

'Yes, but that doesn't mean she killed herself!'

'Of course not, but that's what they'll try to imply. I wish I could stop it, but I can't. It's a distraction from the facts, really. Now, if I call you to give evidence, what hard facts can you add? About the day of her death, I mean?'

'Well, only that he was rude to me at the hospital ...'

'That doesn't help. It shows that he hated you and you hated him. Which helps the defence, not us. What else can you say?'

Kathryn thought for a while, puzzled. 'Well, that Shelley told me two days before she died, that she had dumped him. She sat in that chair where you're sitting ...'

Sarah nodded gently. 'Yes, you can say that, certainly.'

'And like I said, I can tell them how nasty he was. How he took her away from home, how he corrupted her mind, and ...'

'All right. Let's try that out, shall we?' Sarah's tone sharpened. She got to her feet.

'What?'

'Let's try some questions out, as if we're in court, and see how it goes. All right?' She stood in front of the Aga, her fingers touching the warm rail behind her back. 'For instance, let's start with this.' Her voice changed slightly, became more formal. 'Shelley had bi-polar disorder, you say. Did she have treatment for that?'

'Yes. She was on a low dose of medication to keep her stable.' Kathryn clasped her hands in front of her on the table, surprised by the sudden transformation into roleplay. But she seemed prepared to enter into the spirit of it. After all, she had been imagining scenes like this in her mind for weeks. And Sarah was her advocate, not an enemy.

'What effect did this condition have on her schoolwork?'

'Well, her schoolwork was like her character, really. Some of it was quite brilliant, but other parts - the more boring, mundane parts of study - she found very difficult. She needed a lot of help and support with those.'

'Did you and your husband give her that support?'

'We tried, yes. Both of us did, but especially me, I suppose. It was hard work, but we succeeded. She got the grades she needed, she went to York to study English.'

'How did she settle in at the university?' The easy, predictable questions were giving Kathryn confidence, as Sarah intended.

'Well, it was difficult at first, because she was dumped - that's the awful word they use, isn't it? - by a boyfriend she'd had for years, Graham. So that didn't help. But she made friends and was doing well, until she met him, that is.'

As Kathryn was speaking the door opened and Miranda came in and sat down. Sarah wondered for a moment what to do. But it was their house, not hers; and Kathryn might need some moral support in a moment, if things went the way she expected. So she smiled at the girl, saying: 'we're just trying a few questions,' then turned back to her mother again.

'You don't feel her relationship with David Kidd was good for her?'

'No, not at all. He was the worst boy she could have met. Like a monster from the swamp.'

Here we go, Sarah thought. This is the problem, exactly. 'Why do you call him that?'

'Well, from the very beginning, he tried to take control of her. He's a very controlling character: always had his arm round her, always spoke before she did, always decided what she was going to do. It was terrible to see. She was like his little slave, a ventriloquist's dummy, almost.'

'Was there anything else that you felt was wrong with their relationship?'

'Well, yes. The things he wanted her to do. I mean, he has no education, has he? If you gave him a book he wouldn't know which way up to hold it. He wanted her to leave the university and go with him to Africa. After all the work we'd done with her!'

'So it's fair to say that there was a great tension between you and David Kidd, isn't it? With your daughter Shelley in the middle?'

'Well, yes, but she'd seen the light at last. When she found him in bed with that girl, she decided to drop him for good. She came home and told me that.'

'And yet two days later, she went back to see him.'

'Not to see him,' Kathryn protested. 'To collect her things.'

Sarah raised her eyebrows theatrically. 'A nightdress, a few books, and some used tights? Do you really think she went back for things like that?' Their eyes locked across the table. Sarah could see the pain in Kathryn's face as the roleplay became uncomfortably real. 'They were just an excuse, weren't they? An excuse to meet David again, and give their relationship one last try?'

'I .. I don't know. It's possible, I suppose. But then he murdered her.'

'Did he, Mrs Walters? We know they had a quarrel soon after she arrived, and he claims they made love. You've told us how much you disapproved of David, how much pressure you put on Shelley to leave him. And she had decided to leave him, you say. She knew that was the right thing to do, and yet still she went back. And did the wrong thing.'

'Yes, well, she was confused ...' Kathryn's voice broke; she looked near to tears. Miranda reached across the table for her mother's hand. But Sarah hadn't finished.

'It's worse than that, though, isn't it? She was bi-polar, you've told us that. She needed constant love and support. And now the two sources of love and support, you and your husband on one side, and David Kidd on the other, were tearing her apart. Isn't it highly likely that in a situation like that, when she sat alone in that bath after making love to the man she'd promised to leave, that the pressures all got too much for her and ...'

Kathryn was crying openly now. Miranda glared indignantly at Sarah, who relented and sat down. 'I'm sorry. I won't distress you further. But you see, that's the way it will go, Kathryn, if I put you on the stand. And Mr Bhose's questions will be harder than that, they're bound to be if he wants to win. Which he does.'

'That's not the point!' Kathryn grabbed a tissue from a box. 'You think it too, though, don't you? You think she killed herself and it was my fault?'

'No.' Oh God, Sarah thought, I've got this completely wrong. 'No, as a matter of fact I don't. I really don't.' The reassurance didn't seem to be working. She tried again. 'Look, this is an absurd thing to say to anyone for comfort, but it seems crystal clear to me that your daughter was murdered, all right? All the hard facts point that way. It's just unfortunate that she had this history of mental illness which allows the defence to put up this smoke screen of suicide.'

The tears had stopped. Kathryn seemed mollified, but still clung onto Miranda's hand for support. 'But I ought to speak for Shelley, didn't I? I'm her mother.'

'Not if it makes matters worse. Look, the only solid fact that the court needs to hear from you is that two nights before she died Shelley told you she was leaving David. That's in your statement to the police. Now with luck the defence will accept that statement unchallenged. That will mean it's read out in court to the jury, but no one can challenge it or try to twist your words to mean something they don't. That's what I think you should do.'

Kathryn sighed, twisting a tissue in her hands. She had steeled herself for so long to confront David in court. The prospect terrified her, but it seemed like her duty. Could she give it up now without betraying her daughter? She shook her head slowly.

'I don't know. Let me think about it overnight.' She looked down at the table, shaking her head sadly. 'But if you really believe Shelley was murdered, how could you come out with all those questions just now?'

'I'm an advocate, Mrs Walters. I'm trained to argue both sides of a case. But that doesn't mean I can't make up my mind about which one is true. In fact it helps me to do that.'

'All right.' Kathryn stood up. 'So what about David, when he goes on the stand? Will you question him as hard as you questioned me, just now?'

'Kathryn, I was just playing with you, to let you see what it could be like. Don't worry. With him, it'll be the real thing.'

The trouble is, Sarah thought later as she rode away, tough questions only hurt people with soft consciences. Villains like David Kidd have souls made of alligator hide.

21. Queuing Very Fiercely

ON MONDAY morning, the prosecution team met in a hotel for a working breakfast. Mark Wrass, the CPS solicitor, was in bullish mood.

'Just a few more nails to bang into place, and the scaffold is built,' he said cheerfully, through a mouthful of sausage and egg. 'Do you anticipate any problems?'

'A couple,' said Sarah thoughtfully, sipping orange juice. She was finding Mark's cheerfulness hard to cope with today. It wasn't his fault; she had spent the weekend vainly trying to understand Bob's sudden urge to move house; a discussion that somehow, never quite reached the main point. The move, it seemed, was all part of her husband's need to redefine himself, make a new start. But quite why this mattered so much now, was far more obscure. As was the even deeper question: did this new start include her?

She sighed, and brought her mind back to the meeting in hand. She confirmed that Kathryn Walters had decided not to give evidence. 'That's the right decision, I think. But what worries me more is that they're going to call the girl's psychiatrist.'

'Just because she was depressed doesn't mean she killed herself,' mumbled Wrass, mopping up egg with fried bread. 'You can nail that one, surely.'

'I'll try,' said Sarah. 'But the way she insisted on seeing Kidd alone, and maybe had sex with him too - it all builds their case for suicide, doesn't it?'

'How so?'

'Well, look at it this way. She's bi-polar, he claims, so when she's up she's really up - cheerful, energetic, assertive - but when she's down she's the opposite, self-doubting, unsure, a pushover for a bastard like Kidd. That's probably what attracted her to him; he's a strong character with no qualms about telling her what to do. Just like her mother, probably, which explains why those two hated each other on sight. So Shelley tried to dump him, but felt guilty, wondered if she'd made a mistake, and went back to see him one more time - she didn't really need that stuff in her bag. And she did forgive him, didn't she, so it seems? She let him make love to her.'

'Let him?' Terry said. 'More like rape, I'd have thought.'

'Well, we can't prove that. But even if it was, that just helps their case, don't you see? It explains what happened next. He goes out to the shop, and she suddenly realises what she's done, is overcome with remorse, grabs a knife from the kitchen and kills herself. Psychologically, it works fine.'

'Yes, but there are his fingerprints on the knife, the bruises on her neck, and the way her wrists were cut,' said Mark Wrass firmly. 'They all point to him.'

'I agree. They're hard facts, not psychological speculation. But other facts are less good for us. This timing issue, for instance. Terry, I've got the shopkeeper this afternoon. Will he stand up to questions in court?'

'I suppose so.' Terry frowned. 'But Will Churchill interviewed him, not me.'

'Churchill?' Sarah asked, surprised. A worm of doubt stirred uneasily in her stomach. 'I thought this was your case, not his.'

'Yes, but the day I was going to see him, Esther was rushed into Casualty with suspected meningitis.' He shuddered at the memory. 'So Will Churchill took his statement, not me. But it's clear enough, isn't it? What's the problem?'

'Well, you remember how Savendra worried away at Dr Tuchman, cutting down the time Shelley could have lain bleeding in the bath and still been alive when the ambulance crew came? He got him down to fifteen or twenty minutes. So if the shopkeeper says David was out of the flat for more than say, thirteen minutes, then since the ambulance took seven minutes to arrive, our case is blown out of the water. If he'd cut her wrists before he went out, she'd have been dead when he got back.'

'Unless he cut her wrists after he came back?' Terry said. 'That's the other possibility, you know.'

'Not now it isn't!' Sarah glared at him, her hazel eyes making her displeasure clear. *You should know this,* the look said. 'Didn't you see what happened last week, with the priest?'

'No,' Terry frowned. 'I didn't stay for his evidence. What happened?'

Sarah sighed. 'That priest told Savendra exactly when he saw Kidd outside his flat. Six minutes to four, he said; he was late for evensong so he checked his watch. And Kidd called 999 at 3.56 - two minutes later. It's too quick, Terry, he couldn't have killed her in that short time. Anyway, think what he told the operator: "My girlfriend's dead, she's killed herself." He's not stupid - he wouldn't have said that if he'd cut her wrists just a minute before. He'd have waited, given her time to bleed to death first. Which is why he went out to the shop - to give her time to die. So what matters now is exactly how long he was away.'

'He was in the shop for less than five minutes,' Terry replied bluntly. 'The shopkeeper says that quite clearly.'

'Yes, well let's just hope he sticks to that in court,' Sarah said thoughtfully. 'Otherwise we're sunk. You do realise that, don't you?'‘

The shopkeeper, Mr Patel, was a small, rotund elderly Asian gentleman, who surveyed his impressive surroundings with nervous awe. Sarah led him gently through the preliminaries. His shop, he said, was about forty yards from David Kidd's flat. A minute's walk, no more. On the night Shelley died, David came into the shop, and bought some olive oil and flowers. He seemed quite keen to talk, Mr Patel said. He was cooking a meal for himself and Shelley. The flowers were a present for her.

'And what else did you talk about?'

'Football. I had watched Leeds beat Arsenal in the cup the day before. He asked me about the match and I told him.'

'And how did he look, during this conversation?'

'A little agitated, perhaps. Sweating, as though he was hot.'

Sarah smiled encouragingly. So far everything was going to plan. In his statement Mr Patel had said that David had only been in the shop for a maximum of four minutes, meaning that he was away from his flat for no more than six minutes in total, thus making it quite possible for him to have cut Shelley's wrists before he went out, and return to find her still alive. Hesitantly, he confirmed this for Sarah now.

'I think that is probably right, yes. I mean, that is what I told the policeman.'

'Detective Chief Inspector Churchill, you mean?' Sarah had the witness statement in front of her, with Churchill's signature beside Patel's on every page. The shopkeeper's words were faithfully recorded in Will Churchill's smooth, rounded handwriting.

'Yes, I believe that was the officer's name.'

'Very well. And you stand by that statement now, do you?

'I ... well, it's hard to remember exactly after such a long time, you see, madam, but ...'

Don't hesitate now, Sarah thought, for Christ's sake. Not when we're almost there. Yet it seemed if that was exactly what the man was doing. Small beads of perspiration were appearing on his domed brown forehead; he was looking around the court nervously. She was concerned, but not particularly surprised. Many witnesses found it an ordeal to give evidence in open court, particularly in a serious trial like this, with the man accused of murder only a few yards away, glaring at you from the dock as David Kidd was doing now. Smoothly, she moved to help him.

'But at the time you gave this statement, on the 25th of May, your memory of the events was much clearer, presumably? Only four days after Miss Walters died?'

'Yes. Yes, of course.'

'So you were clear enough in your mind then. David Kidd was in your shop for no more than four minutes, you said. Is that correct, Mr Patel?'

'That ... is what I told the Inspector, yes.'

'Thank you.' Sarah gave him a warm, encouraging smile. You have done your public duty admirably, the smile was meant to say. Just stick to your story for a few more minutes and your ordeal will be over. You can go back to your shop and sell baked beans in peace.

But first, the shopkeeper had to face Savendra, who had been watching him like a hawk. Last night Savendra had studied this man's witness statement with unusual care - a task made the more pleasant by the faint traces of Belinda's scent which still clung to his copy of the document. The longer he watched Patel in the witness box, the more his confidence grew. This man was the keystone of Sarah's case; if he couldn't stand the pressure, the arch of evidence she was trying to build would collapse in rubble and doubt. And the shopkeeper had been sweating, even before a friendly advocate.

The man's eyes followed Sarah regretfully as she sat down. Savendra rose and waited, saying nothing, until the shopkeeper reluctantly turned to face him.

'Good afternoon, Mr Patel. My name is Savendra Bhose. I am defence counsel for Mr Kidd.'

'Good afternoon, sir.'

That one word, 'sir', was important. It was an acknowledgement of Savendra's social and professional status; a level far superior to that of this elderly shopkeeper or, probably, anyone in his family.

'Just now, Mr Patel, you told my learned colleague how difficult it was to remember events that took place some six months ago.'

'Yes, sir. I did.'

'I am sure the members of the jury appreciate your difficulty. I doubt if many of them could remember events that took place so long ago. And it's fair to say, isn't it, Mr Patel, that you had no idea, when Mr Kidd came into your shop, that his visit that day was an important one, that you should try to remember. You thought he'd just popped in to buy some food, didn't you? Like any other customer.'

'Yes, sir, of course.'

'Quite. Could you give this court an estimate of how many customers come into your shop every day? In general terms, I mean. How many? Fifty? A hundred perhaps?'

'On a good day, sir, perhaps two or three hundred.' The shopkeeper swelled with defensive pride. 'I have a thriving business. I have a large family and it supports them all.'

'I am glad to hear it, Mr Patel. Very commendable too. So, of these two or three hundred customers, do you remember in detail what each one of them buys, how long they spend in the shop, and so on?'

'Not in detail, sir, no, of course not.'

'Some of them talk to you, no doubt. Do you remember what each of them say?'

'One or two, perhaps. Not all of them, no.'

'And you gave this statement to DCI Churchill when? Four days after Shelley Walters died. Well, today is Monday. Can you remember, for instance, who came into your shop last Thursday?'

'I ... well ... some of them, perhaps. I'm not sure. It's hard to say.'

'You see, the reason I ask, Mr Patel, is that in this statement you gave the police some very precise details about one of your customers who'd been in your shop four days before.'

'Yes, sir.'

'You say - let me see, I have it here...' Savendra looked down at the words he had highlighted in yellow on the fragrant statement in his hand. "...he knew where everything was in the shop and he found it quickly. We had a brief conversation about football but it didn't last long because there were some ladies behind him queueing very fiercely. He couldn't have been in the shop more than four minutes in total." It's very precise, isn't it, Mr Patel. "Ladies queuing very fiercely ... four minutes in total." Do you really remember all of those things?'

'I ... I remembered them when I spoke to the police officer. It's a long time ago now.'

'You remember them less well now, you mean?'

'I am less sure, perhaps.'

'Less sure. You see, this is a very important matter, Mr Patel. You do realise that, don't you? A man could go to prison for life on the basis of your evidence. You have sworn an oath to tell the truth in this court of her Majesty the Queen. With her royal coat of arms above the learned judge's throne.'

Watching, Sarah felt her own concerns increase. The sweat on the shopkeeper's brow was more prominent now, his anxiety greater. The jury were watching him doubtfully.

'Yes, sir. I understand that.'

'Yet you still stand by this statement, do you? You mean to tell this court - this jury - that you remember clearly how long this man, Mr Kidd, spent in your shop more than six months ago?'

'It is very difficult, sir. That is what I told the policeman.'

'I see.' Savendra sighed as though dissatisfied with the answer. 'Let's look at your statement, shall we? You have a copy in front of you. Is that your handwriting?'

'Mine? No, sir. The policeman wrote it.'

'The policeman wrote it? Not you? So he wrote it, and you just signed it?'

'Yes, sir, that was the way.'

Sarah leaned her elbows on the table, massaging her forehead with her fingertips. This was a familiar issue to both barristers. Police regulations advised that, whereever practicable, witnesses should write out their statements in their own hand, but in practice this seldom happened. It took twice as long, and many witnesses were simply not up to the task, crossing things out, including masses of irrelevant details, and being unable to spell or punctuate. So the police officer did it for them, in the process fashioning a statement that simultaneously suited the purposes of the investigation and laid them open to the charge of putting words into the witness's mouth.

The difficulty for Sarah was that it was not Terry Bateson, but Will Churchill, who had written out this man's statement for him. And Churchill, in Sarah's opinion, had about as much respect for the truth as a fox had for the life of a chicken.

'Did you read what he wrote, before you signed?'

'Yes, well ... not exactly. He read it to me.'

'He read it aloud to you, after he had written it. Then you signed?'

'Yes.'

'I see. Did he offer you the chance to correct what he had written, then? To put in a sentence explaining how difficult it was to remember, perhaps?'

'No sir. It was all correct.'

'All correct, was it? And very precise. He couldn't have been in the shop more than four minutes in total. Do you have a stopwatch on your counter, Mr Patel?'

'No sir, of course not.'

'And yet you state very precisely how many minutes this man spent in your shop. Did DCI Churchill explain to you exactly why the timing was so important?'

'Well yes sir, of course. Because the young man had murdered his girlfriend.'

'Oh really? He told you that, did he?'

Sarah groaned softly to herself. Oh Terry, Terry, why didn't you interview this man yourself?

'Well, yes, sir, of course. Everyone knew it. That's why we are here.'

'Let me be clear about this. He told you Mr Kidd had murdered his girlfriend, did he? Not that he was investigating her death, but that it was a murder, and Mr Kidd had done it?'

'Well yes, sir. I think that's what he said.'

'Very well. You are being very honest, Mr Patel. And so that's why you remembered this visit to your shop in particular, is it? Because you knew, or believed you knew, that Mr Kidd had murdered his girlfriend. Did the policeman also explain to you why the length of time Mr Kidd spent in your shop was so important?'

'Yes, I think ... if he had spent a long time in my shop, then she must have killed herself. But if it was only a short time, then he was the murderer.'

'He said that to you, did he? Before you made your statement?'

'I'm not sure when he said it. But it's true, isn't it? I mean, that's what I've heard.'

'Are you telling this jury, Mr Patel, that before you made this statement to the police, DCI Churchill told you that if you said Mr Kidd had only spent a few minutes in your shop, that would be proof that he had murdered his girlfriend?'

'I'm not sure if it was before. Maybe after I made the statement. I don't know.'

'But he did tell you this, did he?'

'I think so, yes.' Something about the reaction to his evidence, maybe the way the judge and Sarah were staring at him so intently, was beginning to unnerve the elderly shopkeeper even more than Savendra's questions. 'Perhaps, yes. I may have got this wrong.'

Savendra studied the witness carefully. The man was sweating, his plump hands clasping and unclasping nervously as he gazed anxiously at the faces in front of him. 'You're being very honest, Mr Patel. That's good, that's very important in a court of law. You're saying you can't remember precisely what the Detective Chief Inspector told you about this crime when he wrote down your statement more than seven months ago?'

'Yes sir, that's right.'

The man looked relieved, but Sarah, watching, guessed that his relief would be short-lived. It was often when he was being kind to a witness that Savendra was at his most lethal.

'And yet you can remember, very precisely indeed it seems, exactly how many minutes Mr Kidd spent in your shop on the 21st May. Is that what you're asking this court to believe?'

The shopkeeper hesitated. 'Well, I'm not sure. I thought ... remembered it then.'

'You remembered it then, when the Chief Inspector was sitting in front of you, writing down words for you to sign. Do you remember it now? Are you sure that these words which the detective wrote down for you are the truth?'

The pudgy hands on the witness stand clasped each other in agony. 'I don't know. It's a long time ago. I thought they were true.'

'You thought they were true, yet you didn't even read them before signing. And you can't remember now, exactly what the Chief Inspector told you before you signed this paper, can you? That's the truth, isn't it?'

'I think he said what I told you. That David had murdered his girlfriend. That's why I tried so hard to remember. It was my duty, you understand. She was a lovely girl. She had been in my shop many times.'

'You tried hard to remember what the Chief Inspector wanted you to remember. That's the truth, isn't it? And he wrote it down for you. Think hard now, Mr Patel. You're on oath, in the court of her Majesty the Queen. Can you honestly tell this court that my client, Mr Kidd there, was in your shop for only four minutes? Could he have been there for six minutes, maybe? Eight minutes? Ten perhaps? Fifteen? Can you really be so sure?'

The man took a folded handkerchief from his pocket and mopped his forehead anxiously.

'It is very difficult to be sure, sir. But he was not there for fifteen minutes, certainly. Ten minutes ... well, perhaps. Possibly eight. But I honestly believed four at the time. I was not lying, sir, you understand. I was trying to do my duty. To help the police solve a murder. That poor girl - she was murdered!'

'You don't know that, Mr Patel. None of us do. It is quite possible that she committed suicide. That is why your evidence is so important, you see. Now, let me ask you one more time. Can you be sure that he was there for only four minutes?'

Patel took a deep breath, and seemed to withdraw into himself for a moment as he searched his memory for the truth. Then he sighed, and looked up.

'No sir. If I am honest, I cannot be sure.'

It was, as both lawyers knew, a terrible admission - possibly the decisive moment in the trial. As Savendra sat down, he smiled at Sarah and made a quiet clicking noise with his mouth. Very soft, but Sarah knew exactly what it meant: you've lost this, darling, he's dropped you in the sewage. If David Kidd had been in that shop for ten or twelve minutes, with at least two more minutes walking to and from his flat and another couple talking to the priest outside his door, then his alibi worked in the way he had always claimed: he would have been away from the flat for fifteen minutes or more, too long for Shelley to be still alive by the time he had returned, phoned 999, and waited a further seven minutes for an ambulance. But plenty of time, on the other hand, for her to have got out of the bath, found a knife, and cut her own wrists while he was away. Mr Patel had just given Kidd a lifeline, by denying the written statement he had given to the police.

22. Recriminations

SARAH STORMED out of court at the lunchtime adjournment, Mark Wrass following anxiously behind. 'Where is that man Churchill? I want to speak to him right now.'

'I rang as soon as this started and left a message,' Mark said apologetically. 'He's out on a case, it seems.'

'Well, ring again and get him here now. This case is going down the pan unless something is done.'

But as Mark began urgently punching numbers into his mobile phone, Sarah spotted Will Churchill running jauntily up the stone steps outside the court. She strode smartly over to confront him as he pushed his way into the foyer. Seeing the scowl on her face, he raised an ironic eyebrow. 'Problems, Mrs Newby, is it? Cock-up on the legal front?'

'I'll say. Come with me, through here, now.'

She led the way swiftly to a small conference room, holding the door open when she got there so that Churchill, following with deliberate slowness, was shown as if into her office. She stood behind the table and glared at him.

'A key witness, a man interviewed by you, has just gone back on his evidence. Unless something is done about it David Kidd is going to walk free.' Briskly, she outlined the events of the morning, while Churchill stood opposite her, stunned, his insouciance blown away by her story. 'He now says that Kidd was in his shop for eight or ten minutes, which means that if Kidd cut her wrists, Shelley Walters would have had to survive for more than twenty minutes with a pierced artery to be still alive when the ambulance came. Which the defence are going to claim is impossible.'

'The little bastard! Why did he do that?'

'He's saying you bullied him into making that statement. Did you?'

'Of course I bloody didn't! What do you think I am?'

A man who wants to get to the top, fast, Sarah thought bitterly. A man who needs successful prosecutions and will bulldoze his way through until he gets them.

'It wouldn't be the first time a policeman has manufactured evidence. If this man had come up with this story before, I doubt I'd have advised the CPS to bring this case.'

'Are you saying I lied, woman?' Always on a short fuse, particularly where women were concerned, Churchill had raised his voice several decibels. The bitter history of their previous conflicts replayed ghostly battles between them.

'*I'm* not saying it,' said Sarah. 'It's Mr Patel who's saying it, on oath, in court. You told him Kidd was a murderer, he says, wrote out his statement for him, and bullied him into saying what you wanted to hear.'

'I didn't bloody bully him, the toe-rag,' said Churchill controlling his voice with an effort. 'I sat him down nice and quiet, helped him make up his mind, and wrote down every word he said. Then he read it all over carefully, and signed it. It's called procedures, Mrs Newby, doing things properly. The way I always operate.'

'Helped him make up his mind?' Sarah said. 'What's that supposed to mean?'

'Just what it says. It's hard to remember exactly how long a conversation took, even you must realise that. So I focussed his mind on the things he did, the words he could remember, and made him think how long each one took. Then we added the times up together.'

'And you call that objective?'

'I call that careful investigation, getting at the truth. Why, what would you call it?'

Putting pressure on the witness to come up with the right story, Sarah thought grimly. That's what I'd say if I had this man on the stand in front of me. But right now, we're on the same side. Gritting her teeth, she said: 'This still looks like a murder but it's going to be a lot harder to prove. Some of those jurors have been brought up on stories of police brutality, and you've just played right into their fantasies.'

'I've done nothing of the sort. I wrote down exactly what he told me.'

'What you wanted him to tell you, you mean.'

'Look.' Churchill pressed his hands to the table and got his feet. 'We're getting nowhere with this. You know it was a murder and I know it was a murder so when that man Patel said Kidd was in his shop for only a few minutes that has to be the truth, however much you lawyers have muddled his brains now. Witnesses get confused all the time, you know that, but it's your job and mine to make sure that wicked murderers like David Kidd get locked away for good. And if you're not up to that, Mrs Newby, perhaps you're in the wrong job!'

Not me, Sarah thought as she watched the door close behind him. Not me, William Churchill, you. She had loathed the man ever since she had met him, but never before, so far as she could remember, had he so clearly condemned himself out of his own mouth.

When court resumed after lunch, Sarah stood up and said, rather lamely: 'My lord, that concludes the case for the prosecution.'

As she had expected, Savendra immediately asked for the jury to be sent out during legal argument, which consisted of his attempt to get the case dismissed on the grounds that there was insufficient evidence to put before a jury. 'My lord, the entire prosecution case rested on the evidence of this morning's witness, who was supposed to disprove my client's alibi that he was out of the flat while Shelley Walters met her death. His original statement, signed it now seems under police pressure, made it possible that the defendant cut Miss Walters' wrists, went out to the shop, and returned in time to find her still alive. This is no longer the case. Mr Patel's new evidence entirely destroys this possibility. Therefore the only rational conclusion is that she took her own life.'

'That is not so, my lord,' Sarah argued firmly. 'In the first place, it seems highly likely that this morning's witness is simply confused, and has no idea how long the accused was in his shop. His evidence is now so contradictory that it should be disregarded altogether. And with Mr Patel out of the equation, we are left with the fact that Miss Walters was found dying in the defendant's bath, in a flat to which no one but he had access, with bruises on her neck and the artery pierced in her right wrist - not her left - and the defendant's fingerprints on the knife. Quite sufficient to put before the jury, my lord.'

'A strong prima facie case, certainly,' said the judge. 'But you must admit, Mrs Newby, your case is damaged. Your chances of conviction seem rather less of a certainty than they did. Do you have witnesses to call, Mr Bhose?'

'Yes, my lord, two. Miss Walters' psychiatrist and the defendant himself.'

Sarah sighed. Earlier she had argued strongly for the exclusion of Dr Giles MacDonald, Shelley's psychiatrist, on the grounds that he had no first-hand knowledge whatsoever of the circumstances of Shelley's death, but the judge, reluctantly, had overruled her. Since the defence relied on the possibility of suicide, he said, the grounds for that possibility must necessarily be explored. After this morning's debacle she saw no point in a further almost certainly futile attempt to reopen that debate. Instead, she bought herself a sandwich and a bottle of water, and phoned Terry Bateson.

'Hi,' she said, sitting on a bench by the riverbank, and ripping open the packet with her left hand while she held the phone in the other. 'What are you doing now?'

'Preparing to interview a drug dealer. Why?'

'I thought you might like to know how things went in court this morning with your shopkeeper. The one whose evidence you were so certain about. Remember?'

Was his mobile clear enough to convey the full bitterness behind her tone of waspish disillusionment? She hoped so. She took a bite of her sandwich and waited. His response, when it came, sounded cautious and wary.

'Why? What happened?'

'He changed his story. Said Kidd might have been in his shop for up to ten minutes. He only said four in his statement because Will Churchill bullied him into it. And not only that, he claimed Churchill told him four would get Kidd convicted of murder.'

'Shit.'

'My sentiments exactly. Only it was me that was dropped in it. I only just managed to stop the judge from throwing the case out altogether.'

There was a pause, during which she bit hungrily into her sandwich and waited for a response which didn't come. What was he doing, she wondered irritably? Shaking his head? Biting his lip? Ignoring her completely while he read some document about his drug dealer?

'Terry?' She unscrewed her bottle of water. 'I trusted you to get this right!'

'Yeah, well. I'm sorry. I'll talk to Churchill. He'll deny it, of course.'

'I'm way ahead of you. I've talked to him already.'

'And?'

'He denied it, of course. Said he did everything by the book, the smug bastard.'

'Yes, well, he would say that, wouldn't he? What did you expect?'

She let him wait for a moment while she sipped from her drink. The water cleared her mouth, so her answer came crisply. 'What I expected, Terry, was that you would double-check everything, and that this case, which I only agreed to take on because you were in charge of it, would be watertight. Now it's holed below the waterline, damn you!'

'Look, Sarah, I'm sorry. You're right, I should have checked.' His voice, she was pleased to note, sounded suitably contrite. She began to feel a little sorry for him, as he went on. ' ... you do appreciate the man's my boss, don't you? I can't just go picking holes in everything he does, you know. Especially when ...'

'He only did it because one of your kids was ill. I know.'

'I wasn't going to say that, Sarah, though it's true. Christ, suspected meningitis - for a few days there I thought Esther was going to die. So I was grateful to him at the time. But what I was going to say was ... well, this is still a murder, Sarah, and Kidd did it, whatever that shopkeeper Patel says now. So when Will Churchill brought back a statement saying Kidd was only in his shop for four minutes, I believed it. I mean, it has to be true, doesn't it?'

'That's not what he's saying now.'

'Well, what is he saying now? That he's sure Kidd was in his shop for ten minutes?'

'No, not really. He's saying he can't remember.'

'Well, exactly. That's the trouble with this kind of evidence. Sod Will Churchill, he's screwed it up by trying to be too precise. But in this case ... well, he's got to be right, hasn't he? I mean, who else murdered Shelley if Kidd didn't do it? There was no one else there.'

'She murdered herself.' Sarah took another bite of her sandwich. 'That's what the defence are saying. Some of the jury are starting to believe that now.'

'Yes, well, she didn't, Sarah. You know that and so do I. It's your job to convince them of the truth, that's all.'

'That, DI Bateson, is exactly what Will Churchill said to me half an hour ago. To cover up the fact that he's been caught falsifying the evidence. Again. In a noble cause, no doubt. Just as he did with my son.'

'Okay, Sarah, look, I'm sorry. We've got to do things the right way, of course we have. But it's not the same as your son, not this time, really. All the evidence shows Kidd's guilty, all the rest of it, anyway. And if he isn't put away, it'll be that girl's family who will suffer, all over again for a second time. Can you imagine what that would be like?'

'I can try, but I don't think imagination takes you very far, do you? The real thing must be so painful it doesn't bear thinking about. Okay, Terry, look, you're right. I think this Patel was just confused, that's all, and Will Churchill's made it worse. But I'll do my best. This afternoon I've got the girl's psychiatrist, God help me. That isn't going to help either.'

Sarah got to her feet, threw the remains of her sandwich to some ducks, and dropped the wrapper in a bin. In a few minutes she was due back in court.

'You'll manage,' Terry said. 'You always do.'

'Do I? We'll see.' Sarah clicked off her phone, drained her bottle, threw it after the wrapper, and strode purposefully back across the road.

23. Trick Cyclist

'STILL FEELING lucky?' Savendra asked mischievously, on the way back into court.

'Of course,' Sarah replied, wishing she felt half as sure as she sounded. 'Trust me, Savvy, your client's going down. There's a cell door with his name already printed on it.'

Dr MacDonald, a lean, grey haired psychiatrist in his fifties, took the stand to explain that he had first met Shelley when she was seventeen, and treated her regularly for bi-polar disorder; previously known as manic depression. He had last seen her three weeks before she died.

Savendra nodded. 'In layman's terms, could you explain what that diagnosis means, please?'

'Well, people with this illness suffer from very extreme, violent mood swings. All of us feel low on some days, when we are ill, perhaps, or things go wrong - and we feel happy when things are going right. Well, for people with bi-polar disorder these moods are magnified hugely: some authorities believe the feelings can be ten, even a hundred times stronger. And this works both ways. Some highly creative people have suffered from manic depression, as we used to call it - Winston Churchill, for instance. When things are going well for them they can be full of energy, their minds buzzing with exciting ideas, as though the sun was shining inside their heads. But on bad days, they can be sunk a gloom so deep that everything seems utterly hopeless. Many people suffer real physical pain, so bad that it frightens them and they want to escape it in any way they can.'

'Even by suicide?' Savendra asked smoothly.

'Sometimes, yes. The suicide rate amongst people with bi-polar disorder is much higher than for the rest of the population.'

'And Shelley Walters suffered from this condition?'

'Yes. Hers was a relatively mild form of the condition, I would say; but even that can be seriously disabling. She came to me in the first place because she was unable to cope with her A levels. Days, even weeks, passed when she was unable to touch a book or a pen, her depression was so bad. And yet when the cloud lifted her teachers confirmed that she was a wonderful student, buzzing with ideas and energy. I saw that for myself, indeed. She was a lovely girl, a real pleasure to talk to.'

'Was your treatment able to help her?'

'I think so, yes, with a combination of drugs and counselling. The drugs were vital - I put her on a prescription of lithium to keep her stable. It prevented her from falling into those black troughs of despair. But not all patients are happy with this treatment, because it also prevents you from reaching those peaks of happiness which are the positive side of this condition. And those can be quite addictive, believe me. So that's where the counselling comes in. I spent a lot of time talking to Shelley, getting her to understand her condition better, and to get used to a more normal range of emotions. And of course we talked about her family, her ambitions, and the things that frustrated or annoyed her. All adolescents have to deal with those things, but it's particularly important for patients with bi-polar disorder to avoid being ambushed by something that can knock them seriously off balance, even with the medication. If they forget to take it, of course, the results can be even worse.'

'Did Shelley sometimes forget to take her medication?'

'Yes, once or twice. If 'forget' is the right word - that's debatable. She may occasionally have done. At least once I think she did it deliberately, because she craved that feeling of intense happiness and creativity which she had experienced before.'

'But without her medicine, she also ran the risk of descending into one of those troughs of severe depression which you described, didn't she?'

'Certainly. I warned her of that risk.'

'And it's because of these depressions, is it, that people with bi-polar disorder are more prone to suicide than the rest of the population?'

'Undoubtedly, yes. It can be an experience so painful, so devoid of hope, that death can seem the only way out.'

Watching from the gallery, Kathryn seethed with fury. She had been incensed that this man was called in the first place, and now, as he described how Shelley found study difficult and the pressure from her parents, particularly her mother, hard to bear, she gripped the rail grimly in front of her. What about patient confidentiality, she wanted to ask - what about the duty of care this creepy psychiatrist owed to the poor girl who'd asked him for help? Was it his duty to blame her family now, help her murderer, when the poor child was dead and could never answer back?

'Could this sort of pressure drive her into depression?'

'Sometimes, yes. All sorts of things could do it - a breakup with a boyfriend, criticism from her teachers, an argument, or just nothing at all. You must remember that these depressions are essentially a chemical imbalance in the brain, so they can begin with no external stimulus whatsoever. As can the highs which are their opposite.'

Savendra glanced at the jury, who were watching intently. It seemed that his witness was going down well. 'When was Shelley Walters discharged from your care?'

'She was never finally discharged. Hers was not a condition from which you are ever really cured. The best you can hope for is to stabilize it, really. The last time I saw her was about three weeks before she died. She came for a new prescription.'

'And how did she seem to you on that occasion?'

'Quite cheerful, positive. She had a new boyfriend, that was the main development in her life. She said he was very attentive, very caring.'

'Very attentive and caring. Did she mention the boyfriend's name?'

'She did. David Kidd.'

'Did she mention any fears she had about this boyfriend?'

'Fears? No, not really. She said she'd had some arguments with her parents but she felt these had been a liberating experience more than anything else. They helped her establish a more independent identity, separate from her parents. It's a normal development for young adults.'

'For God's sake!' Heads turned all round the court, to see Kathryn standing in the public gallery, screaming down at the man giving evidence. 'He didn't liberate her, he turned her into a slave, who could hardly speak for herself! You don't know what you're talking about, do you - you're just here to help Shelley's murderer!'

'Kath, love, please, sit down. Sit down, you can't do this.' Andrew had his arms round his wife, tugging ineffectually with Miranda on the other side.

'It wasn't pressure from us that killed her, it was him - that monster down there!' Kathryn jabbed her finger down at the dock before subsiding into her seat in tears. As the usher nervously entered the public gallery she said: 'All right, all right, I'll be quiet. But he doesn't know what he's talking about, that fool down there. He's just helping her killer.'

As Kathryn sat down, Savendra turned back to the psychiatrist. 'Would you look at this packet of tablets which was found in Shelley Walter's bedroom at the university, please. Is this the medication you prescribed?'

'Yes. I changed the prescription from lithium to sodium valproate on April 30th.'

'Could you tell us, please, how many tablets remain in the packet?'

'Sixteen.'

'And how many tablets was she supposed to take every day?'

'One.'

'I believe there were originally twenty-eight tablets in the packet which you prescribed. So, by a process of simple arithmetic, doctor MacDonald, if Shelley had taken one of those tablets every day from April 30th to 20th May, how many tablets would you expect to remain?'

'Seven.'

'So what does that suggest to you?'

'It suggests that she had missed the medication on nine days.'

'Exactly. What effect would that have on her mental condition, doctor?'

'She would begin to return to the manic depressive state for which she was being treated. Her moods would be more intense and volatile than they had been before.'

'More intense and volatile. And we know that during the week before she died, she found her boyfriend in bed with another girl - that would provide a powerful external stimulus to depression, wouldn't it? Quite apart from the chemical imbalance in her brain.'

'That is possible, certainly.'

'Quite. So, given your knowledge of Shelley Walters' medical condition, doctor, was she the sort of person who, when deprived of her medication and under the pressure of family expectations, academic work, and the break-up of her relationship with her boyfriend, might contemplate suicide as a way to escape?'

'Obviously I have no idea what really happened. As far as I was aware her life was improving and she was taking her medication regularly. But ... my answer to your question, in the circumstances you describe, has to be yes. If she stopped taking her medicine, and then experienced a severe, crippling depression consequent on the break-up of a romantic relationship, then she may have contemplated suicide, certainly. It is a possibility I cannot rule out.'

It was clear to Sarah that the psychiatrist had damaged her case. And Kathryn's outburst had made it worse - at least two of the jurors seemed to have found it more funny than tragic. She had no intention of bandying medical terminology with this man. Her aim was get him off the stand in short order, and refocus the juror's minds on the facts. She confronted him coolly.

'Doctor, you don't know how Shelley died, do you? You never saw her body, did you? Never visited the scene of the crime?'

'No.'

'You never even met her boyfriend - this 'caring, attentive' young man you described.'

'No. That was Shelley's description, not mine.'

'These pills my learned colleague showed you. Do you know when she didn't take them?'

'I can't tell you that, no.'

'So for all you know, she could have missed taking them in the first week of May, just after you prescribed them, and resumed later. That's possible, isn't it? Just as possible as Mr Bhose's suggestion?'

'I can't say when she failed to take them, or why. I can only describe the likely effects.'

'Quite. But she was cheerful and positive when you last saw her. Is that right?'

'Relatively so, yes. That's how she seemed to me.'

'And presumably it would have been more sensible for Shelley to stop taking the medication when she was happy, and then resume later when things started to go wrong for her, rather than the other way round?'

'The medication is supposed to be taken regularly, but yes, if you are going to pause at all, it's safer when things are going well for you.'

'And Shelley was a sensible girl, wasn't she? Not a masochist? She didn't enjoy these terrible low moods that she suffered from?'

'Certainly not. No one could enjoy experiences like those.'

'And she knew that the best way to avoid these was to take the medicine.'

'Oh yes. She knew that, certainly.'

'So if she felt low after breaking up with her boyfriend, the most likely thing is that she did take her medicine then, isn't it? When she needed it?'

'It's quite possible, yes.'

'Very well.' A rasp of scorn entered Sarah's voice. 'So, to sum up, you have no evidence at all that she committed suicide, you don't know when she stopped taking her medicine, and the last time you saw her she was in relatively good spirits. Is that right?'

'In a way, yes.'

'Thank you,' Sarah said, in her coldest, most dismissive voice. She folded her gown about her and sat down, leaving the psychiatrist staring at her, flummoxed. There was nothing on which Savendra seemed to want to redirect. She only hoped the damage he had done was small.

24. Confessions

AS COURT rose for the day, Savendra went down to the cells to meet his client. He was feeling pleased; the psychiatrist, despite Sarah's efforts, had weakened the prosecution case further. If Shelley had been mentally unstable, his client's story might easily be true.

The warder left them together in the 'stable block' area of little wooden stalls. David sat on the bench, tie roughly loosened, boot resting on his knee, and grinned up at Savendra. 'You did well today, mate,' he said. 'That shrink told them what a nutter she was.'

'He made an impression, certainly.' Savendra remained standing, one hand on the wooden partition between the stalls. The warder had left them alone, and the other stalls were empty. 'And tomorrow it's you. Are you ready for that?'

'Ready to give evidence? Sure, why not?'

'Well, just remember what I said. Look calm, and respectable. The jury will be judging your character, as well as what you say.' *And if they see what you're really like*, a voice whispered in his mind, *they'll put you under a stone and stamp on it.*

'Yeah, sure.' David flicked his tie with a finger. 'Proper posh git, I'll be.'

'Nonetheless,' said Savendra cautiously. 'They won't like everything you say. You have to be prepared for that. It may even help, to a certain extent.'

'How d'you mean?'

'Well, look. You admit you were unfaithful and had a noisy argument with the girl in your flat. You persuaded her to stay when she didn't intend to, and to have sex with you. None of that looks good. But it does fit with the psychiatrist's suggestion that she killed herself because she was depressed and ashamed of what she'd just done. Or what you persuaded her to do,' he ended rather lamely.

'So what're you suggesting? That I should play this up a bit, is that it?'

'I'm not suggesting anything,' Savendra answered coldly. 'That's not my job. I'm warning you to be prepared, that's all. It's obvious enough what Mrs Newby's going to ask. How did those bruises get there, for a start? If you weren't holding the girl's head under water, what were you doing? Holding her down while you raped her?'

'Who says I raped her?' A cunning smile crossed David Kidd's face. 'There were no bruises on her cunt, were there? The pathologist said that. No, her head got bruised when I was trying to save her - give her the kiss of life like they said on the phone. I was trying to hold her still in the bath, she was sliding around all over the place.'

Savendra studied him coolly. 'So you didn't hold her down while you had sex?'

'No need, sunshine.' The cunning smile spread wider. 'She was doped. Out of it. Gone.'

'What?' Cold fingers gripped Savendra's spine. This can't be happening, he told himself. *He didn't say that, did he? Not now when we're winning, please.* 'She was drugged?'

'Yeah,' David looked vastly pleased with himself. 'There she was screaming at me, so I slipped some roofies into her wine.'

'You're saying ... you drugged her for sex?' Savendra's voice cracked as he struggled to adjust to this new, horrible reality.

'That's it; got it in one.' David smiled engagingly, as if he was sharing a wonderful secret. 'Worked a treat - calmed her down after all the shouting. Couple of sips and - ping! She's gone. You want to try it, mate. It's brilliant. Do anything after that. Putty in your hands.'

'Oh my God!' Savendra glanced towards the corridor, hoping the warder was out of earshot. 'You shouldn't have told me this, I don't want to hear. I'm sorry, I don't think I can defend you after this.'

'What?' David sat bolt upright, all arrogance gone. 'What you talking about now?'

'You drugged her in order to rape her. You just admitted that to me.'

'Yeah, but I'm not charged with rape, am I? I'm charged with murder, for Christ's sake!'

That's true, Savendra thought desperately. Thank God for small mercies. 'And you're still telling me you didn't murder her?'

'Absolutely. No way. I didn't.'

Savendra confronted the man, thoughts running like rats round his mind. 'Let's get this straight. You drugged her, so she was unable to resist your demands for sex, right?'

'Unable? She was gagging for it, mate. Knees round her ears. What that priest heard, her calling out, she loved it.'

Crawl back under your stone, Savendra thought. *That's where you belong.* 'All right. How did she get in the bath, then?'

'Well, she wasn't completely gone. Just a bit daft and giggly.'

'Could she walk?'

'Yeah, course. I ran the bath for her, and she got in it.'

'You left a drugged girl in the bath?'

'Yeah.' David grinned, uncertainly, as if affronted that his attempt to share a confidence was going so wrong. 'I thought she was happy then, honest. I didn't know she was going to cut her wrists.'

Savendra glared at his client, thinking hard. 'You didn't do that?'

'No. On my honour, I didn't. I came back and found her like that. She did it herself.'

'Your honour,' Savendra mocked bitterly, wishing he'd never met the repulsive little toad. 'So you're telling me categorically you didn't kill her?'

'Yeah.' The conversation was finally beginning to worry David too. 'You won't say this in court, about me doping her, will you? It's our little secret. I'll let you have some if you get me off. Try it on your girlfriend.'

'Jesus Christ! You don't get it, do you? I don't keep secrets for criminals. If this is true then my advice - my professional advice - is that you tell this truth to the court. And let the jury decide what to make of it.'

'Oh, yeah, right. I'm not telling the jury that. They'll think I killed her for sure.'

Savendra turned away in disgust. He wanted to pick up the wretched man and shake him, but he couldn't do that, of course not. Anyway, it would probably result in a fight, and that wouldn't help his career, would it - to have his nose broken by a client? A client who has just admitted rape. The whole thing was a disaster.

David watched him, beginning at last to appreciate the seriousness of what he had done. 'You think that too, now, don't you? You think I killed her?'

Savendra drew a deep breath, and tried to explain. 'Look, what I think's not important. I'm not a detective or a juror. I'm just here to present your case in the best way I can.'

'Well then, how about some help? What should I say tomorrow?'

'Oh no.' Savendra waved a finger, as though to keep the devil away. 'No way, I can't coach you. You must tell the truth, that's all. That's all the advice I can give. I ask the questions, you decide what to answer. Hello? We're finished here!' He raised his voice, to alert the warder that he wanted to leave - to escape, to run as far away from here as possible.

'Well, that's great advice, that is. I thought you were on my side.'

'There are limits, you know.' The warder came round the corner with his handcuffs, to lead David Kidd back to his cell. Where he belongs, Savendra thought, as he watched the man being led away. You should lock the door and throw away the key.

I'm going to have to think about this, he told himself miserably as the warder returned to unlock the gates for him at the end of the underground corridor. If this is true the best construction I can put on it is that Shelley killed herself in shame after this little bastard doped and raped her. And it would have to happen tonight of all nights, when Belinda's dad is taking us out to supper. Where he is undoubtedly going to quiz me about the ethics of defending criminals. Great. That's all I need right now. Bloody marvellous.

When Savendra got back to chambers Sarah was busy working. Her office was opposite his, and she had left the door and window open as she often did for air. Her gown, wig and shoes were strewn on the floor, and she sat on the sofa with her feet curled beside her, studying David Kidd's statements to the police. She was still smarting from the damage the shopkeeper's evidence had done, both to her case and to her confidence in Terry Bateson, but her natural combative optimism was starting to return. She beamed at Savendra brightly.

'Still putting your man on the stand tomorrow, Savvy? Lamb to the slaughter!'

Savendra leaned miserably on the doorframe of her office. 'Yep. Well, you chew him into little pieces if you can. See if I care. I may just sit back and watch.'

'Goodness!' Sarah studied him in astonishment. His body drooped, his face looked grey. 'Not giving up, are you?'

Savendra sucked his teeth, and thought about it. It was a relief to be talking to someone human, someone normal. In other circumstances he would have loved to confide in her, discuss the filthy dilemma he had fallen into. But not now, obviously.

'My client,' he informed her in a voice that was clear, measured, and transparently insincere, 'is a man of the utmost moral integrity. He continues to maintain his complete innocence. Of the crime of murder, that is. And therefore ... ah, sod it, Sarah.'

It was no good. Their usual jokey, ironic relationship was unable to handle a crisis like this. He opened the door of his office, then turned back. 'Just give him hell, Sarah, that's all. And don't even think of dropping the case.'

'Don't worry,' Sarah murmured in surprise, as the door closed behind him. 'I won't.'

25. Harsh Words

THAT NIGHT, Savendra phoned a man he greatly respected, a QC who had been his pupil master three years ago in Leeds. He explained the details of the case, and asked the man's advice.

'It's a simple question, really. Knowing what I do now, can I still represent him?'

'He's charged with murder, you say? Not rape?' Just listening to the fruity, whisky roughened old voice comforted Savendra greatly. It was true what they'd told him when he had been called to the Bar: there was always someone willing to help you out, someone who had met this problem before. This man, in his mid-fifties, had probably seen more criminals, encountered more variations of human mendacity, than an entire rural police force.

'That's the charge, yes,' Savendra agreed. 'And in my view, he probably did it.'

'The court's not interested in your view, old boy, you know that. The questions you have to ask yourself are, one, have you coached him to tell a lie?'

'No. Definitely not.'

'Fine. Good lad. Then, two: has he ever admitted to you that he killed the girl?'

'No, again.'

'All right, and finally, three: now that you know he drugged her, does that make the story he intends to tell the court impossible, or just unlikely?'

Savendra hesitated. 'Well, unlikely, I suppose. I mean, given what I've seen of how he behaves, I think he's still lying ...'

'That's not my question.'

'Yes, I know. But if you say, is it possible that she woke up in the bath in a dazed stupor, was overcome by shame at what had been done to her, got out of the bath, ran into the kitchen for a knife, came back and cut her wrists, then I don't know ... I suppose it's remotely possible. But that still makes him morally guilty, doesn't it?'

'Not your problem. If it's possible his story is true, then you can still defend him.'

'But if the police knew what I know ...'

'It's their job to find things out, my boy, not yours to tell them. However unpleasant it may sometimes be, our duty is to defend the client, not help the police.'

'So this isn't improper conduct, if I continue to defend him?'

'Not if it's the way you've described it to me, no. *You're* not lying, *he* is. So long as he maintains his innocence of the main charge, and you haven't coached him in a lie, you're in the clear. It's the prosecution's job to expose him, not yours. Who's against you, anyway?'

'Sarah Newby.'

'Ah.' A fruity laugh gurgled down the phone. 'The vixen who saved her cub, eh? Well, there you are then! If you really want to help your client, I'd buy him a pair of metal underpants. Otherwise he might lose something important.'

Had Savendra known it, it was not David Kidd but Bob Newby who was being savaged by Sarah just then. The argument had begun with her attempt to re-open the discussion about moving house, an attempt which had been rebuffed by Bob on the grounds that he had an important application form to fill in. It annoyed her. She had already been let down by one man she trusted today; she didn't want it to happen again. But when she came down from the shower she found Bob chatting amiably on his mobile phone, the application form pushed to one side. As she entered the room he clicked the phone shut.

'Who was that?' she asked, crossing the room to pour herself a drink.

'Stephanie, again,' he answered gruffly, as though the call, or her question - which? - had annoyed him somehow. Stephanie was his new school secretary, a childless divorcee in her late twenties. 'She works hard, that woman.'

'You seemed to be getting on all right.'

'What? Yes, she's easy to talk to.' Bob pulled the application form towards him.

'Not just talking, Bob. You were having a good laugh.'

'Yes, well, perhaps we were.' Bob picked up his pen, sighed, and put it down. 'It's good to laugh, once in a while.'

'Depends who you're laughing with,' said Sarah dangerously, perching on the edge of an armchair. She sipped her whisky, a drink she indulged in occasionally when her emotions were raw. 'This woman seems to ring you at all hours of the day and night.'

'She's efficient, that's all. We've got a lot of things on this term. She takes work home just like I do.'

'Mrs Daggett didn't do that.'

'No, well, people are different.'

'Mm.' Sarah stared at her husband coolly. Mrs Daggett, a comfortable grandmother in her sixties, had recently retired after twenty years service at Bob's school. She'd been quiet, efficient, and friendly. Sarah, no great shakes as a cook, had baked an embarrassingly amateurish cake for her retirement party, which had been attended by a surprisingly large number of parents, some of whom had been pupils at the school when Mrs Daggett was young. Sarah had never felt the slightest qualms about entrusting her husband to that woman's care, and so far as she knew the school had run smoothly with only a couple of phone calls to this house each term.

Now, it seemed, there were two or three each day - some, like this, in the evening, others in the morning while they were having breakfast or even at weekends. Bob, having recently discovered how to text on his mobile, did that frequently too, though seldom to Sarah. She had met this Stephanie once at a dinner party in this very same room, to welcome her to her new job, and had not particularly warmed to her. She was young - no more than 28, Sarah guessed - blonde, taller than Sarah, with a slender, bony figure like a model, and liking for striking, ethnic jewellery. It was true that she laughed, loudly enough, and had a fund of amusing stories, many of them quite risqué, but she gave most of her attention to men rather than women.

Certainly not to me, anyway, Sarah thought, recalling the occasion with distaste. I welcomed her into my home but her eyes kept sliding away from me as though I wasn't really there. At the time she'd put it down to shyness or nerves; after all, she was the headmaster's wife and a criminal barrister too, and people could be intimidated by that; but curiously, this shyness didn't seem to extend to her husband. Not if she could gaily ring his mobile at - what time was it now? - nine thirty in the evening for a jolly chat.

'What did she actually ring about?' Sarah asked coolly.

'What?' Bob shook his head distractedly. 'Oh, just some assessment forms we have to fill in. You know, we get so much paperwork nowadays from the government.'

'Couldn't it wait till tomorrow?'

'I told you, she takes work home. What is this, Sarah, are you jealous or something?'

'Should I be?'

The slight, infinitesimal pause before his denial set alarm bells screaming in Sarah's brain. She knew her husband well enough, after eighteen years, to recognise most of his moods, his thoughts, his responses. This one, a tiny hesitation before the correct words were chosen, was one she had never seen before. Not at home, anyway; she had seen it a dozen times on the witness stand and knew exactly how to deal with it there. But here - in her own home?

'Of course not. Sarah, she's my secretary, that's all there is to it.'

'A secretary who rings you at home.'

'Yes. I've explained that already. It's work.'

'Was it work the other night when you took her out for a drink after the parents' evening and didn't come home till - when was it? - twelve!'

'It's not late, twelve, Sarah. A group of us went out for a drink. It's quite a strain for teachers, you know, parents' evening. It's good to let your hair down afterwards.'

'And Stephanie came too?'

'Yes, Stephanie came too. For goodness' sake, why not? She was there all evening, making things run smoothly - better than ever, as a matter of fact. It's a new system she's set up.'

'Did all the teachers stay out until twelve?'

'Some of them, yes.'

'Who?'

'Well, Paul, Melanie, they're ...'

'Having an affair, yes, you told me. Anyone else?'

Again, the awkward pause that gave the answer.

'Did Stephanie stay?'

Bob sighed, sat back in his chair. 'As a matter of fact, yes. We had a few drinks, I drove her home. But that's all it was, Sarah, an evening in a pub. Nothing else.'

Their eyes met. Sarah sipped her whisky, using the scalding warmth to anaesthetise the sudden harsh pain in her chest, the rage in her mind. She imagined the woman's brassy laugh in the car - their car - and the look on Bob's face outside her house. The thoughts in his mind.

'Is that all you wanted it to be?'

Bob shook his head, feigning ignorance of her meaning. 'Yes, of course. What else?'

'Don't pretend to me, Bob. You know very well what else!'

'If you're saying did she invite me in, then no, she didn't. Listen, Sarah ...'

'Would you have liked her to?'

'Would I ...? Look, I've had enough of this, I'm going to bed. She's my secretary, she came out for a drink with the rest of the staff, I drove her home. End of story, all right? All the rest is in your imagination, nowhere else.'

'And yours, Bob.'

'What? Oh, come on now, Sarah, drop this before it gets any worse. Nothing happened, okay?'

'Not then, no. But you want it to, don't you, Bob? And so does she. That's what all these phone calls and meetings and text messages are all about. It's not work, it's flirting, that's what it is. You fancy that woman, and one day soon, if you've got the guts, you'll do what you've been fantasizing about all this time. Well I hope she likes it, that's all! Better than I do!'

'What? What are you talking about now?'

What indeed, Sarah thought, struggling to rein in her galloping anger. You don't say things like this to your husband, but I don't care, he deserves it, the bastard, no one treats me like this.

'Sex, Bob, what do you think? Look, it was fine between us when we were young but it hasn't really happened for years, has it? Certainly not since Simon's trial. It's not really your thing. *You* know that and *I* know that and poor little Stephanie is about to find out too, if you ever get inside her door. It won't be any better, Bob. It'll just ruin our marriage to no purpose.'

Now what have I done, Sarah thought, seeing his appalled face. 'Look, I didn't marry you for sex, Bob, which is all you can offer her. I married you for friendship, and kindness, and loyalty, and that's still what I need. But we've lost it somehow, and you can't give it to Stephanie because that's not what she's looking for, she's divorced already. And even if she was looking for kindness and loyalty she's not going to find it with you, is she - because she'll know, right from the start, that you've been disloyal to me.'

Bob sat stunned, unable to speak. Sarah stared at him for a long moment, aware suddenly of Emily moving around somewhere upstairs. I've broken something that can't be mended, she thought. Not now, maybe not ever. She finished her whisky and stood up.

'She just wants you for a laugh, Bob, that's all. And that's what you'll be. Fine, if that's what you want.'

Upstairs, she took her nightdress into the spare bedroom, and locked the door.

26. Cross Examination

DAVID KIDD, Savendra had to admit, had taken care with his appearance. He wore a clean suit, white shirt and sober dark blue tie. He took the oath in a clear, respectful voice. Savendra began with the most fundamental question of all.

'Mr Kidd, you are charged with the murder of Shelley Walters. Did you kill her?'

'No sir, I did not.'

That's clear, at least, Savendra thought. Start with a lie and keep going. He glanced up at the public gallery, where his prospective father-in-law sat with Belinda. Michael James was a self-made businessman with strong views about lawyers. In the restaurant last night he had reiterated his view that murderers should be hanged, and that lawyers who defended criminals they knew to be guilty should be set to clean toilets for a living instead. Savendra's protests that everyone was entitled to a proper defence had been brushed aside. It had been a lively meal, made worse by the fact that Belinda had decided to goose him with her foot under the table. Now she smiled at him from the gallery.

'Very well. Perhaps you could tell the court how you first met Miss Walters, and describe your relationship with her.'

As David answered, Sarah studied him closely. She was surprised how cool he seemed, unfazed by the eyes watching him, relishing the attention almost. He acted the part of a man trying to clear up a dreadful misunderstanding. He even managed regret. He'd loved Shelley, he said, and was sorry his fling with his old girlfriend had caused her pain, but it had meant nothing. Shelley had a volatile personality and was often depressed. She'd spoken of suicide once or twice but never, he thought, meant it seriously. Nonetheless he knew she was feeling low, and had booked a holiday in Kenya to cheer her up.

It was a convincing performance if you believed it, nauseating if you did not. Several jurors nodded sympathetically. But what surprised Sarah was the way Savendra was conducting the examination. The questions were fine, but his body language suggested that his heart wasn't in it. As Sarah watched, she recalled the scene in her office last night. He doesn't believe it! she thought with delight. He thinks the bastard's guilty and is just going through the motions.

David described how he'd found Shelley's message on his answerphone that afternoon, and begun to prepare a meal. He admitted that they had argued when she arrived, but there'd been no violence, and eventually she had calmed down.

'And what happened next?' Savendra asked, dully.

David smiled, at a pleasant memory. 'Well, we had a glass of wine together.'

Silence. Not a long silence - ten or fifteen seconds, perhaps - but it was long enough for the judge to look up quizzically at Savendra. Why has he paused, Sarah wondered?

'A glass of wine, you say. And then?'

'Well, er ...we took our clothes off and made love.' David turned to face the jury. 'It was brilliant, a reconciliation really. It showed she'd forgiven me, you see. At least that's what I thought. She must have been more depressed than I realised, poor kid.'

Savendra sighed. It was the sort of sigh often used deliberately when cross-examining a hostile witness: one of the standard repertory of tricks that barristers employ to indicate that they don't believe a word that's being said - like never meeting the witness's eyes, or throwing down your notes in disgust. But this is his own client, Sarah thought. Savendra, perhaps unconsciously, was indicating that there was something wrong here, with this particular piece of evidence. But what was it?

'After you had made love, what happened then?'

'She got into the bath, and I went into the kitchen to finish the meal. Then I realised I'd run out of olive oil so I went out to buy some more.'

'And Shelley was still in the bath when you left, was she? Alive and well?'

'Yes, fine.' As Sarah had expected, David exaggerated the time he'd been away: the shop was at least two minutes' walk from the flat, he said, and he'd been there ten minutes, maybe more. Then he'd spoken to the priest for a couple of minutes, so he might have been away for fifteen or twenty minutes altogether. All of which, if true, virtually destroyed the possibility that he could have cut Shelley's wrists before he went out, and found her still alive when he returned. It was the defence's key point, and Savendra brought it out clearly.

When David described his shock on discovering Shelley drowning in a bath full of her own blood, even Sarah was impressed. The jury certainly were. His voice broke, and the horror of the scene came before everyone's eyes. So he's an actor, Sarah thought. No surprise there. After all, if he did it, he would have seen all this for real, so he was only changing the story a little, not making it all up.

'All right. One more question, Mr Kidd. The pathologist found a number of subcutaneous bruises around Shelley's head and neck. Do you have any idea what caused them?'

'I don't know. I never tried to hurt her,' David answered earnestly. 'But I did have to hold her head tight when she was in the bath, so I could breathe into her mouth like the lady told me on the phone. I mean I was in a panic, she was slipping under water all the time, so maybe I held her tighter than I should. I was trying to save her, for Christ's sake!'

'And then you rang 999 to call an ambulance?'

'Yes, exactly. Why would I have done that if I'd wanted to kill her?'

It was a key question, Sarah knew. Several jurors nodded wisely.

'All right, Mr Kidd. Wait there please.'

As Savendra sat down, Sarah stood, her hands trembling slightly with the surge of adrenalin. But her voice, as usual, was calm, husky, controlled. This is where my aggression belongs, she told herself. Not savaging my husband, as I did last night. She'd woken this morning wondering where that outburst had come from, and what, if anything, she could do to repair it. But Bob had left for work early, and here she was, in a theatre where such cruelty was licensed in the interests of justice.

'Do you feel any guilt for Shelley's death, David?' she began sweetly.

'What? Well no, not really. Why should I? I didn't kill her.'

'Nonetheless, according to your story you quarrelled violently, had sex with her, and then she committed suicide. I just wondered if that made you feel guilty.'

'She didn't kill herself because of me. She did it because she was depressed, because her parents were putting so much pressure on her. They wanted her to leave me.'

'I see. So your girlfriend died in your bath, but you don't feel guilty at all. It's useful to establish that point.' Sarah glanced at the jury, hoping they would feel as contemptuous as she did. 'Let's look at some of the details surrounding her death, shall we? The bag in her bedroom, first. How did that get there?'

'Shelley brought it with her. To collect her things.'

'Oh, really? When the police first asked you about this you said she brought it to stay the night. So you lied to the police about that, didn't you?'

'I didn't lie, no. I didn't think about her bag, it wasn't important.'

'Not to you, perhaps, but it was to Shelley. That's why she came. All right, let's move on to another detail. This quarrel you had with Shelley. It was a loud violent quarrel, wasn't it? So loud and violent that Canon Rowlands heard it and thought Shelley was in danger. Yet you told the police it was 'a friendly chat.' That was another lie, wasn't it, David?'

'No. We did have a friendly chat, later. I was talking about that, not the row.'

'Yet the detective asked you quite specifically, didn't he?' Sarah consulted her notes. ''Did you shout at her,' he says. And you answer: 'No, of course I didn't. Why would I?' That was a lie, wasn't it, David?'

'Okay, I may have lied about that, but not about the other things.'

'Oh really? What about the fact that you had sex, then? Why didn't you tell the police about that in your first interview?'

'Well, it was personal, wasn't it? Private, between me and Shelley. It was nothing to do with them.'

'So you lied about it?'

'Not lie, no. I just didn't mention it.' David's expression, she was pleased to see, was dismissive, truculent, as though he could scarcely be bothered to answer. Such insolence suited her fine. The more surly he appeared, the more likely he was to be convicted.

'I see, so when you told the police: 'She said she needed to relax, so she'd have a bath while I did the cooking' that wasn't a lie, then? Or does 'relax' in your vocabulary mean 'we had sex together?''

'No, of course not. I was just ... protecting our privacy.'

'Oh. You're a modest man about sexual matters, are you, David?'

'Well, sometimes. I mean, I didn't want to embarrass Shelley - her memory, I mean ...'

Sarah looked away, refusing eye contact or any hint of sympathy. It was a way of needling a defendant without being openly rude, letting the jury see that his answers were treated with contempt. 'Were you worried about embarrassing Shelley, when she found you in bed with another girl making a porn video?'

'That was different! She wasn't supposed to see that!'

'No, but she did. And she was pretty angry about it, too, wasn't she? She smashed your girlfriend's camera. Did that annoy you?'

'Not really, no. It wasn't my camera.'

'Did you think it was funny, perhaps?'

'Well, it had its funny side at the time, yeah. Not for Shelley, of course.'

'Not for Shelley. She saw her boyfriend in bed with another girl, laughing at her, it seems. So when she came back to your flat a week later, what was this violent quarrel about, exactly?'

'I was asking her to stay. I loved her.'

'Oh really. And would Shelley say the same, if she was here to tell her side of the story?'

'Of course she would, yeah.'

'I see. That's the problem the jury has, you see. You can stand there and tell lies all day, but Shelley can't tell us the true story, because she's dead.'

'I'm not lying. I'm telling the truth.'

'Well, let's talk about another detail, shall we? The knife DI Bateson found on the bathroom floor. He asked you whether you'd touched it, and you said no. Yet there's only one set of fingerprints on that knife, David. Yours. Not Shelley's.'

'Yes, well I meant I didn't touch it in the bathroom. Of course I'd been using it before, to cut vegetables. That's why my fingerprints were there.'

'So you didn't carry it into the bathroom?'

'No.'

'Very well. The jury may think that's another lie. How many is it now? Four? Five? Let's try another detail, shall we? The bruises on Shelley's neck. You claim they were caused when you tried to give her the kiss of life, in the bath.'

'Yes, well, that's all I can think of. They must have been caused like that.'

'Exactly. It's all you can think of. But what would Shelley say if she was here, David? Would she agree? Or would she say, no, he's lying again. He didn't try to save me, he held my head underwater. That's how I got the bruises. He was trying to drown me.'

'No. I didn't do that.'

'Didn't you, David? But how are we to believe you, when you've lied so many times already? Let's take another point, shall we? Canon Rowlands saw you outside your front door, apparently listening for something inside the flat. What were you listening for?'

'I wasn't. He's lying, I was just looking for my keys.'

'Oh, *he's* lying now, is he? A man of the church. Not you?'

'Yeah, well. I mean he's mistaken. I wasn't doing that.'

'You weren't listening to check whether Shelley was dead before you went back in and pretended to give her the flowers you'd bought?'

'No. How could I anyway? There were all those bells.'

'All right. So after all this time we've got - how many lies? Five, six, seven? I've lost count. Each time you say you're telling the truth, and it's other people - the priest, the police, Shelley's friend Sandy - they're all either lying or mistaken, according to you. Yet when we look at things in detail we find that you have lied again and again. You do know what the truth is, do you, David?'

'Of course I do.'

'All right. Well let me tell you what I think the truth is in this case. You're a man who likes to control women, aren't you, David? That's what attracted you to Shelley Walters. She was younger than you, she was naive and vulnerable and she needed someone older to rely on. But in order to get her under your control you had to get her away from her mother and her university, both of which you saw as threats. So you tried to persuade her to give up everything of value in her life: her family, who loved her, and her university, which gave her the chance of an independent career.'

'They pushed her into it. She hated the uni. It was driving her crazy!'

'So you say. But that's not what Shelley's friend or her tutor say, is it? And Shelley can't answer for herself. Your plan was to make her totally dependent on you, wasn't it? With no family or career to fall back on.'

'You're twisting things. I told her, I wanted the best for her.'

'And she believed that, did she?'

'I think she did. Yeah.'

'Well, perhaps she did, for a while. Until one day she found you in bed, making a porn video of yourself with another girl. Not surprisingly that made her angry. She smashed the camera, stormed out of the flat and decided to leave you. The worm had turned, she wasn't under your control any more. You didn't like that, did you, David?'

'No. Of course not. I wanted her back.'

'Exactly. You'd betrayed her with another girl, but you wanted her back. The one thing that you couldn't accept was the idea that this vulnerable young student should open her eyes and see you for the heartless monster that you are. You couldn't stand that. So when she came back to collect her things, you forced her to stay, didn't you, David?'

'Not forced, no. I persuaded her!'

'Well, so you say. She came to your flat to collect her things and you persuaded her to take off her clothes and have sex with you on the floor. It wasn't love, was it? You did it to humiliate her, to show her who was in control. You're a powerful, violent young man, David. The only reason she had sex with you was to appease you, because she was afraid.'

'No!' An odd smile crossed his face. 'I told you, she liked it!'

'She liked it so much that she committed suicide afterwards - is that your story?'

'No, well - I don't know why she killed herself, do I?'

'No, David, of course you don't, because she didn't commit suicide at all. The pathologist has told us that. The lethal cuts were on her right wrist, not her left. The bruises on her head and neck were caused by someone holding her down, underwater, until she nearly drowned. That was you, David, wasn't it? After you raped her, you killed her.'

'No.'

'Didn't you, David? Can you look these jurors in the eye and tell them that? I doubt it. You raped Shelley Walters, on the floor of your flat. You humiliated her, so that afterwards, she got in the bath to make herself clean. To wash the stink of you off her body, I expect. That's what girls do when they've been raped. But you didn't leave her alone even then, did you? You followed her into the bathroom.'

'No! She shut the door, I've told you.'

'You went into the bathroom, David. What did she say to you, when you went in? Something that annoyed you, perhaps - that she didn't want you there, that you'd raped her and she was never coming back? Was that when you decided to kill her?'

'No ... she didn't say anything. You weren't there.'

'So why are there bruises round her neck, then, David? Bruises caused by someone trying to drown her? Because she struggled, didn't she, David? Struggled to get her head above water, trying to breathe - and you held her down with those powerful muscular arms of yours until she stopped moving, she lost consciousness.'

'No. This didn't happen.'

'I think it did, David. You held her down until you thought you'd drowned her. Then you stopped and thought, this won't do, this doesn't look good, this girl's alone with me in my flat and I've murdered her. So in order to disguise what you'd done, you went into the kitchen, found a knife and cut her wrists to make it look like suicide. Then you went out to the shop to give yourself an alibi. That's what happened, isn't it, David? You went out to buy a bunch of flowers for a girl you'd left half drowned and bleeding to death in your bath.'

'Then why was she still alive when I came back, then? You tell me that! Twenty minutes later and she was still alive. It's not possible, is it?'

It was a serious, damaging blow, right at the end when she had him on the ropes. Sarah saw several jurors nodding thoughtfully. She took the only line open to her.

'It's not possible because it's not true. Mr Patel was perfectly clear in his first statement to the police. You were in his shop for less than five minutes. That's the truth, isn't it, David?'

'That's not what he said when he stood here, yesterday.'

'Mr Patel was confused. He couldn't remember how long you were there. But you know, don't you, David? You went to his shop deliberately to create an alibi.'

'No. I went there to buy flowers to show that I loved her. She killed herself while I was out. I didn't know she was going to do that, how could I? She was a mad girl. You heard that psychiatrist. She was depressed.'

'So depressed that you decided to kill her.'

'No! I didn't kill her, she killed herself.'

There was nowhere to go from here, Sarah decided, she had reached an impasse. The only other possibility was that David had driven Shelley to suicide, which would make him morally guilty, but not legally. That was an avenue for Savendra to explore, not her.

She saw no grief on David Kidd's face, no remorse or regret. Only the look of a man who has seen a way to save his own skin, and is determined to do it, whatever the cost to others. His lip curled in a smile of contemptuous triumph. His face was flushed, his eyes shone with the knowledge that she'd failed to break him down.

Sarah stood for a moment, silent, hoping the jury would see in his face what she did.

Then she folded her gown about her, and sat down.

27. Scorn

THE FINAL day of the trial began for Sarah with another row. This time it was about her daughter Emily, who announced that she was going to London this weekend with Larry on an anti-globalisation protest. Sarah was relaxed about this, Bob was not. He claimed to be worried about injury or drugs, but Sarah thought it had more to do with his application for the headship of the Harrogate school. He didn't want his chances ruined by tabloid headlines like 'York head's daughter assaults police. Home discipline fails.'

It wasn't discipline, Sarah thought, that was failing in their home, it was something else. Day by day they were drifting apart. A half-hearted attempt at reconciliation with Bob last night had collapsed. She'd sat up with her speech until one a.m. instead of accompanying him to bed as he'd asked. The two text messages he'd had from his secretary over supper hadn't helped either. The wound to their marriage was not healed, and rows like this morning's scratched the injury raw.

It hurt. She watched enviously as Savendra approached the court with his fiancee, tired and yawning. Young love fades into memory, she thought, marriage into a joint investment, a convenient housing arrangement with a man whose mind slid away from hers as her body slid from his in bed. Work is the best therapy. Maybe if he gets that job, and I send this lad to prison, we can attempt a reconciliation.

Behind Savendra she saw Terry Bateson, approaching court with that long easy stride of his. He smiled as he saw her, and her heart lifted slightly, as it often did when she saw him. Here was a man who at least shared and understood the demands of the work which filled so much of her time, and seemed to value her for what she did. Just as she, on the whole, valued him, despite his irritating carelessness with the evidence of the shopkeeper, Patel. She met him outside the main entrance, and they strolled quietly along the verandah outside the court.

'So, this is it. Judgement day,' Terry said. 'Are you nervous?'

'Always. I wouldn't be any good if I wasn't. There's only my speech left, then it's out of my hands. Have you come to watch?'

'For an hour or so, yes. And I'll try to be back for the verdict. When's that - about three?'

'Sometime like that. Speeches and summing up should be over this morning, and then ... as long as the jury take to make up their minds.'

'A long wait for you. And the girl's family,' said Terry thoughtfully.

'Yes. That's the worst part of every trial - waiting. Oh, God, look at this!' They had reached the end of the verandah, and a sudden gust of wind swirling round the corner of the building set Sarah's gown flapping around her like a sail, and she had to clutch her skirt to hold it down. Her wig blew out of her hand, and Terry ran to retrieve it, while she stepped back into the shelter of the building, laughing.

'Thanks.' They stood with their backs to the wall of the court until the wind died down, watching white fluffy clouds chasing each other through a blue sky behind Clifford's Tower, the Norman castle on its grassy mound. For a second, Sarah wished she could spend the day like this, walking the hills in the open air with this man beside her, instead of the long hours of trauma in crowded rooms which would face her soon. She looked up at him, smiling at the way the wind had ruffled his hair across his forehead. 'I'll need a holiday after this,' she said. 'Not that I'll get one.'

'Won't you? Pity. You deserve it. Where would you go?'

'Oh, I don't know. Anywhere. A day at the seaside would do.' For a moment their eyes met and she wondered, what does he see in me, really? Just a bossy, aggressive barrister, or something more? A woman that if he'd met elsewhere, in different circumstances ...

But the moment blew away as swiftly as it had come. She saw Shelley's parents and sister approaching the court, holding their coats in the blustery wind, and turned back towards the main entrance to meet them. Terry fell into step by her side.

'It's going to be a hard day for them,' she said. 'Even if we win.'

'What do you mean, even if? There's no question of it, is there? He murdered the girl, we all know that. Surely the jury will see it.'

Sarah stopped near the entrance. Shelley's family were at the foot of the steps. She looked up at him, shaking her head slowly. 'Sometimes, Terry, you're charmingly naive for a policeman. This jury contains some of the roughest looking characters I've seen for a long time, and your boss's contribution to this case has given them the perfect excuse for revenge against the police if they want one. It's quite possible we'll lose this case, Terry - I'm warning you now.'

'You'll win, Sarah. You always do, when it matters.'

'Well, thanks for your confidence. I'll do my best, of course. But ... wish me luck.' She touched Terry's hand briefly, and walked past him to meet Shelley's family.

Entering court, Sarah put her doubts behind her and began to take the jury through the evidence for the final time. Several of them - the shaven-headed young men and the girl in the tracksuit - still worried her. She spoke as simply as possible.

'Why do the prosecution say this is murder? Well, firstly, we have the pathologist, who told us how her wrists were cut. The artery in her right wrist was pierced, while that in her left was not. Why is this so important? Because Shelley Walters was right-handed. So if she had wanted to cut her own wrists she would have picked up the knife in her right hand and plunged it into her left wrist, wouldn't she? Think about it for yourselves. No right-handed person would cut their right wrist first; it just doesn't happen.

'So that's it, isn't it, members of the jury? I could sit down now, it seems to me, and the case is proved. She didn't cut her own wrist, the pathologist says. Someone else did it for her. So she was murdered. In David Kidd's bath. In David Kidd's flat. When no one but David Kidd was there. End of story. That should be enough to convict him outright.

'But there is more evidence, equally clear, equally damning. There is the knife that killed her, found on the bathroom floor. A knife belonging to David Kidd, with David's fingerprints on it. Not Shelley's fingerprints, just his, in her blood.

'Then there are the bruises on her head and neck. What do they tell us? Well, the pathologist says, they are pressure marks, caused by someone holding Shelley underwater, so that she would drown. And she was drowning too - she had water in her lungs, bloody froth in her mouth.'

Watching from the public gallery, Shelley's sister Miranda trembled with a sudden memory of the dank, brackish water in that tank in the forest, where she had so nearly drowned as a child. She remembered how it sucked the strength from her body, as her splashes grew feebler; she remembered how it got into her ears and mouth and nose, leaves and small beetles making her sneeze, the water creeping back again, dank and insidious and inevitable

...

Shelley had saved her from all that. But no one had been there in David's flat to save Shelley. Tears misted her eyes, as she listened to the damning words of the prosecutor, describing how David Kidd had first killed her sister, then bought her flowers, to give himself an alibi.

Kathryn clasped Miranda's hand in her own. Mrs Newby, she felt, was putting the case well. Kathryn's initial distrust of the woman had changed to respect. She had treated the psychiatrist with the scorn he deserved, and exposed David's lies. Soon her daughter's murderer would be locked away, and she could relax. Kathryn felt the little diamond engagement ring on Miranda's finger, the smooth wedding band behind it. One child at least was still alive, with a loving husband and daughter. Maybe I'll move to America when all this is over, she thought wistfully. Why not? There's nothing here but memories, horror, and sadness. Why not sell up, and make a fresh start?

Leave Kidd here to rot in his dungeon.

Sarah dealt with the shopkeeper's evidence briefly. The man was confused, she said, that was understandable when recalling events that took place so long ago. Events, moreover, that he had no reason to think were important at the time. 'Use your own experience, members of the jury. Could you say how long you spent in a shop even yesterday, if I asked you now? Two minutes, five, ten - do you really remember? Yet when Mr Patel stood in this court he was trying to recall things from months past. He was not dishonest, he was simply confused.'

Sarah paused to survey the jurors. They were listening, yet she sensed, somehow, that her points were not going home as they should. Several studied her sceptically, with that irritating certainty of youth that everyone in authority is lying - it's only a matter of finding out how, if you can be bothered. Calmly, she controlled her voice. It was all she had to persuade them.

'So we should put Mr Patel's evidence aside, and concentrate on the hard simple facts. Facts that we know to be true. Shelley Walters was killed in that flat. The bruises on her head and neck, the cuts on her wrists, all show that this was murder, not suicide. David Kidd's fingerprints were found on the knife, no one else was in the flat but him. In my view that evidence proves, beyond all reasonable doubt, that Shelley Walters was murdered, and David Kidd murdered her. In the light of that evidence, it is your duty to find him guilty.'

As she sat down, the girl in the tracksuit yawned.

28. Devil's Advocate

As SAVENDRA got to his feet he swayed slightly with exhaustion. He had spent the night wrestling with a speech which had become a nightmare. Always before, the ethics of the Bar had seemed clear: every client was entitled to a defence, and it was his job to provide it. But never before had he defended someone quite so reprehensible, on such a serious charge. It was a vital week for him - his first murder defence, his wedding next week - and yet he was consumed by horror at the thought that the words he was about to speak might save the man who, he was convinced, was morally responsible for Shelley Walters' death.

Morally, and perhaps legally too. That was the dilemma he had wrestled with throughout the night. Did the fact that Shelley had been doped with rohypnol make it impossible for her to have killed herself, or just highly unlikely? Savendra didn't know. It depended, he supposed, on the strength of the dose, her size and bodyweight, and exactly how long before her death she had taken the drug. All of these things could have been debated in open court, if the wretched pathologist had done his job properly and discovered the traces of the drug in her bloodstream. But he hadn't; and so Savendra was burdened with the weight of knowledge which the ethics of client confidentiality forbade him to disclose. He was trapped; all he could do was lay his client's defence before the jury, and hope they were blessed with wisdom. He stood now and faced them - two elderly women, four middle aged men, two with beer bellies, four young men with shaven heads, two vacant looking girls, one surreptitiously chewing gum - and began.

Grimly, he told them that they should convict only if they were sure, beyond reasonable doubt, of David Kidd's guilt. Otherwise, they must acquit. He explained how the bruises might have been caused by David's clumsy attempts at first aid, the fingerprints on the knife by David's picking it up when he found it beside the bath, his lies by panic and distress. He reiterated his theory that Shelley had made a tentative attempt to cut her left wrist first, and then stabbed her right wrist more strongly, causing the fatal injury. The cleverness of this idea no longer impressed him; the words tasted sour in his mouth.

But he had better arguments to make. 'Now that Mr Patel has changed his mind, the whole prosecution case collapses. It is, quite simply, not plausible that she would remain alive, in that bath, more than twenty minutes after her artery was pierced.

'So for all four points of the prosecution's evidence - the bruises, the fingerprints, the cuts, and the timing - there is an alternative explanation, a doubt. And the benefit of that doubt must go to the defendant.'

He glanced at the jurors, several of whom, to his dismay, looked reasonably impressed. Now came the really cruel part of his task. He could feel the eyes of Shelley's family boring into the back of his head. This is why we get paid so much, he thought; to say really nasty things clearly. To tell a lie for a fee.

'Well, members of the jury, if this wasn't murder, there's only one alternative, isn't there? It must have been suicide. But why should Shelley Walters, a healthy young girl with all her life ahead of her, commit such a terrible act? It gives me no pleasure to say this, but here too there is an alternative explanation. One which, if you accept it, doesn't lead to murder at all.'

'This is a tragic love affair. Shelley Walters, in her first year at university, meets David Kidd, and falls in love with him.' He glanced over his shoulder, surveying his client in the dock with distaste. 'You have seen Mr Kidd; you may not like him very much. You may even think like Mrs Newby, that Mr Kidd is a monster - a cold, selfish sexual predator. You may be right. But that does not make him a murderer.'

He ploughed grimly on, going through the psychiatrist's evidence, the stress that Shelley had suffered, with her mother pulling one way, and David Kidd pulling the other. Her discovery of him in bed with another girl.

'Enough to drive anyone mad, wouldn't you say? Certainly enough to trigger depression. And that seems to be what happened. During the week before she died she was happy, highly excited - a symptom, unfortunately, of her illness. She told her mother that she would never see David again, and yet she went to his flat on her own.

'So why did she go? To collect her things - the nightdress, the underwear, the tights, the books, the magazine? Surely not. It seems obvious, doesn't it? They were just an excuse. Her friends offered to come with her, but she turned them down. She went alone because she wanted to meet her boyfriend again. Despite all the ways that Mr Kidd had betrayed her, there was still a part of Shelley that loved him. Part of her that did not believe that he was as bad as people said. She was hovering between hope and despair.'

Savendra paused for another sip of water. The speech, he thought, was going depressingly well. If only he didn't know what he did, he could almost believe it himself.

'So what happened when she got there? Well, they quarrelled, we know that. Then, according to him, he gave her a glass of wine and they had sex. I put that bluntly, members of the jury, because we have only Mr Kidd's word for it. He says it was an act of love, a reconciliation. Well, perhaps it was. Or perhaps, on her part, it was less voluntary. We cannot know.'

Sarah and the judge stared at him in surprise. It was the broadest hint Savendra felt able to give without betraying his client, and the lawyers, he saw, had caught it. Savendra believes this was rape, Sarah thought. But he's not charged with rape, just murder.

Savendra ploughed on. 'The sad truth is that none of us wants to believe that this young girl committed suicide, do we? Because suicide is not something we like to face up to. But we have to face up to it, members of the jury. Because sadly, it is perfectly easy to understand how it happened.

'Shelley went to that flat in two minds - intending to leave, hoping to stay. At some point that afternoon, something stripped the scales from her eyes. We may never know what that was for certain,' he said, glancing gloomily at Sarah and the judge, 'but we can imagine. Against her own better judgement, she allowed him to have sex with her, and then - perhaps when he'd finished - he said or did something which made her see him not as a lover but as a predator, a man who used her for sex, nothing else. And she had walked back into his trap. She felt ashamed, shocked, disgusted with herself.'

He looked up at the gallery, and saw Shelley's sister, Miranda, listening intently. This *could* be true, he thought. It's almost plausible. If only she hadn't been so doped that she couldn't move.

'Isn't it possible that Shelley, alone in that bath, was overcome by a self-disgust so sudden and strong that she decided to kill herself? A feeling combined with the terrible depression of her illness? And in the grip of this strong emotion, she saw death as her only escape, from a cruel, selfish man whom her family loathed. But not a man who'd tried to kill her.'

The more that girl in the tracksuit nodded, the less Savendra liked her, or any of the other jurors who hung on his words. There is another theory, he wanted to say, a perfectly good one put forward by Mrs Newby, supported by one extra piece of evidence that no-one else knows about. He doped her, the bastard, and killed her afterwards, when she didn't know what was happening.

'So she found a knife in the kitchen, took it back to the bath and cut her wrists with two swift, determined blows. She sat in the bath to keep the blood flowing, to die as swiftly and painlessly as possible. As the blood flowed out of her, her head slipped under water.

'Then Mr Kidd came back and found her. He opened the bathroom door and saw this horrific sight, his girlfriend drowning in a pool of her own blood. But she was still alive, he says, so he phoned 999 and made desperate, hopeless attempts to save her.

'Remember, you don't have to like Mr Kidd to believe he's not guilty. If he drove her to suicide, he has some moral responsibility, you may feel. But that doesn't make him guilty of murder. After all, where's his motive?'

He doesn't need one, Savendra thought bitterly. He's a psychopath - he's been charged with rape and kidnap before. The jury should know that. But they won't. They don't know anything important.

'What reason could he possibly have to murder Shelley? To control her, Mrs Newby says. Well, perhaps she's right. Perhaps he really is the monster she describes.' Savendra took a final sip of water, his hand shaking slightly. 'It's for you to decide, not me. But Shelley's motive for suicide is at least as clear. I invite you to consider that too.'

Slowly, Savendra sat down, avoiding Sarah's eyes. That, he thought miserably, was one of my worst ordeals so far. If it works, I'll have enhanced my professional reputation. And set that piece of shit free.

29. Verdict

DURING THE judge's summing up, Kathryn clasped a photograph in her hands. It was a photo of Shelley, riding her pony bare-headed through a river with a freakish effect of the sun making tiny rainbows in the water that splashed around them. Miranda had found it last night, in a family album. The search had been very painful - she had only turned a few, leaden pages before dropping the book in despair. But Mark Wrass had warned them that the press would want photos after the verdict, and no one liked the photo which had appeared in the papers up to now. There was nothing wrong with it, exactly - it was an expensive professional portrait of Shelley on her first day at university - but Kathryn had come to loathe it, and had removed the framed original from her wall.

Once it had symbolized her triumph at getting her wayward daughter so far, to the gateway of higher education at last. But perhaps that was my greatest mistake, a voice nagged in Kathryn's mind now when she saw it. Perhaps Shelley wasn't really suited to study at all and these psychiatrists and teachers and that scum of the earth murderer down in the dock were right - I forced her into it against her will. If only I'd let her work in a bar or a racing stables or any of the other crazy things she wanted to do, she'd still be alive today.

The photo fed that suspicion somehow - the formal pose, the slight tension in the smile - it showed a girl doing what she ought to do, not what she loved. Whereas in the photo Miranda had found Shelley was truly alive - laughing, vibrant, sparkles of watery sunlight in her hair. This was the child Kathryn wanted to remember, this was how she'd be in heaven if the place existed. So she'd brought it for the press, to print with their reports of the punishment handed out to the monster in the dock below.

'Soon it will be all over, darling,' she whispered softly to the photo as the jury were led out. 'Soon we'll have justice at last.'

Sarah and Savendra sat at the leather-covered oak table in the middle of the court, listening to the room emptying around them. Sarah added her notes of the judge's remarks to the rest of her papers, and tied the bundle with red ribbon. She glanced across at Savendra who was doing the same.

'Well, that's it, then. The old buzzard was fair, I thought.'

'Yep. No Alzheimer's there. How old do you think he is, anyway?'

'About nine hundred and fifty, I think. He was a bencher when Moses was born. So he's seen it all before.'

'Yes.' Savendra chewed his lip thoughtfully. 'Unlike the jurors, who just think they have. What do you make of them, Sarah?'

Sarah shrugged. 'Usual mixture. Morons, wasters, and a few sober citizens. Rather fewer than normal, in fact. Which I suppose favours you.'

'You think? True, three are clones of my client. Who isn't a perfect angel. As I believe I mentioned in my speech.'

'You did.' Sarah sighed. 'Several times.' She glanced around the empty courtroom, then fixed her colleague with a beady eye. 'Now that we're all alone and private, Mr Bhose, tell me, how will you feel if your client walks free?'

'*Oh no.*' Savendra waved a finger between them, like a man warding off a witch's curse. 'I don't answer questions like that. Not even to you.' The cupola high above their heads picked up the echoes of distant conversations and footsteps on wooden stairs. He shook his head miserably. 'Still, I sometimes wonder if there's any other job like this. Where you argue as hard as you can for a version of the truth that you don't ...'

He stopped abruptly, stuffing his brief into his case and clicking it shut. When he looked up, Sarah's eyes were still on his face.

'Don't what, Savvy?'

He glanced theatrically round the empty court, then leaned forward and whispered, his mouth a few inches from her ear.

'Don't really believe.'

'Is this really necessary?' Andrew Walters asked irritably, in the conference room where they were waiting. 'This isn't show business, you know. It's real life.'

'Yes, of course.' Mark Wrass sat back, his laptop open in front of him. 'It's just that, with the media outside, it seems best to have something prepared.'

'It seems like tempting fate to me.'

'We can do it afterwards, Mr Walters, of course we can.'

'No, Dad.' Miranda turned away from the window angrily. 'Look, we talked about this on the way in. That's why I found the photo last night. It's best to have a few sentences ready, so we don't burst into tears or ... whatever. So we do Shelley justice!'

'That's what the jury's doing, I hope. But go ahead. I don't mind, if you think it's right.' Her father waved his hand dismissively, and Miranda saw, as they all did, how his fingers shook with tension as he picked up his coffee afterwards.

'How far have we got?' Kathryn asked.

Mark Wrass had thought of this idea, to give them something to do in this terrible empty time. He read what they'd agreed so far. *'Shelley was a lively, energetic, loving girl who we will miss for the rest of our lives. Nothing will ever bring her back or fill that hole in our family. But today ...'* He looked up, seeing tears welling in Kathryn's eyes, and wishing the whole business was over and done with. 'What about *"today justice has been done."?'*

'Yes, put that,' Kathryn nodded grimly. *'and an evil man sent to prison.* Put that too.'

'In bold capitals a foot high,' Miranda added as the lawyer tapped at his keyboard. And then add: *"we hope he never comes out to put another family through the misery we've had to suffer."* Something like that, to finish.'

'Never comes out may be a bit strong,' said the lawyer hesitantly. 'He'll be released one day, I'm afraid. Life never does mean life. Not for one murder, anyway.'

Miranda's face, the solicitor noticed, had gone white with rage. Surely she knew that, he thought. But then of course, she'd been living in America.

'I'll kill him if he does,' she said, staring sightlessly through the solid bars of the window. 'If he comes out, I'll kill him myself.'

'Well, I ... don't think we should say that, exactly.' Normally jovial and avuncular, the solicitor felt ill at ease this morning. The trial, he feared, had gone less well than expected, and the bitterness of Shelley's relatives could easily be about to get worse. He looked up hopefully as the door opened and Sarah Newby came in.

Two hours later, the hands of the clock seemed stuck. Sarah, like Mark, did her best, but she was nearly as anxious as the family. Butterflies were dancing in her stomach; the longer the jury were out, the more her doubts increased. The atmosphere in the room was rank with anxiety, like sweat. The mother and daughter looked worst, she thought. Pale, tense, fidgeting. How much longer ...

'Mrs Newby?' The clerk poked her head round the door. 'The jury are coming back.'

'Thank you. This is it, then.' Sarah stood up slowly. Kathryn touched her arm as they moved to the door.

'Just a few words now. Then he'll be locked away for life.'

'Let's hope so. Fingers crossed.' The family went up to the gallery, while Sarah joined Savendra at the table in the court. Back on show again, she thought. All my life I've been coming on stage for a degree or a ceremony or the end of a trial, and mostly it's praise but sometimes it's blame. What will it be this time? Savendra looked glum, as though certain the outcome would be bad. She turned to smile encouragement at Kathryn, and nodded at Terry Bateson, who'd just appeared in court behind her.

Terry looked nervous, she thought, as well he might. She'd warned him this morning that the verdict was far from certain, and he wanted a conviction as much as anyone here. He'd trusted her to secure one for him, but she was far from certain that she'd managed it this time. Her gaze travelled away from Terry, across to David Kidd in the dock.

The customary arrogance had drained from the young man's face, and she felt an unwelcome rush of sympathy. If she'd won, then his adult life would be over. No more sunshine or sex or safaris: just a festering life in a concrete box. Well, if he'd killed that girl he deserved it. She looked around, seeking his family. Did no one here care about this young man? It seemed not. He was on his own; if he had a family they'd abandoned him. Perhaps that was why he'd clung so cruelly to Shelley, ready to kill rather than let her go.

Sarah watched the jury intently as they filed back into court. She had never entirely believed the myth that if they looked at the accused, they had let him off; some jurors, she was sure, relished the punishment they were about to inflict. But this time four or five glanced David's way. Not just the three young men and the girl in the tracksuit whom she'd disliked from the beginning; an older man in a suit and a middle-aged woman looked his way too, and their faces seemed anxious rather than vindictive, as if seeking reassurance that they had done the right thing and he was not the monster they feared.

A pulse started to beat in Sarah's throat and her chest felt tight. I've lost, she thought desperately, it's all gone wrong! They're going to set the bastard free!

She bowed numbly as the judge came in, then sat as the clerk asked the jury foreman if they had reached a verdict.

'We have, sir, yes.'

'On count one of the indictment, the charge of murder, do you find the defendant, David Kidd, guilty or not guilty?'

Come on now, Sarah thought, there may be a doubt here but it's not a reasonable one, not with those cuts and bruises and fingerprints on the knife! Of course he did it - how could she possibly have done it herself ...

'Not guilty.'

'Oh my God.'

The words, muttered low in despair, sounded so close that for a second Sarah wondered if she'd said them herself, and she put a hand to her lips before she realised they must have come from Savendra, who was the only one close enough for her to overhear. He did indeed look miserable, but before anyone else could notice, a scream shattered the silence of the court. All heads turned, like Sarah's, to the public gallery.

'No! You can't do this, that's not right. *He killed her!'*

It was Kathryn Walters, on her feet, gripping the balcony rail with both hands, screaming down at the stunned jury foreman.

'That's not justice! He killed my daughter! That's not justice! You're wrong.'

Kathryn's fury faded as she faced the dozens of eyes staring at her and realised that nothing was going to happen, whatever she said. She had no power here, none at all. Her husband Andrew had his hands on her shoulders but she brushed him away as she made one last desperate attempt, appealing directly to the judge.

'This is a terrible mistake. Tell them, please, tell them to go back and think again.'

The judge shook his head sadly. 'I can't do that, madam, I'm sorry. I understand your grief, but there is nothing I can do.' He turned to the jury foreman. 'Is that the verdict of you all?'

'It is, my lord, yes.'

'Then stand up, Mr Kidd, if you will. This court has found you not guilty of the only charge against you, the charge of murder. You are free to go.'

'Oh, right. Cheers.' There was a click as the warder unlocked a door at the side of the dock, and David stepped down into the well of the court. He hesitated for a moment, then, as the warder indicated the way out, raised his thumb in a gesture of thanks to the jurors. 'Thanks, guys.' Then he was gone.

The judge turned slowly to the jury. When he had thanked them, he levered himself to his feet, bowed, and walked out through the door behind his throne. Sarah turned to Savendra, as the hubbub of the emptying courtroom burst around them. For once, she had nothing to say.

Both of them turned, and walked slowly out with the rest.

Part Three

Shotguns and Weddings

30. Aftermath

'THIS ISN'T justice, it's a farce. The jury got it wrong. That man's going to walk free and if he isn't stopped he'll do it again. Another mother will go through all this pain. And ...'

The woman on the TV screen broke down in tears, and the clip was smoothly edited to show David Kidd grinning ecstatically outside the court. His solicitor, blinking in the TV lights, read a statement: 'Mr Kidd has always professed his innocence and would like to thank the jury for their faith in him. He would also like to offer his sincere condolences to Mr and Mrs Walters for the grief they have suffered because of their daughter's suicide.'

'Bastard!' Kathryn Walters flung her cup at the set. It hit the wall, scattering tea and broken china liberally around the living room. She buried her face in her hands and wept.

'Kath, come on. We knew this might happen, we talked about it.' Andrew reached out an arm which she brushed irritably away, jabbing a finger at the screen.

'Look at that! Smirking little sod! Someone should kill him!'

'Don't be silly, Kath, this isn't the wild west.'

'Well it should be. Look at him grinning like a pop star. You've got a gun, Andy. It's for vermin, isn't it? Why don't you use it on him instead of blasting away at stupid rabbits.'

'Don't be silly, I can't do that.'

'Why not? If you don't I will.'

'Look, love, we talked about this. We said if it happened, we'd just have to live with it.'

'Well, I can't.' Kathryn got up and rested her face on the window, feeling the glass cold on her forehead. 'Why didn't they convict him? It's so obvious he did it.'

'They didn't know Shelley, mum, that's why.' Miranda put her arm round her mother's waist, staring out at the rain on the lawn. *'We* knew she wouldn't kill herself, but they didn't.'

'And so one day he'll do it again. I should never have listened to that Newby woman, I should have given evidence myself and told them what she was like.'

'It wouldn't have helped, Mum. She's a good lawyer, she did her best. There were guys in that jury who looked worse than David, even. I saw one in the rest room. Whenever the police went by he'd give them the finger behind his back.'

'Then you should report it. We could get them disqualified, have another trial.'

'I doubt it. We're on our own now, Mum.' Miranda gathered her mother in her arms, in a hug that reminded them both of how close they had been in years gone by. She stretched out a hand to her father, who patted his wife's shoulder gently while the TV chattered about football.

It was a strange moment for Miranda. Her parents seemed small, diminished, as if they were the children, not her. They were at a cusp in their lives, all three. She was an adult now, with a husband and child and career of her own; they were at the peak of their journey, with the long downhill slope ahead to old age, dependence, and death. Already her mother felt frail, for all her exercising.

'Come on,' she said, after an age. 'Life goes on, we've got to eat.' She marched into the kitchen and started grimly slicing onions, seeing David Kidd's head in every blow. Something will have to be done, she thought. He can't just get away scot free.

Sarah was watching the same scenes on the television news in her living room. She felt shattered, depressed, exhausted. It was the first major prosecution she had lost, and it hurt more than she had expected. Terry rang her after the 6 o'clock news. He blamed himself, it seemed, not her. And, of course, his boss.

'I spoke to that bastard Churchill just now,' he said, his voice, hard, bitter, angry.

'What did he say?'

'What do you expect? He tried to blame you.'

'Me?' Sarah sighed. 'What did I do wrong?'

'Nothing specific, just everything from start to finish. Not enough experience, should have done better with the psychiatrist, antagonising the jury - it's all rubbish, Sarah, it doesn't mean a thing.'

'You think so? Wait until he starts gossiping with his friends. This could be my last big case for the CPS for quite a while.'

'It's his fault, Sarah, for overcooking the timing with that shopkeeper. I tried to tell him that, but it's like talking to a horse's arse.'

Sarah smiled, briefly, at the image. 'Is that what you told him?'

'Not in so many words, no. But he must know I'm right, though he'll never admit it. Too keen to get promotion, cutting corners to meet his crime figure targets, and bugger the truth. It's him all over, Sarah. I should have seen it coming and I didn't. I should have checked that statement myself.'

Sarah searched for some comfort to give him. The trouble was, she agreed with what he was saying. And this wasn't just a simple matter that could be brushed aside and forgotten. The failed prosecution was devastating for all concerned.

'Well, don't beat yourself up too much, Terry. Learn from the experience instead. Your boss is just a menace. Everything he touches turns sour. So keep him out of your cases in future. And if you can't, check everything he does.'

Terry groaned. 'It's all right for you - you're self-employed. You forget, he's my boss. I'll probably be dealing with parking offences in future, while he does the murder trials. God help the victims, that's what I say.'

'Amen,' thought Sarah, putting the phone down sadly. She was sorry for Terry, but not inclined to excuse him completely. It was too important for that. The local news came on ITV, and she suffered through Kathryn's rage all over again. Sarah looked at Emily, sitting on the floor with Larry's arm round her shoulder, and imagined how she'd feel if it had been Emily who had died, Emily's murderer who had walked free.

It would hurt all over my body, she thought, I'd be a walking wound.

The football came on and Emily pressed the mute button. 'What went wrong, Mum? Why did you lose?'

Sarah explained, briefly, about the devastating effect of the shopkeeper's evidence, and the psychiatrist who she had tried to get excluded. The young people listened seriously. 'I failed, that's all.'

'It wasn't your fault, Mum,' Emily said. 'You did your best, you always do.'

'Did I? Maybe, but it wasn't good enough. Not for the poor girl's family, anyway.'

'Surely, Mrs Newby,' Larry asked thoughtfully, 'even if he didn't actually kill her, he still must be guilty of something. I mean, he caused her suicide, didn't he?'

Sarah smiled sadly. The question was typical of him - thoughtful and straight to the point. Over the past year she had come to regard Larry not as the gypsy who came to steal her daughter away, but as Emily's greatest discovery.

'That's what her counsel argued, Larry - that her boyfriend was such a nasty piece of work that he drove her to suicide without, perhaps, intending to. So he's not guilty of anything.'

'But that's not justice is it? I mean, surely ...'

'It's how the law works, I'm afraid. Unless I could prove he intended to drive her to suicide, he's guilty of nothing. And I wasn't even trying to do that, because the evidence suggests it was murder. Most of it, anyway.'

'Poor Mum.' Emily reached up a hand to her mother. 'You must feel rotten.'

'Yes. Not one of my greatest triumphs, I'm afraid.' Sarah took the hand in her own and squeezed it. 'And tomorrow I'm going to meet that girl's family in my office. What do you think I should say?'

What Sarah actually did say, when Kathryn and Miranda climbed the stairs to her room, was simple and obvious. 'I'm very sorry, Mrs Walters. In my opinion there was enough evidence to convict, but we didn't convince the jury. It happens sometimes.'

Both women looked nervous. Sarah had warned Savendra to be out, so there were no distressing confrontations in the corridors. The two women entered grimly, the clerk closing the door softly behind them. Kathryn was still wearing black; Miranda wore jeans, trainers, and a fleece. Sarah seated them in front of her desk.

'Your husband's not coming?'

'No. He has a lot of work.'

As if that could be more important than this, Sarah thought, remembering how Bob had monopolized yesterday evening with a discussion of whether he should apply to become an inspector if he didn't get the new headship. 'The verdict must be very painful for you both.'

'Yes, it is. Obviously.' Kathryn's mouth was set in a grim, bitter line. 'I don't think I've ever been so angry in all my life.'

'That's very natural,' Sarah said. 'I understand.' She wasn't sure she had the skills or vocabulary to handle an interview like this, with such a justified sense of outrage.

'Can't we appeal? To a higher court?'

'I'm afraid not, no. Not in the present state of the law. We could appeal against an unreasonable ruling by the judge, but it's the jury we're unhappy with here. The government have talked about changing the law to allow the prosecution to appeal against the verdict but that's all it is so far, talk. And even if they did change the law it would only be for cases where substantial new evidence has been found.'

'Such as what, exactly?' Miranda asked. She, like her mother, looked pale, but lacked the bruised eyes, the sense of sleep-walking through nightmare, that her mother conveyed. Perhaps that was just the resilience of youth. The anguish, the barely controlled fury, was much the same.

'Such as for example new DNA evidence, or convincing photographs, a confession, something like that. But even then it's difficult to see how a retrial would work.' Sarah checked herself, realising that the last thing these people wanted to hear was a discussion about how the very statement that compelling new evidence had been found might unfairly prejudice any new jury against the defendant. 'Anyway, it's not something to build your hopes on. The sad fact is that he's been acquitted and there's nothing more we can do.'

'So why did you lose?' Kathryn asked bitterly. She leaned forward on the edge of her seat, anger in every line of her body. 'Everyone knows he did it.'

Sarah kept her voice as calm as she could. 'Because of the psychiatrist, I suppose, and the shopkeeper changing his evidence. Both of those things damaged us badly.'

There was real fury in Miranda's voice. 'That psychiatrist didn't know my sister. He had no idea what she was like. She'd never kill herself, it would never have entered her head.'

'He did say she'd talked of suicide ...'

'He's full of shit! He only met her - what? Half a dozen times in her whole life. Whereas I ...' Tears prickled in Miranda's eyes. She brushed them away irritably. 'I can't believe he was allowed to get away with stuff like that.'

'I did try to point that out,' Sarah said cautiously.

'Yes. Yes, you did, I suppose. I can't blame you for that, only ... why weren't we allowed to speak? Tell the jury what she was really like? My mum wanted to and you stopped her!'

This, Sarah thought, was the crucial point. It was the one big error she could be blamed for - certainly the one Shelley's family would be most aware of. She had spent several hours last night, lying beside a gently snoring Bob, reviewing her decision about it.

'Yes, I know. I've asked myself that, of course - whether the advice I gave you was wrong. But each time I come up with the same answer. I doubt it would have made much difference, truly, Mrs Walters. Except to your feelings.'

'And my Mum's feelings don't matter?' Miranda persisted. 'Is that what you're saying?'

'Not at all, no. Of course not.' If the interview went on like this, Sarah thought, she would have to end it. 'I think Mr Bhose would have humiliated your mother, as I said at the time ...' Sarah turned back to Kathryn. 'He would have tried to make it look as if you drove Shelley to suicide. He would have had to.'

Kathryn shook her head, grimly. 'He works here just like you, doesn't he?'

'Mr Bhose? Yes. He's in court at the moment, though.'

'How can he live with himself, doing a thing like that?'

'It's part of the job.' Sarah shrugged. 'You develop a tough skin.' It was not the most tactful remark; she regretted it instantly. Kathryn stiffened as Sarah's words sank in.

'This is over for you now, isn't it? You just go on to the next case and forget all about it.'

'I'm sorry, I put that badly. Anyway my skin isn't as tough as all that. This is the first major prosecution case I've lost, and it hurts me too, though not as much as you, obviously.' Sarah leaned forward, shaking her head sadly. 'I probably shouldn't say this, but I did want to win this case, truly, because, just like you, I believe the man's guilty. Unfortunately, the jury thought otherwise, and the justice system has let you down. I'm sorry. I know it doesn't help much.'

'Not while that man's walking free, no, it doesn't.' With cold dignity, Kathryn got to her feet. 'It was good of you to see us, but it's just a formality really, isn't it? There's nothing more you can do. We'll just have to deal with this on our own.'

31. Wedding Anniversary

RIDING HOME two days later, Sarah eased the black Kawasaki 500 through a line of blocked traffic on the way out of York, and gunned it into the outside lane of the A64, opening the throttle to somewhere near its limits. She crouched low against the oncoming wind, watching the speedometer creep up towards 90 as she swayed in the sudden alarming swirls of slipstream from the vans and lorries that she passed.

She didn't care if she crashed; she needed this recklessness to purge her of the anger she still felt about losing the case against David Kidd. It had left a particularly nasty taste in her mouth: however Shelley had died, Kidd was the cause of it. Yet the toad was free as a bird, while Shelley's family drank the poison of failure. If I was that girl's mother, Sarah thought, I wouldn't let things rest as they are. If I saw David Kidd in front of this motorbike I'd ...

She swerved, nearly losing control in the backwash from a large van, and slowed at the exit for home. Don't be stupid, she told herself, you could lose everything like that, in a single moment of madness. It's not worth it, not for me or the Walters. But then if the courts, the criminal justice system, have failed them, where else can they go?

Savendra looks sick, too. He knows something, and it isn't making him happy. Out of professional etiquette Sarah had refrained from discussing the trial with Savendra, but she needed to discuss it with someone who understood. Terry Bateson, she thought, I'll ring him.

But when she got home there was no time. She opened the front door, still in her leathers, and stumbled over a vast bouquet of gift-wrapped flowers. Behind it stood her husband, Bob, an anxious, triumphant grin on his face.

'Happy anniversary, darling.'

She stared, astonished. 'Bob! Are these for me?'

'Well, maybe.' He affected to consider the question. 'Yes, I suppose they are.'

It was an unprecedented event. Sarah usually remembered their wedding anniversary, but Bob, until now, had always forgotten. This used to cause rows, until Sarah decided to back off, thinking what the hell, it's the fact of being married that matters, not the ritual, and anyway we're both too busy to make anything special of it. But now, after a fortnight when they'd prowled round each other like bears ...

'What is this, a peace offering?'

'Call it that if you like. It's a gift.'

She bent down to read the card. *Eighteen happy years. With all my love, Bob*. No actual apology then, for the way he'd treated her. But then, her own words hadn't been the kindest. She gathered the colourful crinkly package in her arms. 'I'd better put them in water then. Have we got a vase?'

'All ready, in the kitchen. I'll do it, you get changed. I've booked a table at eight.'

'What? In a restaurant, you mean?'

'Yes, of course in a restaurant. That new French place near the castle.'

'Oh Bob, this is lovely, but I can't, not tonight. I've got a brief to read through.'

'Nonsense. You've always got briefs and trials. This is about us.'

'Bob, I can't. I ...'

'Come on, Sarah. I don't often do this.' His face, the tone of his voice, made her pause. What am I doing, she thought, making him plead? All these years I complain that he takes me for granted, and then when he offers flowers, a meal, I reject it?

'All right, I suppose I've got to eat somewhere,' she said, with less grace than she meant. 'What time did you say - eight?'

'Yes.' He looked wary but eager, like a dog who hopes to escape whipping. Should I admire or despise him for this, she wondered? This is the husband I chose, after all. Shared half my life with.

'Right. Just so long as we don't stay too late.' Halfway up the stairs, she thought no, that's not the right tone either. She leaned over the banisters, flashed him a smile. 'Thanks, Bob. It's a lovely surprise.'

Every year since it was built, York Minster has attracted thousands, sometimes hundreds of thousands of visitors, and not all of them are honest. Many come each day to pray for forgiveness of their sins, others - a small but significant minority - come in the hope of committing more. The cathedral attracts tourists, many of them rich, some of them careless, and from time to time the police are called out to investigate crimes committed against such people.

Terry had spent the afternoon taking statements from an American lady who, as her tour party confirmed, had the unfortunate habit of carrying her open handbag slung over her shoulder, and as a result found herself burdened with considerably fewer worldly possessions when she left the house of God than when she had entered it. After taking the statement, Terry lingered for a while, sitting quietly in a side chapel, listening to the chant of evensong, and the silence of the vast building in the pauses between the psalms. There was peace in here, and comfort: the murmur of voices floated up, indistinctly, between the pillars of the vast stone forest above his head, the sounds losing all clarity and individuality the higher they rose. Perhaps it's like that with prayers, Terry thought; so many millions must have been uttered here, some sincere, some frivolous, all rising and mingling together like smoke joining clouds.

Such faith they must have had, such certainty, those who spent hundreds of years building this ancient cathedral! Raw as he was with the failure of the prosecution, Terry found himself wishing he'd been brought up a Catholic, with the option of anonymous, confidential confession. Would that ease this pain? He'd seen Will Churchill manipulate the truth before, yet failed to check up on him this time. So in that sense, at least, Kidd's acquittal was his own fault, and the pain of the Walters family was on his head. Silently, he slipped to his knees in the empty chapel, rested his hand on his bowed forehead, and tried to remember the formula for prayer. It was so long since he'd tried ...

'Forgive me, Lord, for I have sinned ...'

The muttered words seemed appropriate, but unnecessary, somehow. If there was a God, then He knew the whole story already; and if there wasn't, well, it was a waste of breath. He stayed for a few moments nonetheless, the ache in his knees and his back a minor penance of sorts, then looked up to see a priest approaching with a sympathetic smile on his face.

Terry got to his feet swiftly, but he was too late. To his dismay he recognised Canon Rowlands, the priest from David Kidd's trial. Escape was impossible without blatant rudeness, so he nodded: 'Good afternoon, father.'

'Mr Kidd was acquitted, I hear.' Close to, the man's face looked strained and pale; the smile not sympathetic but anxious. 'I've had to move out of my flat.'

'Really? Why is that?'

'Well, I gave evidence, and he's a violent man ... I still wonder, you know, whether I did the right thing. It's so hard to sleep, but I pray ... I mean, when I heard them quarrel that day, if I'd just gone in. Do you think I would have saved her?'

'It's impossible to say, father. He might have cut her wrists already ...'

'Nonetheless, if I'd done something, I might have saved her!'

The little man was trembling with the intensity of his emotion. Terry put his hand on his shoulder. 'Listen, father, it's not your fault. We all make mistakes, each one of us. It's part of being human. Surely your God ...' He looked up at the forest of stone pillars, bathed in gentle colours as the evening sunlight flowed in through the stained glass windows. '... our God, I mean, He understands that. He won't blame you.'

'That's what the Dean said, when I confessed to him. But though I pray, it's not easy.'

'You did the right thing, father. You gave evidence, you couldn't do more.'

Even as he spoke, Terry was backing away, and with a brief encouraging smile he was off, his long legs carrying him swiftly down the aisle to the exit. As he left he was fuming, muttering to himself. Who the hell do you think you are to give absolution? God? After all if He exists He knows why Kidd was let off and it wasn't that priest's fault, it was Will Churchill's and mine. What the hell happened back there anyway? Did I pray and God send me that priest for an answer? What kind of a sick joke is that? Christ Almighty!

Still blaspheming, he got into his car, and began to move off, crawling slowly through the crowds behind a horse-drawn taxi whose guide was pointing out the sites to the last tourists of the day. Terry turned right into St Leonard's, sitting in a queue behind two large coaches. As he waited, a message on the police radio caught his attention.

'All units, urgent response to Gillygate. Suspicious female reported in gardens under city walls. Any units available to respond?'

Terry snatched the microphone from the dashboard. 'DI Bateson here. I'm in St Leonard's. I'll take that. How far along Gillygate exactly?'

'Just past the pub, sir, under the city walls. Passing through gardens from Lord Mayor's Walk. Woman believed suspicious.'

'OK, I'll check it out. On way.'

Terry looked at the blocked traffic ahead of him and thought, quicker on foot. He pulled the car over onto the cobbled square outside the Art Gallery, leapt out, and ran. But which way? The entrances to the gardens along Gillygate were awkward, often locked, difficult of access. Probably just a burglar or false alarm, but it was a relief to have something to do.

Directly across the road in front of him was the ancient fortified medieval gate of Bootham Bar, a popular site of access to the city walls. Terry sprinted across the road, and ran up the stone staircase, through the medieval gate tower, and out along the narrow footpath behind the crenellated fortifications of the city wall. On his right was the Minster, on his left the backs of the houses, flats and shops in Gillygate. At first, near the Bar, they were only a few metres from the wall, but further along long narrow gardens appeared, partly shielded from view by tall spindly trees, growing in profusion at the end of the gardens, directly under the wall.

Muttering excuses, Terry pushed past some tourists busily photographing the Minster in the rosy glow of the evening sunlight, and climbed a few steps onto a watch tower, where he had a better view. He called control on his mobile phone.

'DI Bateson. I'm on the wall behind Gillygate. Which house exactly?'

'She was reported moving along the wilderness area directly under the city wall, sir. Past the old folks' homes at Lord Mayor's Walk end. Isn't there an acquaintance of yours who lives along there? A David Kidd?'

Kidd? Of course! His flat backed onto the city walls. Terry peered down, between two trees, and sure enough, there was the first floor roof garden which he'd seen when he'd examined the flat after Shelley Walters' death. A light was on in the window too, so maybe David was in.

Bastard, Terry thought. What's he doing in there? Watching TV? Making himself a meal? Cutting meat with the knife we found on the bathroom floor? I could show him what to cut with it, Terry thought. And it wouldn't be steak.

But for the moment, there was this female burglar, or whatever she was. As he looked, something stirred in the undergrowth below. It was shadowy down there; the wall and trees blocked out most of the daylight. But something - or someone - was moving. His pulse began to race with the joy of the chase.

There she was! A woman in a long dark coat, creeping furtively between the trees. She was approaching from the Lord Mayor's Walk end, where no walls divided the gardens from each other. Her attention seemed focussed on the backs of the houses, not on the wall above. Opposite David Kidd's flat she began to step down, cautiously, through the wilderness towards the garden. For a moment she stood behind a tree, studying the windows ahead.

The last rays of the sun vanished and a cold breeze crept along the wall. Goose pimples rose along Terry's arms. What is this, Terry wondered? Why is she approaching Kidd's flat?

A man's figure passed across the lighted window of the flat and as it did so the woman reached the last tree before the wilderness ended, took something long out from under her coat, and bent it with a movement that was suddenly, shockingly familiar. She straightened it with a click, and stepped out onto the lawn with a shotgun in her hands.

For a second, Terry hesitated, wondering what to do. If this woman intended to kill Kidd, why not just watch and arrest her later? But he couldn't do that, of course not, this was a real murder about to happen before his eyes. He looked down from the tower and saw to his right, on the wall itself, the drop was less. He ran back down the steps, climbed onto the wall, pushing through a swarm of Japanese schoolgirls - each mouth a perfect O of astonishment, covered with a hand - and jumped.

He fell ten feet, landing in soft leafmould and pitching forward off balance. Half running, half falling, he lurched down the slope until he managed to wrap both arms round a tree and swing himself to a halt. The woman, it seemed, hadn't noticed. Intent on her own purpose, she had reached the stone steps leading up to the patio outside Kidd's flat. Terry let go of the tree and stepped down onto the lawn.

How do you deal with an armed assailant? Not like this. The pages of correct, cautious procedure flashed through his mind and were gone. No time for that now. And anyway there was something personal here, a mystery that had to be solved. He had only seen the back of the woman, her figure obscured by the long dark coat, but there was something terribly familiar about her. If he knew her they could talk, he felt sure.

She reached the top of the steps and stood with her back to him, staring at the lighted door. He walked towards her, girlish Japanese voices twittering like starlings in the air behind him.

As he reached the foot of the steps she raised the shotgun to her shoulder. The voices behind him rose to shrieks and cries. Hearing them, the woman turned and saw him.

Terry stopped, halfway up the steps. The shotgun was pointing towards him, wavering like a branch in a breeze. Her face was still shadowed but he recognized her, at last.

'Good evening,' he said. 'Kathryn Walters, isn't it? I'm a police officer. Terry Bateson.'

She stared at him for a long, anxious moment. She said something, but the voices on the wall, chattering and shrieking in a crescendo of girlish excitement, made it difficult to hear. Slowly, he climbed the steps towards her.

'Go away.' He was close enough to hear now. Kathryn's voice was low and intense and trance-like. 'I don't need you, go away. Come back when I've finished.'

'Put the gun down, Mrs Walters. Please. You don't want to hurt anyone.'

'Don't I? Why not? You hurt me.' The gun waved unsteadily. 'You got it wrong, didn't you? You failed.'

'I'm sorry about the verdict, Mrs Walters. But this isn't the way to solve it.'

'Go away.' Her voice rose to a sob. 'Just go! There's something I've got to do.'

This is why the procedures insist you call back-up, Terry told himself. I need marksmen to cover me, someone to warn the victim and keep him out of the way. The *victim* - David Kidd, of all people! And this woman a possible murderer. This is what happens when we get things wrong.

'Mrs Walters. Put the gun down for me, please.'

'I can't sleep, you see. If he was dead I could sleep.'

'I understand. Really. But it wouldn't help, you know. You'd only feel worse.'

'How do you know? Has anyone killed your daughter?'

Her voice had risen, and the Japanese were still twittering in the background. Don't be a hero, son, that's what the manuals say. Terry glanced anxiously at the lighted door to his left. Any moment now David Kidd might hear the noise and step out, and then what do I do? Jump on this woman before she has time to shoot, or wait until she's blown his guts across the wall?

'Is that your husband's gun, Kathryn?'

She nodded. '*He* should be doing this, not me.'

'Have you fired it before?'

'I know how it works, if that's what you mean. Go away.'

'If you put it down now, the courts will understand, anyone would. Nothing has happened yet, nobody's hurt. Give me the gun, Kathryn. Please.'

The gun barrel, he noticed, was drooping. For a while she didn't reply. She was breathing heavily, tears trickling down her face. 'Why are you here? You shouldn't have come.'

'Put it down, Kathryn. Please.'

She put the gun on the patio wall beside her and turned away, her arms crossed across her chest. There were shrieks of excitement from the wall behind. Terry took the gun quickly, broke it open, and slipped the cartridges into his pocket. Then he put his hand on her elbow. 'Let's go, love, shall we? Before he comes out and finds us. That would just make everything worse.'

32. Gunwoman

AT FIRST the evening went well. The restaurant was good, the food excellent. Bob talked with amusement of the antics of a group of children rehearsing a school play, and with pride of some others who had won a music prize. His wretched secretary Stephanie did not get a mention. Sarah's gloom about the trial faded, and the quiet murmur of his voice took her back to the days when they had first met; the primitive flat in Leeds, the enormous effort Bob had made with her little son Simon, his joy at the birth of Emily, the way they had scrimped and saved on his teacher's salary while she stole every spare moment she could from childcare to study, ever more books and essays, ever higher grades and new challenges, with nothing but encouragement and support from this man who sat opposite, smiling at her as he used to when they were young.

In those days a visit to an expensive restaurant like this was inconceivable. Yet, Sarah thought sadly, sipping her wine, they had laughed more then, been more easy together. There'd been nothing false about their conversation, nothing strained as there was tonight.

She wondered if she should apologise for her words the other evening, and began to try out phrases in her head that might suit. And yet it was he, after all, who'd betrayed her, not she him. Twice, in fact. Once, eighteen months ago, when he'd believed her son Simon guilty of murder; that wound which would never quite heal. And now, this flirtation with Stephanie. He hadn't actually apologised for that yet, she realised. Flowers and food were fine, but where were the words, and the promise to change his behaviour? After all - the dreadful thought entered her head - this celebration, this meal, was the very thing an efficient secretary would think of, might even suggest to her lover.

Suppressing the unwelcome idea, she reached across the table, intending to take Bob's hand. Then her phone rang. She reached for her handbag instead.

'I'm sorry,' she said. 'I thought I'd switched it off.'

'Well, switch it off now, why don't you? Whoever it is it can wait.'

'Yes, okay, I ... just a minute.' She saw the name on the screen. 'Hi. Terry - what is it?'

She saw Bob frown as Terry answered. 'Sarah, I'm sorry to disturb you, but something's come up. It's Kathryn Walters, I've arrested her.'

'What? Terry, you're mad.'

'No, I had to. Listen, this is what happened.' Briefly, to her astonishment, he described what he'd seen from the wall, what he'd done. 'So I had to arrest her, of course, but the reason I'm ringing is, she wants a lawyer, and she's talking about you. So I don't know what you're doing but if there's any way you can get down to Fulford in the next hour or so ...'

'Terry, I don't do police station work. That's for solicitors.'

'I know it is normally, but in this case you're involved, aren't you? I mean we both are. This would never have happened if Kidd had been convicted, and she's asking for you ...'

Bob, Sarah saw, was getting disturbed and angry. 'Terry, I don't know the procedures. You'd be better off with someone like Lucy ...'

'Please, Sarah.' Terry's voice on the phone became more insistent. 'Look, I know this looks bad, but in the circumstances I want to make as little of it as possible, and you're the only one who really understands why. You're not actually prohibited from doing this, are you?'

'No, I don't think so, but ... I'm in a restaurant, Terry, it's my wedding anniversary.'

'Oh, I'm sorry then, but ... Look, it's a mistake, I'll get someone else. Who did you say?'

'Lucy Parsons. But - Terry, is she really asking for me?'

'Yes, of course. And you do understand this. But ...'

'Okay, look, I'm just round the corner. Bob can drive me. I'll be there in what - fifteen minutes?'

Their arrival at the police station was not harmonious. Bob was furious, and sulked bitterly all the way there. 'This was supposed to be our special evening, Sarah, I made a big effort. You don't like it when I mess you around like this'

'I know you did, Bob, and I'm sorry. But I wouldn't go if it wasn't important.'

'What exactly is so important about this woman - and this detective -

that it can't wait till the morning?'

'I'll explain later, Bob, when I get home. I'll take a taxi back.'

'If I'm still awake. I've got an early start tomorrow. Inspectors - big day, lots of stress.'

Yeah, sure, Sarah thought, getting out of the car. Your pupils don't murder each other, do they, when you get things wrong? She imagined him dialling Stephanie to complain how hard done by he was, then shrugged and strode into the station, still in her smart heels.

Terry Bateson led her down a corridor to a small interview room with a buzzing light. Kathryn Walters sat the table, staring dully at her hands as though she'd forgotten what they were for. She looked exhausted, Sarah thought, and bewildered too, as though all her efforts had gone into getting herself onto that roof garden with the shotgun, and none into what might come after. This is what happens when the justice system lets people down, she thought gloomily. People seek their own revenge.

'Mrs Walters? I understand that you've asked me to accompany you in this interview. As a barrister I don't usually do this sort of thing, but in the circumstances ...'

Kathryn gazed at her bleakly. 'You understand, don't you? You know why I had to do it.'

Sarah glanced quickly to ensure that Terry had closed the door behind him. 'If it was about Shelley, yes, of course. I've been told you were arrested outside David Kidd's flat with a shotgun. Is that true?'

Kathryn nodded dully. 'But that detective came. God knows how.'

Sarah sat down quietly opposite her. 'Do you want to tell me what happened? Don't worry, this is quite confidential.'

'I went there to kill him, didn't I?' Kathryn turned her hand over and peered at her ring. 'I would have done it too, if that man hadn't come. The lights were on in that monster's flat, I know he was in there somewhere.' She looked up, staring straight into Sarah's eyes. 'I told you before, that's what I believe in. An eye for an eye. He killed her, and they let him go.'

'I know, Mrs Walters, and I'm sorry. But ... it might be better not to say that, when the detective interviews you. Not if you want to stay out of prison.'

'Why not? It's true, isn't it? That's what I meant to do.'

The woman's lost touch with reality, Sarah thought. Or at least, what we normally think of as real. 'You can tell the truth to me, of course, but you don't need to say anything to the police. You've a right to stay silent, and that must be better than admitting to attempted murder. Let them prove it if they can.'

'Of course they can prove it. He caught me outside the flat with a gun.'

'Yes, well.' Sarah sighed. This wasn't a situation she was used to. They used solicitors for these early stages. But Terry was right - if she, and he, hadn't got things wrong in court, this woman would never be here. 'Maybe you just went there to frighten him,' she suggested tentatively. 'Did you? Think about that. Remember, it's your intention that counts as much as the facts.'

Kathryn stared at her dully, and Sarah floundered on, wondering how far she could ethically go. 'I'm not suggesting you lie, of course, but you may have been confused, with all sorts of contradictory emotions going through your head, and so to say you intended to do one thing rather than another may not be the whole truth, do you see?' I shouldn't be here, she thought, listening to her voice gabbling, I'm out of my depth. 'So it's far better to say nothing at all. Let them prove your intention, if they can. Otherwise ...'

'I'll go to prison and he'll stay free?'

'Ye ... yes, exactly,' said Sarah, thinking that's not quite what I meant but what do you expect, with a devious twisting Jesuitical argument like that? God knows what solicitors do. The stunned blurry confused disappointment had begun to fade from Kathryn's face, she noted, leaving a ghostly determination behind. Kathryn smiled bleakly.

'Then maybe you're right. That wouldn't be justice, would it?'

'No.' What have I unleashed here, Sarah wondered, in the grim silence that followed. 'That doesn't mean you should try to kill him again, you know. That's not what I meant at all.'

'I know you didn't,' said Kathryn, in her new calmer voice. 'But then it's not your daughter that was murdered, is it, Mrs Newby? Anyway, don't worry. We've only got one shotgun at home.'

For Terry, the arrest of Kathryn Walters was a nightmare. If Kidd had been convicted, this could never have happened. Kathryn wasn't a criminal, she was a victim, the mother of a murdered child. And yet here she was, under arrest and about to be charged with - well, what? Attempted murder? If I hadn't stopped her, Terry thought, she'd have killed him, and been locked up for life. And it's all Will Churchill's fault, and mine for not checking up on him in time!

An hour later, with the cartridges burning a hole in his pocket, Terry led Kathryn and Sarah along the corridor to a different interview room. He paused for a moment outside the door. 'Listen to me, Mrs Walters. In a moment I'll caution you formally again, but first, let me give you some advice. Say as little as possible, just answer me yes or no if you can. Be advised by Mrs Newby, of course, but I'm telling you this for free.'

Sarah glanced at him curiously as she entered the room, and sat beside Kathryn at the table. What had he meant by that? A young female constable watched impassively from a corner. Terry switched on the tape and read the caution.

'Now, Mrs Walters, four days ago a man called David Kidd was acquitted of murdering your daughter Shelley at York Crown Court. That's true, isn't it?'

'Yes.'

'You, as a mother, must have found that extremely upsetting. Traumatic, even.'

'Of course I did. How would you feel, if it was your daughter, and that bastard ...' Sarah put a hand on Kathryn's arm, to squeeze a warning. But Terry, it seemed, was pursuing an agenda of his own, a rather less aggressive one than Sarah had expected.

'Yes, all right, Mrs Walters, I understand. Have you been able to sleep since the trial?'

'Not much, no.'

'So for the past few days you've had hardly any sleep. You're overtired, and understandably very upset. Is that a fair description?'

'Yes, of course it is.'

'Okay. Now the reason you're here, Mrs Walters, is that this evening you were arrested outside David Kidd's flat with this shotgun.' He indicated the shotgun, now absurdly wrapped in a long plastic evidence bag and leaning against the wall. 'Is it yours?'

'It's my husband's.'

'What does he use it for?'

'To shoot rabbits, mostly, and pheasants.'

'Do you go shooting with him?'

'No. I don't like it.'

Where's he going with this, Sarah wondered. He's taking a long time to get to the point. Either there's something wrong with the light in here or the man's looking ill. Grey, haunted almost. Perhaps he's not sleeping well.

'So you're not used to using the gun?' Terry continued.

'No, not really. It's his thing, not mine. He should have ...'

'Mrs Walters, just answer the questions, please.' Terry drew a deep breath. He - and Will Churchill - had put this woman in this position; now he wanted to put things right. But this was the moment of decision; there could be no going back later. He plunged on before he could have second thoughts. It was all being recorded; he had to sound firm and convincing, without the least sign of hesitation.

'I want you to think about this very carefully, if you will. When I took this shotgun from you I was surprised - relieved perhaps would be a better word - to find that there were no cartridges in it. None at all. The gun was unloaded. You knew that, didn't you?'

Kathryn and Sarah both stared at Terry in silence. His face was quite wooden, Sarah noted, quite serious. Even when his eyes met hers they were perfectly still. The devious bastard, she thought. He's lying, he has to be. He means to let her off.

'I ... no, I ... I don't remember.'

'You do know the gun doesn't work without cartridges, don't you, Mrs Walters?'

'Yes, of course I know that.'

'Yes. But you hadn't put any cartridges in the gun, Mrs Walters. So however tired and emotional you were, you must have realised the gun couldn't hurt anybody.'

'I ... yes, I suppose I did.'

'All right.' Terry met Sarah's eyes again, still avoiding a wink or the slightest sign of conspiracy. This can't be true, surely, Sarah thought, he has to be making this up. 'So we need to know what you were doing outside Mr Kidd's flat with this unloaded shotgun. A gun which you didn't really know how to use. Were you trying to frighten Mr Kidd, perhaps, Mrs Walters?'

'I ... maybe, I don't know.' Kathryn glanced at Sarah, remembering their earlier interview. 'I was upset. I may have been ... confused.'

'You were tired, overwrought, and confused?'

'I ... yes.'

'So confused that you made no attempt to load the gun. Nonetheless, Mrs Walters, if Mr Kidd had come out he would have been very frightened, which may be what you intended. Not to kill him, but scare him. Now even taking into account your emotional state, that's still a serious crime, an assault which can't be ignored. Do you admit that's what you intended to do?'

'If you say so. Yes.'

Terry sighed with relief. That's it then, he thought. I've done it. God knows what will come of this in the future but for the moment, this woman can go home. And if I play my cards carefully that's all it will ever be; I'll have made some small atonement at least for the terrible wrong she's suffered. That she suffered because of me.

'Very well. Kathryn Walters, I am charging you with threatening behaviour likely to cause a breach of the peace. Details of this charge will be forwarded to the Crown Prosecution Service. In the meantime I am impounding this shotgun as evidence, and I advise you to stay well away from David Kidd, however you may feel about him. That's it. Interview terminated at ten forty seven.' He switched off the tape. 'I'll type up your statement and when you've signed it you'll be free to go.'

'That's all?' Kathryn said in astonishment. 'I can go home?'

'When you've signed your statement, yes. If you plead guilty the most likely outcome is either a fine, a caution, or both. Do you have any previous convictions?'

'No, of course not.'

'Well then.' He leaned forward across the table, his eyes looking directly into hers, trying to look as stern and intimidating as he could. *'Don't do it again*, Kathryn, that's my advice to you. You may not be so lucky next time. Go home, and don't let me catch you anywhere near David Kidd again, okay?'

Kathryn stared at him in bemusement. 'But you know what happened ...'

Terry took the papers and got to his feet. 'Not another word, okay? Or I'll be charging you with wasting police time.' He glanced at Sarah, wondering if it would ever be possible to explain this to her. Probably not; certainly not now. But maybe she'll appreciate the justice of what I'm doing, even if she doesn't understand exactly why. He picked up the shotgun and left the room.

Sarah watched him go, shaking her head in surprise.

33. Mother's Little Helpers

KATHRYN CAME home from the police station to an empty house. Andrew, she assumed, was with his mistress Carole. She'd thought Miranda would be home, but there was a note from her on the table, something about visiting her friend Lizzie and not to wait up, she might stay the night. Dazed as she was, Kathryn was more grateful than worried. She'd made a fool of herself, and failed; she didn't relish the thought of explaining to either of them. Exhausted, she collapsed on her bed for a few hours' fitful sleep, then drove to Harrogate next morning determined to hide her troubles in work.

The burden of running the pharmacy in recent months had fallen heavily on her partner, Cheryl Wolman, but Cheryl had been in London for the past week with her dying mother. As a result they'd called in a locum, a young man with a reputation for chasing girls who'd already upset several of their elderly customers, and Kathryn sensed the relief when she entered the shop. She was certainly needed: the staff were harassed, customers crotchety, stock control all over the place. Kathryn felt like screaming at the lot of them, slamming the door and running away down the street. Instead she went into the stock cupboard and helped herself to some Valium. Then she floated through the rest of the day like a hologram, empty of feelings. She took some more before she drove home, to find Andrew waiting in the kitchen.

'Where've you been?' he asked anxiously.

'At work. Sorting things out. That young locum's a disaster.'

'Your mobile was switched off. I was worried.'

'Were you? Why? Has Carole found someone else?'

'Oh come on, Kath, that's not fair.'

'Isn't it?' She took off her coat. 'Look, you may as well know. I was arrested last night.'

'What?' She made herself a coffee, sat at the table and explained. The Valium made her feel cool, lighthearted, calm. Everything mattered, and yet it didn't. She watched everything from the kitchen ceiling, encouraged by the performance of her body below.

'You meant to kill him, you mean!'

'I couldn't, could I? That detective lost the cartridges for me.' Andrew's horror amused her. Kathryn giggled, and fumbled in the pockets of her coat. 'There are still some gentlemen left in the world.' She pulled out some cartridges and lined them up, one by one, on the table. 'How many does it take to kill a man? One, two, three ...' She flicked the cartridges down with her finger, one by one like toy soldiers.

As she did so a taxi drew up outside and Miranda came in. At least, it was someone who looked like Miranda, but with her shoulder length brown hair cut brutally short to a two inch length all round, teased into little curls and spikes, stiffened with gel and dyed blonde, with red and orange highlights. Miranda had expected a strong reaction, but to her surprise, her mother contemplated her with disconcerting calm.

'Ah, here's another one. What happened to your hair?'

'I saw it in a fashion magazine. Thought it would cheer me up.'

'Well, I hope it does. Bruce will get a shock.'

'Yes.' Miranda's husband's conservative tastes were well known. 'I'll manage him.'

'You were out last night, were you? Just got home?'

Miranda nodded. 'I stayed over at Lizzie's. I did phone, but you weren't here. And then we spent the day in town.'

'That's all right. I saw your note. Anyway, I was out last night, too. At the police station.'

'What?'

Astonished, Miranda collapsed in a chair, as Kathryn explained it all over again. She even made it sound funny at times, with the new chemical grin on her face. You want irony, take the irony tablets. Kathryn was so distant from her real feelings, that she could observe Miranda's shock with pride. Her daughter's startling new hairstyle just seemed to fit in with the dreamlike mood of the evening.

'But Mum, what if he'd opened the door and come out?'

'I'd have blown a hole in him, to let the truth out.'

'My God.' Her mother's words sounded surreal, insane. And yet similar hazy thoughts of vengeance had been circling in Miranda's own mind; nothing as violent as this, but the search for a way to make David Kidd pay for his crime. She had one half formed idea, which had been the reason for getting her hair cut. 'Did you ... look? See him inside?'

'I saw a man moving. If that detective hadn't come, I'd have done it.'

'And then what? Mum, it would have been murder!'

'Yes, well.' Kathryn picked up a cartridge from the table. 'I'd have still had these left, wouldn't I?'

They stared at her in horror. 'Kathryn love,' Andrew said. 'Are you all right?'

From an immense distance, Kathryn considered the question. 'No, probably not. But don't worry, life goes on. That's what they say, isn't it?'

'But what about this charge, the police?'

'They let me go, with a warning. Don't shoot people, the man said, it's wrong. I must remember that. It's good advice, don't you think?' Kathryn laughed - a short, nervous laugh that threatened to run out of control.

'You're not well, love. You need a doctor.'

'No I don't. I need a daughter.' With a dizzying jolt, Kathryn fell from the ceiling back into her body, and slumped forward, head in her arms on the table. *No, please, not again, the pain's coming back. Where are those pills, I'll take some more.* She felt Miranda's arm round her shoulders.

'You've still got me, Mum. For a few more days, anyway.'

'Yes, that's good.'

'Maybe, love,' Andrew said hesitantly. 'With your mother in this state, you could stay a few more days.'

Miranda considered. She had an open ticket, but before the trial she'd been planning to go back this week, soon after the verdict which should have seen David Kidd locked away for life. Now, everything was changed. Her mother was clearly unbalanced and if she was to do anything about this plan which she had been hatching all day she would need a little more time. But this wasn't something she wanted to discuss with her parents. They needed care, she thought, and freedom from further worry.

'Yes, of course I can, Dad. I'll give Bruce a ring tonight. Sophie won't be pleased but ...'

'Don't stay just for me, darling,' Kathryn said. 'I mean, it's lovely to have you but I'll manage. I always have before.'

'You've never had this before, though, Mum, have you? None of us have.'

'No. But don't worry, I'm not mad. I just thought - it was perfectly rational - that man deserves to die. Unfortunately I failed and ...' She shook her head wearily. 'I don't think I could do it again.'

Andrew reached across the table for her hand. 'It's not normal to think like that, love. You've been under a lot of stress, of course you have. See Doctor Pegg, he'll give you something for it, he'll understand.'

And bring Shelley back, too, will he? Kathryn thought, hazily. I don't need a doctor, I've got the pills in my bag. What I want now is to be left alone. She smiled at Andrew through her tears. 'Yes, all right. I'll ring doctor Pegg in the morning.'

'Good. And no more shooting, okay?'

'I can't, can I? They've got your gun.' Kathryn smiled and hauled herself to her feet. The pills were working again. She felt a blissful ease, an exhaustion. 'You're right, I do feel strange. Tired, more than anything else. Find something in the freezer, if you're hungry. Right now, I'm going to bed.'

Terry, too, was feeling strange - depressed, and light-headed, both at once. The depression was fairly easy to account for - it came from guilt, and the shock of not only failing to secure David Kidd's conviction, but of having betrayed his own principles. Now he too, had tampered with evidence. Naturally he felt depressed. Yet since the arrest of Kathryn Walters, he'd also felt light-headed - infected by an absurd, almost cheerful fever which overlaid the guilty gloom beneath. At least he'd been able to put matters partly right, he thought. If anyone else had arrested Kathryn Walters she'd have been charged with attempted murder; as it was, she'd been released on bail.

I'm becoming a gambler with the truth, Terry thought, as he knocked on Will Churchill's door - a high wire artist. If I slip, I'll lose my job.

Will Churchill, looking up from Terry's report, was incredulous. 'Threatening behaviour likely to cause a breach of the peace? Are you mad? The woman had a shotgun!'

'An unloaded shotgun, sir.'

'Well, she must be mad, too. How d'you know it wasn't loaded?'

'First thing I did, sir, was break it open.' Terry spread his hands wide. 'Zilch.'

'What about her pockets? Did you find any cartridges there?'

Terry shook his head, using the eye furthest from Churchill to wink at a photo of a nubile young woman in a wetsuit to the right of his boss's head. 'I found no cartridges there either, sir,' he said, which was true, since he had deliberately avoided searching Kathryn's clothing. The two cartridges he had extracted from the gun were now in the bin outside his house.

'Well, what the hell did she think she was doing?'

'In my view, sir, she was overwrought, and possibly hallucinating from stress and lack of sleep. The main thing is she didn't cause any harm.'

'You could have charged her with attempted murder.'

'She admitted she wanted to scare him, sir, and that's what she's charged with.'

Churchill sat back in his leather chair, shaking his head in disbelief. 'No wonder you don't get any convictions, Terence. First Kidd, now this. Ever think of joining the social services? They'd take you like a shot.'

There was no answer to this, so Terry studied the young woman in the wetsuit instead. Churchill glanced back at the report. 'She had a lawyer, of course. Who was it? My God, Mrs Newby! I thought barristers didn't lower themselves to this sort of thing.'

'They don't normally, sir, but she was, er, available at the time, and Mrs Walters requested her services.'

'Available at the time?' Churchill smirked. 'What's that supposed to mean? Not what I think it means, surely?'

'She was at a restaurant in town, and I reached her on her mobile.'

'The number of which just happens to be saved on yours.' Churchill's grin broadened. 'Give it up, Terence, you haven't got a hope with a bird like that. Go on, get out of here, now.'

He waved a pencil imperiously. Then, as Terry reached the door, he laughed. 'You'd never afford her anyway, on a social worker's salary.'

34. Travel Writer

WHEN SARAH got home from the police station, Bob was already asleep. Next morning he listened sourly to her explanation, before driving off grumpily to his school. The following two evenings were no better; Sarah worked late in her chambers, Bob at the rehearsal of a school play. They snapped at each other in passing; the flowers he had bought her wilted and died. Waking the following morning, Friday, Sarah found Bob's suitcase neatly packed in the hall. For a moment she stared at it stupidly, wondering if things were even worse than she'd thought, and he was really intending to leave. Then she remembered; he'd said something about a conference this weekend, which clashed with Savendra's wedding. She'd meant to discuss it with him but the turmoil of the last few days had driven it out of her mind.

As usual, Sarah was up at six, ready to catch the early train for a committal hearing in Newcastle. Bob was still comatose, his tousled head under the duvet to avoid the noise she made showering and drying her hair. Normally, she let him sleep, but today there was no time. Doing her face in the mirror, she began to talk.

'I see you've got your suitcase packed. Is that for this conference in Harrogate?'

'Mmn.' He groaned and turned over. 'Told you about it last week.'

'What is it, three days?'

'What? Yeah. Shut up, love, I'm asleep.'

'I'm sorry, but if you're leaving today I won't see you, will I? When do you get back?'

'Sunday evening, I think. Sarah, it's six fifteen.'

'Tell me about it.' Sarah brushed her eyelashes with mascara, peering into the mirror at the tousled creature hunched like some huge chrysalis under the duvet. 'The point is we're going to Savendra's wedding tomorrow afternoon. Saturday. Remember?'

'What?'

'I did mention it, Bob. You just didn't listen.'

'Well, I can't go. Obviously. I'll be at this conference.'

'Where is it? Harrogate? It's only an hour away, max. Look, surely you can skip a few seminars and come to the ceremony at least, can't you? They're expecting us both, after all, and he is one of my closest colleagues.'

'I thought that copper was. The one you were with the other night.'

'What?' She swung round, hairbrush in hand, to stare at him. He had emerged from the duvet now and was lying slumped against the pillows, unshaven and grumpy. 'You mean Terry Bateson? Bob, for Christ's sake, I've told you about that. It was work.'

'Since when do you go out with detectives investigating crimes? You're a barrister.'

There was no obvious answer to this. He was right, of course, but it had eased her conscience to help Kathryn, and as for Terry, well ...

'This was different, that's all.' She turned back to the mirror, brushing her hair vigorously. 'Anyway, what about this wedding? I don't want to go on my own, it'll look bad. Surely you can spare a few hours?'

'Maybe. I'll look at the programme and give you a ring.'

'Do that, Bob.' She put down the hairbrush and pulled on her motorcycling leathers over jeans and teeshirt. She had her smart trouser suit neatly folded in a briefcase; she would change in the ladies' room at the station. Having gained her point she felt a little more conciliatory. 'What's the conference about, anyway?'

'Administering larger schools. That's why I'm going. It'll help with this job application.'

'I see. Not teaching then.' A cold thought struck her. 'Is Stephanie going?'

'Yes, it's for secretaries too. They help with administration, after all - in fact half of them are called administrators now.' A defensive look crossed his face. 'It's just a conference, Sarah.'

'Is it?' She strode smartly to the door. 'I hope so. Well, do one thing for me, Bob, will you? Me, your wife. Find time for Savendra's wedding. You've got all the rest of the weekend to work with Stephanie.'

Her mother's action strengthened the idea that had begun to germinate in Miranda's mind. If David Kidd had killed her sister, then since the justice system had failed there must be some other way of making him pay. There simply had to be. There could be no forgiving what David Kidd had done, not ever. Over the next few days, she developed the details of her plan.

Miranda worked as a freelance journalist, mostly local stuff in Wisconsin, but she'd seen enough exposés of serious crime to know that a not guilty verdict was sometimes just the necessary opening gambit in a series of conspiracy articles that could run and run, exposing police corruption, the incompetence of lawyers, blackmailing of witnesses and the hounding of those who'd been acquitted, often for the rest of their lives. All that was needed was a little evidence; not as much, at first, as was needed in a court of law, but enough to give the story legs so the public would read it. Then dozens of journalists would come pouring out of the woods to follow the scent that one had started. Often, Miranda had felt cynical about this business, which was more about the selling of newspapers than the pursuit of justice, but in this case, she was convinced, David was guilty, so an injustice had been committed. If she could convince the press of this, he wouldn't have got away with it after all.

And then there had been those words in Sarah's office. The law might change one day, she'd said. So if she could just find proof of David's guilt, there could be an appeal sometime in the future. Maybe five, ten years later - it didn't matter how long, if David knew that justice would reach him one day.

What sort of evidence had Mrs Newby mentioned? DNA was no good here - but what about a confession? That was it, surely! If David could be induced to confess to the crime - and to Miranda he looked exactly the sort of cocky little loudmouth jerk who might do just that - then there's your newspaper scandal, there's your grounds for appeal!

But first, she had to get in touch with him. Without, of course, letting him know who she was. That was her plan for today. David, she knew, was a tour guide for an adventure travel company. Among the sad clutter of Shelley's things, stored in her parents' house, she had found a brochure with the company's name, and an address in South London. She fingered it now, remembering Shelley's excitement about the promised holiday in Kenya. It was this that had given her her plan.

With the brochure on the table in front of her, she cleared her throat nervously. She would have to do this in a good American accent, the sort she heard all around her at home. She dialled the number on the front. A young woman answered.

'Sunline Tours, Sandy speaking. How can I help?'

'Oh, hi. My name's Martha Cookson, I'm a journalist for the Washington Star. You may have seen my stuff, it gets syndicated in English language papers worldwide.'

'Maybe, I'm not sure ...'

'You probably have without noting the name. See, I write for the travel supplements mainly, and I'm in England just now, saw one of your brochures, looks real cool, so I thought I might do a piece on you if you like.'

'You need to speak to our manager. Hold the line please.'

Miranda relaxed. The American accent made it seem like a game. Her friend, Martha Cookson, was indeed a travel journalist for the Washington Star, far grander than Miranda's local paper. But Sunline Tours would never know the difference, and anyway they deserved all they got for hiring a lowlife like David Kidd.

'Nick Tranter here, Miss Cookson. What can I do for you?'

Miranda repeated her spiel, which the man swallowed hook line and sinker. 'But of course. Come round tomorrow and we'll show you everything you want - videos, references, the works. Guarantee a big spread and we'll fix you a free holiday.'

'Sure, but I'm in Yorkshire right now. You don't have anyone in this part of England that I could visit with, do you? Someone who's been on the trips, knows what he's talking about?'

'Er, not sure. Let me think. There is one guy, matter of fact, in York - would he do?'

'Sure.' Miranda grinned in delight. 'York's not far.'

'OK. He hasn't worked for a bit but he knows his stuff. Give me your number and I'll see what I can do.'

Half an hour later the man rang back. He sounded a little more cautious. It was only tourism she was interested in, wasn't it? Yes, of course, she laughed innocently. What else? In that case their representative David Kidd would meet her at the Slug and Lettuce in York on Saturday at eight o'clock.

Where she could try to worm her way into his confidence. And find out, perhaps, what really happened to Shelley. In which case, she really would have an article to write.

35. Wedding Invitation

WHEN TERRY had first been invited to Savendra Bhose's wedding he had been surprised and flattered. Although he'd met the young barrister professionally and at a few social occasions, he didn't count him as a close friend. And then, of course, Savendra had been defending David Kidd, in a case which Terry, at the time he received the invitation, fully expected to win. It showed the young man in a good light, he thought, magnanimous even in the face of defeat. It was not often a defence lawyer extended the hand of friendship to the police, so Terry had responded in kind. He penned a gracious letter of acceptance, and bought a handsome cut glass bowl as a wedding present.

Now Savendra had won his case and it was for Terry to display magnanimity. He no longer wanted to go, but it seemed graceless to refuse at the last moment. So he pinned a carnation to his buttonhole, put the cut glass bowl in the back of his car, and set out.

Savendra's family, although Indian, were Catholics, one of the few good things about them as far as Belinda's parents were concerned. A Hindu or Sikh for a son-in-law would have strained her father's tolerance to the extreme - it was bad enough that his daughter was marrying a boy who defended murderers for pay. But at least he had been educated at Ampleforth, the top Catholic school in the north of England. So the wedding was in York's Catholic church, and there was a fine show on either side of the aisle.

Terry crept alone into a pew at the back, and was relieved when Sarah Newby joined him with her husband Bob. She greeted him with a tight little smile; her husband nodded genially. Yet something jarred; the couple seemed ill at ease. I probably ruined their wedding anniversary, Terry thought sourly; well, they should be grateful they still have one.

The wedding couple looked stunning, Savendra dark and suave in morning dress, Belinda in a white wedding dress styled like an Indian sari, with a veil and long floating scarf fringed with flowers of pink and cornflower blue. As she walked up the aisle, the church pulsating with organ music, Terry recalled the cheap cassette recorder in the registrar's offices where he'd married his wife, Mary. So young they had been, so long ago.

One fine day in heaven, he promised her silently, we'll do it again, like this.

Afterwards, at a hotel by the river, they sat at round tables for eight. Terry, a solitary male, found himself next to a long-nosed stick-like spinster aunt of Belinda's in a low cut dress which revealed skin and bones and nothing much between. Sarah and Bob were there too, with a clutch of jolly Indians, but Terry could find little to say to anyone. By the main course he had consumed most of a bottle of wine and was calling for more to dull his desperation. After the speeches a spat erupted between Sarah and Bob, about what he couldn't tell. When they drifted out later onto the lawn, Sarah's husband was nowhere to be seen. Seeing Terry, she smiled at him brightly.

'Staying for the dance?'

'That was the intention, but now ...' He swayed on his feet. 'I don't know.'

'If you do, I'm short of an escort.' She shrugged. 'Bob's gone, I'm afraid. Family row.'

'Oh. Well, in that case, who could refuse?' Together they found a table on the lawn, overlooking the river. Terry fetched drinks from the bar. They sat in companionable silence, watching ducks pick up crumbs round their feet.

'Remind you of your own wedding?' Sarah asked, twirling her glass between her fingers.

'A bit. This is ten times more posh. Makes me feel like a failure.'

'Me too, especially when my husband's not here.'

He studied her thoughtfully, wondering whether to probe. 'Major argument?'

'Fairly major. It's been going on for some time, I suppose ... ever since last year, when he thought Simon was guilty, nothing's quite been the same. And the other night didn't help.'

'I'm sorry.'

'Oh, we all have bad patches, but thanks.' She sighed, and sipped her drink. 'I've been wondering. Was that true what you said, the other night, in the station?'

'About the shotgun, you mean? And Kathryn Walters?'

'Mmm.' She studied him carefully. 'I shouldn't ask, I suppose. Can you tell?'

'Not sure if I should.' He stared across the river, thinking. What would she think, if he admitted he had tampered with the evidence? Understand his reasons, or despise him for betraying his principles? She had probably guessed already, but part of him longed to confess. 'Well, the woman deserved a break, didn't she? It was the least I ...'

'Hey!' A hand slapped his shoulder. 'So glad you could make it! Parents both. Dragged you away from the kids, have I?'

The groom, Savendra, collapsed into a seat beside them, groaning with happy exhaustion. His collar was loose, his hair mussed by the fingers of bridesmaids. 'Enjoying yourselves?'

'How could we fail, Savvy? Seeing you reach your heart's desire!' Sarah smiled, and Terry remembered how these two, professional rivals, were nonetheless good friends. It was hard for a policeman to imagine - that someone on the opposite team could be your closest pal.

'Belinda looked beautiful, didn't she?' Savendra beamed, a smile of flashing white teeth. 'Not as lovely as you, Sarah, of course, but I got the next best thing.'

'Of course you did, Savvy, and she'll be much more fertile than me too. You have told her your plans?'

'For the family of eight? I'm saving that up for later. I mean, that's what you do, isn't it, on the wedding night? Tell me.' He leaned forward, drawing them close together in conference. 'You both know about kids, don't you? What's the best and the worst of it?'

And so Terry's chance to confess was gone, lost in an hour of pleasant banter, during which they were joined by Belinda's mother and then the bride herself and several Indian cousins, and the subject of children and weddings was tossed around with cheerful laughter. It was already early evening. As the sun set behind the trees a maitre d'hotel advised them that the dancing would start soon, and the hotel's facilities were available for those who felt the need to freshen up. Sarah took Terry's arm.

'Just what I need. Look, I'd better phone Bob, try and smooth things over. But I still want to dance. Will you wait?'

'Of course,' Terry said. 'So long as there's no crisis at home. I'll ring the girls while you're changing.'

'Fine. See you here at what? Seven then.'

'It's a date.'

Terry waited until she'd gone, then picked up his mobile.

Arriving for the interview just after eight, Miranda felt her heart pounding faster than normal. What if David recognised her, what would he do? He won't, she told herself firmly, he's only seen me a couple of times in court and each time he looked right through me as if I wasn't there. Anyway I looked quite different then. Each time she looked in the mirror her new punk hairstyle gave her a fright. In court she'd worn a sober navy suit; now she wore jeans and a black leather jacket with straps and zips, in the lining of which she'd sewn a mini tape recorder, which she'd bought last year for an investigative radio program. She also wore two large hooped ear rings and black wraparound shades. In other circumstances she would have enjoyed the disguise; now she chewed gum to still her nerves.

Entering the restaurant she saw him immediately, at a table near the window. She walked to the counter, ordered a coffee and pastry, and looked around as if searching for someone. Another young man was sitting alone in a corner. She took her tray over to him.

'Excuse me, I'm looking for a David Kidd. Would that be you?'

The man grinned. 'No, sorry, love. But I could be. Why not sit down and wait?'

Miranda smiled. 'Some other time, maybe.' Appearing to notice David by the window, she approached him in the same way. 'David Kidd?'

'Yeah, that's me.' He waved her to a chair. 'You're the journalist, are you? Martha Cookson?'

'That's right.' Miranda held out her hand. 'Pleased to meet you.'

The handshake nearly betrayed her. Bile rose in her throat as his soft, moist palm, her sister's murderer's flesh, touched hers. She pulled back instinctively, sending a subliminal signal of distaste. 'So. You're the intrepid explorer?'

'I'm a tour guide, yeah.' He lounged in his chair, resting one boot on his knee in the arrogant pose she remembered from court. It's all right, she thought, he just wants to impress me, the jerk. She took the gum from her mouth, and sipped coffee. 'Where do you guide, exactly?'

For the next half hour he described his safari tours, while Miranda made occasional notes. Much of it matched what she'd heard from Shelley, although David spoke as if he was the safari leader rather than a hired help. But he was funny, in a slightly snide way, telling stories of his rich, elderly clients - the American lady who'd feared that vampire bats might nest in her hair at night; a Dutchman who had climbed a tree to escape a rabid hyena. Not the best way to recruit my readers, Miranda thought. But she didn't care; her mind was focussed on the next stage of her scheme, winning his confidence so he would talk about Shelley.

'So, what d'you do when you're not saving rich ladies from scorpions?' she asked, with what she hoped was a friendly, inviting smile. 'Can you have a good time in York?'

'York, Leeds, Sheffield. Sure, there's plenty of action if you know where to look.'

'That's my problem, see. I'm staying with friends of my parents, so ...' She shrugged expressively. 'Not much of a guide to the night life.'

Will he take the bait, she wondered. He studied her coolly, trying to pierce her shades with his eyes. Cocky little bastard, a voice murmured inside her head. As if he'd have a chance with me normally. But to her relief, David's cold scrutiny relaxed into a calculating smile. 'What sort of night life are you interested in?' he asked at last. 'Maybe I can help you there.'

'Hi there! Come and join us.'

Sarah waved to Terry from the bar, where she stood with the newlyweds and several other couples whom he took to be lawyers or family friends. The room was large and noisy; a band was tuning up at one end, and the guests stood in groups shouting in each other's ears to be heard. Sarah, he noticed, had changed; the formal dress and hat she had worn for the afternoon ceremony had been replaced by a low-cut black evening gown which clung to her figure like a sheath. The plunging neckline left no room for a bra, and he saw no hint of a panty line either. She noticed his stare and blushed, mocking her own embarrassment with a shy pirouette.

'My birthday present. What do you think?'

'It's lovely. Stunning, in fact.'

'Don't flatter me, Terry, or I won't believe you. I had to wear it soon before I collapse into middle age. Kids okay?'

'Fine. They're watching Harry Potter with Trude. Esther told me the whole story on the phone.'

'They're sweet, your girls. Want a drink?' She passed him a glass of champagne.

'Just the one. I've brought the car.'

'Leave it here. Take a taxi.'

'Maybe.' He sipped the drink and smiled at her. The flush had not entirely faded from her cheeks, and the sparkle in her eyes suggested that she was several glasses ahead of him. 'Did you make things up with Bob?'

'Not really. He's at a conference. I think his phone's switched off.'

'Oh, I'm sorry.' The suggestion of a rift was obvious. 'So he doesn't get to see you in his birthday gift?'

Sarah shook her head. 'It's not his gift anyway. Simon gave it to me - my son, remember? With grateful thanks to his mum for keeping him out of prison.'

'Good lord!' Terry thought back to the surly young bricklayer who had stood in the dock, with his feisty mother defending him. His fingers brushed the soft satin gown. 'I'd never have thought ...'

'That an oaf like him could buy such a thing? Neither could I. It brought tears to my eyes, Terry, I can tell you. Nice ones, for a change.' She bit her lip, and put her glass down on the bar. 'Come on. That's a waltz they're playing, isn't it? Let's dance to celebrate his freedom.'

Terry had danced with Sarah once before, he remembered as he pressed his hand against the small of her back, at a ball in the Judges' Lodgings. Only one dance then, for Bob, her husband, had scowled possessively beside her that evening like a sullen bear; but tonight, it seemed, the fool had absented himself. Sarah was light, easy on her feet. She smiled up at him brightly, shy, a little nervous.

'You've done this before, I see.'

'I took lessons at uni. Hoping to meet girls. How I met Mary, matter of fact.'

After several dances they sat down for a rest, at a table on a patio outside. Sarah drank a third glass of champagne. Terry stuck to orange juice. She studied him, the thrill of the dance in her eyes, but a touch of sadness underneath.

'You were going to tell me something earlier, weren't you?'

'Was I?' Terry's eyes lingered for a second on the decolleté of her dress, where a hint of perspiration beaded the outline of her breasts. 'Oh yes. About Kathryn Walters, and her shotgun. You don't want to talk about that now, do you?'

'Don't you trust me? Promise, I won't tell.'

He sighed. 'All right, yes, it was loaded.'

'You lied, you mean? Concealed evidence?' Without meaning to, she'd switched to her courtroom voice, sharp and concise. Their eyes met; hers bright, his anxious.

'If you want to put it like that, yes. So you hold my career in your hands.'

'Hardly, unless I want to damage my client.' Sarah watched his face, regretting the impression she had given. There was no need to be cruel; this man hadn't hurt her, like Bob. Softening her tone deliberately, she said: 'That was a kind thing to do, Terry. And brave, too - I couldn't have done it. Any more than I could have arrested her in the first place.'

'More foolish than brave, if it goes wrong. But I doubt if she'll try it again.'

A cool breeze blew off the river, fingering its way along Sarah's bare shoulders. She shivered. 'She feels very bitter, you know. Anyone would, in a situation like hers.'

Terry thought back, to the moment when he had confronted Kathryn on the roof garden outside David Kidd's flat. Would she have fired that shotgun, if he had handled it differently? Or had it all been just a bluff, a scream for help? 'Anyone can lose their mind, under pressure. But they don't always mean what they say.'

'Don't they? Who can tell?' That applies to so many things, Sarah thought, not just this. They fell silent for a moment, staring at the dark water flowing by. 'These are strange careers we pursue, in our different ways,' she resumed pensively. 'Look at the happy bridegroom in there, winning his first murder trial. You'd think he'd be proud, wouldn't you? But he's not. I think he's disgusted with the whole business.'

'Does he think Kidd was innocent?'

'No, that's just it, I don't think he does. Judging by the way he behaved in court, he thought his client was guilty as sin. But unless the man actually confessed to him, he had to defend him to the best of his ability. You hate us for it, I know, but that's our job.'

'Even policemen stretch the truth sometimes,' said Terry reflectively. 'Nobody's perfect.'

'No one except you and me, eh?' said Sarah lightly. 'And even you're a bit tarnished.' She glanced back into the ballroom where Savendra, flushed with pride, stood hand in hand with Belinda about make an announcement.

'Ladies and gentlemen, while the band take some well-needed refreshment, we are pleased to announce an addition to the programme. The groom's sister and cousins will treat us to an exhibition of Indian dancing, after which you are all invited to follow their lead in a simple Indian folkdance.'

Three girls in saris came to the front of the stage, and a tape recorder began to play Indian music. Sarah got up and took Terry's hand. 'Come on. No more shop, for this night at least. Let's watch this, and then you can squire me for the rest of the evening.'

'My pleasure.' That word - 'squire' - intrigued him; he wondered what she had in mind. She had always been a woman of surprises, able to switch moods in a moment. Her sideways mischievous glance for his reaction as she dragged him with her bare arms towards the ballroom might have been just a parody of the Indian dance, but on the other hand ...

She tugged his hand and he followed, his heart pounding strangely.

36. Wedding Night

THE CLUB David took Miranda to was all very well, and the music and the dancing made it easy enough to hide her revulsion for him. But it was impossible to talk except by yelling in your partner's ear, so after a while she pleaded hunger, and David suggested an Indian restaurant. Here, as they nibbled at the tray of yoghurts, pickles and popadums, she was able to begin the conversation which she really wanted to have.

'So, Dave, what do you do with yourself when you're not on safari? Sunline Tours said you hadn't been out with them for a while.'

'Oh, this and that. Import and export. African art, mostly.'

'Really? What about a regular girlfriend? Am I treading on someone's toes here?'

'Getting nosy, are we?' He dipped a piece of popadum in the yoghurt, popped it in his mouth, and stared at her coolly.

'Just interested. If I meet a guy I like to know where I stand.' She had pushed the shades to the top of her head now; they might look cool but she couldn't really see with them on.

'I had a girlfriend, yeah, but she's dead.'

'Oh? I'm sorry. What happened?'

'She killed herself. And I was tried for her murder.'

So it had started, at last. Miranda clicked the button in her pocket to start the mini recorder, and stretched her right arm, the one with the microphone sewn into her jacket sleeve, towards him across the table. David was watching her closely, perhaps wondering if she would get up and leave. Or maybe - she shuddered at the thought - he was proud of what he had done.

'What - you mean a real trial?' she asked, in fake astonishment. 'With lawyers and all that jazz?'

'With lawyers and all that jazz, yeah. Are you sure you want to hear this? I might be a murderer for all you know. She even looked a bit like you.'

No, don't say that, Miranda thought. I'm just a tourist journo from the

States. 'Tell me about it,' she said, faintly. He was grinning at her, for Christ's sake, as if he fancied himself as Hannibal Lecter. Dammit, the slime bag's enjoying this!

'You really want to know?'

'Sure, if it's a good story.'

So he began, while Miranda acted her role, and hoped the tape was working. It was okay to seem shocked, she thought, and even a little nervous and afraid - after all, what girl wouldn't be nervous of a man who'd been tried for murder? His words burned into her memory.

'Shelley was a sweet kid, but all messed up. She told me, night after night - how her Dad had these affairs, and her Mum kept on at her all the time to study like her sister, go to uni and get those exams which - you know, they're all crap really. All those dead poets and novelists and crap - I mean who gives a shit, really? If you want a book buy one, but don't write essays about it - what's the point? That's why she was coming to Kenya - to get away from it all.'

The half truths hurt, more than Miranda had expected. Shelley had been difficult at school - but in Miranda's view it was brilliance, not stupidity, that had caused her problems. Where Miranda had been diligent, industrious, well-organized, Shelley had been the opposite - impatient, chaotic, insolent. She cheeked the teachers and refused to do homework, but often it was because the task was boring, too tedious for her to dignify it with her attention. And then, just when everyone was exasperated with her, she would redeem herself with an essay or presentation that was brilliant - rainbow coloured where everyone else's was grey.

It was her illness that caused it: Miranda understood that now. But it was an illness that she shared with William Blake, Sylvia Plath, Winston Churchill. It wasn't an excuse for failure, as this moron seemed to believe, it was a spur to genius. That was why their mum had worked so hard with Shelley - because she'd really believed she was someone special.

'So what happened then?'

As they began the curry David elaborated on how Shelley had adored him. 'I was opening her eyes to things she'd never dreamed about,' he said. 'Stuff that really turned her on. I thought we were going places together.'

Miranda choked, and took a drink of water to cool her throat. Bastard, she thought. If only I'd been here, to protect her from this boasting!

David described the quarrel the week before Shelley's death, but to

Miranda's disappointment it was the same tale he'd told in court. At the end of the meal she was no further on than before.

When he asked her back to his flat she had a further decision to make. The way he phrased it was cunning. 'I know what you think when a guy says this, but really, it would mean a lot to me. Not for sex, but for someone to trust me again, you know, not be afraid. Just to treat me like a normal human again. Have a cup of coffee and go.'

It was quite the creepiest proposal she had ever had, and in any normal situation ten alarm bells would have been ringing in her head at once. But this wasn't a normal situation: she was stalking him, after all, and so far she had nothing to show. Perhaps in the flat he would tell a different story, provide the evidence she wanted. And it was where Shelley had died: irrespective of this little jerk before her, something inside Miranda needed to see it. Once, at least.

So she took the risk. He was a runt, after all - not half the size of her husband. She could manage him if necessary, she thought. They walked the short distance to his flat, and she climbed the stairs to the door where, she remembered from the trial, a priest had found this man bending at the keyhole, listening for something inside. Was that priest upstairs now? Would he hear if she screamed? Miranda shivered, and followed David in.

It was a long time since Terry had had the undivided attention of a woman his own age, and he felt uncertain how to handle it. Ever since he had first met Sarah Newby he had fantasized about her, wondering what she would be like to kiss, to undress ... now it seemed he might be about to find out. As the evening wore on she danced closely with him, hung on his arm as though they were a couple, drank two more glasses of champagne ...

Several times over the past year he had made gauche, unsuccessful attempts to take their relationship further, arranging pre-trial meetings in pub gardens or by the river rather than in her chambers or his battered, overcrowded office. On these occasions their conversations would extend into their family circumstances and history, the way they had reached the present stage in their lives, he through university and police college, she by fighting her way up from the slums after leaving school pregnant at fifteen. They had become friends as well as colleagues, comfortable in each other's company, gradually learning more about each other's separate lives.

But that was how they had remained until now: quite separate. She had a career which she cherished; a husband whose support had made it possible;

two children; and a pleasant home which she loved for its contrast with where she'd begun - in a damp, drug infested slum on the outskirts of Leeds. She had climbed a ladder out of that abyss; she had no intention of falling back down.

Sometimes he kidded himself that she fancied him, but his occasional clumsy attempts at flirtation had always been briskly knocked on the head. The idea of an affair, if it entered her mind at all, was rejected as a threat, something that would sweep away the pillars of marriage, career, and reputation that kept her safely above the chaos of the world she had left.

But tonight, it seemed, something had changed. For once it was not he hunting her, but she him. She touched his arm, hugged him close in the slow movements of the dance, smiled up at him seductively. Perversely, it made him uneasy. He knew she had quarrelled with her husband, but not the details of it. She was drinking steadily, too. The glasses of champagne came and went, her face was flushed, she pulled him energetically into wild, noisy line dances with the younger guests, while the older ones looked on indulgently, or made their excuses and left.

Midnight came, and bride and groom were escorted boisterously to their suite. As the band played something slow and romantic, Terry circled the floor with Sarah resting her head on his shoulder. He bent his head closer to hear what she said.

'You're a good friend,' she said. 'I've had a great time.'

'Me too.' He smiled, then, thinking perhaps she expected it, attempted a kiss. She turned away, so his lips brushed her cheek.

'Not here, Terry. Everyone's looking.'

As the band began to pack up, she led him out onto the lawn by the river. A waiter moved around picking up glasses, the moon peeped through clouds above the trees, the grass was damp with dew. She stumbled and clung to him, hobbling, then bent to adjust the strap of her shoe.

'Damn!' she swore. 'Look at that!' She held up the dangling broken heel in disgust. 'To think how much these things cost!'

'You can get it repaired, can't you?'

'Maybe. But for now ...' She bent to unfasten the other, and stood barefoot, both shoes hanging from her finger. She squirmed her toes in the moist grass. 'There! Back to nature. Emily would love it.'

They walked away from the windows, Sarah taking little skipping steps on the grass. Suddenly she ran round him in a circle, three times, as if he were a maypole. Then she stood, panting, and slid her arms slowly round his neck.

'Come here, my tall policeman.'

She reached up on tiptoe, and this time they kissed. They were tentative at first, her lips hot and warm, his nervous and firm. He felt big and clumsy in his shoes and suit, holding this woman barefoot, light and frail and suddenly passionate. She pulled back, and laughed.

'You don't mind, do you?'

For answer he kissed her again, this time for longer. The sound of the music ending, the clatter of the waiter putting glasses on his tray, did not disturb them, but as a group of other guests came out on to the lawn they drew apart. She twined her arm around his waist, still holding her shoes.

'Party's over, it seems,' he said. 'What now? Back to real life?'

'If you like. Or ... we could have one more drink. In my room.'

'What room?'

Seeing the expression on his face, she laughed, and squeezed his arm. 'I booked one, to avoid going home. Why shouldn't I? Emily's in London, Bob's away at his conference, and I'm too sozzled to drive. So, a night in a hotel. Come on, Terry. Why not?'

Sometimes, alone in bed at night, Terry had imagined things like this, but they never happened, not in reality. He was too busy with work and the children, and for years his mind had been filled with memories of his wife Mary. But she was dead, he told himself firmly, as they embraced once more in the lift. Long gone, never to return in this life. If Mary was watching surely she'd understand, and wouldn't begrudge him this - sex with a woman he'd admired and respected for years. A professional, mature woman who had chosen him because ... well, that was just it, it didn't bear thinking about too closely.

Because she fancied him, he wanted to believe - because ever since she'd met him she'd dreamed it was him making love to her, not that bearded lummox Bob. But of course Bob was the problem behind all of this. She's a married woman, she's drunk, she's using me for revenge on her husband. Added to which all her professional colleagues have seen us together. What if I screw not just her but her reputation too - will she thank me for that tomorrow?

He went to her room nonetheless. The temptation was strong and it was, after all, her choice. The feel of her body pressed against his, naked under the satin gown, drove all thought from his mind.

In her room she broke away, smiling, and opened the door of the mini bar. 'Vodka, whisky, gin - all at a thousand pounds a bottle. What do you fancy?'

'You,' he smiled. 'If you mean it.'

'In a minute. We've got all night, after all. And it seems perhaps I do need something ...' She poured herself a vodka and drank, the laughter in her eyes slightly shaded, as if scared of what she planned to do. 'You don't want one too?'

'No. Don't drink that. Sarah, come here.'

She knocked back the drink, and stepped unsteadily towards him. 'I need courage, you see.'

'I never thought you were short of that.' They kissed on the sofa, and somehow the straps on her gown came down over her shoulders exposing her breasts. He buried his face in them, kissing and fondling while she stroked his hair like a child. As he fumbled for the zip in the back of her dress, she suddenly pulled away. 'I'm sorry, I - don't feel quite ...'

'What's the matter?'

She stumbled to her feet in search of something - the bathroom. She collapsed to her knees in front of the toilet and the bowl echoed to the sound of her retching. She was crouched on her knees, her gown round her waist, her head in the toilet. He put one hand on her bare back, and stroked the hair out of her eyes with the other as the puking continued. Vodka, countless glasses of champagne, wine, wedding feast, all on their way to the sewage works at Naburn. He felt the cold sweat on her back under his hand.

'Oh God. I'm ... so sorry.'

'It doesn't matter.'

'Yes it does. I feel awful.' She reached up to flush the loo, and slumped on the tiles beside it, her hair hanging bedraggled round her face. 'Christ. What a mess.'

'You had too much to drink. Don't worry. It happens.'

'Not to me it doesn't. Oh God.' She bent urgently over the bowl for a second bout. When it was over she collapsed, weaker than before. He found some moist tissues by the basin and crouched beside her, wiping her face. She tugged fretfully at her dress, trying to cover her breasts, then shook her head feebly. 'God. What do I look like.'

'You look lovely.' Terry smiled gently. 'Look, why don't I get you a glass of water, and then run you a bath, or a shower if you prefer. I'll stay outside till I'm sure you're okay.'

'Yes. Water. Just a sip.' She took the glass, then clambered to her feet and stared at herself in the mirror, all dignity gone, while he ran the taps for the bath. 'Look, Terry, I'm so sorry, I wanted to but I don't think I could possibly ...'

'No, of course not. What do you think I am, Frankenstein?' He met her gaze in the mirror - draggled hair, death white face, shaking hand holding a glass of water over naked breasts no longer enticing but infinitely pathetic, and grinned. 'It's the thought that counts, you know.'

The faintest hint of an answering smile crossed her lips and was gone. She put down the glass, gave him a brief, sisterly hug, then pushed him urgently towards the door.

'Just go now, Terry, please. Just go. You're a nice man but I'm humiliated beyond belief already. I'll never live this down.'

He backed out of the sitting room. 'Just as long as you're okay?'

'I'll be fine. Terry, please. I'm so sorry.'

He kissed his fingers and touched them to her lips. 'Another time, perhaps?'

'Yes. Maybe. I don't know.' She closed her eyes, and when she opened them, he was gone.

37. Mickey Finn

THE FLAT was lighter, and more modern than Miranda had imagined it. There were wall lights in the living room, which he switched on, as though to dispel her fears. There were African masks on the wall, and framed photographs of lions and giraffes. There was a pale green sofa and armchair, a wide screen TV with DVD player, and a white coffee table with plastic flowers on it. Near the far window and patio door was a dining table and two chairs.

'Shall I take your jacket?' he asked, oddly polite.

'No, it's okay. I'm only staying for a minute, anyhow.' She shrugged her hands into the pockets of the leather jacket and strode across the room, staring about her with unfeigned curiosity. So this was where it happened!

'Up to you. Black or white?' he asked, hovering at the door of a clean, well-appointed kitchen just to the left of the short entrance lobby.

'Black, please. One sugar.' There were two doors out of the living room. Through one, to the right, she saw a double bed, with a shirt and pair of jeans strewn across it. The other door was in the left-hand corner of the room near the window. The bathroom. She touched the handle tentatively with her hand and pushed the door open. It was shadowy inside, whitish tiles on the floor, a decorated blind pulled down over a window, a bath ... Resolutely, she pulled the cord. A light came on and a fan started up in the ceiling.

'Need the loo? Help yourself.' He had come out of the kitchen and stood close behind her. Really he was two or three feet away, but any distance felt uncomfortably close in here.

'No, thanks. I just wanted to see ...'

'Where it happened. Yeah, well, that's it.' He sighed, a decent imitation of grief. 'Right there, in that bath. That's where I found her when I came in.'

'But ... you said she cut her wrists, didn't you? How did she get the knife?' Miranda re-activated the mini recorder in her jacket.

'She must have got out of the bath, walked to the kitchen and picked it up, then got back in the bath to kill herself. Then I picked up the knife when I found her. That's how my fingerprints must have got on it. That's all I can think.'

'It seems a long way.' Her voice trembled slightly, but that was okay. Any girl's would, in a set up like this. He grinned, enjoying her fear.

'You're a tough chick, I'll give you that. What do you think happened?'

'How should I know? I wasn't there.'

'No. Well, neither were the jury, but they said I was innocent.' The kettle boiled, and he turned back into the kitchen, busying himself with cups. He set two down on the coffee table. Cups with saucers, she noticed, and spoons. 'Here, sit down. Yours is black, mine has the cream.'

She sipped her coffee and looked around. 'Have you lived here long?'

'Three years. It took me a while to get the place right.'

'And you shared it with this girl. What was her name - Sheila?'

'Shelley.' He grinned. 'She looked a bit like you, in a way.'

'Really?' Not that again. Just a clumsy attempt to scare me, she told herself. He's enjoying this, the spook. She sipped the coffee and searched for a question to take her further. 'So, don't you feel guilty, about her death?'

'I would if I'd killed her, but I didn't.' He shrugged. 'So ...'

'It would be a natural reaction, though. I mean, you were here with her.'

'Are you accusing me?'

'No, of course not, I ...' Outside the window, the deep bell of the Minster clock tolled twelve, interrupting her train of thought. She drained her coffee, seeking stimulation to clear her mind. She had got herself in exactly the position she had aimed for, and yet she had nothing, so far. He was just playing, spooking her for fun. And all the time she had to maintain this pretence of an innocent American, who had never heard any of this before. The tape spun, but recorded nothing useful. Perhaps her whole plan was misconceived.

'Why all these questions?' He leaned forward, watching her intently. She stared back, thinking, his eyes weren't that big before, were they? Oh God, they're slipping around ...

'I think I'd better go.' She stood up, but as she did so the coffee cup crashed to the floor. How did that happen? She bent to pick it up, and strangely, without understanding quite how, found herself sitting on the table, the cup a long way off. A voice somewhere, not unlike hers but much more brainless and girly, began to laugh. 'This is crazy. Get it yourself, will ya?'

'You'll be safer on the sofa. Here, pet, this way.' She felt his hands slide under her arms, cupping her breasts as he pulled her back. She tried to resist, but her limbs wobbled like jelly. Nothing seemed to be working. 'You'll be more comfy without that heavy jacket, now, won't you? And the rest of these clothes too.'

The ceiling, it seemed to Miranda vaguely, was more interesting than she had realised at first. In fact, it was probably the answer to the entire puzzle, if only she could remember the question. Whatever it was, this ceiling was fascinating. She had never understood before how these swirls of Artex were really continents and galaxies, that moved in such amusing ways.

She giggled as he stripped off her clothes. When his face came close to hers she turned aside, concentrating on the wonderful ceiling. The sound of his voice was wonderful, intricate, a surreal pattern of noise vibrant with vivid colours but devoid of all meaning. So only the faithful machine in her jacket recorded what he said.

'Now you can let yourself go, sweetie. No inhibitions, and no memory in the morning. At least I hope not, not like Shelley. She woke up too soon, but you - you've had twice as much. So just relax, darling, and enjoy ...'

There was a waterfall outside the window. Or was it a fountain? The sound rose and fell, splashing and trickling and setting off rainbows of colour in her mind - sparkling crimson, aquamarine, viridian, and black. Ouch! the black ones hurt - there was another, a little hammer thumping the inside of her skull, like a woodpecker trying to get out. Yes, that was it - birds were taking over the world. She sat up abruptly, rubbing her skull to still the knocking inside, then winced at another loud black thump from the mighty church clock. She shook her head and the kaleidoscopic images in her mind fell into a clearer pattern. She understood now - she was in a flat, behind the Minster. The sound wasn't waterfalls or fountains - it was birdsong, in the trees under the wall.

The room was light; it must be morning. She stood up, and the hammers inside her skull thumped so hard that she felt dizzy and her eyes went blind for a time. When sight returned, a soft woollen rug fell to the floor around her feet and she saw she was naked. Dimly, she tried to recall why she was here but no reason answered.

Her mouth was parched and sandy, her limbs ached. If she could find something to drink and paracetamol, that might help. There was a kitchen. Clutching the rug around herself, she tottered into the kitchen and saw clean tiles, cupboards, a cooker and fridge, but all in unfamiliar places. Had she been here before? She couldn't remember. There was a glass, anyway, and orange juice in the fridge.

Paracetamol? Nowhere. Coffee, she thought, that might help, strong sweet coffee. She found a kettle and switched it on, spooned coffee into a mug, searched for sugar. Whose kitchen was this? A face came into her mind, and swam away again. Not a nice face. It was talking, laughing at her as it vanished, with words she couldn't decipher.

The kettle boiled. She poured water into the mug, hot droplets scalding her naked arm so that she jumped. It was all wrong, to be here like this. In a moment she would remember and sort it out. Where was the sugar? There it was, in a jar with *Sugar* on the side. She tugged the wooden lid which seemed to be stuck, then - whoosh! - sugar sprayed everywhere, all over the side, crunching under her toes on the floor. What the hell, spoon some into the coffee anyway, stir it. And the white pills? What about them?

She sipped the scalding coffee, and studied the white pills in the mounds of spilt sugar on the side. Had they been there before? Surely not - they'd come out of the jar with the sugar. She scraped around in the sugar jar, found some more in the bottom. She picked one up and studied it, searching for what it might mean. As she did so the face swam back into her mind. A sneering face, laughing at her, saying something she couldn't quite grasp. But it had to do with the pills, she felt sure.

Why am I here, like this? She sipped more coffee and her brain began to clear. Shelley's boyfriend, that was it! He killed her and I came here. Oh God. He gave me coffee too. Not this coffee but ...

She poked at the pills with her finger. This is it, of course, this is why I feel like this. I must keep some, find out what they are. But he'll come in, she thought suddenly, he'll see I've got them. Then what? Christ! Maybe he gave these to Shelley. Think what he did to her!

Urgently, she scooped as much of the sugar as she could back into the jar, pushing the pills to one side. Then she found a dustpan and brush under the sink and tried to clean the floor. As she did so the rug fell off, leaving her naked again. She emptied the pan in a bin, drank some more coffee, picked up the pills and the rug, and wove her way unsteadily back into the living room. Her clothes were strewn all around the sofa on the floor. The horrible African mask on the wall glared as she unzipped a pocket in her leather jacket, stuffed the pills inside, and sat down, exhausted.

The hammers in her head throbbed with renewed energy, the birds outside the window resumed their waterfall impressions. She felt a powerful urge to sleep. But that's no good, I've got to get out of here now. This is a dangerous place, Shelley died here. She saw her panties on the floor, put them on, and as she did so she realised she was wet, sticky between the legs. How can that have happened? Bruce isn't here, he's four thousand miles away, this is all wrong. If it wasn't Bruce, who was it?

She found her bra and struggled with the clasp like an insuperable chess problem. Only when she stopped thinking and let her trembling fingers do what they done a thousand times before did it work. It was the same with the buttons of her blouse - if she looked at them they became alien Mensa puzzles with no solution, but her fingers remembered.

What had happened to her mind? She was trying not to think about how her shoes were put together or which way round they went when the bedroom door opened and a man came in. Not a man she knew or liked. She shrank back on the sofa, hugging her knees under her chin.

'Hi there, sweetie! Not thinking of leaving, are you?'

She considered the words and didn't like what they meant. He was naked under a blue silk dressing gown that hung open all down the front. His face was darker with stubble than the face in her dreams. He was her sister's murderer, she remembered that now. Was this how Shelley's last moments had been?

'Go away. Who are you?'

'Don't you recognize me?' His grin broadened. He took a step closer. 'You liked me last night, sweetie. Liked me a lot.' He sat on the sofa beside her and put his hand on her knee. She shrank further into the corner, feeling the shameful stickiness on the inside of her thighs, hugging her arms across her stomach to protect herself. 'So what now?'

Now you kill me, she thought. Just like you killed Shelley.

'Let me go, please. I want to go home.'

'Home? Where's that? Back to America?'

'Yes. Please. I don't feel well.'

'I thought you liked me, you muppet. You did last night. Want to do it again?'

She shook her head silently. All the strength she had left went into clutching her knees tight to her chest, a little ball of fear. But the hammers still beat inside her skull and her arms shook feebly. She felt weak as a baby.

There's nothing I can do, she thought, whatever he wants I can't stop him. If only he'll give me time.

'I'd like breakfast.'

He stared, then laughed aloud, gloating at the shivering figure beside him. 'Oh, you'd like room service, would you? Orange juice, boiled egg, slices of toast?'

She nodded, meeting his smile with what she hoped was one of her own. 'Yes. Please. I'll feel better then.'

He leaned forward, his face an inch from her own. 'You know what? You stink.'

Here it comes, she thought. This is the end.

He stood up, drew his dressing gown together, covering himself. 'Tell you what. I'll make the breakfast, you have a bath.' Again, a mocking smile. He walked - strutted almost - into the kitchen. 'Towels in the airing cupboard next to the bedroom. Go on, clean yourself up.'

'I don't want a bath.' She said the words so softly, she scarcely heard them herself. There was no way she was going into that bathroom. Not unless he dragged her in there with his hands around her neck. Was that what he'd done to Shelley? She stayed in her protective ball, relaxing the arms around her knees slightly. To her astonishment, she heard him light the gas on the cooker, clattering plates and cups. She heard him press down the toaster, smelt the toast.

Will he let me escape? Very slowly and carefully, she lowered her feet to the floor.

'Go on. Have a bath. I told you where the towels are.'

'I ...' She got to her feet, stumbled to the kitchen door. 'I've got a headache. Have you got any paracetamol?'

'In the bathroom cabinet. Help yourself.'

Shit. 'Okay. I'll, um ... then I'll have breakfast.'

He grabbed her right shoulder, pushed his face into hers. In his hand was a knife, she saw - table knife with butter on it, no harm there. 'Wash yourself. That's what girls do in the mornings. Or weren't you brought up right?'

'All right.' If you can't escape, humour them, she remembered from some self-defence course at journalism school. Defiance just provokes more aggression. She found a towel, and crossed the living room like a girl walking to her death. He was still in the kitchen. She entered the bathroom and bolted the door behind her. Now what? There in front of her was the bath that Shelley had died in. All clean and white with little fish and seaweed on the tiles and blind.

Her head throbbed, a tide of nausea rose in her throat. She fell to her knees in front of the loo, and retched. Her head felt like it would split apart. As she crouched waiting for the second wave which she could feel building inside her, she remembered how her mother used to hold a cool flannel across her forehead at such times, and wait quietly until the fit passed. Such a small thing to do, such a world of comfort. She vomited again. The door rattled behind her.

'Are you okay in there?'

She struggled to her feet and flushed the bowl. 'Yeah, I'm okay. I've been sick.'

'Open the door if you need help.'

'No, don't come in, please. Make the breakfast. I'll be better soon.'

To her relief he went away. She opened the cabinet above the washbasin, found some paracetamol, pressed two capsules out of the foil, and washed them down with water from the tap. Then she stared into the mirror on the back of the cabinet doors.

The face that looked out at her was pale and terrified. Her freckles stood out on the white skin, her eyes were huge and dark and smudged with mascara. She was puzzled to see her hair so short and spiky and blonde, then remembered how she had restyled it to deceive the monster outside. The mirror reflected her fear back at her, making it worse. Trying to encourage herself, she wrenched her features into the shape of a smile. Not much of a smile, it looked pretty awful, but better than the panic stricken rabbit face before.

She splashed water on her face until a trace of colour came into her cheeks. You can do this, kid, she told herself, you can get out of this alive; you must for Shelley and Mum. You've proved what a monster he is, get out now and you can do something later, get your revenge.

With trembling hands she undid the bolt and stepped into the living room. On the table by the window he had laid two places with orange juice, boiled eggs, toast and coffee.

'Wash yourself properly?'

'Yes. I found the paracetemol. That looks great.' She picked up her jeans from the floor and put them on. He sat in the blue silk dressing gown, watching her curiously.

'Been sick, have you? Probably drank too much last night.'

No, that's not it, Miranda thought. Her mind was still fuddled but things were becoming clearer. She slumped into the chair opposite him and sipped the orange juice cautiously. He gave me those pills and raped me, she thought. I can't remember anything but he says I liked it. Is he mad, or does he really believe that?

'Have an egg. They're free range.'

He murders my sister and cooks me breakfast. This is so strange. She pulled the egg towards her and tried to crack its top with a spoon held in wobbly fingers. Those white pills - has he found them? She darted a guilty glance at the leather jacket on the sofa, then dipped her spoon in the yolk.

'This is good.'

'I like to treat my girls well. Encourages them to come back.' He smiled across the table at her, a parody of charm. 'Will you show me the article, when you've written it?'

'What article?' She gazed at him, bemused. What new madness is this?

'Your travel article, about the safaris. I'd like to see what you write.'

'Oh yes, that.' She remembered now, he thought she was a journalist. Does he think I don't know what he's done? 'I don't know, I ...'

'Bring it and show me. Why not? We could do this again.' He leaned forward and squeezed her knee. 'I could take you for a drive, show you a bit of the country before you go back to the States. Ever sat in a Lotus, honey? If not, you haven't lived.'

38. Morning After

WAKING SUDDENLY in the hotel, Sarah moved swiftly to the bathroom. She'd got rid of most things last night but her stomach wasn't convinced. She retched dryly and then as she got to her feet a vice tightened around both sides of her skull at once and she groaned. She poured a glass of water, averting her eyes in disgust from the cruel huge mirror in the hotel bathroom, and stumbled back to bed.

So this is it, she thought, this is how it all ends. Seventeen years of marriage and study and struggle all wasted, for a fuck in a hotel bedroom that didn't even happen, oh my God what did happen though? He saw me puking in the loo, I'll never live this down, never!

She fumbled in her bag for Nurofen and gulped down three, you shouldn't do that but then you shouldn't get pissed either and offer yourself to random men just because your husband's behaved like a total shit and ruined everything you ever had; but he can't do that, can he? He can't because I won't let him. This was supposed to be my way of teaching him a lesson and having a little fun but the only one who's learning a lesson here is me. The lesson is don't do this you're too old and ugly and can't hold your drink. God that man must be laughing at me now and Savvy too and all his guests - how will I ever dare step out of this room?

And as for fun ... Sarah lay very still with one arm across her eyes while the throbbing in her head subsided by infinitesimal amounts which suggested she would be well and healthy again by the time the sun had swallowed up the solar system and disappeared down a black wormhole in space.

Aeons later, she woke with a dry mouth and the faint memory of a headache. Cautiously, she sat up and looked around. Her ball gown was strewn across a sofa, her kitten heels lay broken on the floor. Sunlight was streaming through the curtains. She got up and peered outside. A rowing eight slid past on the river, their blades making little rainbows in the sunlight.

Savendra must be here with Belinda, she thought, and the families who stayed. Do I dare face them at breakfast? What on earth will they think? I suppose it depends on how much they saw and imagined. If they care about me at all.

She pondered the problem as she showered and dressed. She could slink away like a guilty tramp but how would that help? She'd probably meet someone in reception anyway and now her stomach was totally empty she was hungry again. She'd paid for the hotel breakfast so she might as well have it. I'll need something before I go home.

She glanced at her mobile, wondering whether to ring Bob, but decided against it. Let him wait; he's at his conference with Stephanie, he hasn't rung me. Anyway this can't be fixed over the phone. For Emily's sake, if for no one else, we've got to stop behaving like a pair of teenagers and sort this out properly.

She finished her make up, and opened the door. To find, outside in the hall, a large bunch of flowers, gift-wrapped with a ribbon and a card. Which read, when she opened it:

Thanks for a wonderful evening. Still friends, I hope. Terry.

Miranda slumped in the back seat of the taxi as it crossed Lendal Bridge. The pavements were full of hurrying people, heads down, immersed in their own interests. Maybe I shouldn't go home, she thought. Why not ask this taxi driver to take me to the police?

'Had a long night of it, did you, love?'

'Yes. With my boyfriend.' Christ, she was lying already! What did he mean by a question like that? He looked a decent enough man, mid thirties, clean shirt, short hair, pot belly, probably a wife and kids at home - what did she look like to him? Slumped in the back seat of his cab with spiky hair, bleary unmade up face, leather jacket - like a hooker with a habit to feed, perhaps?

'Off to work this morning then, is he?'

'Yes. Look, I'm sorry, I don't want to talk.'

'Suit yourself.' He turned up the radio and concentrated on the road. Boyfriend, she thought, that's a laugh. So why did I say it? Because the truth's too difficult, too messy, too dreadful altogether. What will I tell Mum when I get home? I'll have to say something but I can't - even a fraction of the truth will hurt her badly. What time is, it? Ten. Pray God she'll be at work, I can't talk about this now, not to anyone.

Who could possibly understand?

She dozed off until the driver woke her to ask for directions to the house, which clearly surprised him when he saw it. Not the sort of place junkies usually live, she thought wryly. Her mother wasn't there, thank God; presumably out at work. She found the key under a plant pot, stumbled inside and collapsed on the hall floor. The collie, having seen off the taxi, licked her face in an ecstasy of welcome and worry. It was an old dog, which had known her all its life. She hugged it back hungrily.

'Oh Tess,' she murmured. 'What have I done?'

But a dog couldn't solve this problem. She dragged herself upstairs to the bathroom, adjusting the shower head to massage until it stung, little hard rods of water drilling into her skin and tearing away his smell, his slime, every trace of where he had been. She drenched herself with shampoo and conditioner and lemon-scented shower gel and stood there until the hot water tank was drained, and then she ran it cold. She stepped out glowing and clean, wrapped herself in towels, and dried her poor short hair until it was soft and smooth and all the spikiness was gone. Then she made up her face until it looked, well, if not like a model then human at least. More like a younger version of her mother, if truth be told, with this short fair hair, than the face she was used to. But nothing like the girl of last night.

So what now, she thought, staring into the mirror at her wide, shadowed eyes. Do I go to the police and cry rape, having scrubbed all the evidence away? Well, they could test my blood I suppose, that might still show traces of whatever he slipped me in the coffee. I can show them these pills. But then what? If there's a trial some public schoolboy in a wig will ask me why I went to see my sister's murderer - no, they won't call him that, will they? - my sister's boyfriend in the first place. Was it because I fancied him, like she did? That's what he said, last night. Was I jealous, did I want him for myself? Or was I trying to compensate him for the trauma he suffered when Shelley thoughtlessly killed herself in his bath?

It won't work, the jury will let him off, just like they did before. And it's not just me that will suffer. Mum and Dad will be humiliated all over again and Bruce too if he hears about this. God knows what he'd do. Probably fly over and tear the bastard limb from limb.

Which is what should happen.

Only none of us should be hurt, not any more. This guy's burrowed into our family like a grub, he's eating us from within. Mum's right, he's got to be destroyed.

So how?

She took the tape from the leather jacket and slipped it into the player in her bedroom. I may as well hear it, she thought grimly. If only I could prove that he killed her, and drugged her first with these pills, that would be the thing. The one thing that might do some good.

She sat, staring out at a tractor peacefully working in a field the far side of the river. She listened to what David had said and done to her last night, and thought about what had happened this morning.

It didn't lessen the pain, but it gave her an idea.

Come back, he had said, let me take you for a drive in my car.

Part Four

Retribution

39. A Walk in the Woods

MIRANDA'S FIRST resolve was to hide what had happened from her parents. When they came home from work they were bound to ask where she had been last night and with her mind bruised with shock it would take enormous resolve to say nothing. But that was what was needed. However much she longed for comfort she must stay silent. No running to her mother's skirts, not any more. Nothing to suggest that she planned to do anything other than return to America with her grief. Nothing to involve her parents at all.

If anything was done, it would be done by her alone.

She put on her mother's old wax jacket and went for a walk to put colour in her cheeks. It was a blustery day; cloud shadows chased each other across the fields. The trees bent and swayed with the wind, and every now and then flashes of sunlight darted from behind the clouds. It was the sort of day she and Shelley would have gone for a wild gallop on their ponies, leaping ditches, tearing across fields, leaning into the wind on hilltops, coming home muddy, glowing, exhausted. Their mother would make them tea and toast, and then they would slump on the sofa attempting to clean their tack but, as often as not, falling fast asleep in the fuggy indoor air.

It had been a good childhood, Miranda thought, as she walked away from the river towards the woods. Wild and innocent. We never feared paedophiles or rapists or any of the horrors parents worry about today. When we did imagine monsters in the dusk Mum told us they weren't real, nothing could hurt us here.

Her feet led her away from the river towards the woods where they had ridden as children. It was a wide area, several hundred acres transected by dirt roads, footpaths, and the narrow trails of deer, badgers and foxes. She and Shelley had spent hours here, riding, picnicking, playing hide and seek, watching the wild duck on the lakes and marshes.

She reached the deserted, overgrown strips of concrete which were all that remained of the wartime RAF airfield. Were they monsters, the men who flew from here to kill Germans, thousands each night, burnt to a crisp by fire bombs? No, they got medals. They were ordinary men just like grandad. They were killing others to defend their own families.

She found the deserted reservoir and stood for a while staring at it. Spilt aircraft fuel and oil from the runways would drain in here, she'd been told, and float on the surface until it was skimmed off, to avoid polluting the land. If Shelley hadn't saved her she'd be an oily skeleton mouldering at the bottom of this in the mud. She shivered, turning up the collar of the wax jacket she'd borrowed from her mother, and pulling a pair of gloves from its pocket.

There was a barbed wire fence around the reservoir now, put up by the farmer after the accident. But it was a flimsy construction, less of a barrier than the brambles that grew all around. She rested her gloved hands on a post and rocked it to and fro, widening the hole until she could lift it out by hand. She did the same to another, laid the fence on the ground, and stepped over, looking down into the dark, dirty waters where she had so nearly died. The panic of those moments came back to her, the splashing and neighing of her terrified pony, the fear of drowning, the overwhelming love and gratitude she had felt to Shelley for hauling her out. It could all have happened yesterday.

She turned towards home, listening to the wind roaring in the trees above, revelling in the vast loneliness. Yet these woods had not always been empty, she knew. As children she and Shelley had imagined kings and knights, outlaws and sheriffs fighting here. Murder and rape were not new inventions. She wondered how many bodies lay under the leafmould beneath her feet, unknown and untraced, killed by ordinary people driven beyond endurance by their enemies. Real people with families, just like Shelley and me.

She tramped grimly back across the fields towards her parent's house. The sun was setting behind a stand of beech trees on a tumulus to the west, sending long bars of shadow across the countryside. Miranda stood awhile, watching the rooks soaring and diving above the trees, croaking hoarsely as the sun sank behind a purple band of cloud. She felt strong here and clean, as she had not done in town.

Strong, but very lonely. She stood alone in the gathering dusk, until she saw the lights of her mother's car on the road below, coming home from work.

When Sarah got home she arranged the flowers in front of the fireplace and launched herself into a storm of housework. By mid afternoon her kitchen and bathroom were gleaming, every floor was hoovered, every surface dusted and polished. The house reeked of bottled pine, and Sarah stood in the living room, a huge pile of shirts, trousers, and teeshirts on the armchair behind her - crumpled ones on the left, ironed and folded ones on the right. Steam hissed ferociously from the iron in her hand.

Sarah had never reacted tamely to defeat and she didn't intend to do so now. The problem she was trying to work out, though, was exactly what victory she wanted. In the neat immaculate room the flowers glowed wild, radiant, extravagant; her face flushed with pleasure and shame when she looked at them. Yet she had disposed of Terry's card, had not rung to thank him. What would she say when she did? He'd screwed up the investigation, of course, but it wasn't that. Where did she want this to lead?

She and Bob had several divorced friends, and each separation, so far as Sarah could see, had brought misery. Bitterness, tears, hassle, house sale, hardship - usually a dramatic, immediate and sustained collapse in both partners' standard of living. Each time she'd thought why? How can anyone be so foolish, fail to see what they're losing?

Her own distant divorce didn't count: they'd been children themselves, penniless, and Kevin an unredeemed thug. But the friends who split in later life had substantial investments in houses, children and careers; everything that Sarah thought marriage was about. And yet they had thrown it all up. Traumatized wives and husbands had sat here, dabbing their eyes, telling her their stories, and dropping damp tissues in the fireplace where Terry's flowers now blazed. And each time, Sarah realised now, she'd missed the point. She hadn't understood why it happened.

She understood the bitterness, the loss, the betrayal well enough. What she hadn't understood before, was why anyone would put themselves through it.

People left their families not because they felt bored or badly treated or couldn't stand their partner's dirty underwear; that was only a condition in which break-up could grow - not even a necessary condition, perhaps. The reason they left - totally destroying everything they'd built up for so many years - was because they fell in love with somebody else.

It was as strong and simple as that. Love was a disease, as it said in the books, it made people so drunk or happy or totally self-absorbed that they smashed things up like teenagers.

I could be like that, Sarah thought, gazing at her flowers while the steam hissed from her iron. If I hadn't been sick last night I would have made love to Terry for certain, I wanted to so much and he did too and he's such a lithe, easy dancer and where would it lead? First a one-night stand, then a series of hurried, secret meetings, always dreading discovery and exposure. That's not what I want - after all he's free, a widower with two little girls, I could care for them too, and Simon and Emily, well, they're almost grown up, they could come and visit my new family, it would be full of life and love and colour and ...

'Hi, Mum. We're back.'

A pair of grubby, smelly, paint-sprayed global protesters shambled into her living room and collapsed in happy exhaustion on the sofa. Her seventeen year old daughter Emily was wearing some sort of ex-army battledress fatigue, torn and ripped and covered with pink and purple day-glo painted slogans - for extra camouflage, no doubt - and her hair, Sarah saw, was bright green. Beside her, his fingers locked through hers, lounged Larry, with his wispy beard and ponytail, in black jeans, combat boots, and ancient leather jacket. Both young people's faces shone with simple happiness.

'Did you see the demo on telly?'

'It was tremendous. Three hundred thousand, the pigs say, but it must have been nearer a million. There were banners and music everywhere ...'

'You couldn't hardly move ...'

'People from all over Europe - China even!'

'And huge balloons in Trafalgar Square!'

Sarah had given little thought to this since the quarrel with Bob last week. She had seen the TV news briefly in the hotel, but had forgotten what the protest was about. It looked like fun, though, and they were back safely - that was all that mattered. For a while she carried on ironing, asking questions and listening to their cheerful responses, then they made themselves something to eat and took it up to Emily's bedroom where the music started booming away.

Bob came in, looking shattered. She switched off the iron, all the clothes in a neat pile, and boiled the kettle for tea. 'How did it go?'

'Oh, fine, I suppose.' He slumped at the table wearily, listening to the sound from upstairs. 'Emily's back, I see.'

'Yes, they've been telling me about it. They had a great time.'

'I'm glad someone did.'

She made two mugs of tea and joined him, studying his face carefully. He looked drawn, weary, sad. '*You* didn't, you mean?'

'Not really, no.' He sipped the tea gratefully. 'Oh, the conference was all right - boring, of course, but then administration always is.'

'And the hotel?'

'Fine.' He helped himself to a biscuit, avoiding her watching eyes. So it's Stephanie, she thought vindictively. Well, serve the bastard right. But then ...

His eyes met hers, then looked nervously away. 'We, um, said some rather unpleasant things yesterday, at the wedding ...'

'*You* did, you mean.'

'We both did, Sarah, be fair. I've been thinking about that over the weekend. I ... probably shouldn't have said what I did.'

'Sorry, I think is the word you're looking for,' she prompted, when no more followed. But then I said those things too. Worse, probably, last week.

'Yes, all right, sorry then.' He looked up, searching for forgiveness. 'I wish I'd stayed at the wedding now. Did you have a good time?'

'Yes, pretty good. I danced with Terry Bateson. He sent me flowers afterwards. Look - in that vase.' So there, she thought, I've said it. No concealment necessary.

'Your admirer, you mean?' He gazed at the extravagant, expensive bouquet, the painful thought clear on his face: a woman doesn't get flowers like that from a man unless ...

'My admirer, yes. He was very kind and attentive.'

'Sarah, you didn't ...?'

'How did it go with Stephanie, Bob?' There was a time, Sarah thought, that I looked up to this man. He was older than me, wiser, endlessly patient and attentive. If it wasn't for him I wouldn't have anything I value. Not this house, not these children, nor my career either. I could never have even begun studying without Bob's support. He was my rock, my foundation, my safe haven. He was never forceful or aggressive, but I never wanted him to be; I could do that for myself. Yet I always respected him, until now. Something's changed: perhaps he feels age creeping up, or the world's altered and he doesn't understand it any more.

Or he fell in love with someone else and broke the thing that mattered.

Either way this isn't a man to look up to; it's one who's uncertain, hurt, afraid. Afraid of me. The foundations of our marriage are shifting; I don't need him any more, I could leave if I choose. And I might, too.

'Stephanie ... oh, she had a great time, I think. As far as I could tell.'

'But not with you, Bob, you mean?'

'Not with me, no.' He heaved a long, weary sigh. 'There were several younger men there, Sarah, and she spent a great deal of time with one of those. Wrapped around him, in fact; it was quite embarrassing. And, er, rather painful, I must admit. It showed me what a fool I've been for the past few weeks. It must have been painful for you, too, I should think.'

He gazed at her like a man waking from a dream. But Sarah wasn't about to forgive him just yet. I could make him crawl, she thought. Will that help, or make things worse? How could I stay with a man I despised?

'Painful?' she said, 'Yes, it was. But what's sauce for the gander, Bob, might just be sauce for the goose as well.'

'Don't say that, Sarah, please.' Bob glanced at the flowers. 'Don't start something that might go wrong.'

'Why not? You did.' Even when I threw up, she thought, my lover was a perfect gentleman. I could ring him now, if I dared; leave Bob here, show him how much it hurts.

Bob reached across the table for her hand, his fingers warm from the tea, his grip firm. 'I'm not going to plead, if that's what you want.' Sarah considered pulling away but didn't. Their hands knew each other, after all; had done for eighteen years. 'I've been a fool, I see that now. But I could never have left you for Stephanie, that wasn't what it was about, at all.'

'Oh, so she was just a bit of fun, was she? A shag on the side?'

He winced. 'You always had a cruel way with words, Sarah. But if I wanted that it never happened. Never will now.'

Poor feeble sheep, Sarah thought. But then who am I to talk? Neither of us seem to have the gift for adultery.

But if I want to, I will. Next time. If there is a next time.

'Ooops, sorry!' Emily poked her head into the kitchen, saw her parents holding hands across the table, staring earnestly into each other's eyes. 'I'm just going into town for a while with Larry, okay? Be back before ten.'

'All right,' Sarah said. 'Take care.'

'Will do, Mum, Dad. Aged parents.' Emily beamed at them, Larry's arm draped carelessly round her shoulder. 'Behave yourselves now, while we're out.'

'We'll try,' said Bob. 'We'll try really hard.'

40. Flight Plan

'IT'S A pity you had to leave so soon,' Andrew Walters said.

'I know, Dad, but I have to think of Bruce as well. And Sophie. Look, Dad, I've been here a week longer than I expected, but I have to go home some time and ... I can't bring Shelley back to life, can I?'

'No. No one can do that, sadly. Or get revenge, as your mother seems to want.'

Miranda looked out of the car window as the high, bare hills of the Pennines flashed by in the early morning light. It wasn't a line of conversation she wanted to encourage, and besides, her father needed all his attention for the driving. Since the trial he had been sunk in gloom, sitting alone in his study when he was at home, but frequently out of the house, either walking the dog or God knows where - most likely with the mistress her mother had told her about. Well, she was welcome to him, Miranda thought; he was the shadow of the father she remembered, a broken, exhausted, incommunicative man barely able to stumble through everyday tasks, let alone give support to his wife and daughter. And her mother was little better. Since her arrest she had seemed defeated, more like a child than the forceful mother she had once been. The verdict had diminished both parents, kicking them violently down the slippery slope towards second childhood. The only responsible adult left in the family was Miranda herself.

Responsible. Miranda smiled bitterly to herself. The plan that obsessed her now was the opposite of that. I'm a mother with a child and a husband - those are my responsibilities. Not this, not ...

But it was a perfect plan, and it filled her mind, to the exclusion of everything else. It had come to her like that, clear and simple and deadly, at four o'clock in the morning. For hours she had tossed and turned, consumed by fury and frustration, knowing what she wanted to do but unable to work out how. And then suddenly there it was, all the details exact and precise, the result beautifully satisfying, the escape route certain, the revenge - if it all worked out as it surely must - so sweet she could taste it on her tongue.

It was risky, surely, but possible - more than possible, certain, if only she made no mistake - and if she achieved it, as she surely would if she kept her nerve, then no one else need ever know. And that would make it perfect.

But first she had to attend to each detail, one by one. And this trip with her father was the first.

In the car park at Manchester airport she hunted up a trolley while he lifted her suitcase from the boot. At the check-in desk she turned to wish him goodbye. 'I'll send you a text when I get there, Dad, all right? And if you want to ring me use the mobile, all right, or better still, send a text, it's easier. You know how you and Mum are always getting the time difference wrong and waking us up in the middle of the night. I'll be jet-lagged, I'll need my sleep.'

'All right, love. Just so long as we know you're safe.'

'I will be. But I may be in a hotel in New York, if the flights are all full to Wisconsin. If you ring too soon you'll upset Bruce, you know what he's like.'

'Okay, love. Take care. You're all we have now, you know.'

'I know, Dad.' He hugged her tightly, tears in his eyes. Then she walked away, through the security check, into the international lounge. Her father went for a coffee until the flight was called, then went outside onto the viewing platform to wave as the plane took off.

Entering Gillygate two days later, David Kidd crossed to the sunny side of the street. It was only a hundred yards to his flat, but after so many months locked up on remand, the warmth of the sun on his skin was important to him. Every little sensation - the roar of a bus, the scent of bread from a bakery, the chime of the Minster clock - helped him to savour his freedom. It was a freedom he didn't intend to lose; prison and the trial had scared him, and the rational part of him knew that next time - and there was bound to be a next time - he might not be so lucky.

Entering his flat, he saw the little red light flashing, which meant he had a message. He picked up the phone and dialled 1571. To his surprise, he recognized the voice of the American girl who'd come to his flat the other night. He hadn't expected to hear from her again, but here she was - speaking from a train station or airport, to judge by the background noise.

'Hi. It's me. David, it was sweet of you to make me breakfast that morning and I left rather suddenly, I'm afraid, without thanking you properly. I think I was a bit woozed probably, had too much to drink. Anyway, I enjoyed our evening together and I've got a draft of my article to show you. So wondered if we could go out again, maybe in that fancy car you mentioned. If you're free, that is. My mobile number is ...'

He was pleased. It seemed the roofies had worked this time, wiped the girl's memory clean so that she had no idea what had gone on under the influence. Either that or she'd enjoyed it. Anyway he'd liked the girl, and why not? She'd be going back to the States in few days so there'd be no ties. All he had to do was be careful, not let himself get out of control.

So he rang back, and made a date to meet that evening.

David went into the bathroom to wash his hands, glancing casually at the bath to his left as he did so.

41. Lotus

'SO YOU came?'

'Sure, why not? I brought the article.' Miranda pulled two sheets of folded paper from her bag.

'I'll read it later. Over a meal.' David stood in the door of his flat, devouring her with his eyes. He seemed to have dressed for the occasion - pressed jeans, snakeskin boots, a soft silk shirt. But he looked flushed and nervous, too, more than Miranda had expected. Was some part of his strange perverted mind worried about the impression he was creating, perhaps? Hoping she would love him while he abused her, was that it? Too late for that now, sonny boy.

Miranda had dressed carefully too, in a way that she hoped would give her control. She wore tight black trousers, a short white top showing her belly, and a soft suede jacket of her mother's. Enough, she hoped, to give him the message that she was respectable, persuade him to take her out somewhere decent. At least make him pause before he jumped her.

She wasn't wearing heels though, but old black trainers. She carried a small handbag slung over her left shoulder. All the rest of her luggage she'd left in New York two days ago. 'It's my last night,' she said with an attempt at a smile. 'I've got to fly home tomorrow. I thought maybe you could drive me to the station.'

'What, you're not staying?'

'In the morning,' she said as sweetly as she could. 'The train leaves at nine.'

'Oh yeah? You're hoping to be up by then?'

'It doesn't matter. I can take a taxi. I just thought ...'

'Don't worry. Where you flying from? Heathrow?'

'Manchester. At 12.30.'

'Okay. No worries - I'll drive you. It's quicker in the Lotus.'

It was the reaction she had hoped for. Her plan hinged around the boasts he had made about his Lotus last time they had met. It was his biggest toy, it seemed; he had to show it to her. 'What about tonight?'

'Well ...' He slid one hand round her waist and pulled her to him, urging her lips apart with his own and forcing his tongue into her mouth while his other hand squeezed her bottom. This was the worst part; she was expecting something like this but still she tensed, every part of her rigid with fear and rage. He laughed, pressing her hard against him. But it was no use fighting; she had to go through this, or her plan would fail. She forced herself to relax, closing her eyes and letting her muscles go limp as though she was in a yoga session and not here at all, jammed up against the wall with his thumb inside her knickers and ...

'No! No, wait.'

'What for? Come on, now, darling.'

'I've got a better idea. Let's do it in the Lotus.'

'What?'

'That's what I've been thinking about ever since you told me you had a car like that, I ...'

'Are you crazy?' He paused, considering the idea. 'There's no room.'

'I'll make room. It's speed that does it for me. Please, David. It'll be ...' Words failed her for a second. 'Like nothing you've ever had in your life. I promise.'

'All right.' He pulled back, grinning, while she adjusted her clothing. 'It better be good though.'

'It will. Ever since I was a kid I've liked screwing in cars. Come on, let me see it.'

Somehow she had regained the initiative. He was only an overgrown boy, after all, she had managed enough of those in her youth. Not half as strong as Bruce - God if he was here, this jerk would be a pile of bones on the floor. Well, he will be.

'Where do you keep this car?'

'In a lock-up at the end of the road. I'll show you.'

They walked along Gillygate to Lord Mayor's Walk, the little man swaggering assertively beside her. Two ivy covered garages nestled under the city wall behind the houses. 'How did you get this?' Miranda asked as they approached the one on the left.

David jerked his thumb at one of the houses on the right, where an elderly man was watching them through a window. 'Old guy over there can't drive, lets me have it for a tenner a week. It's worth it, you'll see. Car like this left outside, the wheels'd be gone in five minutes.'

The door slid up smoothly. David flicked a switch and a covered shape appeared. That's him, she thought, fussy bastard. A brick garage isn't enough, he needs a dust cover too. As he pulled back the cover the nose of the gleaming grey Lotus Elise emerged. David touched it with his fingertips gently.

She was glad it was grey. She'd feared it might be bright yellow or red, the sort of car no one could easily forget. A Lotus was conspicuous enough, but she didn't get to choose. For her plan to work, she had to use whatever car he owned. A Mini would have done just as well.

She waited while he drove it out and opened the driver's door. 'Come on, get in.'

He locked the garage door, then climbed back in beside her. 'There, what do you think?'

'You're right, it's quite snug.'

'All the power's in the engine.' He put his hand on her knee, squeezing it roughly. 'I'll put her through her paces on the way to the coast. Then I'll put you through yours.'

As Terry sat at his desk, gloomily considering his situation, his phone rang. A woman's voice - light, husky, slightly nervous.

'Hi, Terry. It's Sarah. Not interrupting anything, am I?'

'No, not at all.'

'Just rang to thank you for the flowers. That was a nice gesture, Terry. I appreciated it.'

Flowers? He struggled to remember what she was talking about. 'Oh, good. I'm glad you liked them.'

'Exactly what I needed to restore my confidence after the fiasco of the night before. I do apologize for that, Terry, really.'

'Nothing to apologize for.' He smiled at the memory. Sarah's voice, however, sounded embarrassed.

'I, er, felt pretty silly next morning. I hope you don't think too badly of me for it.'

'Sarah, don't torture yourself. I was flattered, really.' Terry struggled to find the right words. 'I've always ... I mean, perhaps we can meet for dinner sometime.'

'I'd like that but ...' she hesitated awkwardly. 'You should know I've patched things up with Bob, a bit, anyway, and er ....'

Don't get your hopes up. Terry sighed. No luck here, then. The gods seemed set to crush him again. In the calmest voice he could manage, he said: 'I understand. But we're still friends, I hope. I mean, that's all we were ...' No, that's not quite right. ' ... good friends, I mean?'

'Yes, of course.' Sarah sounded relieved. 'Terry, you're sweet, really. I'd like to meet for lunch. You can tell me how things are going since David Kidd's acquittal.'

'All right then. How about Thursday at one. In Marzanos?'

She leafed through her diary. 'It looks free at the moment. Okay, it's a date - you're on.'

'Fine. I'll look forward to it.' So that's it, Terry thought gloomily as he put the phone down. A lunch date, not with a lover, but a friend, who's patched things up with her husband. A bit, anyway.

What does that mean?

42. Lovers' Lane

THE PUB he chose was larger than Miranda would have liked, with a dozen cars parked outside. That was probably why David chose it; other customers would see the Lotus and be impressed - exactly the opposite of what she wanted. But she had no choice.

Everything, so far, had gone exactly his way. He had taken the car out onto the long empty roads on the Wolds towards Bridlington, where there were no speed cameras and the road lifted and fell like the waves of the sea. The little car with its light, fibreglass body took off at times like a speedboat. For him it was exhilarating, for her terrifying - he was not a particularly skilful driver and several times almost lost the back of the car on corners. On a blind bend he missed an oncoming tractor by inches. She could do nothing about it - he was fondling her leg most of the way and when they finally stopped on a ridge overlooking the sea she had no choice but to give him the blow job he wanted, while he lay back and revved the engine in ecstasy.

In the pub she sat opposite him, trembling, sick and furious. She picked at her meal while he sawed at a steak, trying to impress her with tales of travel which she guessed were mostly fictitious. If I don't do it now, she thought, I never will. She had never hated a man more but her fear was disabling her. Two young men had been watching them since they came in; surely they would remember? And the barman too. But she had no other plan and in twenty four hours she would be four thousand miles away.

When he went to the gents she slipped two of the pills in his lager.

She watched, fascinated, as they fell to the bottom of the glass. Two white tablets beaded with bubbles. She stared, willing them to dissolve. Slowly, before her eyes, their texture began to crumble, the shape become less distinct. Soon ...

'All right? Ready for the drive home?'

'Sure.' She picked up her gin and lemon, drank deep for courage. 'Let's finish these first.'

She watched him swallow the lager, fascinated. The beer looked darker - would it taste foul, would he spit it out in disgust? No, no more than she had with the coffee in his flat. Half of it was gone already. Would he see the pills in the bottom? No, they'd dissolved now.

'What you staring at?'

'Nothing. Just thinking.'

'I bet you are. We'll do it again on the way back. Maybe I'll show you another trick.' He hesitated, grinning oddly as if he'd forgotten what he meant to say next, and slouched slightly in his seat.

'Drink up then, if that's what you want.'

He looked at the glass in surprise as if he'd not seen it before, then lifted it and swallowed the rest. That's it, she thought, it's inside him now. Now to get him to the car before it takes full effect.

She stood up, hitched her bag on her shoulder, and touched his left arm. 'Come on then, Shumacher, let's go.'

'What?' He got up, stumbled, and started to laugh. 'Schumacher, yeah, that's right, I ...'

The sentence dissolved into a stupid, high pitched giggle. He stood, swaying on his feet, then lunged for her shoulder. Christ, I've given him too much, Miranda thought. She took his weight, wrapped his arm round her shoulders, and propelled him towards the door.

To get there they had to pass a table with four young men. As they approached it David, still giggling, raised his free arm in mock salute, then swung it wildly, sending a bottle of beer spinning on the table, spraying its contents in all directions.

'Hey! Watch what you're doing, stupid bastard!'

'Look at my trousers!'

'Come here and I'll smack your stupid face!'

Just what she didn't need. She was surrounded by four angry young men while David leaned across her shoulder, giving them the finger. His body was growing heavier and floppier by the minute. It took all her strength to keep him upright. She urged him towards the door, his feet wandering haphazardly beside hers.

'I'm sorry, he's drunk,' she said, desperately wishing they'd go away. 'He can't help it, it's an illness he gets sometimes.'

'What, too much beer? Give over, love - we all get that!'

'Stupid prat! What's so bloody funny?'

'You're not going to let him drive like that, are you, love?'

'No, of course not.' She reached the door, turned to smile at the least aggressive man of the four. 'I'll drive him home, it gets him like this sometimes. It's a sort of allergy.'

'Shall I call a doctor?' The young man held the door while his mates resumed their seats, ostentatiously brushing beer off their damp trousers. He followed her into the car park. 'He looks pretty sick to me.'

'He'll be okay. A cold shower and a sleep and he'll be right as rain.' She propped David against the Lotus, slumped with his face between his arms on the roof, chuckling to himself at some incomprehensible joke, and searched his pockets for the keys. They must be here somewhere, dammit, try the other pocket, yes here we are. She pressed the button on the fob, watched the lights flash and opened the passenger door. Her good Samaritan was still there, watching every move.

'If you can just help me get him in the seat...'

'Yeah, sure. He's really gone, isn't he? You sure he's okay?'

'He'll be fine, really.' She strapped David in. 'I'll take care of him now. I'm sorry about the beer.' She fished in her bag for a fiver. 'Here, buy your mates a drink.'

'No need for that.' He took the money anyway, but didn't go. Just my luck to meet a nice guy now when I don't need one. 'You sure you can drive that thing?'

'I'll manage. Look, thanks for your help, but I'm fine.'

She got in the car and searched for the ignition while he stood there, watching. Where is the damn slot? Okay, here. Shall I move the seat forward? No, David's not tall. He looks like an idiot, slumped there, dribbling. Maybe I've killed him already. How does this work? Standard H shift, three pedals like any other car. She started the engine, touched the accelerator slightly, felt a deep throated purr. Okay, where are the lights? Pull, twist, what the hell do you do - ah, that's it, full, dipped, fine. She let in the clutch. The car jerked forward and stalled. The young man stepped helpfully towards her.

Oh no, please no more help, don't watch me any more! She restarted the ignition, let in the clutch more gently, and waved her thanks to the young man. Just don't take the number, please don't take the number. She turned smartly out onto the road and drove away. Thank God. He knows it's a Lotus but that's all, I hope. I really hope.

What now?

As she reached for the gearstick David's hand seized hers, pressing it down so that she ground the gears, making a horrendous noise that her Samaritan might easily hear at the pub.

'Get off!' She flung his hand away. So he wasn't completely out after all. He stared at her, a manic grin on his face, then reached across and grabbed her hair.

'Christ, David, let go!' His fingers were clenched in her hair and he was leaning forward, trying to paw at her breasts. As they approached a bend the car swerved wildly and she dragged it back to the left just in time to avoid a van going in the opposite direction. She heard its horn fading in the distance as she dragged her head loose from his hand and shoved him back into his seat. 'Get off me, you maniac!'

'You want it, don't you?'

'No!' This bloody drug was supposed to subdue him, not turn him on. Maybe this is why I did those things in his flat, it wasn't just him, it was the drug as well. But I can't drive like this. As he fumbled feebly towards her like some sort of randy jellyfish, she fended him off with one hand while peering ahead for somewhere to pull in and deal with him properly. Why is this road so straight and full of cars? Several passed in the opposite direction and then at last there was a turning to the left down a country lane. She drove half a mile and pulled onto a layby by a heap of stone chippings. She switched on the inside light. 'Now then, you bastard.'

'Fuck me, baby.' He giggled and stroked her leg.

'I'll fuck you all right.' She reached in her bag and pulled out a syringe. It was filled with whisky in which she had dissolved three more tablets before she left home. With the syringe in her right hand, she climbed out of her seat on top of him, letting him paw her breasts and fumble his hands in her hair. 'Come here, puke face.'

She kissed him, pressing his head back against the seat rest and forcing her tongue into his sloppy mouth until his jaw was open and his head tilted back beneath her. Then she slipped the syringe into the side of his mouth and pressed the plunger. It was a technique she'd learnt, without kissing, when worming horses.

'Aaaagh!' He gagged and spluttered, spraying some in her face but most of it, she thought, went down. She shoved one hand under his chin, clamping his jaw shut, and stroked his throat until he swallowed. Then she pulled his nose and jerked his head from side to side beneath her until his eyes wobbled in their sockets.

'You're going to die, little fart. Do you know that? Die like Shelley died. In a place where no one will find you.'

He was still partly conscious, and in the dim passenger light she saw his eyes watching her and thought she detected fear. He struggled feebly, but she had her full weight on top of him, and with that and the drug there was no way he could get her off now. She gripped both hands in his hair and stared down at him, waiting for the new dose to take effect.

'You're scum, you are. A nasty evil excrescence. You don't deserve to live and you won't.'

His eyes closed and he began snoring. She climbed off carefully, switched off the inside light and got out of the car. The night air was cool, quiet, refreshing. She had the appalling thought that someone might have been outside the car watching everything she did but there was no one here, no one it seemed for miles. Occasional car lights passed along the road she had left half a mile back, and there was a single light from a house on a hill two miles away, but apart from that, nothing. Just a munching sound which might be cows in a field, and the screech of an owl hunting somewhere ahead. The silence and the darkness comforted her. It was what she had grown up with at home.

She got back into the car and turned it round. David lay snoring in his seat, long streaks of dribble falling from his mouth. She was getting used to the little car now and her thoughts came easier, but a hint of drowsiness began to set in. She opened the window to get more air and a police car passed, going the other way. She wished she hadn't drunk the gin, but she'd needed it for courage. But how much had she drunk? It would be ironic to be breathalysed now.

She drove back to York and round the ring road, keeping carefully to the speed limit. Several drivers zipped past, proud to be overtaking a Lotus, one or two passengers giving her admiring, envious looks. If only it wasn't such a conspicuous car. But it was his personal pride and joy, that was what made it such a fitting place for him to die. In a fancy fibreglass coffin.

As she approached Wetherby she came nearer to her parents' home. A brief rain shower spattered the windscreen, then stopped. The countryside was dark but familiar; the roads narrower, quieter, more remote. It was after eleven now. There were no cars and few lights in the houses. She turned down another lane into a forest.

It was a dirt road, with potholes and grass growing in the middle. It was used by walkers and horse riders and the occasional tractor, but very few cars - especially ones slung as low as the Lotus. Twice she felt a nasty scrape underneath. She laughed softly to herself.

'New exhaust, David, maybe a new sump. Cost thousands, that will.'

Deeper in the forest she came to the abandoned airfield. All overgrown now, covered with moss and birch, pussy willow and elder, leading nowhere in the night. A dog fox stared for a second, eyes glowing in the headlights, before loping away into the dark.

A few yards further on the road forked, just as she had remembered. The main track went on to a farm about two miles distant. The track to the left was where she had walked the other day. Brambles scraped the paintwork as the car forced its way through. One particularly loud screech seemed to pierce the fog in David's brain. He sat bolt upright, staring around in alarm. Miranda drove on grimly. Only a few more yards. Slowly, like a deflated tyre, David slumped back to unconsciousness. Thank God.

Here it is.

Right in front of them was the concrete tank, dark water glistening in the headlights behind the flimsy barbed wire fence. She switched the engine off, got out and stood for a moment, listening. Small insects fluttered and swirled in the headlights' beam, and a dog barked far away near the farm. Shut up, dog, don't wake anyone now. She turned off the lights; the barking continued for a while, then subsided to a few puzzled yips, and silence.

She put her bag on the ground beside the car and took out a torch. She shone the torch on the fence posts which she had loosened the other day, tugged hard and in a couple of minutes had all three on the ground. But the barbed wire refused to lie flat as she wanted it to. It rose in awkward loops and whorls between the horizontal posts, ready to snag a wheel or a bumper or number plate. She needed something to hold it down. Stones, that would do, or logs - there must be some around here.

She hunted around with the torch and found one large stone - two - and a large rotten log that was snagged by brambles and weed so that whichever way she pulled it would not quite come out. Time was moving on. Her breath came short and sweat prickled under her breasts. She gave one final, desperate heave and the log snapped with a loud crack!

'What's going on?'

At the sound of the voice she whirled around and saw David - *NO!* - climbing clumsily out of the passenger door. She snatched up her torch to see better. He had the door open, one foot on the ground, and was leaning around the side of it like with a dazed grin on his face like some lunatic playing hide and seek. In a second he'd be out altogether and then what? She'd have to shove him back in if she could. If the drug hadn't worn off completely.

'David, no. It's all right. I just stopped for a second.'

'Where are we?'

'I ... I needed a pee. Get back in the car, David, please.'

'I wanna piss too.' He hauled himself to his feet with the door, then started fumbling with the zip of his trousers.

Shit! This isn't what happens. What do I do now? She stood irresolute in front of him, torch in one hand and the rotten log in the other, while he hauled out his prick and sprayed an endless jet of urine on the concrete between them.

'Like watching, do you?' he leered. 'Here gimme that, I want to see ....' Still pissing, he made a sudden grab for the torch which missed, and the momentum took him round in a circle so he ended up with his back to her, pissing into his car. 'Shit, where'd it go?'

This has to stop now, she thought. She put down the torch, lifted the log and hit him as hard as she could across the base of his skull. Rotten splinters flew everywhere. David slumped forwards, banging his nose on the roof, then fell to his knees. She hit him again and the log broke in two. Then with her hands under his armpits she heaved and strained until he was somehow inside the car. He slumped sideways in the seat, moaning softly. She touched the back of his head which was sticky with blood.

I've got to do this now, she thought, it's getting out of hand. She slammed the door shut, found the torch, and went over to the fence and used the remaining piece of log to press down the wire. Then she got in the car and leaned forward to start the engine. A hand grabbed her arm.

'I wanna drive.'

'What? Get off me, you jerk!'

'No. S'my car and I'm driving.' Somewhere he had recovered much of his strength. As the engine purred into life he leaned over, wrestling her with both arms so that she was pinned in the seat and couldn't get out. Then his leg caught the gear stick and with a grinding crunch the car shot backwards into a tree. The impact jolted them both forwards. David's head smashed into the windscreen while the top of her head caught him under the chin.

'Bloody hell.' She pushed her foot down on the clutch and reached around his limp body to take the car out of gear. He lay across her like a sack. The windscreen was starred into fragments by the impact, but it hadn't burst. Her head hurt but there was no time to think of that, not now. This was her chance, the last chance probably.

Carefully, she heaved him off her so she could reach all the controls. Then she turned on the headlights and eased the car forwards in first gear until it was just on top of the flattened fence, its front wheels a foot from the lip of the tank. Now the hardest part. She put on the handbrake, opened the door and squirmed out from beneath him. He was beginning to moan again and thresh about. Damn! She grabbed him round the waist and heaved his backside into the driver's seat. A foot flopped on the accelerator and the engine revved loudly. Christ, shut up, no, you'll wake that dog! She switched off the engine and leaned across him to let off the handbrake.

He grabbed her hair. No get off me bastard let me go! But his strength was returning again even if his mind was switched off. He wound his fingers into her hair and pressed her face down into his crotch. She reached up and tore his fingers loose, one by one. 'Come on, Shelley,' he said. 'One more time.'

At last she was free. Almost free. He snatched her hand just as she was closing the door and there was a further tug of war. Then her hand slipped free and she was out. She slammed the door in his face, ran round the back of the car and leaned all her weight on it.

It wouldn't move. Dammit come on what's the matter with it now? She pushed harder until every muscle in her body trembled with the strain and then slowly, slowly the little car rolled forward. Two inches, four ... she heard the grit crunching under the tyres and then the door opened and David's arm and head popped out.

'Shelley? What's going on?'

I'm not Shelley you bastard heave come on please come on please come on yes! Oh yes yes, that's it *yes!* The front wheels slipped over the rim, the rear lifted slightly in the air, and with a final crunching heave the entire car tipped over the edge, stood on its nose, and began to sink. For a long terrible moment she thought it would stand there like that, half in and half out of the water like the Titanic on its way down, but the water was so deep that the bonnet and then the passenger compartment and then the entire car slid slowly inexorably out of sight and was gone.

Is David still in or did the bastard get out? Where's the damn torch I need it now! Her breath rasping in her chest she hunted in the darkness for nearly a minute before she found the torch and shone it down on the dark bubbling water. Great gouts of air and weed and oil rose to the surface, but no car and no man. She picked up the log in her right hand and stood there ready. How long can he stay down there and live? If he doesn't come up in a couple of minutes it'll be too late. It must be two minutes already, what's the time? She shone the torch on her watch - twenty past twelve. Remember that, twenty past, twenty past, five minutes and he'll be dead for certain. She stood there playing the torch on the water and muttering to herself, twenty past twenty past, while the breath rasped in her throat and her body shook and the surface of the black water gradually subsided. Four bubbles, two, one big one, none. Twenty five past twelve.

He's gone.

The sound of the midnight woods came back to her. The dog in the distance, a mile away, barking sporadically. The shriek of a rabbit caught by a stoat. The wind in the trees overhead. A girl sobbing softly. Shut up, no time for that now, you've got to clean up and get out of here.

Moving like an old woman, she hauled the fence posts upright and dropped them into their sockets until the rickety fence looked much as it had done before. She tamped earth around the foot of the posts and covered her efforts with leaves. Then she shone her torch carefully around the gritty concrete, looking for things that might arouse suspicion. She found her handbag - just think, if I'd forgotten that! - and a mark on the tree which the car had hit, but nothing else. She rubbed moss onto the tree to hide the mark, then used a handful of ferns to brush grit across the tyre tracks so that they were less obvious to the naked eye. It might look different in daylight, of course, and none of it would deceive a forensic scientist but that wasn't the point. The point was to avoid attracting attention to the tank in the first place.

When she had finished this housekeeping she stood still and listened. The dog had stopped barking. The wind still soughed in the trees. Somewhere to her right the fox gave its hoarse, coughing bark. A barn owl screeched.

Why so quiet? She strained her ears but could hear nothing else - just the faint singing of blood in her ears and the scrunch of her shoe on the grit when she moved, loud as thunder in the silence. An uncertain, nervous grin played on her face in the dark. Just the owl's hoot and the cricket's cry. There should be loud knocking, a porter opening the gates to a messenger for the king, barking dogs, the wail of police sirens, helicopters clattering overhead with searchlights, loudspeakers and men in black swarming with guns, but

nothing.

There was something wrong with her face, though, it was twisting and giggling and making her want to shout and scream and ... *shut up shut up*, I've got to hold this together. It's not over yet, I've got a long way to walk and the danger isn't police cars or helicopters or anything like that it's in my own mind. My God I've committed a murder.

But he deserved to die ten times over. I did it for you, Shelley, and now he's in that tank where I would have died long ago if you hadn't saved me. You understand that. He was scum, he was filth, the world is better without him but not without you, you deserved to live and he killed you. Now I have to hold all this together and leave. It's a long walk but I'm not afraid of the night and I know where I'm going. Just hold it together in your mind, that's what matters. Not like Lady Macbeth she cracked up but I won't I can't I've got a child who needs me unlike her. She did it for greed and power but I did it for revenge and justice that makes the difference - it's got to. Everything's changed now, I'm changed too, but I've got to look the same. Work that out later.

She stood for a while longer, listening to the wind in the trees, the owl hunting, the bark of the fox. They didn't care, they killed routinely, every night. The deafening silence in the tank behind her meant nothing to them.

She took one step, the first, away from the scene of her crime.

Four thousand miles to go.

43. Nightwalk

IT WAS a long walk through the night. The moon appeared fitfully, sometimes bathing woods and fields in cold white light, sometimes hiding behind clouds so that all was black. Once Miranda slipped up to her knees in a ditch; as she climbed out a bramble snagged her tight black trousers, tearing them across her thigh. In her mind the walk had seemed easy, but she'd been away in America for years, and the half-remembered landmarks seemed to have moved in her absence.

She took a wide loop around the farm to avoid disturbing the dog, but then, crossing a pasture, a blurry white shape erupted in front of her, and in a moment the field was full of a bleating flock of similar creatures, confronting her in panic and defiance. The distant dog barked furiously, leaping to the end of its chain, and a light came on in the yard. Miranda ran until the breath sobbed in her chest. Had she been seen? She couldn't tell; too late she realised she'd crossed open fields in moonlight. She stood with her back to an oak tree until the yard light went out, then crept away, hiding her silhouette against the dark line of a hedge.

By the time she reached the road she was muddy, bedraggled and cold. She crouched in a ditch while a car went by, then another, their headlights carving tunnels through the night. She couldn't risk being seen, not like this, but it was easier to travel along the road. She stepped out cautiously, buttoning her jacket over her white top, looking ahead for a ditch or gate to hide in if a car should appear.

Towards dawn she reached the racecourse near Wetherby. She went through the car park, climbed a fence, and walked along the damp thick grass of the steeplechase course beside the road. The grandstands slumbered on a rise to her left, a hint of lemon yellow behind them in the sky. Ahead, traffic swished north and south along the A1; to her right were the floodlit fences and huts of a juvenile correction centre.

She sat down and rested her back against the brushwood of a jump, waiting for dawn. No one would see her here. She watched the light grow above the roofs of the town, and checked her watch. 4.35. The first bus wouldn't leave for hours yet, and before she dared enter town she'd have to improve her appearance. She fumbled in the pockets of her coat and found a safety pin to patch the rent in her trousers, along with a hanky of her mother's which she moistened on the wet grass and used to clean her clothes.

If only it wasn't so cold! She folded her arms under her armpits and rolled into a ball, like a lost forgotten jockey. The sun will come soon, she told herself. Then the bus with its heater, the comfortable airport and home - central heating as hot as you like it! We'll have Christmas together as a family, me and Sophie and Bruce, we'll go skiing and come home to the sauna and no one will ever guess how cold I once was, shivering under a steeplechase fence in England, with icy dew trickling along my hair and black oily water creeping into my lungs until I can't breathe and I'm clawing my way up to the surface but the car door won't open and ...

Stop it! She sat up suddenly, shaking her head violently to prove she was still here and not drowning in nightmare sleep. He's the one with icy water in his lungs - not me. Look about you, girl, it's light. Her hand and her jacket had colour now, they weren't just grey. A car swished by on the road. The prison floodlights across the road cast less glare. She glanced at her watch. Maybe the bus station would open soon.

She dragged a mirror out of her bag, improved her haggard face, hauled herself to her feet and set out for the town.

Kathryn was cooking supper when she decided to ring Miranda. Over the past few days the Valium had spread a thin film of oil over the surface of her mind, smoothing the seething turbulence beneath. Andrew was out, probably with his mistress Carole, and Shelley was in her little urn at the crematorium. This was what life would be like from now on. The home she had created had been violated, destroyed, yet it was still here, all around her. The tiles on the floor, she noticed sadly, were chipped and cracked; the paint on the walls faded. Like a pensioner's kitchen, she thought, with memories that no longer comfort. I tried here and failed: maybe I should follow Miranda across the Atlantic, sell up, start afresh.

'Hello.' A vigorous masculine American voice answered the phone.

'Hello, Bruce. How are you?'

A brief pause, then recognition. 'Oh, hi - Miranda's mom, right? Good to hear you, Kathryn. Hey, I was sorry to hear about the trial, you know. Real bummer.'

'Yes, it was terrible. Miranda told you about it, did she?'

'Sure, she rang me a couple of times. Bastard got off scot free, she said. Should have been strung up.'

'Our courts don't do that any more, unfortunately. Anyway, how are you, Bruce?'

'Oh, struggling, you know, with the old child care. It's amazing the energy it takes.'

The thought of her big son-in-law blundering around the house after a two year old made Kathryn smile. Yet he could be surprisingly gentle too; that was what she liked about him. 'You'll be glad to have Miranda back then.'

'Miranda? No, she's not back till tomorrow. That's what we're doing right now, matter of fact. Me and Sophie together. Tidying the place up to look good for her mom. You want to talk to her? Hey Sophie, come here, it's granny K on the phone.'

'But I thought ...' Kathryn was still puzzling over these words when the voice of her distant granddaughter came lisping down the line.

'Hi, granny.'

'Hello, Sophie, is that you?' She tried to put warmth and love into her voice, but it came out hoarse and croaky. 'What are you doing now?'

'Tidying. For mommy come back.'

'Good. Mummy's back tomorrow, is she?' There's something wrong here, Kathryn thought. Why isn't she home yet? What's happened?

'Yes. Bring presents. Bye, granny.'

'Is that all? No more for granny?' Bruce came back on the line, proud and embarrassed. 'Okay - she's shy, Kathryn, hiding her face right now. But she does help with the chores - some of them anyhow. You must visit again soon. She's growing so fast you wouldn't believe.'

'Yes, I'd like that, Bruce.' Kathryn's voice was faint. 'Really I would.'

'Yes, well do it then. You deserve a break after all you've been through this year.'

'Bruce, you say Miranda rang you. When was that?'

'Couple of nights ago, I think. She's stopping over in New York on the way back, doing some shopping. What's this thing you wanted to tell her about? Can I take a message?'

'No. No, it's nothing really, Bruce, I just wanted a chat. I ... I must have got the time wrong, I always forget how far it is. Don't worry her when she arrives, it's nothing, really. She'll need support, you know, when she gets home. It hit her hard, the trial. So if she seems a bit tense and het up ...'

'Yeah, I understand. Lots of hugs and TLC, eh? Coffee and cuddles.'

'That's it, exactly.' Kathryn felt tears start in her eyes, at the thought of Miranda safe in the arms of this bluff, friendly man. 'She's lucky to have you.'

For a few more minutes, Kathryn managed to string the conversation along, asking about Bruce's job, the improvements they planned to the house, his boat, but all the time she was wondering, *why isn't she home yet?* Andrew had taken her to the airport three days ago, so where was she? Shopping in New York? Perhaps, but it seemed oddly callous, after what they'd all been through. Miranda wasn't like Andrew, surely, she couldn't have a lover in the city? That would be the final betrayal, everything good in the family destroyed.

Kathryn tried Miranda's mobile but it was switched off. She put the phone down wearily, and bent to check the casserole in the oven.

The plane, to Miranda's relief, was half empty. There were few women on board: leaving La Guardia just after midnight, it was used largely by weary, crumpled businessmen, students, and people who, from the raw, anxious look of their eyes, were in the throes of some emotional crisis. She had changed into clean clothes when she had retrieved her luggage at Manchester airport, but the eyes she saw in the ladies' room mirror at La Guardia were red and staring from weariness, her face pale and lined with exhaustion. She had splashed cold water on it and done what she could with some moisturiser and eye-liner she found in her bag, and now, she thought, it looked presentable.

Not the face of a murderer, anyway. She judged that from the looks she got from a few of the businessmen, one of whom had taken the aisle seat beside her and essayed a few jokes which she ignored, staring ostentatiously away into the darkness outside the cabin window. Just night out there, and the lights of cities far below - less and less of that, as they flew further west across the lakes. They would arrive about 3 a.m; she planned to check into the airport hotel, sleep until noon, and then face her husband and daughter.

Life would begin again - real, ordinary, everyday life to do with cooking and cleaning and new shoes for Sophie and visits to K-mart. And Bruce - his big, powerful arms, the deep voice - how she longed to rest her head on his strong hairy chest and let him hold her. She would weep, for certain, but that wouldn't matter - she'd been through a terrible time, after all. It was just that he had no idea how terrible.

And she mustn't tell him. Not now, not ever. She had thought about this all the way back, on the flight across the Atlantic - her second in less than a week. Bruce might understand, even sympathise with what she had done. In his world justice was simple - an eye for an eye, a killer deserved all he got - but all the same she had no right to burden him with it. No right and no need.

It was all, already, so very far away. Something that happened in a wood, in the night, on a little island thousands of miles from her home. No one had been there - no one but herself and David, and he was dead. Dead, and sunk among the mud and water snails fifteen feet below the surface. With luck no one would find him for years, perhaps never. After all, who loved him, who cared? Nobody. So why would anyone even look?

So if she kept silent, no one would ever know. She knew about secrets - they were like the box in which Pandora kept the winds. Once tell Bruce, and her secret would spread to the four winds; she would have to rely on his discretion, his self-control, to keep the horror to himself. And Bruce was the bluffest, most honest, most hopeless liar in the world.

If only her hands didn't tremble so, the tears choke her chest. But that was natural, surely, just reaction after the shock. In an effort to hide from the man in the aisle seat, who kept glancing her way, she tried on the courtesy eye shield. But that led to horror - she was back in the wood, by the Lotus, watching David clamber dopey and drugged from the driver's seat all over again. She relived the way she had hit him with the log, shoved him inside, heaved at the heavy car as though her lungs would burst. Only this time it all went wrong. As she ran across the midnight fields, dodging the dog and the sheep, David's face rose from the water behind her, his dank hair full of sticks, fish swimming out of his nose and worms in his eyes, but somehow still alive!

She tore off the mask with a scream, shaking. The man beside her leaned over, concerned. 'You okay, there, ma'am? Something wrong?'

'No. No, I'm ... fine, thanks. Just a bad dream.'

'Try a Scotch - here. Chase them old bogies away.' He pulled a flask from his pocket.

'Yes, all right. Thanks. Maybe I will.' This isn't going to be so easy at all, she thought, as the warm alcohol flooded through her veins. I've done the hard bit, the main thing, but now ... I'm alone with my secret for ever. She stared out at the clouds and lights below, a distant scream that she hoped was exhaustion and not panic whistling like tinnitus in her ears.

Part Five

The Choice

44. Tyre Marks

THE FARMER, Arthur Dixon, had had a restless night. Several times the dog had woken him, and once he had seen lights in the woods. Men out lamping for rabbits or deer, he guessed, and considered chasing them off. But if it was deer they were after, they'd be a gang from Bradford or Barnsley, equipped with rifles and poaching to order. Too much for an old man of sixty four. So even when the dog barked the third time he contented himself with a tour of the byres. All quiet there; cows munching contentedly. It was not until the following morning, when his son arrived for work, that the two of them drove out to search the woods.

Dan saw the tyre marks first, in a patch of mud near the concrete of the old airfield. Nothing too dramatic; just a track suggesting someone had driven through the brambles near the old fuel pit. Several long thorny runners had been snapped off or crushed.

'Why drive through here?' Dan asked. 'Not the best place for lamping, is it? Too many brambles, for a start.'

They stopped at the old fuel pit and got out. No sign of cartridges anywhere, but then Arthur hadn't heard any shots. Just an engine, and lights in the night. He looked at the old pit uneasily. He'd felt guilty about it ever since that day, ten years before, when the little girl and her pony had nearly drowned it it. He'd seen her sister galloping and known at once something was wrong; no one would ride like that across the winter wheat straight towards the farmer who owned it without good reason. When he'd seen what had happened he'd felt cold all over; not just because the child might have drowned but for the insurance claim that could have resulted. But the parents had been decent, and hadn't blamed him though he owned the land. So he'd praised the children's courage, and erected a fence with a sign saying 'Danger - Keep Out.' He looked for the sign now and saw it, rotting on the ground. He hadn't been here for ages. It was a place he preferred to forget.

So what had a car been doing here last night?

'Dad? Here, look at this.' Dan had wandered behind the pickup and was looking a pine tree at the edge of the concrete. A foot from the ground there was a gash in its bark, partly covered with mud. Dan ran his fingers over the gash, picked up some mud and spread it on his palm. 'That's paint, isn't it? Grey metallic paint from some vehicle.'

Arthur nodded. 'What d'you think? They got stuck and smashed the truck into a tree?'

'If it was a truck.' Dan, who loved everything mechanical, was more of an expert than his father. 'Looks like car paint to me. There, see? Gun metal grey.'

'All right, a car. So where did it go from here?'

'Same way they came in, I reckon. No other choice.'

Immediately beyond the fuel pit the brambles had grown into an impenetrable thicket - a better defence than anything health and safety could have devised, in Arthur's view. He'd hoped it was like that on the western side too, but clearly not.

'So what were they looking for here?' Dan asked, gazing around the clearing.

'Lost, probably. Turned round and went back.' Impelled perhaps by guilt, or the desire to look in the pit which he hadn't seen for so long, Arthur wandered across the fence, and tested a post with his thick, gnarled hand. To his disgust it was loose, the bottom snapped off, just hanging there supported by wire. He tried another the same. The whole fence was basically rotten. Well, posts did rot; maybe he should put in some new ones. Then, as he turned away, he saw it.

A glove, floating on the water.

He stared, chewing his lip, an unpleasant taste in his throat. That shouldn't be there, that didn't look good. He grunted, stepped over the fence, and hauled the glove in with a stick.

'What you got there, Dad?'

He held the dripping glove up to show his son. Not a working glove or one that would keep you warm. Not the sort of glove a lamper would use on a night out for deer. Not unless he was some kind of pansy. It was a man's driving glove with decorative holes in the back. They studied it in silence.

'See anything else?' said Dan at last. 'What about this?'

He pointed to the edge of the pit, and the old man sucked his teeth. Something had scraped away the concrete lip above the water, tearing away moss and leaving a clear white scar. There was another mark, too - a large cushion of moss near the edge had been flattened, a tyre print clear in its surface.

Dan frowned at his father. 'Looks like they tipped something in.'

Arthur nodded, feeling queasy. The excitement of the search vied in his mind with fear of the consequences. 'They've ripped out the fence there and put it back after.'

'For what?' Dan looked at the glove. 'Maybe hiding drugs, Dad, cocaine and that?'

'In the water? Don't be daft.'

'They could be, though. In sealed containers.' Dan had seen more films than his father. 'Worth millions, that sort of stuff. We'd get a reward. Here, give me that stick.'

He crouched, and began to poke down into the depths. 'Fifteen foot deep, this, isn't it? Maybe more. I remember you warning us about it when we were kids. Here, what's this?'

Five feet long, with Dan's arm extended to the elbow into the water, the branch snagged on something. Dan hauled it out, measured the length, and tried again. 'That's not fifteen foot, nothing like. There's something down there, all right.' He prodded slowly to the left with the branch. After about a yard, he couldn't find bottom any more. One arm dripping with water, he confronted his father triumphantly.

'Something there all right. Come on, let's haul her out!'

'How're you going to do that?'

'We've got a towrope, haven't we, and a hook. You lay the fence down, Dad, I'll back up to the edge and snag it with the hook. If the pickup won't lift her, a tractor will.'

45. Regrets and Dreams

THEY MET in an Italian restaurant opposite the Judge's Lodgings in Lendal. It was a place popular with lawyers, and Sarah wished he had chosen somewhere else. Twice she considered ringing to ask Terry change it, then put down her mobile in frustration. She'd made enough of a fool of herself in front of him already. Anyway, what did it matter if she was seen lunching with him? Lawyers entertained clients, police and solicitors all the time; it was part of the job.

So why feel so guilty - so girlish - approaching this restaurant now?

The reason, she knew very well, lay not in the act itself, but the intention behind it. It was a point she argued regularly in court. When my client took the watch out of the shop into the street, my lord, he didn't intend to steal it as the prosecution say, he simply meant to examine it more clearly in natural daylight. It was intent which distinguished between a naive, innocent act and one which was infected with *mens rea* - a guilty and criminal mind.

Sarah, entering the restaurant and looking round for Terry Bateson, felt guilty. As he smiled at her from a quiet table in a corner she noted with relief that no one else she knew was there. It was absurd, really - she'd known Terry for years, and never thought of him as anything but a friend; a charming, handsome, occasionally infuriating detective, whom she sometimes worked with in court. He'd helped her in her son's case and she'd been grateful, but that was it; there'd never been anything more. Not until that stupid, drunken, wonderfully embarrassing night at Savendra's wedding.

When she thought back now she found it hard to believe that it had really been her, that woman dancing barefoot on the grass, drinking glass after glass of champagne before taking him up to her room with such embarrassing results; but that memory was real, just as real as the flowers and the card Terry had sent her afterwards, and her unresolved quarrel with Bob.

So even though nothing had actually happened between them, she'd intended it to happen, and so had he. The context of their meetings was changed. She could see it in his eyes, the way he stood up to pull out her chair, his smile as she sat down. There was hope in that smile, and an intimacy that had not been there before.

Well, that will have to end, Sarah thought. That's what I came here to tell him. Only ...

Only she didn't really want to.

Normally, Sarah was a decisive woman; it was the defining feature of her character. She identified her goals and set out to attain them, overcoming every obstacle in her way as swiftly as possible. She believed you should never, ever, make a mistake, particularly in love or sex, because, as she knew only too well from her teenage years, that could destroy you utterly.

And yet that was what she had so nearly done with Terry Bateson. Something which could have destroyed both her marriage and her reputation. I was insane, she thought; I lost control. So it has to be brought to an end: here, now, today.

The dominant, logical part of her mind knew that and accepted it. The trouble was that there was another annoying, emotional part of her which didn't accept it at all. A part of her which for years she had managed to subdue, and which now wanted - intended - this meeting not to be a brisk businesslike end to their flirtation at all, but the beginning of something new.

'Hi. How are you?'

She sat nervously opposite him, fending off his smile with the first cliché that came to mind. 'Busy, as always. Rushed off my feet.'

'Tell me about it. Crime never stops.'

'No. Look, Terry, maybe we should order. I haven't got long.'

'Fine. Waiter! Over here.'

The words, brisk, meaningless, batted between them like ping-pong balls, kept them apart. But it was the look in the eyes, the unspoken thought behind them, that mattered. When the waiter had gone Sarah leaned forward, keeping the talk on neutral, serious, ground.

'So. Lots of crime, you say?'

'Yes. Burglaries, shoplifting, theft. The usual round. But I've been demoted, it seems. There's a suspicious death over towards Wetherby, and slick Willie's told me to keep away.'

'Will Churchill, you mean?'

'Yes. He's taking charge of all murder enquires from now on. After you and I cocked up the last one, he says.'

Sarah frowned irritably. 'But that's absurd. How does he get away with it?'

'You know why we call him slick Willie? Because his ego's made of Teflon. Nothing sticks. So if he says we cocked up the trial, that's what people believe. And then, that business with Kathryn Walters the other day was the last straw.'

Sarah studied him thoughtfully, noting the lines of pain on his face. Once, a couple of years ago, she remembered boasting cynically to this man about how every trial was just a game of proof, in which a lawyer could argue either side without caring about the truth. She'd learned humility since then, and looked back on that moment with embarrassment. Terry had argued passionately for the work of the police, saying that society would only be really safe if burglars and murderers and rapists were locked up. Yet only a few days ago, he had risked his own career to protect a woman who was, undoubtedly, intent upon vengeful murder.

'None of this is simple, is it?' She stretched her hand impulsively across the table. 'You're a good man, Terry. You don't deserve this.'

'Don't I? Who knows?' Terry took her hand in both of his, stroking her fingers gently, touching the wedding ring. 'Anyway, Sarah, how are you? You've made things up with Bob, you said.'

'Yes, just a family quarrel, you know. They happen from time to time.' She flexed her fingers in his, delighting in the touch, knowing she should take her hand away. 'You must have ... well, quarrelled with Mary sometimes?'

As soon as the words were out she realized how thoughtless they were. But she was no good at these situations. Look what happened last time, for heaven's sake! *I came here to end this. But ...*

'Yes, once or twice, I suppose.' He released her hand, sooner than she wanted. 'A long time ago ...'

'I'm sorry, Terry. I shouldn't have said that.'

'No, it's all right, it brings it back to me.' He looked away out of the window, then back to her. 'I'd have hated it if anyone had come between us. No doubt Bob feels that way too.'

'Yes, but he ...' *He deserves it*, the emotional rebel within her almost blurted out. Swiftly, her rational self regained control. '... he doesn't have anything to worry about,' Sarah continued firmly. 'I mean, nothing's going to come between him and me, really. We've been married for eighteen years and that's how it's going to stay.'

There, she'd said it, the thing she came here intending to say. She met his eyes coolly, her rational ego standing with its foot firmly planted on the dissident teenage emotional id, which lay bound and gagged on the floor of her heart, kicking wildly to be let out. She was surprised Terry couldn't hear the knocking on her rib cage.

'Yes, of course.'

She saw the disappointment in his eyes, and his mind wondering exactly what she was trying to tell him. As if she hadn't made it clear.

'But then ... there are other possibilities. A long way short of divorce, I mean.'

She gazed at him for a long moment, to be certain she understood what he meant. Slowly, she shook her head.

'No, Terry.' She looked down, partly to avoid his eyes, partly to still the pain in her chest. 'No, no, it's sweet of you, of course, don't think I haven't thought of it, but it wouldn't work. I don't think I could manage deceit. Could you?'

The question, she saw as soon as she'd asked it, was a mistake. For herself, because it left the door open which she was trying to close. The prisoner in her chest twisted violently, trying to get free. But also for Terry, because it gave him hope.

He smiled ruefully. 'I think everyone can manage deceit, if they want to enough. Just as everyone can change their mind.'

'I have changed my mind, Terry. I'm staying with Bob. You must understand that, surely?'

'Of course I understand. But that doesn't mean I have to like it, does it?'

'No. We can't always have what we like.'

'Can't we?' He leaned forward, looking directly into her eyes. The pain in his eyes faded into amusement. 'I can still keep asking the question, though.'

'Oh Terry, please!' Again she looked round the half-empty restaurant.

'Please what?' He laughed softly. 'Please ask me again?'

'*No!* One more crack like that, Terry, and I'm out of here. I mean it!'

'Sure you do.'

The trouble was the smile in her eyes, responding to his. It was not the expression she intended to have, nor did she intend to let him reach forward and take her hand again across the table. She dug her nails into his palm, to make him let go. But not very hard. Despite herself she was laughing. With an effort she sat back in her chair.

'Look, Terry, I like you very much, and I admit that the other night I nearly did something I shouldn't have, but today ...' She shook her head.

'You're not going to do it.'

'No.'

'How about tomorrow?'

'Not tomorrow either, or the day after that. Or any day in the foreseeable ...'

'Sssssh!' Terry put his finger to his lips to silence her. 'Don't say that, life's too short. Things can change. Leave me some hope, at least.'

This is ridiculous, Sarah thought. I'm trying to be serious and he's making it into a game. The trouble is it's such fun. So long as nothing happens. 'Hope ...' she began hopelessly.

'... is what we all live for. Where would we be without it?'

'Terry, you talked about deceit. Well, you can deceive yourself if it makes you happy, but that's all it is, it's never going to happen, okay? If you want to call that hope, go ahead.'

'Okay, it's a start.' Terry grinned. 'I'll live in hope, then.'

'Much good may it do you.'

'And memories, of course. You can't take those away.'

'No, please!' Sarah closed her eyes and shuddered. 'Don't think about that!'

'Why not? You were charming. Still are.'

'Okay, that's it.' Sarah glanced at her watch and stood up, trying to regain some of the rags of her dignity. The trouble was she was still smiling. 'I've got to go, I'll be late for court. I've said what I've said. If you want to sit here and dream, that's up to you. That's all it is, just a delusion.'

'Sure,' Terry called after her. 'In your dreams.'

46. Unwelcome Visitors

MIRANDA PHONED home the day after she arrived to say that she had, indeed, stopped off in New York to spend some time with a friend. She hadn't answered her mobile because the charge had run out. The explanation did not go down well with Kathryn but what, after all, could she do about it? Her elder daughter - her only daughter now - was a grown woman, she could do as she chose. She had always been stubborn, determined - qualities of self-reliance and independence that had taken her across the Atlantic to marry her American vet. But now, it seemed to Kathryn, she was ignoring him. Her response, on the phone, was cool.

'Bruce will be pleased to see you then, at last.'

'Yes, of course he is, Mum. And Sophie. I brought her a bear.'

'Good. Well, take care of them, darling. They matter to you, more than your friends.'

'I do realise that, Mum. Honestly.'

In the conversation it seemed to Kathryn, somehow, that there was an invisible barrier she could not get past. Perhaps it was just that Miranda was tired - after all, a four thousand mile journey could cause that easily enough; but after she put the phone down she wondered how close she had come to Miranda even during the time she was here. They had been together a great deal, of course, spending long tearful evenings reminiscing about Shelley's childhood; but the trauma of the verdict, and her own failed revenge with the shotgun, had changed things somehow. Even through the haze of the Valium, it seemed to Kathryn that Miranda had become more distant, withdrawn further into herself in a way she had not noticed before.

Perhaps it was just her own way of coping. She hoped so. The other possibility - that Miranda, like her father, had a lover outside her marriage, perhaps in New York - was not one she wanted to face. A small thing, perhaps, after the death of a daughter, but it was the small things, sometimes, that could tip you over the edge.

Andrew, at least, had been more attentive since her arrest, but that did not mean he was home every night. So when he was, as now, she tried to treat the evening as a celebration rather than a normal event. She had bought a chicken, a bottle of wine, and was preparing a proper roast meal in the kitchen. It was an effort, even to focus her mind on the cooking. Everything she did at the moment was like that, as if she carried a huge boulder of grief on her shoulders.

But she had to go on, she told herself grimly. If she was to survive, and walk away from this horror that had happened, she could only do it one step at a time.

She was draining sprouts when she glanced out of the window to see their collie barking at a woman who was closing the gate at the end of the track behind a car which had just come through. There was something disturbingly familiar about the woman which set Kathryn's heart beating anxiously. She watched as the woman got back into the car, which drove swiftly down the track, the collie streaking exuberantly alongside.

'Someone coming, Andy,' she called to her husband. 'Can you see who it is?'

'All right.' As the car pulled up outside the front door Andrew stepped outside and called the dog to heel. The young woman got out, followed a man in a suit, and a uniformed police constable. They came towards him, their faces grim but polite.

'Mr Walters? DS Tracy Litherland. We met before, you may remember ...'

'On the night Shelley died. Yes, of course.'

'This is Detective Chief Inspector Churchill. Is your wife at home?'

'Yes, she's inside. Why?' A pulse beat uncomfortably in Andrew's throat. Not more bad news, surely?

'Could we come in? We have a few questions.'

'About what? She's had a lot of strain recently, you know. We both have.'

Will Churchill spoke for the first time. 'It would be easier to explain inside, sir. If you don't mind.'

'Oh, all right.' Reluctantly, Andrew led them through to the farm kitchen. Kathryn's eyes darkened as she saw it was the police. 'What now, for heavens sake? Not that gun again, surely? Is this my official warning?'

'I'm afraid not, no, madam,' Churchill said solemnly. 'If you'd like to take a seat? A few days ago we found a body. In the woods, a couple of miles from here.'

'Oh, that.' Paradoxically, the announcement came as relief to Kathryn. She had read about the incident and dismissed it as a tragedy that, for once, had nothing to do with her. The name of the dead man had not been released. 'Yes, it was in the Press. A man in a car, wasn't it? You must be busy.'

'We are.' Churchill studied her coldly. 'We thought you might be able to help with our enquiries. The dead man's name, you see, was David Kidd.'

'Good God!' Kathryn stared at them unseeing, as a stream of emotions swirled through her mind - shock, horror, joy, relief. 'David's dead?' she said, her voice croaking hoarsely. 'Really? Are you sure?'

'He appears to have drowned in his car, in a pit on a disused airfield in woods two miles south of this house.'

'Thank God!' Andrew squeezed Kathryn's hand in warning, but the relief in her voice was plain. 'Did he kill himself, then, is that it? Out of guilt?'

'No. We believe he was murdered.'

'Oh. Well, whoever did it should be given a medal.' She brushed away tears, meeting their cold, disapproving eyes with a bleak smile of delight. 'You don't expect me to be sorry, do you? That bastard killed my daughter.' She laughed, a high, shrill laugh half out of control. Andrew squeezed her hand tighter.

'Not according to the court, he didn't,' said Churchill coolly. 'He was acquitted, as you know very well. And you told the world how wrong it was on prime time TV. Shortly after which, Mrs Walters, you were arrested outside his flat with a shotgun registered to your husband. Now David Kidd has been found dead, a few miles from your house.' He took out his notebook. 'So perhaps you could tell me where you were on the night of Wednesday 16th October. Both you and your husband. From say, six in the evening till six the next day.'

Kathryn shook her head, dazed. This was all crazy, and it was happening too fast. David was dead - she wanted to savour the wonderful news, not account for herself to this obnoxious young man with his questions and notebook. Where had she been, anyway, and what did it matter? The Valium made it hard to remember. 'I got home from the pharmacy at about seven, I think, and then I was here, all evening.'

'Was anyone with you?'

'I'm not sure ... I don't know ...' Something was knocking at the back of her mind, a terrible, shocking question wanting to come in.

'I was here, all the time.' Andrew answered smoothly before she could say any more. 'All evening, don't you remember, Kath? I came home shortly after you. We had a meal, watched TV for a while, and went to bed.' His hand tightened on hers as she turned to him in surprise. What the devil is he saying that for, she wondered. He didn't come home at all on Wednesday, did he? Or have I got the days mixed up?

'Is that true, Mrs Walters?' Churchill's eyes were focussed intently on her, as though he could see inside her mind. She glared back, hating him. Surely Andrew can't have done this? But if he has, my husband's been a hero, for once. Rashly, she decided to agree.

'Yes, I think so. It was just like tonight, only we weren't interrupted by policemen.' She smiled again, more vacantly this time. 'We didn't kill him, much as we might have liked to. How did he die, exactly?'

'He drowned,' Churchill answered shortly. 'His car was found in a fuel pit. You didn't go anywhere that evening, then? Not out for a walk, for instance, with the dog?'

'It's not necessary,' said Andrew. 'She exercises herself, as you saw.'

'So you were both here. What did you eat?'

Andrew glanced hesitantly at his wife, who answered coolly for them both. 'Shepherd's pie. Followed by apple crumble. And cream. Oh, and coffee of course. With mints.'

'A lot to cook after a long day at work.'

'I like to cook. As you see.' Kathryn nodded at the Aga, where the chicken was roasting in the oven. Potatoes were steaming on the side, sprouts ready drained in the sink. 'I was just about to serve up. Unfortunately we can't ask you to stay.'

'Can anyone confirm this story?' said Churchill, ignoring the hint. 'Your other daughter, Miranda, perhaps? Where was she?'

A door opened at the back of Kathryn's mind, and the terrible question crept in. *Why wasn't Miranda at home when I phoned?* Three days after she left here?

'In America,' said Andrew, coming to the rescue again. 'I drove her to Manchester airport myself, on Monday. Even watched her get on the plane, as it happens.' He smiled with obvious relief. 'So you won't be bothering her, I hope.'

'You don't happen to remember the flight number, do you sir?'

'I can tell you the time. 08.37, British Airways. Good enough?'

Churchill wrote it down. 'We'll check. After all, she had a motive too.'

'A motive? So you're saying one of us killed him, are you?' Kathryn glared at the officious little detective, real hatred in her eyes. The threat was out in the open now. 'Look, we're glad to hear he's dead, of course we are, both of us. That may not be Christian, but it's true. That man killed our daughter, whatever the jury said, and he deserved to die. But that doesn't mean we killed him. My husband and I were here together in this house and Miranda was thousands of miles away in America. So if he was murdered it must have been someone else. A nasty little sod like that must have dozens of enemies. Why don't you go out and find them instead of wasting our time?'

'We're pursuing several lines of enquiries, madam.'

'Are you? It doesn't look like it. What makes you so sure it wasn't an accident, anyway? Or suicide - he had enough to feel guilty about.'

Churchill put down his pen and looked at her carefully. 'Well, for one thing, Mrs Walters, the post mortem. He didn't just drive into that pit in the darkness, you see. He was drugged. We had the laboratory results today. And you're a pharmacist, I believe.'

Kathryn shook her head slowly. She felt sick. 'That's a serious accusation.'

'It's a serious matter, Mrs Walters. I have a warrant here to search your pharmacy. So if you don't mind, I must ask you for the keys.'

'The keys to my business? What on earth for?'

'As I say, Mr Kidd's body was drugged, and we need to determine whether the drugs came from your pharmacy. We could do it now but it's late and I imagine you're tired. So if you give me the keys we can start in the morning. Don't worry, you can hand out prescriptions while we search.'

This is nonsense, Kathryn thought. How could David Kidd have taken drugs from my pharmacy? Even if he did, how would he get up there in the woods, in a car? It doesn't make sense. But if it's got nothing to do with me, it can't have anything to do with Miranda or Andrew either, can it? Stunned, she handed over her keys. 'What about my partner, Cheryl Wolman?'

'Someone's calling on her at the moment.' Churchill got his feet. 'I've a warrant to search this house, too. We'll begin straight away, if you don't mind.' He strolled out into the hall, pausing by a rack of coats, shoes and boots in the porch. He picked up a shoe, turning it over in his hand and peering at the sole. 'This yours, is it?'

'Well it's obviously not my husband's.'

Churchill nodded. 'Size six, I see.' He dropped the shoe and its pair into a plastic evidence bag. 'If you stay down here with this officer, I'll take a look upstairs.' He waved casually at the Aga as he left the room. 'Eat, if you want to. It's going to be a long night.'

It was the shoes which upset Kathryn the most. They were a pair of black trainers which she wore sometimes for running or walking the dog. They were stronger, more waterproof than those she used in the gym. But the most important thing was how she had got them. They were a gift from Miranda. She'd seen her daughter with a pair like that and liked them so much that Miranda had bought her some for Christmas. She remembered them running together, mother and daughter dressed alike, a perfect match. They both took the same shoe size, six.

So why had the policeman taken them? Not to match with a shoe he'd found, surely - that wouldn't make sense. So what else did shoes leave? Footprints! If he'd found a size six footprint matching those trainers in the woods near where Kidd had died then ... of course he would think it was her. Especially since she probably had been in those woods wearing those trainers with the dog some time in the past month - and she almost never cleaned them, so the bits of mud and leaves in the soles or trapped between the laces might easily be the same as those on the feet of whoever had killed him.

Someone else who hated him as much as she did. Well, there must be plenty of those. But not so many who wore size six trainers.

Why wasn't Miranda at home in Wisconsin, four days after she'd left? What could she possibly have to do with drugs from my pharmacy?

For an hour she and Andrew sat silent together in the kitchen, watched by a young constable. Neither of them felt like eating, so she took the chicken out of the oven and put it in the warmer with the vegetables. When the police eventually left Andrew fumbled for the mobile in his pocket.

'Don't worry,' he said, 'I'll ring Carole now.'

'What?' Kathryn stared at him, dazed. 'What are you talking about - ring Carole now?'

'To tell her what story to tell. Don't worry, she'll do it for me. She does care, you know.'

'You mean - it was you and Carole who did this? My God, Andy - how?'

'Did what?' He frowned, his fingers paused above the mobile.

'Killed David, of course. Drowned him in that pit.'

For a moment, hope sang in her heart. Above the fear and horror she felt pride, that her faithless husband had done something for once, had cared enough about Shelley's death to wreak the revenge she herself had failed to do. If his mistress had helped him, well at least for once she had done something good. But the frown on his face killed her hope.

'Kill him? No, of course I didn't, Kath. I thought you did. That's why I told them I was here.'

Kathryn groaned. This nightmare was just getting worse. 'You mean, you were with Carole that night, and you want her to lie and say you were here with me? Andrew, you idiot, you don't think I actually killed him, do you?'

The lack of an instant answer made her want to laugh and scream at the same time. What was the matter with the man, to tangle things up so badly? But then, she scarcely understood him at all these days. 'Oh Andy, don't be so stupid, how could I possibly have drowned him in a pit in the woods? What am I - Superwoman?'

'It's not me who suspects you - it's them.' Andrew persisted stubbornly. 'After all, you had a motive, you took my shotgun into York - and now they say he was drugged. What are they likely to find in your pharmacy, anyway?'

'God knows. It's been in the hands of that wretched locum for the past month. I'm still trying to sort out the mess. It would help if I knew what drug they were looking for.'

'Yes, well, maybe you should phone Cheryl now, to let her know what's happening. After all ...' He looked at her carefully. 'You were here that night, weren't you?'

'Of course I was. Andy, I didn't kill him.'

'That's why you need an alibi. I'll ring Carole now, before it's too late.' Holding his mobile, he walked out into the study.

Kathryn sat down, her heart beating wildly. So now I'm to be rescued by my husband's mistress, she thought. Or more likely, convicted by her when this stupid alibi fails. But it's too late now, and anyway, that's not what matters, not really. What really matters is that policeman, and what he makes of that shoe. If it wasn't me who killed David, who did? Andrew says he took Miranda to the airport and saw her get onto the plane. But what if she gave him the slip somehow - it's not impossible, she's run rings round her dad since she was eight. What if she didn't get on that plane, and came back?

47. Arrest

THE SEARCH of the pharmacy went a long way to ruining Kathryn's business. Neither she nor Cheryl Wolman, students together at Imperial College, London, had inherited or married wealth; they had saved and borrowed on their own, remortgaging their family homes when their children were small and the venture far from certain to succeed. They had worked hard, building up an appreciative clientele in a town not short of aggressive competition; and their efforts had paid off, making them prosperous and well respected amongst the discerning elderly population of Harrogate.

All this was threatened by the intrusive presence of four detectives inside next morning. By eleven the news was all over the town: those nice ladies at Walters and Wolman's were being busted by the drug squad. Even people with no business at the chemist's took a diversion down the street to see for themselves, and those who came at lunchtime were particularly rewarded to see computers and bags full of ledgers being carried out to a waiting van, while the pharmacists watched, white as sheets.

'How long are you going to keep this stuff?' Kathryn asked. 'We can't run a business without records.'

But Churchill was unsympathetic. This was a murder enquiry, he insisted; his warrant empowered him to impound any evidence he deemed relevant. To him, as he explained to Tracy and the rest of the team that morning, the situation already seemed quite clear. Kathryn Walters had both motive and means to dispose of David Kidd; now, as the evidence began to fall into place, it was clear that she had had the opportunity as well. A witness had seen a woman with Kidd getting into his car; a partial footprint found in the mud matched Kathryn's trainer; and there were several packs of rohypnol unaccounted for in the pharmacy records as well.

The arrest came at six the next morning. Kathryn was in her dressing gown feeding the dog, when two cars drew up outside. Churchill got out, three other detectives behind him.

'Kathryn Walters,' he said. 'I am arresting you on suspicion of the murder of David Kidd. You don't have to say anything, but it may harm your defence if you do not mention when questioned something which you later rely on in court. Anything you do say may be given in evidence.' He nodded at Tracy behind him. 'This officer will stay with you while you get dressed. Is your husband at home?'

'Yes. He's still in bed.'

'Well, he'd better get up, smartish. I want a word with him.'

Tracy followed Kathryn upstairs, and Andrew came down, red-faced and blustering. 'What the devil do you think you're doing? It's six o'clock, for Christ's sake.'

'Justice never sleeps,' said Churchill smoothly. 'Though you do, sir, it seems. At your mistress's flat, most often.'

'I don't know what you're talking about.'

'Don't you? You told me that you spent the night of the 16th with your wife, a lie that she confirmed. We checked with your mistress Carole Robinson, who claimed that she was alone that night. The trouble is, sir, times being what they are, her apartment building has CCTV cameras installed to protect female residents from harm, and guess what? We checked the film of that night and who should we see on it but you, sir - arriving at seven in the evening and not leaving until eight the following morning.'

'There must be a mistake ...'

'Yes, sir. The mistake of a liar who got found out. But a mistake which gives you an alibi too, as it happens. You can hardly have been murdering Mr Kidd if you were rogering Miss Robinson in her flat all night, can you? The details of which she is probably confirming to a woman PC about now. I'm afraid your wife is coming with us.'

In the interview room Will Churchill sat with Tracy Litherland facing Kathryn and Lucy Parsons, the solicitor Sarah Newby had recommended, across the table. He switched on the tape, and repeated the caution. 'Mrs Walters, on Thursday the body of a man, David Kidd, was recovered from a disused wartime drainage tank in woods two miles from your house. How do you feel about that?'

Kathryn glanced at Lucy Parsons, whom she had met for half an hour before the interview began. Say as little as possible, the lawyer had advised her. If you're innocent, keep telling them that. If you don't want to answer a question, say nothing. If you're glad about Kidd's death, don't emphasize it.

'Shocked, I suppose.'

'Just shocked? You said you were glad yesterday, at your house.'

'Yes, well. You and I both know he killed my daughter.'

'He was acquitted, Mrs Walters, by the court.'

'The court got it wrong. I said that after the trial.'

'You did, yes.' Churchill read from a paper on his desk. '"This isn't justice, it's a farce. The jury got it wrong. That man's going to walk free and if he isn't stopped he'll do it again. Another mother will go through all this pain." Do you remember saying those words?'

'I remember it, yes. I was upset.'

'If he isn't stopped. That sounds like a threat to me.'

'Does it?'

'Yes. Come on, Kathryn. We both know you were arrested with a shotgun outside David Kidd's flat. You went there to kill him, didn't you?'

'How could I? I didn't have any cartridges.'

'So you say.' Churchill gazed at her coldly. He had confronted Terry Bateson again about that incident earlier this week. Terry had stuck to his story but Will Churchill didn't believe a word of it. The man was a sentimental fool. 'What was the point of taking a gun then, if you didn't intend to use it?'

'I was upset. I wanted to frighten him, I suppose. Show how badly he'd hurt me.'

'Are you pleased that he's dead?'

'I'm not sorry.' Kathryn felt Lucy's fingers on her arm. 'How could I be?'

'So you admit you had a motive for his death?'

Kathryn felt tears welling in her eyes and brushed one away from her cheek. She didn't want to be here, she didn't want any of this. If Andrew had done this, I'd be proud of him. But he didn't, he's not man enough to. So that leaves Miranda. And if she was here instead of me, that would be ten times, a hundred times worse. I couldn't bear it. Overnight her suspicions about Miranda's involvement had grown stronger, together with her desire to protect her. Miranda must have done it: how, Kathryn didn't know and didn't want to. All that mattered was that this policeman didn't find out.

A picture came into her mind of the lapwings who nested in the fields near their home in the spring. When she went out with the children or the dog the mother bird would appear ahead of them, screeching, trailing a wing as if it were broken, flapping and falling to the ground again, risking its life in front of the dog's jaws, but always drawing it a few yards further away from its chick. That's what a mother is supposed to do, she thought. That's what I'm doing now.

'All right.' Churchill turned to another subject. 'Where were you on the night of the 16th?'

'At home with my husband.'

A cool grin stretched Churchill's lips. 'You're sure about that, are you?'

'Yes. Why, don't you believe me?'

'As it happens, no, I don't. You see, we have CCTV pictures of your husband entering the flat of a Miss Carole Robinson at about seven that night, when you say he was at home with you. We also have pictures of him emerging from the flat at eight the next morning.'

'Oh.' Things could always get worse, Kathryn realised. It was bad enough guessing - knowing - where Andrew had been that night, but to have this man salivating as he twisted the bruise was a new form of torture altogether. She looked at the two detectives sadly. 'I must have got the night wrong.'

'You admit he has a mistress?'

'He has graduate students who he does research with. I think she's one of those.'

'Research. Is that what he calls it?' Churchill smirked. 'So you were alone that night?'

'I must have been, yes.'

'And you lied about your husband being home.'

'I made a mistake about the day, that's all. So did my husband.'

'All right.' Churchill reached beneath the table and produced a pair of black trainers in an evidence bag. 'Do you recognize these shoes?'

Kathryn shuddered. She examined the shoes through the plastic. 'I have a pair like this, certainly. Where did you find them?'

'In your house, yesterday afternoon.'

'So?'

'The scenes of crime officers have found several partial footprints around the tank where David Kidd's body was found. They appear to match the tread on those shoes exactly.'

'It doesn't prove it's me.' Hundreds of women must have shoes like these, Kathryn thought. But she didn't say it, because she guessed whose shoe had left the footprints. And she felt with a sudden, urgent panic that if she did say that, Churchill would instantly realize his mistake and start looking for the real murderer, which would never do. The lapwing flapped its wings in her mind. She shook her head, confused.

'Kathryn? How do you account for that?'

'I don't. I have no idea.'

'The tread on your shoes matches the footprints found at the scene of the crime. So you were there, weren't you?'

Kathryn shook her head, wordlessly. Churchill persisted, his voice louder. 'You were there, weren't you? Wearing these shoes? I need an answer, Kathryn.'

Lucy Walters put her hand on Kathryn's arm, facing Churchill firmly. 'Inspector, my client is distressed. She needs a break.'

'In a minute. Let her answer first. Were you there, wearing these shoes?'

Kathryn looked up, meeting his eyes, so close to her own. If she confessed, Miranda would be safe for ever. But she couldn't do that either, it seemed. Not yet, anyway. Maybe a time would come ... it was so hard to think what was right, in this cold, impersonal room, with this man firing the same question again and again. All she wanted to do was escape. Shaking her head, she whispered: 'No. I wasn't there.'

Churchill sighed, as if tired of all this pretence. 'Why not confess now, Kathryn, and make it easy for yourself? You have a motive for this crime, you have previously threatened the victim with a shotgun, you have conspired with your husband to lie about your whereabouts on the night of the murder, and your footprints were found near the crime scene. In addition to which you're a chemist with a pharmacy in Harrogate. We searched your shop yesterday, as you know. We were particularly interested in the drug rohypnol. Do you know what that is?'

'Yes. It's occasionally prescribed as a sleeping pill. Flunitrazepam.'

'Do you stock it in your pharmacy?'

'We usually have a few packs, yes. For private prescription.'

'You know it has illegal uses, too, don't you?'

'As a date rape drug? Yes, that's why it's strictly controlled.' Kathryn frowned. 'Why are you asking about this?'

'The pathologist found significant traces of this drug, rohypnol, in David Kidd's blood.' Churchill studied her reaction carefully. 'Perhaps you could tell us what the effects of this drug are, Mrs Walters.'

'It makes people dizzy and confused, unable to control their body properly. They lose all inhibitions, like someone who's drunk, but still look as if they're awake although they don't know what's going on. Normally they don't remember anything afterwards, which is why rapists love it, I suppose. How could David Kidd have taken it?'

'That's what I hoped you might tell me.' The two detectives, watching Kathryn, both saw a shudder, tightening of the lips. In Kathryn's mind the answer to the question was clear; of course, what better way for someone like Miranda to disable a man than slip him some roofies. The perfect feminist's revenge. She shook her head slowly.

'You see, I did a little research on this,' Churchill resumed grimly. 'It seems that this drug, fluni ...' he looked down at his notes. 'Flunitrazepam, is subject to strict record keeping by the World Health Organization, no less, as well as the UK government. Yet when we checked your records, Mrs Walters, we found no less than two packs of this drug unaccounted for. Not covered by any prescription. Can you explain that?'

Kathryn stared at him, stunned. 'No, I can't. Are you sure?'

'Quite sure, Kathryn. We checked very thoroughly.'

'I'd have to look at the records myself to explain it.'

'You'll have plenty of time for that, before the trial.' Churchill leaned forward across the table, a wolfish grin on his lips. 'How did you do it, Kathryn? Trail him to a pub and slip the pills in his beer, is that it? They dissolve in a couple of minutes, I'm told. Tasteless, odourless, invisible. Then what? You steered him out to his car, and drove him to the woods near your home while he lolled in the seat like a dummy? Was it difficult to drive, a Lotus? Had you driven one before?'

Kathryn stared at him, like a rabbit watching a stoat. She could deny all this, even his description of the drug, which in its legal version released a blue chemical dye, but she didn't want to. Not now, not yet. In the horror of his mistaken accusation, she thought, lay some safety. For herself, because she was innocent; for Miranda, because she was unsuspected. There was another possible reason why this drug might be missing from her pharmacy; a fortnight ago her partner Cheryl had sacked a young male locum who had harassed the female staff. But she said nothing of this now.

'Then what? You drove him to the woods where this awful pit was, got out, moved the fence, heaved him into the driving seat, put the car in gear and stepped back, is that it? The perfect crime, except that you made too much noise and the farmer heard you. Otherwise he'd still be down in the mud today.' Churchill studied her, his eyes a few inches from hers. 'That's what you did, isn't it, Kathryn? You stopped him, just as you said you would outside the court. You killed him because he killed your daughter.'

'No.' She spoke so softly that Churchill doubted it would record.

'No? For the benefit of the tape, Mrs Walters is shaking her head. But you're glad he's dead, aren't you? You told me that earlier.'

'If anyone deserved to die, he did.' This time the words were clear, quite clear enough for the recording. Lucy squeezed Kathryn's arm in warning.

'So you don't regret killing him?'

Kathryn stared into Churchill's eyes, a cauldron of emotions bubbling inside her. There was only one thing she was certain of, in all this horror and chaos. She was not going to lose another daughter.

'I regret nothing.'

The cold smile of triumph on Will Churchill's face broadened slightly. 'Very well. Kathryn Walters, I am charging you with the murder of David Kidd. You do not have to say anything, but it may harm your defence if you do not mention when questioned something which you later rely on in court. Anything you do say may be given in evidence.'

48. Personality Clash

TERRY BATESON and Will Churchill were like oil and water, unable to mix. They had clashed the moment Churchill was appointed, parachuted in from Essex while Terry was disabled by the shock of Mary's death. Since then, despite initial attempts to get on, the conflict between them had become personal. Churchill grated on Terry every time they met. Brash, cocky, ambitious, unencumbered by wife, children, or self-doubt, he focussed relentlessly on his own career when on duty, and his personal enjoyment when free. Nothing else mattered. And yet, it seemed to Terry, the future was with men like Churchill, not himself. The younger officers admired him for his mastery of buzz words, his skill at jumping through the promotion hoops. Targets mattered more to him than the crimes themselves, or their victims. For him, the failure of Kidd's prosecution was a catastrophe not because of the pain suffered by the Walters, but because of the damage suffered by the crime figures.

Terry's own reputation was damaged too, perhaps terminally. Crossing the canteen, he imagined muttered conversations: 'past it', 'too much time with the kids', 'can't hack it any more'. He'd seen it happen before, to an old DI with a legendary string of convictions to his name. Suddenly, in his fifties, the fire had gone out of the man. The younger detectives saw not a star but an old buffer who didn't understand new procedures or technology. He was shifted sideways into administration, and when he retired, there were more balloons in the canteen than colleagues.

That could be his future too, he thought sadly. Kathryn Walters' arrest had brought a buzz to the department, as the arrest of a murder suspect always did; but most of Churchill's team looked at him with eyes that were pitying, embarrassed rather than friendly. It wasn't his case any more; it was his mess they were clearing up.

Yet he was desperate to know what was going on. The arrest of Kathryn, of all people, was a dreadful blow to him. After all, she was the original victim, not David Kidd. None of this would have happened if Kidd had been convicted, as he should have been. And that, of course, was largely Churchill's fault, although no one else saw it like that. Terry had been in charge of the case, so its failure gave Churchill an opportunity to crow over him once again.

Grimly, he squared his shoulders and knocked on his boss's door.

'Come.'

Terry entered and stood before the broad desk, noting the mocking surprise on the younger man's face as he looked up from in the comfortable leather office chair. 'Ah, Terence. What can I do you for?'

'It's about the Kidd case, sir. I understand you've made an arrest.'

'Yes. Kathryn Walters. She was charged this morning.'

'I ... wondered what the evidence is, sir.'

'Oh, you wondered, did you? Well, it's not your case now, is it?'

'No sir, but it was, and ... obviously I feel some concern.'

'So you bloody well should, too! For Christ's sake, man, if you'd thrown the book at Kathryn Walters when she was arrested with a shotgun outside his flat, then Kidd would probably be alive today. And that woman wouldn't be facing life imprisonment, either. You've got a lot to answer for, old son.'

The accusation, as Terry had expected, was brutal and directly on target. He'd reflected on it long and bitterly last night. He'd destroyed evidence to spare Kathryn, and now it seemed she might be guilty of a murder. If she had committed that crime it was largely his fault, first for failing in the prosecution and then for hiding those cartridges. And yet he still could not fully believe she was guilty. But if she hadn't killed Kidd, who had? These questions consumed him like a fever, the more insistent for the fact that they had no answer. Certainly he could expect no sympathy from Churchill.

'We discussed that fully at the time, sir. The shotgun was unloaded; I had no reason to suppose that it was anything but a futile gesture.'

'Well, it's not so futile now, is it? The man's dead, at the bottom of a stinking pit. You know, if I wasn't so soft, I'd send you back to traffic duty. Might be a good idea, at that. The shift patterns would be easier for your kids, and the decisions less taxing for your brain.'

Terry drew a deep breath, driving his fingernails into his palm to control his temper. Churchill loved to goad him; an outburst of temper would make the wretched man's day. And he deserved something like that, after all; that was the worst of it.

'What I wanted to know, sir, was whether you're sure Mrs Walters is guilty.'

'Sure?' Churchill sat back in his chair and laughed. He spoke in a tone adapted to the understanding of a three year old. 'Well, yes, Terence, as a matter of fact I am. That's why I've charged her with murder, do you see? Because of the evidence, and so on. It's what policemen do.'

'And that evidence is what, exactly?'

For a moment Terry thought his boss wouldn't answer. The idea of telling him to get lost flitted across the younger man's face. But the opportunities for mockery, for rubbing his subordinate's face in it, proved too strong. Churchill leaned forward, counting out each point on his fingers. Terry listened numbly - the motive, the threats Kathryn had made outside court, the shotgun attempt, her husband's failed alibi, the rohypnol in Kidd's body, the missing drugs from Kathryn's pharmacy, the partial footprints which matched a pair of her trainers, and a witness who had seen a woman answering Kathryn's description getting into Kidd's car the night before he died. Churchill smiled grimly.

'Good enough for you yet? To say nothing of the fact that it happened in woods a few miles from her house, in a place she knew well. Oh yes, and in case you're wondering, the only other obvious suspects, her husband and daughter, have rock solid alibis for the night of his death. Hubby was tucked up in bed with his mistress, and daughter flew home to the US of A two days before. I checked, you see. That's what detectives do.'

Terry thought about what he had been told. 'This witness, where did she live?'

'It was a he, actually. An old colonel who lives off Lord Mayor's Walk. Knew Kidd, had had several conversations with him. His window overlooks the garage where Kidd kept his car.'

'How far away is it?'

'About forty yards. He didn't claim he recognised Mrs Walters directly, of course. But he saw her face briefly under a street lamp and picked her out from a list of possibles we showed him. Same height, same age, same colour hair. What more do you want?'

'And his eyesight's all right, is it?'

Churchill shrugged. 'Seventy years old, wears glasses. But he's still got his marbles, the old boy. Commanded a battalion in Korea.'

Terry shook his head doubtfully. 'So what was she doing in the car with Kidd?'

'Planning to kill him, I presume. She'd probably doped him already. You're too soft on this woman, Terence. You don't understand how devious the female can be, when she plans a crime like this.'

There was a case, Terry could see that. But he didn't want to accept it; it didn't fit the Kathryn Walters he knew. Something was wrong here, somewhere. 'It's not good enough, it's all circumstantial. Even those footprints, they could be anyone's. You haven't got anything which puts her at the scene of the crime.'

Churchill looked up at him, the smile cool, controlled, devoid of doubt. 'Not yet, Terence, no, but we will. Don't worry, SOCO are still working on it. I've sent them back to scour the site for another day, or as long as it takes. If she was there - and take my word for it, she was - they'll find something, you know. They always do.'

49. New Client

'KATHRYN WALTERS?' Sarah said. 'I'm not sure I can do it. I prosecuted David Kidd, remember? For the murder of her daughter.'

'Yes, I know. That's why she asked for you, apparently. She wants you and no one else.' Lucy Parsons laughed, a cheerful, encouraging sound. As Kathryn's solicitor, she was ringing to ask if Sarah would defend her client in court. 'Heaven knows why, but you seem to have this effect on some people, Sarah. They trust you. It seems you were nice to her during David Kidd's trial, and she thinks you're the best there is.'

'Even though I lost?' Sarah answered wonderingly. 'Surely it's partly my fault that all this has happened.'

'She doesn't see it that way,' Lucy assured her. 'She blames the police, not you. And she thinks you'll be able to defend her better because you know so much about the background.'

'Well, I'm flattered, Luce, and intrigued. But I'll have to check with the judge first, to see if he thinks there's a conflict of interest. If he doesn't, I'd be happy to do it, of course.'

Sarah put down the phone and leaned back in her chair, thinking. In the months since David Kidd's acquittal many things had happened. Her career had begun to pick up; she had been involved in several high profile cases. Her husband had got the job at the school in Harrogate, and seemed absorbed by the new challenge. Emily had been to Cambridge for an interview, and been offered a place to study environmental science if she got two As and a B in her A levels. And her son Simon had a new girlfriend, Lorraine, a shy girl who seemed so terrified of Sarah that she'd scarcely uttered ten words on the two occasions they'd met so far.

But for all this time Kathryn Walters had been in prison on remand, charged with murder. Sarah had never quite forgotten her; David Kidd's prosecution had been her first notable failure, and the results that had flowed from it made everything worse. Just like Terry Bateson, she wished she could put things right, and this unexpected request to be Kathryn's defence counsel gave her the opportunity. She contacted the judge who was listed for the case, and was relieved when he made no objection. But as she sat reading through the brief which Lucy sent over, her sense of relief and excitement drained away, to be replaced by a burden that pressed on her brows like a migraine.

The prosecution case was stronger than she had expected. If she took on Kathryn's defence and lost, Sarah realised miserably, then she'd feel doubly depressed: for failing to convict Kidd in the first place, and then for failing to defend his victim.

For victim was what Kathryn Walters was, whichever way she looked at it. Even if she had killed David Kidd, she'd only done it to avenge her daughter's murder; and if she hadn't, well ... the injustice was ten times worse. Sarah began to jot down a few phrases for a speech in mitigation, then stopped as she realised what she was doing. Her task was get Kathryn Walters acquitted, not to minimise her sentence out of pity. Not yet, anyway. Though it might come to that in the end.

When she met Kathryn in prison her sense of pity increased. The woman looked thin, grey, diminished. Her body, once trim and muscled by regular visits to the gym, had begun to sag; her mind, previously kept sharp by the demands of running a business, seemed dull and blunted. Sarah had come equipped with a pad of vital questions, but to her surprise, the answers were vague, hesitant, rambling. Several times Kathryn stayed silent, as though she had not heard the question at all.

'Your defence is, simply, that you didn't do it, you weren't there. So why did you give a false alibi?'

'That was my husband, it was his idea. I panicked, I suppose, and went along with it.'

'Not the best decision by either of you. The trouble is, the prosecution will use it to imply that your husband knew you were guilty. Or at least, that he thought you were capable of murder. Is that what he thought?'

'He may have done, I don't know. He was probably just trying to help me.'

'Then they'll bring up your motive: your words outside the court, and your arrest with your husband's shotgun.' Sarah frowned, remembering her earlier interview with Kathryn in the police station. 'You'll have to be careful what you say about that. If you tell the court what you told me that night, it can only help the prosecution.'

'That I went there to kill him, you mean?'

'Yes. You can't afford to say that, Kathryn. Even if it's true. Is that still how you feel?'

'Am I glad he's dead, you mean?'

'Yes.'

'Well ... I always thought I would be, until it happened. But now that I've had time to sit here for months and think about it - think about nothing else, really - it doesn't help.' She sighed, looking down at her hands. 'Nothing brings Shelley back. All I think about is her.'

'Yes, of course.' Watching, Sarah remembered those terrible moments when she'd believed her own daughter was dead. Every second of that time was still vivid to her. She still had dreams about it from which she awoke trembling, tearful, afraid. Occasionally she crept out of bed at three or four in the morning, to listen outside Emily's door and check she was still breathing. All that for a child who hadn't died. How much worse it must be to grieve for a child that had.

'But how do you feel about David?' she asked gently, after a moment's silence.

'Him? Oh ...' Kathryn shook her head, as though distracted by an irrelevance. 'Well, he deserved punishment, of course he did. But you failed to get it for him, didn't you? I don't mean just you on your own; I mean the police and the jury as well. The whole rotten system. So ...'

So I killed him myself, Sarah thought. Is that what she's going to say? If she says that I can't defend her. Not on a not guilty plea. It's best to make that clear now. Then if she does confess I can make a strong plea in mitigation.

She waited, and the moment passed.

'So now he's dead,' Kathryn continued wearily, 'and of course I'm glad he can't harm anyone else's daughter. But it doesn't make me happy, if that's what you mean. How can it? Shelley's still dead and I'm locked up in here. The damage he's done doesn't end.'

'Did you kill him, Kathryn?'

Lucy Parsons looked at Sarah in surprise. This was not a question she, or any barrister, usually asked: not as bluntly as this, anyhow. Normally if a defendant decided to plead not guilty, their barrister would argue the case accordingly, however tenuous or incredible that defence might appear. It was a useful convention, because criminal barristers regularly found themselves defending clients who they were virtually certain were guilty; but so long as the client hadn't actually admitted that guilt, the barrister's duty was to suspend judgement and defend the case as instructed, whatever her own opinion. Judgement was for jurors, not lawyers.

Now Sarah had deliberately broken the convention. If she was going to take this case, she had decided, she wanted to believe in it.

Kathryn met her eyes. She appeared to be thinking, weighing things up. But she didn't give the impression of lying. 'No,' she said at last. 'I didn't. I had my chance, and I failed.'

That's another thing it would be better not to say in court, Sarah thought. She nodded slightly, accepting Kathryn's assurance, but wondering about the cautious, almost balanced way it had been given. There was something strange here, which wasn't quite clear. Maybe it would become clear later. She turned to the evidence.

'Did you know David Kidd had that car? The Lotus Elise?'

'Yes, of course. He drove Shelley to our house in it once. To show off, no doubt.'

'And this drainage tank in the woods. You knew that was there, I suppose?'

'Of course I did. I used to take the dogs for walks in those woods. Lots of people knew it was there.'

Kathryn thought about saying more, but decided not to. In her mind she saw again, as so often over the past few months, the images of two little girls, sodden, filthy, and exhausted, their clothes dripping, their hair hanging in rats' tails, on that terrible day when Shelley had saved Miranda from drowning. That was when Kathryn had first learned about the pit, and she had regarded it with horror ever after, avoiding it herself and forbidding her daughters to go there; but it was a story she didn't want to tell her lawyers, because she guessed what they would make of it. This barrister, Sarah Newby, had children of her own; she would know how strong childhood impressions could be. If she heard that story she would realise how powerful an impression the drainage pit must have made upon Miranda, as a place so nearly associated with her own death - a place where a body could so easily drown under black, filthy water, far from any possible help. And with luck, never be found.

Kathryn didn't want Sarah Newby, or anyone else, to think about

Miranda just now. Like the lapwing feigning injury in the fields, she was still trying to draw attention further away from her nest, until finally she could escape, sure that her chick would never be found. But she knew that at any moment her deception might fail, and she would face a terrible choice. To see her daughter devoured by the jaws of justice, or to throw herself in front of them instead.

That was why she had chosen Sarah Newby to defend her. Not because she thought she was the best barrister in the world - she had failed, after all, to get David Kidd convicted - but because Sarah had defended her own son in court before, so Kathryn thought she would understand, better than most, how much a mother would do to save her child.

But it had not come to that yet, and Kathryn hoped it never would. If Sarah could save her from the clutches of Will Churchill, she might never have to mention Miranda at all.

'The police found partial footprints near the tank, matching the tread pattern of a pair of your trainers,' Sarah continued. 'And they have this forensic report saying the mud on your trainers matched that of the soil in the woods.'

'So?' Kathryn smiled faintly. 'I often went for walks in those woods. Just not near that tank, that's all.'

'And you don't know anyone else who has trainers like that?'

'No.' It was the first direct lie. Kathryn met Sarah's gaze and found she could hold it quite well. She'd had practice, after all, with the police.

Sarah nodded. 'Well, there must be thousands of people with trainers like that - possibly millions. Lucy will check, get the exact figure from the manufacturers. Now, what about this other point they're going to focus on - the rohypnol David Kidd was drugged with. It doesn't help that a couple of packets are unaccounted for in your pharmacy, does it? It's circumstantial, of course, like all of this stuff, but ...'

'Yes, well, I've been thinking about that.' Kathryn interrupted with, for once, a trace of eagerness. Here at last was a trail which led away from Miranda. 'You see, in the months after Shelley's death, as you'll imagine, it wasn't easy at work. I took some time off, and even when I was there, I wandered round like a ghost. My partner, Cheryl, did what she could, but she has troubles of her own: her grand-daughter's autistic, so she had to help there. So we hired a young locum. Neither of us liked him much, but he was the best we could get. And, well, there were several complaints from the girls in the shop, and when Cheryl rang round the places he'd worked before it was the same story. So ...'

'You're suggesting he may have stolen the rohypnol for use as a date rape drug?'

'It's possible, yes. From the way he behaved and what the girls said.'

'Did you tell the police this?'

'Yes. They weren't interested.'

'Well, that's useful, at least.' Sarah made a note. 'The other main detail is this hair bobble of yours, that was found under some leaves near the tank. It had your hairs on it - they've established that by DNA. That's the only thing that puts you indisputably near the scene of the crime. How do you account for that?'

'I don't.'

'Not at all? It's the one thing that's likely to convict you.'

'Then the police must have put it there themselves. That's the only possibility, isn't it?'

Sarah'd had the same thought herself, when first reviewing the papers; and the fact that DCI Will Churchill was in charge of this case increased the possibility considerably. But there was a deep gulf between suspicion and proof. She sighed. 'Yes, but it's going to be hard to convince a jury of that. Let's go through exactly how it could have happened, shall we? When did the police first visit your house?'

For the next half hour they went through this in detail, Sarah making extensive notes. The police had searched Kathryn's house and the pharmacy as well, and she wanted to know the names of all the officers involved, and exactly where each of them had been, as far as Kathryn could remember. It was a difficult business, because she had not seen everything that had happened, but Sarah had a sense that Kathryn was being more helpful than before - perhaps too helpful, at times, claiming to remember details that she couldn't easily have known. Nevertheless, she wrote it all down: if her client was being a little creative with the truth now it didn't matter; she could weed out the bits the jury were least likely to believe before she challenged Will Churchill in court.

Kathryn, watching, was pleased. The more her lawyers accepted the possibility of police corruption, the better. It was of course quite plausible that the hair bobble had indeed been planted at the crime scene by the police; she'd seen enough of DCI Will Churchill to believe him capable of anything.

But there was another, equally plausible explanation, which Kathryn was trying to hide. Since they had been teenagers both of her daughters had regularly borrowed not only each other's clothes but hers too. They would wear any top, shoes or jacket that took their fancy, as if clothes were something owned in common, rather than individually. On the day after the shotgun incident, for example, Miranda had wandered in from a walk wearing an old wax jacket of her mother's. The more Kathryn thought about it, the more she realized how many things were stuffed in the pockets of that jacket - tissues, coins, gloves, dog biscuits, wisps of hay. A hair bobble too, perhaps. Kathryn could remember several occasions, on a windy walk with the dogs, when she'd pulled her hair back in a ponytail to keep it from blowing in her eyes. Whereas Miranda, of course, had cut her hair so short after the trial that she'd have had no use for such a thing.

So what if Miranda had put her hand in her pocket for something - a tissue, say, or a glove, or a biscuit for the dog - and the hair bobble, with Kathryn's hair on it, had dropped out? It could have happened any day, of course; but what if Miranda had been wearing that coat on the day David died? Or perhaps she had visited the tank a day or two earlier, on one of her walks with the dog. Either way, it would explain why the bobble was there.

Her lawyers, however, concentrated single-mindedly on the other explanation - that the police had put it there - and the more they explored this possibility, the more Kathryn came to believe in it herself. After all, if Miranda had been so clever, so determined as to do this thing, surely she would have been careful not to make a mistake. She had made no other mistake, as far Kathryn could see - her alibi was perfect, there were no clues, no traces other than these inconclusive footprints. And in the absence of the real murderer this policeman, this DCI Churchill, had every reason to suspect her, Kathryn, and every incentive, too, to go that little bit further to provide proof of her guilt.

Sarah, reviewing her notes at the end of the interview, was convinced that the detective had done exactly that. She'd seen how he behaved in David Kidd's trial with the shopkeeper Patel, stretching the evidence in the way he wanted; and before that with her own son, interviewing him in a police car in defiance of all regulations and then trying to present his words in court as a spontaneous confession. But how to challenge it; that was another matter.

Rising at the end of the interview, she gave Kathryn a tight, determined smile. 'Very well, Mrs Walters, I think we've reviewed all the evidence. But this is the key to it, certainly. If we can shake them on this hair bobble, all the rest is circumstantial. So if anything else comes to mind, for goodness' sake let me know.'

'I will, of course. Do you think we have a chance?'

Sarah considered, knowing how her final words, after an interview like this, could echo in a client's mind, late into the lonely night. 'Yes, we have a chance, certainly. But I'd be lying if I said it was going to be easy. A lot will depend on the impression you make on the witness stand. If the jury believe you're just an innocent victim of this whole affair, then they're more likely to turn their suspicions on the police.'

'So I should be careful what I say, you mean?'

'Yes.' Sarah studied Kathryn thoughtfully. The woman looked pale, gaunt, and anxious. 'Careful, but not too careful, if that makes sense. Think about what they're likely to ask you, and how you'll reply, and then ... tell the truth, as genuinely as you can.'

'I'll try.'

'Good. I'll see you in court then. And don't worry. I'll be doing my best.'

She smiled encouragingly, but on the way home, the interview echoed in her mind just as her words, perhaps, echoed in Kathryn's. There had been something not quite right about it which she couldn't quite put her finger on. Kathryn had maintained her innocence quite firmly, and yet ... there was something that didn't quite fit. It was a sense, familiar to her from less reputable clients, that the whole truth was not being told; that their conversation only dealt with what was on the surface of the woman's mind, that things more momentous by far were going on beneath.

She frowned, sat back in her chair, and wondered.

50. Wisconsin

THE LONG months before the trial had been a torment for Miranda. When she had first heard the news of her mother's arrest she had been distraught. It was not what she had imagined would happen, at all. The body should have remained buried in that tank for months, years even, until it dissolved into mush; instead, just as her nightmare on the plane had foretold, David's corpse had crawled out, pallid, bloated, relentless, to threaten her family again. And she had certainly not expected her mother to be arrested. I'll have to go back, she thought; I did this, I'll have to sort it out.

But then her mother had phoned from prison - a three minute call, probably recorded by the authorities and made in a public corridor to judge from the background echoes. Kathryn had been adamant: 'It's all for the best, darling. He's dead and I'm glad of it. Proud. If I met the person who did it I'd hug them to my heart and ... well, never mind. I'd love that person forever. The main thing is not to worry. They can't prove I'm guilty because I didn't do it, and the best thing you can do for me is to stay in America with Bruce and Sophie, and *not come here*. Do you understand? I love you deeply, darling, more deeply than ever before, but I don't want you to come back here until it's over. Promise me, please darling, promise me that.'

So Miranda had promised. What else could she do? Letters had followed in similar vein, all of them circumspect because of the prison censor, but it was clear, without saying it, that her mother guessed who had done it and was prepared to sacrifice herself, if necessary, for her daughter's happiness.

Only Miranda wasn't happy, not at all. She couldn't say anything, even to Bruce, without incriminating herself. She hid from him behind a wall of silence. Once allow a trickle of truth to escape, she thought, and it would prize the floodgates open and drown them all. Her mother was right - she would lose Bruce and Sophie - all would be drowned, torn away from her for ever.

But the secret consumed her like a cancer. If only there was someone she could tell! She went for long walks alone in the forest, whispering her confession to beavers in dams, screaming it aloud to eagles on hilltops, throwing stones disconsolately into lakes. Nothing helped for long; no one understood. There were weeks when she scarcely spoke to Bruce at all; their marriage seemed drying up for lack of love. From her, at least; he remained kind and considerate, ascribing her snappish moods to the strain she had been through in England. He rocked her in his arms, his big hands holding her like a child, until she shoved him away, tears starting again in her eyes.

If it had not been for Sophie she would have gone back. But the little girl needed her now, it seemed, more than ever. In the first few weeks after Miranda's return the child had been a nightmare, alternately clinging to her mother's jeans or slapping her face and running to hide in her bedroom. To Miranda it seemed as if the child was fey, smelt the mud and oil of the drainage pit on the hands that reached out to embrace her, saw the ferocity of a killer in her mother's eyes. But it wasn't so, she told herself, it couldn't be true; Sophie had been upset the first time she'd gone to England, for Shelley's funeral; this was the same effect magnified, an attempt to punish her mother for going away. All her friends said the same: her long absence had damaged her daughter's security, it was to be expected. All she had to do was stay patient and calm, and her daughter's trust would return.

So Miranda tried, and slowly, grimly, it worked. Gradually, Sophie settled, until, occasionally, a whole day would pass without a tantrum, a week without a damp little girl coming in to her at midnight from sodden sheets. But it was not straightforward, and with Bruce often working late, most of the burden fell on her. Once it became so bad she took the child to a therapist, but that was awful; after conducting various tests on her daughter the man turned his gaze on Miranda, asking increasingly probing questions about her emotional state, her behaviour, her relationship with her husband and parents. Miranda met his eyes with a blank, non-committal stare, while the panic-stricken truth burrowed away to hide in a cave deep in her brain. It was too early, the man said, for Sophie to be exhibiting the symptoms of bi-polar disorder; the best thing by far would be consistent, patient parenting, in a secure environment shielded from the pressures of the outside world.

But to do that Miranda had to grow a shell to shield herself. She became adept at deflecting all talk about events in England; friendly enquiries from friends and her husband's family slid off her like water from a duck's wings. Perhaps she seemed cold to them, indifferent; she didn't care. To her the subject was so sensitive that part of her mind thought about nothing else; and yet, to survive at all, to get through the day, above all to care for Sophie, she had encysted her secret within her, so that it lived in its own little world like a globe, a cherished disease. A monster whose existence she could acknowledge to no one.

It was hardest, of course, for Bruce. As things with Sophie improved, he wanted to try for a second child. Miranda shuddered and shrank from him in bed.

'No,' she said. 'Not yet. I'm not ready.'

'So when will you be? After your Mom's trial?'

'Maybe. I can't say. I'll let you know.'

'You'll let me know? This is a thing for us both, honey. Not just you.'

'I know, love. But not yet. I just can't.'

As the trial approached the cyst within her threatened to burst. Her mother's letters insisted that she should stay away, but Miranda knew, more and more clearly, that it would be impossible. She had to go back, even if meant abandoning Sophie yet again, just at the time when the little girl was really settling down. But the thought of allowing Bruce to put another baby inside her, another responsibility to grow alongside the monster of guilt she kept hidden, made her feel sick. She hadn't dared discuss this with him yet, let alone tell her daughter she was leaving. But she had to go back, she couldn't leave her mother to face this alone. Even if it meant abandoning her family for ever.

'Sophie's nearly three now,' he persisted. 'We agreed that would be the best time, you know we did. A little brother or sister for her to grow up with might be just what she needs.'

And a mother in prison, if things go wrong, Miranda thought. Yes, terrific. With an enormous effort she turned in the bed to smile at him.

'Maybe you're right, love. After Mum's trial. I'll feel better about things then.'

'Is that it? I know it's a lot of strain for you, honey. But you never talk about it. Maybe it would be better if you did.'

'Nothing to talk about. She didn't do it, she's not guilty. I'm tired, Bruce, I'm sorry. I've got a headache.'

It was not the first or the fortieth time he'd been brushed off like this. Tonight, with the trial less than a month away, he was determined to pursue it further. Bruce admired his mother in law, regarding her as a tough old bird, but he didn't regard her guilt as totally impossible. She had a clear enough motive, after all. It might be wrong but he could understand someone killing for revenge.

'Have you never thought she might have done it?' he asked. 'After all she had good reason, didn't she? If anyone did that to Sophie, I'd probably do the same.'

'You're a man, Bruce. She's a woman in her fifties.' Miranda turned away, feigning sleep.

'Even so, Shelley was her daughter. You'd do it too, wouldn't you, love?' he persisted. 'Fight to protect your children, if there was no other way?'

Miranda shook her head numbly, feeling the tears prickle at the back of her eyes. For a moment she was tempted to confess; if he really felt like that perhaps he would understand her, even forgive. But she didn't trust him; the burden was too great. He might have broad shoulders but she'd been married to him long enough to know that his opinions changed according to the people he was with, and his mother in particular had powerful religious views that saw the world clearly in terms of the ten commandments. Once her secret was out, she could never call it back. Bruce would be shocked, appalled, uncertain what to think; he would seek advice from his family and friends, and soon the whole world would know.

She loved him so much; she was killing everything she loved.

'Maybe you should go back for this trial after all,' he said thoughtfully, after a pause. 'You're no good here, just worrying. You should give your mom support, not just shrivel into yourself like this.'

'I do give her support!' she snapped, so loud that their dog barked in the garden. 'Haven't you seen all the letters I send her, the cards? What more can I do, Bruce, if she doesn't want me there?'

'I know she says that, honey, I've seen the letters too.'

'And what about Sophie? Just when she's doing so well at last.'

'I'll manage. I managed before.'

'Until I came back, yes. You know what she was like then.' Abandoning the pretence of sleep, Miranda sat up in bed. He was only advocating what she knew she had to do anyway.

'You needn't be away long. If your Mom's acquitted, you could even bring her back here for a holiday. She likes Sophie; that might help.'

'Yes, sure.' Miranda stared numbly out of the window, watching the moon rising over the trees at the end of the garden. Why was it so red tonight, of all nights?

'If it was my mom, I'd be there no matter what. Christ, Mandy, what can go wrong?'

'Oh, nothing.' Gratefully, Miranda watched a cloud darken the blood red moon. 'Nothing at all, Bruce.' She mouthed the words emptily, grateful that he'd made the decision himself. It might be the last burden he'd ever take from her. That, and a lifetimes's care of Sophie, if things went wrong.

Miranda shuddered, exhausted by the months of struggle. She'd borne her secret for so long, but it just grew stronger. Bruce was right, she belonged in England, not here. She'd done her best with Sophie, but she was no good to her husband any more; she was a husk, a ghost of the wife he deserved. To hide here with him while her mother was locked up for life would be intolerable.

Her only hope now was that Kathryn would be acquitted. And I have to be there to see it, Miranda thought. There's no other way.

They sat silent in the dark, their minds as distant as continents. The first red rays of the moon emerged from the far side of the cloud.

'You're right,' she said at last. 'I do have to go.'

51. New Trial

ANOTHER DAY, another trial. Sarah Newby placed the red ribboned brief on the ancient oak table in the centre of York Crown Court, and sat down to await the entrance of the judge. Beside her, counsel for the prosecution, Matthew Clayton QC, a short, dapper man with the spare physique of a long distance runner, smiled at her politely. She had not met him before, but he came with a formidable reputation. He surveyed the court with interest.

The public gallery was full, the air humming with the buzz of eager whispered conversation and feet hurrying over wooden floors. The jury were on Sarah's right, the clerk and ushers ahead of her, the security guard and shorthand writers all in place.

The talk hushed as the accused came up from the cells between two security guards. Sarah turned to smile encouragement to her client as she entered the dock. Kathryn looked pale, calm and composed. She wore a blue two piece suit, with a brooch and a scarf at her neck. She looked what she was - a respectable educated woman in her early forties - except that she was thinner now than when they'd first met. So thin and pale, that Sarah had wondered if she might have cancer. But the stress of losing a daughter could do that to anyone - not to mention being tried for murder. Kathryn stepped forward to the edge of the dock and looked around her - a tense, frail figure surrounded by eyes - like Joan of Arc at the stake, a martyr to the mob.

The judge, his Lordship Robert McNair QC, entered, bowed, and took his seat, resplendent in red robes, sash and wig. The clerk read the charge:

'Kathryn Elizabeth Walters, you are hereby charged that on the night of 16th October last, you did kill David William Kidd, contrary to Section 1 of the Homicide Act 1957. How say you? Are you guilty, or not guilty, of that charge?'

'Not ... I'm sorry.' Kathryn coughed to clear her dry throat. 'Not guilty.'

'Very well. You may be seated.'

So that's over at least, Sarah thought. Throughout their pre-trial conferences Kathryn had been so withdrawn, tense, and uncommunicative, that Sarah had sometimes wondered if she wanted to be convicted, and would surrender at the first challenge. Sarah dreaded putting her on the stand. Any competent prosecutor could make that sort of behaviour look like guilt; it was not a chance that Matthew Clayton QC was likely to miss.

He rose now to outline his case. Addressing the jury with a clear, resonant voice, his pleasant everyday tone somehow emphasized the horror of how David Kidd had died.

'The pathologist will tell you that the cause of his death was drowning. Not surprising, you may think, for a man trapped inside a car under six feet of dirty water. Physical examination shows how he clawed at the roof and doors of that car, trying to get out, but failed. His lungs filled with water and he drowned.'

He explained how the presence of copious quantities of rohypnol in David's blood made it impossible that this was an accident, since he would have been incapable of driving a car or performing any normal actions, let alone escaping from a car when he suddenly found himself trapped in it under water. And the car was far from the road, in the middle of lonely woods.

'So, a suspicious death, at the very least. But what led the police to treat this as murder, and crucially for us, to identify Kathryn Walters as the murderer? Well, as in the best detective stories, a number of small clues led inescapably, so the prosecution say, to Mrs Walters' door. The police witnesses will lay this evidence before you.'

The best detective stories! Sarah snorted, just loud enough for Matthew Clayton to hear. He looked, she thought, faintly abashed. This was a serious matter, after all, not an entertainment, and he must know that the tightrope of logic he was about to lead the jurors across was painfully thin. One weak thread and they would fall into an abyss of doubt.

Glancing over her shoulder, Sarah saw Will Churchill sitting at the back of the court, so sure of himself, so smug - a man on the make, who needed convictions to rise to the top. He was the man she would have to challenge, if she was to have any chance at all of winning this case. And so far, the prospects looked far from good.

'The first of these clues, from careful examination of the crime scene, showed a number of marks, on trees and the concrete around the tank, to suggest that the driver of the car - not Mr Kidd - had got out to move a fence, before driving the car over it. Then the fence had been replaced to make it look as though nothing had happened. Mr Kidd couldn't have done that, clearly. Then secondly, footprints - or partial footprints - were found in the area, made by a size six training shoe - the same size and style as trainers found in Kathryn Walters' house. And most conclusively of all, you may think ...'

Matthew Clayton paused, milking the moment like an impresario, meeting the eyes of each of the jurors in turn to ensure he had their full attention.

'Several hairs were discovered, a cluster of female hairs, on a blue elastic hair bobble near the fence. And these hairs, when subjected to DNA analysis, proved to be identical to hairs taken from the accused, Kathryn Walters. Proof positive, you may think. How could Kathryn Walters' hair possibly be near this abandoned fuel pit, unless Kathryn Walters had something to do with the murder of David Kidd?'

There was a soft intake of breath, and the eyes of the jurors, all twelve at once, turned towards Kathryn, where she sat pale and defiant in the dock. She must feel it, Sarah thought, like heat burning into her - or cold, perhaps, sucking her life away.

It was a lethal question, all right. That hair bobble might lock Kathryn away for life. And Clayton had introduced it in just the right way - as the killer clue in his detective story. The jurors would love that, just as Churchill would. After her conferences with Kathryn, Sarah had rung Terry Bateson to ask his opinion about the case. They'd met on a bench by the river. Over the past few months Sarah's conflict with Bob had died down as he threw himself with apparent enthusiasm into his new job, and her relationship with Terry had reverted, more or less, to the professional friendship they had had before. Slightly to her regret, he had made few attempts to progress it further. He seemed too depressed to try.

The failure of David Kidd's trial, followed by the arrest and prosecution of Kathryn Walters for his murder, had undermined Terry's faith: both in the police service, as an organisation devoted to justice, and in himself, as a canny, successful detective. If Kathryn Walters *had* killed David Kidd, then a significant part of that was his fault; but if she was innocent, then someone, somehow, had fabricated the evidence against her.

'I never believed it was her, perfect motive or not,' he'd told Sarah when they met. 'I mean, a woman of her age, how could she get near him, for a start? He loathed her, he'd have crossed the street to avoid her. If it had been Shelley's father or daughter, perhaps. But he was with his mistress and she was in the States. So ...'

'It has to be Kathryn?'

'That's what Churchill thinks, yes. But there could easily be someone else, couldn't there? That's what I told him. Some junkie or hooker like Lindsay Miller, the girl Shelley found him in bed with; some boyfriend or business associate he'd cheated - anyone really. This lad was one of nature's pondlife - he was under every stone you could find. But I'm off the case, and slick Willie, he doesn't want to know. It would take time, energy and resources to track down someone like that. Whereas if you can build a case against Kathryn Walters - bang! You've got it in one. With lots of choice headlines as well.'

'But apart from these hairs, the evidence doesn't stand up.'

'Exactly. The day after she was arrested, SOCO wanted to close the crime scene down. But little Willy's not satisfied. All they'd found was a few footprints, so they had to go over it again. Much moaning and strong words, but they do it because he's the boss. And guess what? He was right all along. Next day they find these hairs, on an elastic bobble, that they missed before. Hairs with roots, that can be tested for DNA. And that's it, done and dusted. Kathryn Walters, placed at the scene of the crime.'

Sarah studied him carefully. There was a bitterness in his face that she hadn't seen before, a resentful, frustrated cynicism. 'You think he planted the hairs?'

'Why not? It's not as though he hasn't done this before. Think of how he exaggerated the statement of that shopkeeper Patel, for instance, in Kidd's case. And Nick Bryant's no idiot. His team had combed that site already. Churchill was the one who arrested Kathryn, searched her house. Easy to pick up a hair bobble.'

'Terry, if you're right, this isn't a mistake. It's a deliberate attempt to pervert the course of justice.'

'I know. And if I could prove it, I would, but I can't. So unless you can do something magic, your client's going down.'

Sarah had walked back to her office deeply depressed. Churchill had interviewed Kathryn a number of times, been to her house - it would have been so easy to pick up a hair bobble, take it to the woods, and leave it for the SOCO team to find next day. Easy, and almost impossible to challenge.

She and Lucy had spent hours checking the chain of evidence that led from the scene of crime to the laboratory. Almost everything suggested that it was exactly what it appeared to be - a piece of brilliant, painstaking forensic detection, locating this tiny, vital clue in a dirty and unpromising crime scene.

Over the next few weeks Terry had tried, in the time he had left from the minor cases assigned to him, to investigate David Kidd's death on his own account. But it was difficult; it was not his case, and few people on the team would talk to him about it. There was a wary, pitying look in their eyes that Terry was becoming used to. Everyone understood about the conflict between him and his boss, and what was happening to his career as a result of it. It could happen to them as well.

Nick Bryant, the SOCO, had agreed, cautiously, that his team had conducted a thorough examination of the crime scene the first time, they always did. But it was a messy place, with mud from the tractor that had hauled the car out, leaves, insects, and animal droppings everywhere. They were not supermen, they got tired and bored like everyone else. It was not impossible that they could miss a small elastic hair bobble. No one had seen Churchill anywhere near where it was found.

So Terry went back to the beginning, trying to see who else might have killed David Kidd. Surely he must have had other enemies than Kathryn.

He went back to where Kidd had kept his car, in a garage under the city wall, fifty yards or more from his flat. Churchill's team had found an elderly colonel who'd seen David on the night he died, driving his Lotus out of the garage. There'd been a woman with him, the old man said, in her thirties or forties, he thought, though he couldn't be sure. She had fair hair, he was sure of that. How long it was, he was less certain. He'd glimpsed her face under a streetlamp and had picked Kathryn's photo as resembling it more closely than the others he'd been shown.

Terry checked all the other flats and houses with windows overlooking the garage, and struck lucky - a woman, younger than the colonel and with arguably better eyesight, had seen the same thing, but with a subtle difference. She didn't know David Kidd, but she remembered the Lotus Elise. And she described the female she'd seen getting into the car as a *girl* - a young woman in her twenties, she insisted, certainly not her late forties. She was certain of the date because it was the night before she went away on holiday; that presumably, was why Churchill's team had missed her.

It wasn't much, but it was a start. He looked at the map, and went for a weekend walk in the countryside, wondering how the murderer, whoever she was, could have left the scene of the crime without being traced. He enquired at the bus station in Wetherby, to see if anyone unusual had turned up that morning. Again, a young woman, bedraggled, tired, this time with short fair punk style hair.

But who was she? And how had she arranged to meet him? One night, thinking about this, Terry remembered suddenly that David Kidd had worked for a travel agency, leading safari holidays in Kenya. A trawl through the files of the case yielded a name: *Sunline Tours*, with an office in Hammersmith. Next day he rang them and, to his surprise, a lead opened up.

Yes, they confirmed, after a long search through their records, a woman had arranged to meet him, as a matter of fact. A travel journalist had rung their office about an article she intended to write, and they'd fixed an appointment for her to meet David Kidd at the *Slug and Lettuce* in York.

'Do you have a name?' Terry asked, pen poised above his notebook.

'Yes, I think so. Just a minute ...' There was the sound of paper rustling on the other end of the line, and pop music playing in the background. 'Here it is. Martha Cookson. She writes for the *Washington Star*. I'm looking for her article, but the cuttings agency don't seem to have sent it, unfortunately ...'

'Never mind,' said Terry. 'I'll give her a ring, see if I can trace it that way.'

Matthew Clayton QC was approaching the end of his opening speech. Having described Kathryn's failed alibi, he moved on to the question of motive.

'But why, you may ask, would a woman like Kathryn Walters - a mother, a respectable businesswoman, a pharmacist - do such a terrible thing? What would drive her to hate David Kidd so much as to cause his death? Well, unfortunately, the answer to that is all too clear.'

Sarah switched off while he described the events of the previous trial, Kathryn's outburst on the steps of this court, her arrest with a shotgun outside David's flat. There was no doubt whatsoever that Kathryn wanted him dead; she'd been quite clear about that in their last pre-trial conference. It was the one point she'd been really animated about in their conversations.

'I don't hold with Christian forgiveness. Not now. I doubt if I ever did. That man took my daughter away from me, exploited her, and killed her.

There's nothing worse you can do to a parent, nothing. He didn't deserve to live after that. You tried to send him to prison, Mrs Newby, and failed, so somebody killed him. I'm glad he's dead; I hope he rots in hell. If there is a hell. There should be, for people like him.'

It was a line of argument unlikely to benefit her in the witness box. Yet despite Sarah's warnings, Kathryn seemed determined to stick to it. Sarah shook her head glumly. If six months on remand hadn't purged Kathryn of her bitterness, she doubted if the shock of finding herself in court would do it. Sarah glanced over her shoulder at her client, sitting pale and intense in the dock, then let her gaze rise upwards to the public gallery, where, to her surprise, she thought she recognized another face.

A young woman in her mid twenties, with wavy brown shoulder length hair, a dark blue coat, and a striking resemblance to her mother sitting below in the dock. Kathryn's daughter Miranda, Sarah thought after a moment - the sister of Shelley who died. I thought she was staying in America, that's what Kathryn said. Well, good for her. Perhaps she can talk some sense into her mother. Someone needs to, if she isn't going to go down.

Sarah turned to the front, to listen with increasing gloom as the prosecutor outlined the final part of his case, the faulty stock control procedures at Kathryn's pharmacy which could have allowed her to obtain rohypnol without anyone tracing it. She pondered the options open to her in defence.

They seemed less encouraging than ever.

52. Mother and Daughter

THE FIRST day of the trial passed in a haze for Kathryn. She hadn't anticipated how lonely she would feel, isolated in the dock at the back of the court. The lawyers, clerks, ushers and jury busied themselves in the well of the court below her, leaving her raised on high in this strange wooden tower, conspicuous, alone. Behind her sat her guard, a dour burly woman in grey uniform with handcuffs, keys and sturdy sensible shoes; directly in front of her, across the valley where the lawyers toiled, sat the judge in his wig and red robes. His eyes were the only ones on a level with hers and once, when she caught his gaze resting on her, she had nodded at him out of reflex politeness, but met no response. She was here to be judged, after all, not acknowledged.

She had met Sarah Newby, of course, in the morning, but all she saw of her barrister for most of the day was her black gown and the wig at the back of her head. A succession of witnesses came and went: the farmer who had found the body, the pathologist, the scenes of crime officer, a forensic scientist, the old colonel who had seen a woman resembling Kathryn get into David Kidd's car. With the first two there was little to say, but Sarah worked hard with the last three, chipping away at crucial details: why exactly had the SOCOs not found the hair bobble on their first examination of the site? Wasn't it possible that the mud and leaves on her trainers came from the fields near her house, or indeed other fields and woods twenty miles away? Did the seventy five year old colonel, wearing strong glasses in poor light late in the evening, really recall the face of the passenger who got into David Kidd's car? Could he really be sure of her age, or even remember the date?

Kathryn followed the legal battle with the surface of her mind only. Isolated at the back of the court, it scarcely seemed to concern her. Her lawyer was doing well enough, but it didn't matter any more to Kathryn.

What mattered, was that she had seen Miranda.

She had told her daughter not to come so many times, in carefully guarded phone calls and letters from the prison. The whole basis of her sanity was that Miranda was safe, four thousand miles away, out of reach. She had promised to stay away. But this morning, when Kathryn had looked up to the public gallery, she had seen her. All morning she had thought about that, and then, at lunch time, her cell door had opened, and there she was. Smiling anxiously.

'What are you doing here?'

'Mum, I had to come.'

'No, you didn't. I told you to stay away. Go home, back to your family.'

'Mum, you don't know how it feels. I can't just leave you here alone. If you're convicted - I couldn't live with that.'

'Look, I've got a good defence team, a good barrister, she thinks she can get me off. So there's no need for you to worry. I'll be free soon.'

'It's not worry, Mum, I've got something to tell you. I have to say this ...'

'I don't want to hear it. Please, darling, *no!*'

'What I did ...'

'*I don't want to know* what you did, or how you did it, or anything at all. Look, it's *my* trial, I'm the one locked up in here, and for all we know these walls have ears. Tape recorders, hidden microphones, anything. So *keep your mouth shut*, Miranda, please, and listen to me. Listen, all right, please? If you love me.'

'All right.'

'Right. Now I've lost one daughter already, and you've lost a sister. We both know how badly it hurts. That man killed her for certain, so whoever killed him, Mandy, did a good thing, a right thing. Because he was a monster - if he hadn't been stopped he would have gone on to do it again and again. He was a killer, and the world's a better place without him.'

'Mum, I know, I know, but that's not how it *feels*. Promise me, if it looks like you're going to lose, let me confess. It would be the right thing, you know it would. It would bring me peace.'

'No, it wouldn't. Look, just wait a few more days and I may be acquitted. Then we'll both be free. I've been thinking about that, what I might do if that happens.'

'What, Mum?'

'Well, they have pharmacies in Wisconsin, don't they? Maybe I could sell up and come out to join you. Start again. If you'd have me, that is.'

'Oh, Mum!'

'I wouldn't live too close, don't worry. It's a big country, they say.'

'Mum, that would be lovely. But ...'

'Good. So go out of here, fly home, and stay there until this is all over. Then if it's the right verdict I'll put the business on the market and start things rolling.'

'Mum, I'm not going. I can't. Not unless I can take you with me.'

'Well, you will, love, if I'm acquitted. I'll be out of here in a couple of days anyway.'

'Yes, that's right, Mum, that's what I've come to see. I'm not going now until it happens. Don't you understand? I can't. I've got to see it through with my own eyes.'

'Then ... just sit somewhere quiet out of the way and keep your mouth shut, darling. Promise me that at least. I don't want anyone here thinking about you. Not for a second.'

'I'll talk to Dad. He's here too, you know. I've got to talk to him.'

'Of course you must. But you haven't told him, have you? I never breathed a word.'

'Neither did I. Oh Mum, I've never told anyone, not even you, not properly. It's so hard - sometimes I think my brain will burst. But you *know*, don't you?'

'Sssssh. Darling, *don't say it*, not here. Not anywhere. Not until I'm free and we're alone on a mountain somewhere. Just a few more days now, that's all. You can manage that, can't you? You can be strong, for me?'

'I'll try, Mum. But I can't let you be convicted. I won't.'

'Then we'll just have to make sure I'm not, won't we? Hope that lawyer of mine does her job.'

But all that long afternoon, as she watched Sarah Newby battling with the prosecution witnesses, trying to build a shaky platform for reasonable doubt, Kathryn thought *it's not going well enough, she's coming off second best*. From time to time a juror would look up at her thoughtfully, trying to gauge her guilt from the expression, the tension in her limbs, her body language. And each time Kathryn had the impression she'd sent the wrong message; the juror would turn away dissatisfied, disapproving, no hint of sympathy on their face.

Sarah, coming down to see her at the end of the day, remained ebullient, forceful, combative. 'No guarantees yet,' she said, 'but it went about as well as expected. The old colonel was good - very honest, decent man, I thought. No attempt to bluster or make his evidence better than it was; he admitted it could have been a woman of any age he saw.'

'He said it could have been me, though.'

'Yes. That was a smart trick for the prosecution to pull.' A frown crossed Sarah's face as she remembered the moment when Matthew Clayton QC had persuaded the judge to ask Kathryn to stand up while the witness confirmed that she looked *not unlike* the woman he had seen with David Kidd all those months ago. *Not unlike* in terms of identification meant virtually nothing, as Sarah had sought to establish at length in her cross-examination, but before she had a chance to do that Matthew Clayton had ensured that every single member of the jury had studied Kathryn carefully, standing nervous and alone in the public dock. 'I'm sorry the judge allowed that to happen. It must have felt awful.'

'It did. But I'm getting used to bad things, by now.'

'Tomorrow will be better. That scenes of crime officer, Nick Bryant, was difficult, but he admitted enough in the end. So did forensics. The case isn't proved yet, not by a long way. If I can just manage to shake their boss tomorrow - DCI Churchill - then we've got a good chance.'

'A chance?'

'Yes. You know I've always tried to be honest with you, Kathryn, I can't put it higher than that. But it all comes down to him and you, in the end. If I can make the jury distrust him - and he's the sort of man jurors *can* be suspicious of, with good reason - then all you have to do is go on the stand and not alienate them, like I said. Win their sympathy without saying you're glad Kidd is dead, then the seeds of doubt are sown. All of their case rests on those hairs; if they doubt those, then the case ought to be withdrawn, and I'll do my best to get the judge to do that. But otherwise, it's going to turn on who the jurors trust most; DCI Churchill, or you. Just tell the truth, as clearly as you can, and it'll be no contest.'

The two women stood silent for a moment, each assessing the sincerity of Sarah's words. Both knew Sarah was trying hard to be encouraging; both knew there was more to the truth than Kathryn, so far, had told. But only Kathryn knew what that was.

'I saw your daughter in court today,' Sarah said. 'Sitting with your husband.'

'Yes. She came to see me.'

'That must have been a comfort. Flew in from America, didn't she?'

'Yes. I wish ...' They heard men's voices in the corridor outside, the rattle of a large bunch of keys. Kathryn stopped abruptly, turned her head aside.

'It would be nice to see her in better circumstances. I know,' Sarah said, standing aside as the cell door opened and the wardress came in, and handcuffed herself to Kathryn's left wrist. 'But it's good that's she's here, to give you support.' Sarah put her hand on Kathryn's arm as she was led past. 'Get a good sleep, if you can. I'll do my best for you tomorrow, I promise.'

All I need now, Sarah thought, as she walked slowly upstairs to the robing room, is to find out who really did kill David Kidd. That would save Kathryn, for sure.

53. Martha Cookson

IT PROVED harder than Terry had expected to make contact with the American journalist, Martha Cookson. She had left the *Washington Star* three months ago, it seemed, either to go freelance or join another paper; their personnel department wasn't sure. Several calls to the answering machine at her home address brought no reply. It was not obvious to Terry what else he could do, or indeed how relevant an American journalist, gathering material for a travel article, was anyway. A second call to *Sunline Tours* confirmed their impression that the woman had not asked for David Kidd when she called, or appeared to know that he even existed until they suggested she call on him. The chances of Kidd so offending a perfect stranger that she murdered him three days after they met, seemed highly remote. If they had in fact met at all. After some grumbling, the archivist at the *Washington Star* rang back to confirm that no story by Martha Cookson about *Sunline Tours* had ever been filed.

Terry's other leads also led nowhere. He tracked down and interviewed Lindsay Miller, the girl Shelley had found in David's bed. But she not only had a perfect alibi for the night of David's death - she was being visited by an educational welfare officer who was concerned about her son's behaviour at nursery - but also failed to come up with any suggestions about other women who might wish David dead. Yes, he had other girls, she admitted that, but he wasn't the monster Terry seemed to believe. Shelley Walters had committed suicide because she knew that David would come back to her, Lindsay, and his kid. And if Shelley's mother had accepted that, she wouldn't be on trial for murder now. In Lindsay's view, she deserved all she got.

So it was not until Martha Cookson rang him, two days after the start of the trial, that Terry got the first scent of a trail. She rang late in the afternoon, when he was putting together a burglary file to send to the CPS, and at first he couldn't work out who she was. The American accent seemed out of place.

'That is Detective Bateson, isn't it? You left several messages on my answering service.'

'Cookson, you say? Oh yes, you're the journalist. From the - what was it? - *Washington Star.*'

'Got it at last. But you're behind the times - I left there months ago. Anyway, how can I help the British police?'

'Well, I understand you were here in England six months ago. Staying in Harrogate, I believe. While you were here you contacted a company called *Sunline Tours* to write a feature article about their safari holidays, and they sent you to an employee of theirs called David Kidd. Well ...'

'Are you crazy?' Even over the international phone line there was no mistaking her tone of amazement. 'Hold on there, detective, you've got me confused with someone else.'

'You *are* Martha Cookson? The Martha Cookson who writes feature articles for travel supplements?'

'Yes.'

'And you were in Yorkshire last .....'

'Yorkshire, England, right? That's where you're speaking from now?'

'I'm in York, yes.'

'Well, that's great for you, sir, but I'm sorry to disappoint you. I've never been to Yorkshire in my life. London, sure, several times, Scotland once, the south west of England a couple of times, that place up in the north west where they have those dinky little lakes, but Yorkshire, no sir, I've never had the pleasure.'

'What about *Sunline Tours*, a travel company in London? Do you recall talking to them?'

'I talk to so many companies. What did you say their specialty was?'

'Safari trips to Africa. You rang them from Harrogate, they say, and they put you in touch with a tour leader who lives - lived - in York.'

'Well, I can assure you that wasn't me. I wasn't in Europe at all last year, as it happens. I was in New Zealand, and before that the Himalayas. There has to be some mistake.'

'Can you think of anyone who might want to impersonate you?'

The woman laughed. 'Hardly. I'm not a film star, you know.'

'Maybe not, but - just borrow your name, perhaps?'

'Anyone could do that. Just buy a paper and read it.'

'Yes, I suppose so, but ... You say you've never been to Yorkshire. You don't know anyone who lives here, do you?'

'Detective, I meet hundreds of people in my job. Probably thousands. Anyone could steal my name. What's this all about, anyway?'

'It's a serious matter, Ms Cookson. The man that you met - were alleged to meet, that is - has been murdered. So if there's any way you can help us find out who did it ...'

Terry could almost hear the woman thinking in the silence that followed. 'Murdered, you say? How, exactly? Who killed him?'

'That's what we're trying to find out. All we know is that a woman was seen getting into this man's car with him, and a few days later he was found drowned inside the car at the bottom of a drainage tank in some woods.'

'And this happened shortly after someone impersonating me went to see him?'

'So it seems, yes.'

'Then I understand your concern. But whether I can help or not ...' Again the phone fell silent, Martha Cookson apparently deep in thought. 'I do know someone from that part of the world, as it happens. She was one of my students on a course I taught at college once. But she wouldn't hurt anybody. Matter of fact her sister was killed last year, poor kid.'

Terry waited, conscious suddenly of a pulse beating in his throat. When nothing further was said he asked: 'You wouldn't happen to recall her name, would you?'

Again the silence. Followed, surprisingly, by a flat, flustered denial. 'No. I'm sorry, detective, I don't. It was a long time ago, and names have never been my strong point, anyhow.'

'Think harder,' Terry prompted urgently, not believing a word. 'It's really very important, Ms Cookson ...'

But to his surprise, after a further silence, the phone went dead. And when he tried to ring back, the caller's number was hidden.

54. Hair Bobble

THE PROSPECT of cross examining Will Churchill would have filled Sarah with a harsh pleasure, if she had thought she could shake him. This man, who had done his best to put her son behind bars, epitomised everything she most disliked about the police. He was smug, deeply insensitive beneath a veneer of surface politeness, and, most frightening of all, successful. It was a success which she suspected was built largely on political talent rather than skill as a detective. He was young for the job - in his mid thirties - clever, well dressed, capable of deploying charm when it was useful, yet ruthless and vindictive when need be. She had heard several rumours of officers in Essex - his former force - who had crossed him and suffered, and now Terry Bateson, it seemed, had gone the same way.

But it was not enough to dispose of his rivals and pass exams. What he needed to further his career was a string of successful, high profile investigations. This trial, no doubt, was just such an attempt. And to Sarah's dismay, it seemed likely to succeed. As her opponent, Matthew Clayton QC, took Churchill smoothly through his evidence she watched the jury lapping up the story they were being so competently fed, and fiddled nervously with the two handwritten sheets of paper on which were scrawled the few weak questions she had to challenge it.

When she rose at last, Churchill faced her with polite contempt. He was immaculately dressed, a little red handkerchief in the breast pocket of his tailored suit, a touch of mousse in his hair giving it that fashionable look that would appeal to the younger members of the jury. None of the jurors would have noticed the hatred that scorched their eyes as they met. It was invisible, a laser that burned only those who stood in each other's way.

'Inspector Churchill,' Sarah began, deliberately diminishing him in rank, 'when you interviewed Kathryn Walters, you suggested that she must have trailed David Kidd to a pub, is that right? And slipped the rohypnol tablets into his beer while he was there?'

'That is one possibility, yes. Not the only one.'

'Oh I see. There are others, are there? What are they?'

'She may have gone to his flat, as she did before, and met him there.'

'I see. And what do you suggest she said to him, when they met?'

Churchill shrugged. 'I have no idea. I wasn't there.'

'Indeed. You have no proof that they actually met at all, have you, in either place?'

Churchill turned away from her, addressing his reply to the judge. 'We know that they met, my Lord, because hairs bearing Mrs Walters' DNA were found on a hair bobble near the fence, and her footprints were found nearby.'

'Footprints of shoes *similar* to hers, you mean.' The jury had already heard an exhaustive cross examination of the forensic scientist on this point, in which Sarah had established that fifty thousand size six pairs of that particular trainer had been sold worldwide last year, and that the mud and plant fragments found in the soles and crevices of the trainers were similar to mud and plants found in Kathryn's garden, as well as near the scene of the crime.

'Footprints of shoes *identical* to hers, my Lord,' Churchill replied wearily, his tone suggesting impatience with such nitpicking.

'And to thousands of others,' Sarah insisted doggedly. It had taken two hours of forensic cross-examination to establish these points; she wasn't about to abandon them now.

'To thousands of others whose owners had no connection with David Kidd whatsoever, so far as we know.' Churchill glanced at the jury where, to Sarah's chagrin, several concurring smiles met his own.

'Have you investigated any of these other people?'

'No.' Churchill smiled patronizingly. 'We had no reason to.'

I'm losing this, Sarah thought. *Getting drawn into petty battles I can't win.* 'Let's return to this alleged meeting between Mrs Walters and David Kidd, shall we? You admit that you have no evidence that it actually took place?'

'As I said before, Mrs Walters' hair was on the hair bobble, and her footprints - or footprints identical to hers in every way, if you insist - were found near the drainage tank. So if they were together when he died, it follows that they must have met some time earlier, my Lord.'

'That's your idea of logic, is it, Inspector?'

Churchill gazed at her blankly, refusing to answer the question. Sarah heard a discreet cough from Matthew Clayton, and noticed the judge watching her intently. She could imagine the reprimand forming in his head. *'If you could refrain from insulting the witness, Mrs Newby, and question him instead, things might move along a little faster.'* She hurried to forestall him.

'There is no proof, is there, that either the hair bobble, or the footprints, got there at the same time as Mr Kidd and his car entered the drainage tank?'

Churchill hesitated. 'It seems logical enough.'

'To you, maybe, but it's a long way short of the standard of proof required in a court of law. If we take the footprints first, not only are you unable to prove that those footprints were made by Mrs Walters, you cannot prove exactly *when* they were made either, can you? They could have been made several hours *before* David Kidd died, or some time *afterwards*, for all you know.'

Churchill smiled coldly at the jury. 'I checked the weather forecast for that week, Mrs Newby. As it happens, there were showers that evening. Enough to wash out any traces of footprints, I would have thought. The showers ended about ten p.m., after dark. So Mrs Walters would have had to be taking her dogs for a walk in the dark, wouldn't she, to get those footprints in place just before he died. Bit of a coincidence that, wouldn't you say? Especially if she dropped a hair bobble at the same time. What are you suggesting? That she did all that, and then rushed home for a cup of cocoa before someone else, *a completely different person*, drove up there and tipped David Kidd in the pit *without leaving a single trace behind?'*

One of the jurors laughed openly, choking off the sound quickly at a frown from the judge. Several others nodded. Churchill turned his bland, smooth face back towards her. Sarah felt sick. All the way up the hill and then straight back down again.

'Nonetheless, I repeat, you have no way of proving exactly when those footprints were made, have you? They could have been made some hours before the murder, or after it.'

'By an innocent person wandering around in the middle of the night?' Churchill sneered. 'Yes, I suppose so.'

I could have been an air hostess, Sarah thought. *A secretary, a fashion model, shop assistant, nurse, anything but this.* The point she was trying to reach in her cross examination seemed to be sailing further away, across oceans of contempt. She glanced at her notes, seeking for a different tack to approach it.

'Inspector, you have already told us how much Mrs Walters hated David Kidd, believing as she did that he had murdered her daughter?'

'Certainly. She threatened him publicly outside this court, and was found later outside his flat with a shotgun. That seems to me to provide a motive for murder.'

'And Mr Kidd was aware of how she felt? He had heard these public threats?'

'I believe so, yes. They were reported in the media.'

'Yes. So why does it seem plausible to you, Inspector, that he should take her for a drive in his car?'

'I'm not saying he did that, exactly. I'm saying she put a drug in his drink and then drove the car herself.'

'Even so, Inspector. How do you think she got close enough to drug that drink in the first place? Are you seriously asking this court to believe that he opened the door of his flat and invited her in? Or sat down with her for a drink in a pub?'

Churchill sighed, turning to the judge. 'The truth is, my Lord, we have been unable to establish exactly how Mrs Walters managed to get close enough to David Kidd to drug him. We can only infer from the forensic evidence that she did so. And that she had a clear motive for wishing him dead. As she admitted several times in interview.'

'You haven't found this pub, then?' Sarah asked.

'No, unfortunately not.'

'Have you found any witnesses who saw them together?'

'No.'

'What do you imagine she said to him when they met? *Hello, David, remember me? You killed my daughter. Let me buy you a beer?*'

This time the suppressed smiles were on her side. Churchill's face stiffened. 'Obviously not. But she might have apologised.'

'Apologised? For what? She'd done nothing to him.'

'I'm only surmising, of course, my Lord,' Churchill said carefully. 'But if Mrs Walters had formed a definite intention to kill him, as I believe she had, she would have worked out a plan. Perhaps she approached him and pretended to apologize for her previous remarks. She might have claimed she'd had time to think about the jury's verdict and come to realise that he was innocent. And since he *was* found innocent ...' Churchill's eyes bored into Sarah's at this point, reminding her that she had prosecuted David Kidd and failed to convict him. ' ... and had always said how much he loved Shelley and how sad he was at her death, perhaps he believed her. At least enough to, as you say, sit down somewhere and have a drink with him. At which point she, as a fully qualified pharmacist, would have been able to slip the drug into his drink, steer him out to his car, and drive him to his death.'

To her disgust, Sarah saw several jurors nodding wisely. There were always one or two in every jury, who appeared to reject the obvious in favour of the fantastic. As though a trial were not a search for the truth but an improvisation on the possible.

'You have no evidence of that whatsoever, do you, inspector?' she responded in her harshest voice. 'What we actually *know* is that there was considerable antagonism between Kathryn Walters and David Kidd even before her daughter's death. Even if she faked an apology, why would he believe her?'

'This was a cold-blooded, calculated murder, Mrs Newby. It's my belief that Kathryn Walters set out to deliberately deceive David Kidd so that she could drug him and get him in her power. How she did it, I don't know. What I am quite convinced of is that she was there, in his car, when he was incapacitated by this drug rohypnol. Perhaps when she gives evidence she will tell the court how she did it.'

If she goes on the stand, Sarah thought to herself wryly. This was a further weakness in her case, a huge bone of contention between Sarah and her client. Sarah was still trying to persuade Kathryn that she would make a good impression on the jury only if she acted a part - that of a bereaved mother, a quiet, dignified figure who had no desire to see anyone dead. That way, she might enlist their sympathy. But Kathryn, so far, refused to consider it. If he asks me, she insisted, I'll say what I think. Why should I stand there and pretend I'm sorry he's dead when I'm not? The answer - *to avoid a life in prison* - was so obvious that Sarah scarcely bothered to make it. It almost seemed as if the woman *wanted* to lose.

But she still had a few cards to play before the strongest one, the most open challenge of all. 'Very well, let's turn to this drug, rohypnol, shall we? You told my learned friend that you searched the records of Mrs Walters' pharmacy and found two packets of rohypnol that were unaccounted for?'

'I did, yes.'

'Very well. You are aware, of course that this is a perfectly legal drug in the UK, available on private prescription for insomnia?'

'Yes. But it is banned in the USA and many other countries, because of its illegal uses, particularly in crimes of date rape.'

'Yes. But since 1998, Inspector, the makers of this drug, Hoffman la Roche, have altered their formula so that the tablets take longer to dissolve and release a blue dye as they do so. You are aware of that, are you?'

'I am, yes. But you may not be aware, Mrs Newby, that it takes nearly twenty minutes for this dye to be fully released. So if someone swallows the drink quickly, in a noisy, crowded pub ...' Churchill shrugged, smiling, and one of the jurors laughed.

Shit! I should have known about that, why didn't anyone tell me? I'm losing this, Sarah thought, it's time to go for the throat. Now or never. Let's see if I can draw blood.

'Very well, let's turn to this hair bobble, shall we? When was it found?'

'It was found by the scenes of crime officers on the afternoon of the 20th, three days after Mr Kidd's body was discovered.'

'Quite. And we've heard from Sergeant Bryant, the officer in charge of that search, that he'd completed his initial search on the 19th, the day before. When he had found no hairs whatsoever. But you ordered him to go back again.'

'That is correct, yes.' Churchill turned to the judge. 'It was a very difficult, complicated site, my lord, with a lot of leaves and small sticks and plant and animal debris everywhere. It was very easy to miss something. This was an important enquiry, and as the officer in charge I felt it was important to, as it were, leave no stick or stone unturned.' He smiled, pleased with his attempt at wit.

'You were dissatisfied, you mean, with the result?'

'I was concerned that the searchers might have missed something. As it turned out, my lord, I was right.'

'Yes, indeed. Mr Churchill, after Sergeant Bryant completed his initial search, was there a police guard left at the site?'

Churchill hesitated. 'There was a constable on duty guarding the site at all times while the site was being actively investigated.'

A small, tight smile crossed Sarah's face. The evasive answer betrayed a certain arrogance, a belief that she had not done her homework. For a moment she decided to humour him. 'By *at all times* you mean day and night, do you? Twenty four hours? And that constable's duty is what, exactly?'

'To ensure that no unauthorized personnel enter the site. To preserve the integrity of the evidence.'

'Quite. To ensure, in fact, that no one contaminates the site by, for example, bringing in evidence from elsewhere?'

Again the cold intimate look of hatred flashed between them, invisible to the jury, perfectly clear to them both. He guessed where she was going now. She watched his body stiffen as he attempted a casual, rather awkward shrug, body language that she associated with guilt.

'That would be one thing, yes. Another would be to prevent people trampling evidence into the mud by stepping in the wrong place.'

'I see. So this is quite a vital job, guarding the site?'

'It's a small but crucial part of the investigation, yes.'

He thinks he's got away with it, Sarah thought. She sprang her trap. 'But you didn't quite answer my earlier question, inspector. Isn't it true that after Sergeant Bryant completed his initial search, the police guard was withdrawn on the assumption that the search was completed, and not replaced until the following day, when Sergeant Bryant and his team went back?'

'I believe there may have been a gap of some hours, yes. But only overnight. Sergeant Bryant ended his initial search on the afternoon of the 19th, and began again on the morning of the following day.'

'Only overnight.' Sarah smiled coolly. Her next few questions established precisely the times when the guard had been withdrawn - 6 p.m. on the 19th - and reinstated - 10 am the next day. 'And so we are to understand, are we, that this was only a brief hiatus, a time when nothing important could happen?'

'I didn't say that. But it's fair to point out that this is a very remote, isolated site in the middle of a wood. Hardly anyone goes there in the day, let alone at night. So the chances of contamination during that brief period are really very low.'

'Yes. Of course the murder happened at night, didn't it, inspector?'

'What?'

'Well, you say no one goes there at night, nothing happens, but the whole basis of this case is that David Kidd was murdered in that wood in the middle of the night. That's a fairly significant event, isn't it?'

A low murmur of laughter came from the public benches and one or two jurors. Sarah smiled, waiting for her answer. It came in a tone of heavy sarcasm.

'If your suggestion is that Mrs Walters visited the site during those hours and somehow innocently contaminated it, then you are forgetting, Mrs Newby, that she spent that night in police custody. What are you saying, that she escaped custody in the middle of the night and went for a walk in the woods without anyone seeing her?'

'I'm not saying *she* did that, Mr Churchill. I'm suggesting *you* did.'

So now it was out in the open. A gasp of surprise went round the court. All eyes were focussed on their exchange now, no one was dozing.

'I resent that.' Churchill looked as angry as she had expected him to. But then, there was no other credible response. Sarah continued, her voice cool, hard, relentless.

'The reason for these questions, Mr Churchill, is the very surprising, very strange discovery of an elastic hair bobble with my client's hair on it *after* the crime scene had already been searched thoroughly by Sergeant Bryant and his team, who found no hairs whatsoever, nothing to incriminate Mrs Walters except a few footprints which could have been almost anyone's. He reported this to you and you told him to go back the next morning where, surprise surprise, he found a blue hair bobble in a place he'd already searched. Now, as you say, Mrs Walters couldn't have put it there, so *who did*? That's what this jury would like to know.'

Sarah *hoped* the jury wanted to know it. *She* certainly did. Churchill's smooth face was pink with rage. Or possibly fear. He turned to the judge. 'I find that question offensive, my lord.'

'Nonetheless, Chief Inspector, you should answer it.'

'All right. You've seen the forensic report. The hairs on that bobble came from Kathryn Walters' head. The only way it could have got near that pit was that she dropped it while she was committing this murder.'

'So what are you suggesting, Mr Churchill? That my client drugged Mr Kidd, pushed his car into the pit, and then stood there calmly brushing her hair?'

'Of course not.' Churchill's answer came back swiftly, stilling the giggles from the public gallery. 'Probably Mr Kidd tore it loose during the struggle. Or it fell from her coat or her bag.'

The answer was strong and reasonably convincing. If Sarah lost this point, she knew, she would lose the case. 'The body was discovered on the 17th, Mr Churchill. On the 18th and 19th, Sergeant Bryant's team searched that site very thoroughly and found no hairs whatsoever. They completed their search and left the site unguarded. Then you told them to go back and look again and - lo and behold! - a blue hair bobble is there.'

'As I have already explained, this was a difficult site to search. Small items were easy to miss. As the senior officer in charge of the investigation I took the decision to search the area one more time. The likelihood of contamination overnight was very small. As a Detective Chief Inspector I am engaged in a search for the truth, and I resent extremely the suggestion that I or any of my officers could manufacture evidence, my lord.'

Again he turned away from Sarah, but he could not escape her for long. 'I am not suggesting that your colleagues did it, Mr Churchill. I am suggesting that *you* did.'

Assaults on police witnesses don't get much more raw than this, Sarah thought, the adrenalin making her hand tremble on the pad of questions in front of her. She saw the judge draw breath for a comment and, realising she not really asked a question, continued: 'Let me ask you this. On the day you first searched Mrs Walters' house, did you go into her bedroom?'

'I did, yes.'

'Were you there alone, or with other officers?'

'Sometimes alone, sometimes with others. The search took some time.'

'During that search, did you see Mrs Walters' dressing table?'

'Really, my lord, this is absurd ...'

'It would only have taken a moment, wouldn't it, for you to have picked up this hair bobble and slipped it into a bag in your pocket, without anyone seeing?'

'I had no reason to do that, my lord. None whatsoever.'

'I suggest you had the perfect reason. The need to supply yourself with DNA evidence where none might otherwise exist.'

'I did not do that, my lord. Of course I did not.'

'No, Mr Churchill? I suggest that is exactly what you did. From the first moment you visited the crime scene you knew it would be difficult to find convincing forensic evidence, and you took this elastic hair bobble to keep in reserve in case you needed it. Then, when Sergeant Bryant completed his first search, you realised you had nothing, nothing except a few inconclusive footprints, to put Mrs Walters anywhere near the scene. But you weren't prepared to accept that, were you? You weren't prepared to see the police fail once again. So you slipped out that night, when you knew the crime scene was unguarded, dropped the hair bobble near the barbed wire, and sent Sergeant Bryant back to find it. That's what happened, isn't it, Inspector Churchill?'

'No,' said Churchill coldly. 'It is not.'

And since she had nothing more to say, Sarah sat down.

Immediately Sarah sat down Matthew Clayton had stood up to re-direct, and in a smooth, emollient voice fed Churchill a number of questions designed to reestablish his reputation as a conscientious senior detective concerned only to uncover the truth. He did it well, but Sarah was gratified to see several thoughtful, if not openly cynical expressions of the faces of the watching jurors. I did the best I could, she thought; I've sown the seeds of doubt; let's hope they flourish.

At the end of the afternoon, Sarah ran briskly down the stairs to see her client. She was feeling confident, determined, optimistic.

'Well, I think we did as well as could be hoped,' she began, taking off her wig and picking at a tuft of horsehair that was working loose. 'Now we have to talk about tomorrow.'

'What about tomorrow?'

'Your evidence. How you behave on the stand.' She noted how Kathryn sat dejectedly on the bench, looking pale and strained. Had this afternoon's performance really seemed that bad to her? In Sarah's opinion it had given them a real chance. 'Now look, before you say anything, I know you're worried about it, but really, this is the moment of decision. In my opinion that man Churchill looked shifty today - too smooth, too sure of himself by half to appeal to the average juror, and some of them are certain to believe he planted that evidence, whether we can prove it or not. So what we've got to do now is reinforce their impression of his character by comparing it with yours - a decent, respectable mother who's been through terrible suffering because of the death of her daughter and then framed by the police to disguise their own incompetence. If you can just make them feel sorry for you as well as telling the truth, we've got a good chance.'

'And what if I refuse to give evidence? I've a right to do that as well, haven't I?'

'Refuse?' Sarah shook her head in surprise. 'Then we lose, it's as simple as that. The prosecution and the judge will both comment on it, and the jury will be wondering what on earth you've got to hide. It's not an option, Kathryn, not this time. Not unless you want to spend the rest of your life behind bars.'

'Maybe I do.'

'What?' The words were said so softly that Sarah wasn't sure if she'd heard them. 'You don't mean that?'

'I don't know what I mean.' Kathryn sat hunched on the bench avoiding Sarah's eyes, twisting her wedding ring on her finger. She's more depressed than I thought, Sarah realised. She sat down beside her, taking Kathryn's hand in her own. She didn't have much time; she could hear footsteps and loud laughter along the corridor, where the van crew had probably arrived to take Kathryn back to prison for the night.

'Kathryn, listen to me. You pleaded not guilty because you didn't do this, all right? If that's the truth then you have a duty to yourself to give evidence, however hard it may seem. A duty to yourself and your family. We're talking about a long time in prison for a crime like this - ten years at least - for a murder you didn't commit, however glad you are that it happened. So give yourself a chance tomorrow, okay? At the very least it will help when we go to appeal. Whereas if you say nothing ... you'll have a long time to regret it.'

A long time to regret it, perhaps, but no more time to talk. The security guard came in with her handcuffs, and Sarah watched Kathryn walk away. Still wondering, as she had since she took the brief, exactly what her client had to hide.

55. Frequent Flyer

TERRY HAD seen Miranda in court, sitting in the public gallery next to her father. He'd thought nothing of it at first; it was natural for her to be there. He realised of course that she, like her mother, had a clear motive for killing David Kidd, but she was no more on his list of suspects than she was on Will Churchill's. In the first place, as Churchill had pointed out, she had the perfect alibi. Two days before David Kidd died, Mrs Miranda Ward had landed in New York.

And in the second place, she had shoulder length wavy brown hair.

The first eye witness, the elderly colonel, said the woman he'd seen getting into David Kidd's car had fair hair; he wasn't sure if it was short or long. The second, the woman Terry had found, said her hair was 'a sort of spiky blonde', which agreed with the description he'd had from Wetherby bus station. Forget the spikes, and it was the colour of Kathryn Walters' hair, exactly. Not her daughter's. Nothing like it.

But Terry only had to walk into his bathroom at home to see the flimsiness of that evidence. His Norwegian nanny Trude, when she'd arrived, had been blonde, but there was another time when her hair had been almost white, and another when it had sported streaks of orange and blue. He had no idea what her natural colour was. And now, after a brief, hopeless battle from her father, his own daughter Jessica had begun to join in the fun, spending hours locked in the bathroom with Trude, involved in some mysterious alchemy which, to Terry's relief, produced no more than a few delicate streaks of auburn in her naturally dark locks. So far, he had to admit, it didn't look too bad. By the time she was fifteen, she might look like a walking rainbow.

He picked up a tube of dye in the bathroom and looked at it. The colours, it promised, would last for weeks. No doubt it did exactly what it said on the tin. But however carefully he read, he couldn't find a promise to transport the user across four thousand miles of ocean. Not even the most extravagant advertiser claimed that. But it was the key point. Until yesterday's phone call from Martha Cookson, Terry, like Will Churchill, had ruled Miranda out of the picture. Now, it seemed, he might have to think again.

But how could she have done it? He'd been back to BA, checked her flight to New York. It tallied, just as his boss had claimed. Her father had driven her to the airport for an early morning flight, she'd got on the plane and flown home - two days before David Kidd died. So why had the Cookson woman been so nervous, then, rung off so abruptly? It didn't fit the facts. And after all, if Miranda *had* done it, why risk coming back now? The wise thing would be to stay in America. But only if she was guilty. Perhaps the very fact that she *was* here argued her innocence. Come to support her mother, like a loving child.

It can't be her, Terry thought. I'm clutching at straws. And this particular straw is one I don't want. And yet ... Terry's motives for continuing this unofficial enquiry were mixed. Partly, he wanted to put things right for Kathryn Walters. If Kidd's trial had succeeded, she wouldn't be in this position in the first place. But equally strong, in Terry's mind, was the urge to expose Will Churchill, and the dangerous way he treated evidence. Any suspect, even Kathryn's own daughter, would serve to do that. And after all, he told himself grimly, whoever killed Kidd, it wasn't me. The killer did it on her own.

He had a nightcap and went to bed, trying not to confront his own feelings. How would it feel, to see your own mother in the dock accused of a murder you'd committed yourself? He'd seen the girl in court; she looked so still, so calm. It couldn't be her; this was all a stupid fantasy. He was probably as far from the truth as Churchill was. But how would it feel, to arrest Miranda in front of her mother? What sort of triumph would that be? Shit.

He dozed off into a dream in which he was shouting at the judge while his own mother drove a Lotus with a drowned man in it across a ploughed field. As he ran behind her, black water rose up to his neck.

A long time later the phone rang. He fumbled to pick it up. 'Hello. Who's this?'

'Terry Bateson? Hi. This is Larry. Larry Eagleton. Sorry, did I wake you?'

'Who? Oh, Larry - yes, of course.' The man was his sole contact in the

New York Police Department, someone he had met on a training course a few years ago. Terry had rung him earlier in the week. 'You did wake me, matter of fact. It's ... er, 3 a.m.'

'No kiddin'. Sorry, guy, me being insensitive again. But you did say ring anytime ...'

'Yes. Yes I did. What is it? Have you found something?'

'Have I found something? Wait till you hear this. Listen, your question was did this lady, Miranda Ward, fly on to Wisconsin after she landed in New York, right? And the answer is no - not for three days. Then she catches the redeye straight down there to land four in the morning central time. So there's a question to ask, straight off. I mean, why the redeye?'

Terry sat up, feeling a dull ache behind his eyes. 'The last plane, you mean? Leaving in the middle of the night?'

'That's it. Flies out of La Guardia at 12.09 Eastern Standard Time on Friday 18th. I mean, this chick's been in the Big Apple three whole days, right? Sure it's a big attraction for a babe married to some hick vet in a cow town out west, she probably wants to do some shopping, see the sights, all that stuff - but why the redeye? Why not take some normal flight that would get her home in time to kiss the kiddies, ball hubby on the couch, you know - things a married lady might expect after a few weeks away. So that sets me thinking.'

'What did you come up with?'

'Get this, feller. A lot of those people on that flight, they're flying straight on from somewhere else, right? Land in New York without an onward booking and take a standby, you follow? So since this lady's English, I check back, and guess what? She flew in from Manchester two hours earlier.'

'What?' Terry was wide awake now. 'On the same day?'

'The same day exactly. Thursday 17th October. Three days after she arrived before, here she is again, flying British Airways from Manchester, England.'

'But that means she wasn't in New York at all for those three days. She was back here!'

'Looks like that, doesn't it? But just to make sure, I went back to the 14th and checked again. Last time I was looking for connecting flights on from New York to Wisconsin, and what did I come up with? Zilch. Because I was looking in the wrong place. This lady didn't fly on to Wisconsin at all.

She got off the plane from England, went straight over to the booking counter, and took an Air France flight to Paris. From there, I'm willing to bet, she hops over the Channel back to your neck of the woods. I guess you can check that out for yourself.'

'I certainly can. Larry, you're a genius. You've just solved a murder mystery.'

'I have? Tell my boss, maybe I'll get a raise.'

'I'll do better than that, Larry. Next time you're in the UK I'll show you the sights of North Yorkshire, and buy you a five star dinner every night.'

'You mean that? Hey, you're on. Can I bring the wife, too? She eats for America.'

'Sure. Bring the whole family - in-laws, dogs, horses - the lot. I'll look forward to it.'

But even as he put down the phone Terry was thinking: *anyone but her.* I'm not looking forward to this. Kathryn Walters may be safe but she's not going to thank me this time.

Miranda, next morning, approached the court in some hope - insofar as hope could survive in the toxic cocktail of tension, guilt and fear that she had come to regard as normal everyday emotions. She had slept for several hours last night, reliving in her dreams the way Sarah Newby had cross-examined that loathsome detective, Will Churchill. In her dreams it went even better at first: Churchill's face, smooth and arrogant at the beginning, gradually developed new seams and lines with every question, black wrinkles which criss-crossed his face like a net, and began to ooze some foul dark liquid, until quite suddenly his head and then his whole body burst and became a dark pool on the courtroom floor. A pool which she dared not look into, and which, when she turned to leave, followed a few yards behind her.

She woke up shaking, as she often did now in the night, and told herself *it was him who was destroyed, not me.* Not me, it was him, and he deserved it.

Only a couple more days, she told herself, approaching the grim elegant courthouse with the statue of Justice on the roof. Then Mum will be acquitted and we can escape. Never see this place again.

There was a man standing beside the main entrance. A tall, lean man, in a loose-fitting double-breasted suit. As she came closer she recognised him as the detective who had given evidence in David Kidd's trial. She had seen him once before at the court, but paid him little attention. But as she climbed the wide stone steps he seemed to be watching her, and when she reached the top he came up and blocked her way.

'Miranda Ward?'

'Yes.'

'Detective Inspector Bateson. I've a few questions to ask, if you don't mind.'

He put his hand lightly on her elbow and steered her through the foyer to a small conference room with a table and six chairs. It was horribly like the one in which she had waited with her parents for the verdict in the earlier trial, preparing a press release to tell the world how pleased they were at the conviction of Shelley's murderer. If only Kidd *had* been convicted, as he should have been! Everything would be different. The detective pulled out a chair but she refused to sit, her first sign of resistance since he'd surprised her. 'What do you want?'

'I think you know, Miranda, don't you?'

He stood a few feet from her, the grey-blue eyes in his lean, unforgiving face watching her intently.

'No. Of course I don't know.'

'Why are you here, Miranda?'

'For my mother's trial, of course. What do you think?'

'How does it feel to be watching her? Sitting in the dock for something she didn't do?'

'Terrible, of course. But it went well yesterday. That policeman lied about the hairs, the jury could see that. I think she'll get off. I hope so, at least. Then ...' Her voice, which had been running away with her, suddenly stopped. Those cold grey eyes sent a chill to her heart.

'Then you won't have to make a decision, will you?' he said after a pause. 'That's what you're hoping for, isn't it?'

'I don't know what you mean.'

Terry smiled; a thin smile which to Miranda looked as cruel as the grin of a crocodile. But it was only a surface reflex prompted by her choice of a phrase so common with suspects whose game was up. But this time, it was a particularly nasty game. Terry might look cold and unforgiving to Miranda, but the expression on his face was a sign of his own weary disillusion at the role he found himself forced to play. There was no satisfaction in this discovery, only despair.

He took a sheet of paper from his pocket. 'You flew from Manchester to

New York on Monday 14th October, flight BA 349. Correct?'

'Yes.' Miranda felt the blood draining from her face as she guessed what was coming.

'Where did you go from there?'

'I ...' Her mind was racing. He must have phoned Bruce, she thought. So he knows I didn't go home. '... stayed a few days in the city. Seeing friends, doing some shopping.'

'I see. Did you stay with a friend?'

'No, I ... stayed in a hotel.'

'Really. A hotel in New York, you mean?'

'Yes. I ... don't remember the name, though. It was a small one ...'

'Not a hotel in Paris?'

'What?' There was no blood in her face at all now. In a moment, Terry guessed, it would all come rushing back in a flood. '*Paris?*' she said in a whisper.

'Oh come on, Miranda, the airlines do keep records, you know. The same day, Monday 14th October, you flew from New York to Paris, arriving 8.37 p.m. at Orly. But you didn't stay there long, did you? Because three days later you flew from Manchester to New York again, on the same flight, BA 349, from where you took the night flight home to Wisconsin. Quite the globe-trotter, aren't you?'

Miranda stared at him, speechless. In her mind thoughts and emotions were running wild, crashing off the walls in panic - *confess, escape, deny, cry, hide, scream, say nothing.*

'Want to tell me what you were doing?'

She shook her head. Her secret had encysted itself so deep it was hard to release, even if she'd wanted to. She had admitted her guilt to no one so far except her mother. And she had come here this morning in such *hope!* She looked into Terry's eyes and saw something there flicker in response to the heightened consciousness in her own mind - pity, perhaps, doubt, reluctance, compassion, uncertainty. Something in her own brain screamed *he doesn't know yet, he's not sure, don't tell him!*

'I don't want to say.'

'I'll bet you don't. You see the thing is, Miranda, on the day you left Manchester the first time, the 14th, your sister Shelley's killer was still alive. But by the 18th he was dead. And you weren't in New York on the day he was killed, as everyone thought. You were in *old* York, Yorkshire, England.'

'Was I? How do you know?'

Terry stared at her as the silence lengthened. The blood had begun to flow back into her neck, but her face was still blotchy, pale. So she was going to deny it! And she was right, he thought grimly, he had no proof she'd actually been in York. Only that David Kidd was dead, killed by a young woman with fair hair. Fair hair and a motive.

'Do you know a lady called Martha Cookson?'

'Maybe. I don't know.'

'She knows you, she says. She taught a course you attended once. And someone used Martha Cookson's name to get an introduction to David Kidd. On the 11th October.'

'So? You can't prove it was me.'

'But it *was* you, wasn't it, Miranda?'

'Why would I go to see David Kidd? I loathed the man, he killed my sister.'

'Just *because* he killed your sister. You went there to kill him.'

'On 11th October, you say? He died five days later.'

'When everyone thought you were in America, but actually you were back here in York.'

They stared at each other coolly, standing either side of the table. Miranda had one hand on the back of a chair. She was clutching it unconsciously, with a grip that would have broken one less solidly made. The turmoil in her mind was still swirling, thoughts going this way and that, but for the moment defiance was uppermost. The part of her that had brought her to England - the part that longed to confess, to end the tension and hiding and deceit, to stand up and bear the burden of what she had done - that part was still alive and breathing, but paralyzed, like a body that's forgotten how to move, a prisoner buried so long in a cell that when the door is opened she flings her arm across her eyes against the sunlight and backs away, unable to face the world she longs for. And in front of her the guards of deception, the defences she'd nurtured so long, sought to protect her as they'd always done, close the door and shut her secret away, deny it ever existed.

She realised, as she watched him, that there were weaknesses in his position too. The very length of his silence was more like a question than an accusation. He *believed* she was guilty, but he still wasn't sure; he couldn't be, or he'd have arrested her by now. *He didn't really know!*

'If you think I murdered David, you'll have to prove it, won't you?'

As she watched the effect of her words on him she marvelled at how calm and controlled her own voice sounded, how detached from the turmoil within. Terry shook his head slowly.

'You'd let your mother be sentenced, would you? For a crime you committed yourself?'

'What makes you think she'll be found guilty?'

There it was, the final reason to keep up her defences. She remembered - her thoughts still racing for escape like rats in a maze - how she'd felt just ten minutes before. She'd been approaching this court not in fear but *in hope*, thinking her mother might easily be acquitted. And if that happened what would be the point of throwing everything away for a detective who had no proof, no real proof, that she was actually guilty? All he could prove were her strange, suspicious travel plans. That made her eccentric, certainly, but not a killer. She could say she had a lover in Paris! Now that the danger was here, in the open at last, there was a strange exhilaration in defying it.

'Are you arresting me or am I free to go?'

Terry thought about it. This wasn't his case; if he made the slightest mistake Will Churchill would be down on him like a ton of bricks. And the girl was right, he had no real proof, after all. Just very strong circumstantial evidence that, linked with her obvious motive, added up in his own mind to a certainty. A *virtual* certainty. But in a court of law that wasn't enough, as Will Churchill was finding already. Churchill believed, with circumstantial evidence probably stronger than Terry's, that this girl's mother was guilty - and unlike Terry, he had real solid evidence, the DNA from those hairs, to put his suspect at the scene of the crime. How the hairs had got there, that was another matter entirely. But Terry had no hairs at all, nothing to prove that Miranda had been within fifty miles of the crime.

But he knew she'd done it. And she, surely, knew that he knew.

'It's a matter for your conscience, really, isn't it?' he said, watching her closely. 'Whether your mother goes to prison, or you do.'

'Or neither of us do,' said Miranda, unclenching her hand slowly, finger by cramped finger, from the back of the chair. 'We still have a good lawyer, don't we?' she added, quietly leaving the room.

A lawyer who I'm about to go and see, Terry thought grimly. God knows what she'll make of this.

56. The Choice

'ARE YOU sure?' Sarah asked. 'You'd better be sure.'

They were meeting in another conference room, half an hour before the case was due to resume. Sarah was dressed in a smart black trouser suit but had not yet put on her gown and wig.

'Sure as I can be without her admitting it,' Terry answered. 'But she's right. I haven't got enough to make it stand up in court. Not yet, anyway.'

'Even so.' Sarah leaned against the side of a table, shaking her head slowly. 'Her own daughter, Terry! What will that do to Kathryn, I wonder?'

'She won't want to believe it,' said Terry. 'I don't, either. Anyone else and we'd have the perfect result. Your client goes free and Will Churchill gets screwed. But this way ... She's not going to be happy, is she?'

'Maybe she knows already. That would account for some of the things she's said - and not said - to me in conference. But if she doesn't know, it'll knock her sideways. Still, either way I have to tell her. I've no choice.' Sarah pushed herself away from the table, and made for the door, then turned back. 'Terry?'

'Yes.'

'Who else knows about this, so far?'

'Just me. That's all.'

'Can you keep it like that, for a while? Kathryn's going to have to make a decision about this, and it won't be the easiest one. My God, I'd hate to be in her shoes now.'

Sarah had sat up late last night planning how best to lead Kathryn through her evidence, trying out one question after another in search of exactly the right tone to help Kathryn catch the sympathy of the jury, and avoid unnecessary expressions of hatred for David Kidd. She had intended to see Kathryn this morning, to warn her against the tricks Matthew Clayton was likely to use to provoke her.

Now, instead, she found herself describing Terry's discovery. At first Kathryn sat on the bench, listening in stunned silence; but halfway through, the tension became too much. She sprang to her feet, hands over her ears as if she couldn't bear to hear any more, and stood with her back to Sarah, facing the concrete wall at the end of her cell.

'I'm sorry,' Sarah said as she finished. 'I didn't want to tell you this, but I had to.'

There was a silence, broken by the sound of a guard whistling cheerfully in the corridor outside. Sarah wondered if Kathryn was crying, but when she turned her cheeks, pale with shock, were quite dry.

'It's not true,' she said simply.

'You don't believe it?'

'Of course I don't believe it. My own daughter? Anyway she was in America at the time.'

'I've explained that,' Sarah said patiently. 'DI Bateson's checked with the airlines. She flew back to Paris the same day she arrived. October 14th.'

'Paris isn't York, is it? Maybe she went to visit someone there.' Kathryn brushed a hand across her face, as if bothered by an irrelevant detail. Sarah noticed the first hint of tears in her eyes.

'Look, Kathryn, I know how painful this must be ...'

'You don't. You have no idea.'

Kathryn turned away, avoiding her gaze. Sarah persisted, keeping her voice as low, sympathetic and reasonable as she could manage. She felt like a doctor telling a patient she had cancer.

'I can't feel it myself, no, but I can see and imagine. What I am bound to say to you, as your counsel, is that this is new evidence which could help your defence. It might be difficult for me to get it admitted into court because DI Bateson isn't part of the investigating team, but I can certainly try. And if the judge does allow it then it's bound to create doubt - more than a little doubt - in the minds of the jury. So ...'

'It'll send Miranda to prison, won't it?'

Sarah sighed. 'Not immediately, but yes, I suppose if you're acquitted because the jury believe your daughter did this, not you, then she's quite likely to be charged at a later date, if enough evidence can be found.'

Kathryn paced anxiously across the narrow cell, once, twice, three times, shaking her head. She slapped the wall in frustration and turned to Sarah, her eyes wide and desperate.

'You're a mother, Mrs Newby. What would you do, if you were in my position?'

For once the correct professional answer coincided with the personal one. But even as she spoke the useless words Sarah hated herself, wishing she had more to offer.

'I can't answer that. I'm sorry, it's impossible to say. It's a terrible decision, I know, but it's one that you'll have to take on your own.'

Kathryn shook her head bitterly, indicating Sarah's irrelevance. There are some divides which can never be crossed, some places where we're always alone. She turned away, sat down on the bench.

'Before I do that, I want to see my daughter.'

Dismissed, Sarah turned, and tapped on the door. 'All right. I'll see if I can find her.'

When she left Terry Bateson Miranda ran to the first place of safety she could find, the ladies' loo. The face in the mirror frightened her; for a few moments she stood there torn, unable to look at herself, unable to look away. Those eyes: she wanted them to seem firm, determined, defiant, as she hoped they'd appeared to the detective. And so they did at first; she held her expression triumphantly. *I'm a killer and I lied and I'm still in control*, she told herself grimly. *I can do this and survive.* But the moment didn't last; mist rose on the mirror from the hot water tap, and when she brushed it away with her hand the determination on her face had dissolved. She could see too far into those eyes; they weren't shields keeping the world at bay, they were windows into the terror of her soul.

I can't do this any more, she thought. *I can't look. But where is there to hide?* Then two women came in, loudly discussing something to do with knives and a brawl in a pub, and Miranda fled, out into the foyer and down the steps across the grass of the Eye of York towards the car park, against the flow of people visiting the Castle and the Castle Museum. But where can I go, she thought? I can't just run back to the States, I have to brazen this out now, see it through. I didn't admit anything to that man and he didn't arrest me, so all that has to happen now is for Mum to be acquitted and we'll both be free and safe.

That won't happen. Yes, it will. Well, it might. *No, it won't, you know it won't.* It still could, you know it could. *But it won't.*

Three times she walked around the circular mound of the Castle, as though it were a roundabout and she didn't know which exit to take. But each time she came back to the Court, with the statue of Justice on the roof and the prison van outside and a barrister and policeman strolling on the stone balcony before the door. And next to it the Castle Museum which had once been the prison where Dick Turpin was kept before his execution, and female murderers had been hanged from the great gable opposite the car park. They don't do that any more, Miranda told herself, thank God they won't do that to me or to Mum, but it's almost as bad. If this goes wrong one of us will be locked up for years and years in a cell like the ones in there.

And it *will* go wrong, I know it will. This is where I belong.

At the top of the wide stone steps under the columned entrance Sarah Newby was waiting for her.

'Your mother wants to talk to you,' she said.

Miranda nodded. 'I know. But first, I've got a question for you.' She turned and looked Sarah in the eyes, wondering, as she did so, what expression the lawyer could see in hers. 'It's a very important question, so I need you to tell me the truth, as best you can. I don't want you to give me the polite answer or the encouraging one, but the true one. Can you do that?'

Miranda could hear the guards in the corridor outside her mother's cell, but Kathryn had abandoned her fears that they might be taped or overheard. It was too late for that now. They would just have to take the risk.

She had tried, as soon as Miranda entered, to persuade her that nothing had changed.

'Just keep on as you are, darling, that's the best way.'

'Mum, I can't. I spoke to the barrister, that Newby woman, before I came in here ...'

'You spoke to her! What did she say?'

'Just answered my question, that's all. I asked her to tell me honestly what chance you had of being acquitted if I didn't ... if things stayed as they were yesterday, before the detective came up with this stuff about the air fares and so on. If the jury didn't know about that.'

'And?'

'She said ... she said she thought you'd be convicted.'

'She said that?' Kathryn sat down abruptly on the bench, and Miranda sat beside her. She reached across and grasped her mother's hand.

'Not in so many words, no, she hedged it about like they all do, saying if the jury think this and if the jury think that, but in the end what it boiled down to was that juries usually believe the police. So she reckoned you had a twenty or thirty percent chance of being acquitted and a seventy or eighty percent chance of being convicted. That's not good enough, Mum!'

Kathryn returned her daughter's grip for a moment, then smiled, gently patted her hand, and pushed it away.

'I still have a chance of getting off.'

'Not much of one, though. One chance in four or five!'

'She probably said that to put pressure on you, Miranda. She was trying to help me.'

'I don't know. I just think she was trying to be honest. Look, Mum, *you* didn't do this. *I* did. And that detective *knows* I did. I might as well go and confess right now.'

'*No!* For heaven's sake, Miranda, listen to me, please.' Kathryn got to her feet, crossed the narrow cell, and turned to face her daughter, with her back to the wall. 'This is so important and I mean what I say. If they find me guilty it'll be hard, but I've thought about it and I can bear it. After all I'm in prison already and it's - nasty but not impossible. But to think of you in there - that would be a hundred times worse. Look, darling, I've had my life. I've had two daughters, and lost one; had a husband and more or less lost him as well. I've got one daughter left - the best one, the bravest ...'

'No, Mum, don't say that! Shelley was much better, much braver than me!'

'I put that wrongly, love, I'm sorry. Of course she was brave, she was a wonderful girl. But so are you. Don't forget that, I mean it. And you've got everything to live for - a fine husband and daughter, and probably more to come. Bruce wants a big family, doesn't he?'

'Yes, but with all this ... how can I?'

'You think like that now, darling, but you won't always. You'll see; time changes everything. So you mustn't do anything stupid, not now, when we're so near the end. Don't even speak to that detective.'

Kathryn came back to the bench, sat down, and took both Miranda's hands in her own. 'Look, I may still get off - Mrs Newby's a good lawyer, she was just being cautious when she spoke to you. But even if the worst happens and I'm convicted, I can still survive in prison knowing that you and Bruce and Sophie are safe, growing up free and healthy in all that sun and fresh air. That'll keep me sane, I'll be able to take it. Whereas if it was the other way round, you see, love ... if I was free and you were locked up inside, separated from little Sophie, your family broken apart - well, I couldn't bear that. Don't you see that, darling? I'd be free but in prison for ever.'

Miranda shook her head, desperately, staring round the cell. 'But that's just it, Mum. Don't you understand - that's what it's like for me, too! I'm free, but I'm in prison all the time. All day, all night. Especially all night. I get such dreams.'

If it hadn't been so serious, it would have been as though she were a little girl again, Kathryn thought fleetingly. Like when Miranda had come into her room at night after a bad day at school. She put both arms around her.

'I'm so sorry, love, but you did the right thing. I'm proud of you. The dreams will go one day, I promise. You've been so brave and kept this secret so long. Just keep quiet a little longer and we'll be free, both of us. I'll come and join you in Wisconsin.'

'I don't know, Mum.' Miranda moved out of her mother's embrace, shook her head sadly. 'I don't think that's going to happen.'

'It can if you just hang on a little longer.'

'I'll try, Mum, but I don't know.' Miranda got to her feet and moved towards the door. 'You say I did the right thing but I just don't know any more. Perhaps it was right but I ran away from the results, didn't I? If you're convicted I'll have run away again.'

'No you won't.' Kathryn said desperately, sensing she was losing the argument. Miranda was moving away from her as she spoke. 'You'll be living for me. Every day I'll think of you and be glad, knowing you're free.'

'But how will *I* be, Mum? That's what you don't think of. How will it feel to be *me?*'

She tapped on the door for the warder. Her decision was almost made.

57. Unwelcome Verdict

'I CAN'T believe I'm hearing this. Any of it.' Will Churchill's colour had been rising rapidly ever since Terry steered him into a quiet corridor of the court to explain what he had discovered about Miranda. Now, his face pink with fury, his temper threatened to boil over. But Terry was determined to get his point across.

'I had to tell you, sir. In my opinion it makes this prosecution unsafe.'

'In your opinion! Who the hell asked your opinion in the first place? You're off this case, Terence. It's nothing to do with you.'

'Nevertheless, sir, I've uncovered this information. It would be wrong to ignore it.'

'In your opinion again, I suppose?' Terry's cool, insistent, rational tone only served to inflame his boss further.

'Yes, sir, in my professional opinion. The daughter had as clear a motive as the mother, after all. You would have suspected her yourself, if she hadn't set up this most elaborate alibi which I only uncovered by chance, really ...'

'By meddling in a case that didn't concern you!'

'Out of professional curiosity, sir.'

'Professional curiosity my arse! Professional jealousy more like!'

'Well, however I uncovered it, it changes everything, sir, don't you see?' Terry sighed, enjoying his boss's discomfiture. 'The daughter was back in York - she could have been, anyway - and the defence have a second eyewitness who saw a young woman get into Kidd's car, someone under thirty ...'

'A witness uncovered by you, I suppose? Behind my back.'

'The point about this witness, sir, is that the woman she saw was young ...'

'And had fair hair, as well,' Churchill snapped. 'Which agrees with the colonel. Forgive me for pointing this out, Terence, but Mrs Walters is blonde. A fact which I managed to establish early in my investigation of this case by the simple but well-known technique of looking at her, old son. It works wonders, you should try it sometime. While her daughter, I believe, is a brunette.'

'She could have dyed her hair, sir.'

'She could have walked on water, too, or run off to the south of France with an Eskimo.' Churchill shook his head furiously, contempt fuelling his rage. 'What we're supposed to be dealing with, Terence, is facts, not remote possibilities. And the facts are that even if this girl did make these flights as you say, all that proves is she went to Paris and Manchester, not York at all. Nor is there any evidence whatsoever that she dyed her hair, impersonated a journalist, or met David Kidd even once, let alone killed him. Has she admitted any of these things?'

'No sir. She denies them.'

'Exactly. Whereas we do know, for a proven fact, that the mother - not the daughter, mark you, but the mother - not only publicly threatened Kidd but turned up outside his flat armed with her husband's shotgun. An allegedly unloaded shotgun, Terence. You remember that, now?'

'I do, sir, yes, but ...'

'And in addition, if you'll allow me to finish, she and her husband both took the earliest opportunity to lie about their whereabouts on the night of Kidd's death. Lies which they persisted in until they were exposed, and genuine actual footprints and hairs were found, placing the mother squarely at the scene of the crime. Need I say more?'

Clearly, Terry saw, his boss was not persuaded. He made one final try.

'It's quite possible that the daughter takes the same size shoes as the mother, sir.'

'Oh, you've measured her feet, have you?'

'Not yet sir, I couldn't. She wasn't arrested.'

'Quite. So you have no idea of the size of her feet and even if you were to strike lucky there, you'd still have to produce a pair of her trainers with exactly the same tread, stained with the same soil and leaves as were found on her mother's. You're not claiming she wore her mum's shoes, I take it?'

'No, but ...'

'And then of course there are the hairs, containing DNA that precisely matched that of the mother and therefore, by definition, differed from that of her daughter and everyone else on this planet. Added to which, as I recall, the hairs were genuine blonde, not dyed. But I suppose you account for those in the same way as your sweetheart does, Mrs Newby. You think I planted them there, is that it?'

The longer the silence lasted, the clearer Terry's answer became. The two men stared at each other, the hostility between them naked and open now.

'Get out of my sight, Terence. I'll have you suspended for this, by God I will if I can. In the meantime, this case goes ahead as planned.'

For half an hour Miranda had been walking outside, replaying the morning's events in her mind. She knew she ought to confess, and yet, and yet ...

It was a crisp spring morning, the leaves just coming out on the trees, with that spice in the air which recalled a night of frost. She crossed the street to the river, where the sun sparkled on the water, and two swans drifted lazily under the arches of Skeldergate Bridge. A small boy, about Sophie's age, ran past her laughing while her mother pushed a buggy with a baby in it slowly behind. That might have been my future, Miranda thought, but not now. I'll lose all this in prison. But then Mum has lost it already. Voices warred in her mind.

I did this, it's my responsibility. I ought to confess.

But what if she's acquitted, and we both walk free? That could still happen.

She'll be convicted if I don't confess soon.

If you confess now they'll stop the trial. You'll always wonder what the jury would have done, and never get the chance to know.

Four chances in five of conviction, her lawyer said. That's too big a risk to take.

Mum begged me to let her take that risk. Just a few more hours and we'll know.

In a few more hours it'll be too late.

However many times she went around the circle the dilemma was the same. Once, all those months ago, it had all seemed so clear. She'd been trapped in a tunnel with only one exit, David Kidd's death. No one had been in there with her, no other solution had entered her mind, no choice had come to confuse her. She'd been single-minded, resolute, certain.

Since then, her will had been debilitated not by action, but the lack of it. Deceit, deception, denial. Do nothing, let others decide. Soon her fate would be in the hands of the jurors. Who would decide with the wrong information.

If only someone would decide this for me! She walked back to the court like a child, dodging the lines between the paving stones. If that detective comes out now, I'll confess. *If he doesn't, I won't.* I can't bear it any more, it'll be a sign. Come out, DI Bateson, please. *No, don't.* Let the trial go on and Mum be acquitted.

But he was there waiting for her.

'Looks like you're safe after all,' he said. 'Your mother's changed her mind. She's going back into court in a few minutes to change her plea to guilty.'

So then at last, Miranda knew what she had to do.

'All rise. All those having to do with the case of the Crown versus Kathryn Elizabeth Walters draw nigh and give your attendance. My lord Robert MacNair presiding.'

As the judge bowed and took his seat Sarah remained standing, her heart heavy as lead. Despite a further adjournment she had been unable to either change her client's mind, or alter her decision. Her very shocking decision. She was aware, somewhere behind her, of Will Churchill watching developments with delight.

'My lord, there has been a development. My client wishes to change her plea.'

'Very well, Mrs Newby. Change it how, exactly?'

'She wishes to enter a plea of guilty.'

Sarah sighed. She felt surprisingly weary and, unusually for her, close to tears. But she was angry, too. Nothing quite like this had happened to her before. Despite the difficulties she'd explained to Miranda, she had still hoped to win this case for her client. She understood the reasons for Kathryn's decision, but was convinced it was the wrong one. Especially now that Terry's discoveries had made her more certain than ever that Kathryn was innocent. But it was the client, not the lawyer, who decided on the plea.

'Indeed. Kathryn Walters, stand up please. I am advised that you now wish to plead guilty to the charge of murdering David Kidd. You understand what this means, do you? You have discussed it with your counsel?'

'I have, yes.' Kathryn stood in the dock, calm, pale, determined.

'If you plead guilty to murder, that is the end of this trial. All that remains is for me to pass sentence, and the only possible sentence for murder is one of life imprisonment, with or without a recommendation for how long that shall be. You understand that fully?'

'Yes, my lord.' Now that she had decided it seemed easy. All that had gone before seemed a waste of time.

'Very well. The clerk of the court will now put that charge to you.'

But before the clerk could speak Sarah noticed, to her surprise, that Matthew Clayton had risen to his feet. Throughout the last few minutes, Sarah had been dimly aware of an urgent whispered conversation between him and the CPS solicitor; now he apparently wished to interrupt proceedings.

'My Lord, if I might crave the court's indulgence for a moment?'

The judge turned to him in surprise. '*Now*, Mr Clayton?'

'Yes, my Lord. A significant legal matter has arisen which should, I feel, be addressed before the plea is put to the defendant. If I might request a further adjournment to digest this matter and ... a conference in chambers, my Lord?'

The judge turned to Sarah. 'Mrs Newby?'

Sarah stood, looking at her opponent curiously. She had been so occupied with Kathryn that for the past half hour that she had spoken to no one else except Terry, who she had met briefly in the corridor as she was preparing to go into court. Now she noticed that he, too, was standing at the back of the court near the entrance, with Kathryn's daughter Miranda beside him. Like Matthew Clayton, he was staring at her urgently as though willing her to agree.

She looked to her left, where Kathryn Walters stood trembling in the dock, ready to confess to a murder she had almost certainly not committed. Once she had formally entered a plea of guilty in this court she would be convicted, and only the Court of Appeal could overturn that conviction as unsafe, whatever new evidence came to light. And that was a process that might take years.

Sarah knew what her client wanted, but a few more moments of delay, however painful, could hardly be refused.

'I have no objection, my Lord.'

The comfortable judge's chambers, lined with leatherbound tomes and panelled with ancient oak, looked out across a roundabout by a small park near the river. The late morning sunlight sparkled from the early spring leaves on the trees. The judge sat at a long table with his back to this view, Sarah Newby and Matthew Clayton QC side by side facing him. Both looked stunned, shocked by the arguments they felt compelled to advance.

'My lord,' Clayton began. 'This is a highly unusual situation. I cannot recall one like it in all my time at the Bar. Nor, I believe, can Mrs Newby.'

'You intrigue me, Mr Clayton. What is it that puzzles you so?'

'This morning, my lord, as you know, Mrs Newby informed the court that Kathryn Walters wished to change her plea to guilty, a development that the prosecution would normally welcome. However, at the same time further evidence was brought to my attention which began to cast doubt on the validity of that plea, which was why I requested an adjournment. Since then I have had more time to look at this evidence, which in my opinion casts so much doubt on Mrs Walters' intended plea that it seems to me unsafe to continue with this prosecution.'

'Unsafe, Mr Clayton? You astound me.' Robert MacNair leaned back in his chair, long bony hands clasped under his chin. 'Explain yourself, please.'

'My lord, not to put too fine a point on it, there has been a confession. Mrs Walters' daughter, Miranda Ward, has made this written statement confessing to the murder. Her mother, she says, had nothing to do with it.' Matthew Clayton passed the statement that Miranda had given Terry across the desk - a detailed description of why, how and when she had murdered David Kidd. He and Sarah sat silent, each busy with their own thoughts, while the judge read slowly through it. He looked up, a faint smile on his lips.

'This exonerates your client, Mrs Newby.'

'If it is true, my lord, yes.'

The judge raised a quizzical eyebrow. 'You surely cannot mean to cast doubt on it? Evidence that will set your client free?'

Sarah sighed, and leaned forward earnestly. This was a truly terrible situation but she had to play the game out to the end. She had spent the last half hour trying, and failing, to convince Kathryn of the absurdity of her position. But since it *was* Kathryn's position, she had promised to argue it to the best of her ability.

'My lord, I find myself in an invidious situation. Mrs Walters is aware of this confession and the other evidence that supports it - Mr Clayton can apprise you of that - and she is very shocked by it indeed. She has already lost one daughter and stands to lose another, if this is true. She has asked me to tell the court that it is not true. Her daughter Miranda did *not* murder David Kidd, she says - she did it herself, in exactly the way the prosecution allege - or did allege until now. She wishes to plead guilty to that crime and is prepared to confess to it on oath, if necessary.'

'Mr Clayton?'

Briefly, Matthew Clayton recited the evidence of the airline tickets and the witnesses Terry had told him of when he produced the confession, while the judge shook his head in a surprise which, both lawyers suspected, contained a faint trace of hidden amusement. 'I see what you mean, Mr Clayton. This is an occasion wholly without precedent, in my experience, at least. You cannot really be asking this court to convict your client, Mrs Newby?'

'My lord, as her counsel I must represent her wishes.'

'Yes, but you are also an officer of this court, with a duty to assist in the search for truth.'

'Indeed, my lord. Clearly this new confession and the supporting evidence of the airline tickets and the witness who saw a younger woman with David Kidd are important evidence which I would call in Mrs Walters' defence, if those were my instructions. Unfortunately, they are not. She is adamant that she *did* kill Mr Kidd, and wishes me to point out that *her* hair, not her daughter's, was found at the scene of the crime. That is - or was - the key to the prosecution's case, after all. She believes her daughter felt pressure to confess out of a misplaced sense of loyalty to her mother. That is why she wishes to change her plea to guilty.'

'To protect her daughter?'

'To ensure that her daughter is not wrongly convicted of a crime which she, the mother, committed, my lord. That is her position now.'

'Well, well. She has a point, I suppose, Mr Clayton. If this new evidence is to be trusted, how do you account for the hair bobble found at the scene of the crime?'

'My lord, we seem to have switched roles here. You will recall that in her cross-examination of DCI Churchill, Mrs Newby did her best to persuade the jury that the hairs on that bobble were the result of deliberate contamination of the crime scene by the police. I have no opinion on the truth of that other than to say there is a doubt, I put it no higher than that. But without the DNA evidence from those hairs, I concur with Mrs Newby's arguments earlier in the week - the prosecution case fails. All the rest is circumstantial. So when we combine the doubt about those hairs with this startling new evidence of a confession, supported by eyewitness accounts and a return trip to America, deliberately concealed, I cannot in all conscience allow this prosecution to go forward.'

'Even when the defendant intends to plead guilty?'

'Even then, my lord. In the interests of justice, this must be stopped.'

Lord Justice MacNair thought for a moment, cracking his long bony knuckles under his chin. Then he smiled. 'Very well, I agree. Mrs Newby, if you will call your client into the dock, I will deliver the apparently unwelcome news that the charges against her have been dropped, and she is now free to go.'

58. Riverside Talk

THEY MET, as so often, on the riverside walk. It was quiet here, and private; they could stroll along, watching the birds and boats on the river, stepping aside for joggers and cyclists as they passed with a quiet nod of thanks. Such meetings had an indeterminate feel to them; they could walk for miles if they chose, south out of the city past the A64 to the fields opposite the Archbishop's palace; or they could go nowhere, just sit on a bench and watch the sunlight flicker through the leaves of the ancient alders and horse chestnuts.

Both were still bruised by the case, Terry perhaps the most, for he had Churchill's fury to cope with at work, and the man had been understandably enraged at the way the case had ended: Kathryn set free, weeping, her daughter Miranda arrested, reporters crowding round with their cameras and microphones and tapes while DCI Churchill stormed away to his car. It had been a two day wonder in the news - two days of horror for Churchill, his hopes of promotion gone; two days of savage schadenfreude for Terry, his boss publicly humiliated, unanswered questions buzzing around the station about how the hair bobble had got there, and when the charge of fabricating evidence would be brought. Never, was Terry's guess, though time would tell. Churchill was too well connected, too good a politician for that; and the powers above, those he so longed to join, were too skilled in ambiguity, maintaining the reputation of the service by washing their dirty linen in private, or not at all. Churchill would stay, but he was wounded, and like a bear tied to a stake he saw tormentors everywhere, and was prepared to lash out again.

Particularly if he could damage Terry or Sarah.

In the intervals of fending off Churchill and dealing with Miranda's arrest, Terry had phoned Sarah several times without success. Either she was refusing his calls or too busy, he wasn't sure which. When he'd finally got through, her voice had been cool and businesslike; no hint of shared triumph or sympathy. She'll have had Kathryn's grief to deal with, Terry thought; perhaps this case has damaged us all. But she'd agreed to meet, and here they were at last, strolling uneasily together. Her face was tired and closed, her manner brusque and bitter. But they both needed to understand.

'You really didn't suspect her before?' she asked, stepping aside for a cyclist.

'Only when Larry rang from the States,' he replied cautiously, kicking a stick into the river. 'Until then I thought her alibi was watertight. A lowlife like Kidd - it made sense he'd have dozens of enemies. I just couldn't find them. I was off the case, remember - I had plenty of other matters to deal with.'

'Don't make excuses, Terry, it doesn't suit you.'

He looked at her - a slim dark woman with hazel eyes, staring at him coolly, her hands thrust deep into the pockets of her coat.

'We destroyed that family between us, you realise that.'

They'd stopped walking, stood facing each other on the path, theleaves of a huge horse chestnut tree rustling above. Terry threw a stone into the river, watched the ripples rush away downstream.

'*I* did, you mean. I bungled the investigation into Kidd. Missed crucial evidence. *You* didn't do anything wrong.'

'I could have ridden that psychiatrist harder. If it wasn't for him ...' She paused, glanced at Terry in surprise. '*What* crucial evidence, Terry? The shopkeeper, you mean?'

'Not him, no. It's worse than that.' He looked at her, wondering how to say this. All this time he'd blamed his boss, Will Churchill, for David Kidd's acquittal and the dreadful consequences which had followed it. But it wasn't as simple as that, after all. Life never was. 'I found out something yesterday which, if we'd only known it at the time, would have saved all of this. Every bit of this tragedy.'

'What? Terry, tell me.'

He drew a deep breath. If only I could go back and put this right, he thought. It would have changed things from the beginning. 'You remember the roofies?'

'The rohypnol, you mean. Which Kathryn was supposed to have given David Kidd?'

'Yes. Well, he *was* drugged with it, the post mortem established that. Only it wasn't Kathryn who slipped them in his beer, it was Miranda, and here's the thing: she didn't get them from her Mum's pharmacy, as Churchill tried to make out.'

'From where, then?'

'From David Kidd's flat. That's what she told me yesterday, when she went through her confession in more detail.' They resumed walking slowly downstream, and Terry told her the story of how and why Miranda went to David's flat where he'd drugged and raped her just as he'd done to her sister. 'Only when she woke up, she found them at the bottom of the sugar jar, and took them away.' He shook his head bitterly. 'The sugar jar, of all the obvious, simple places. The first place every junkie thinks to hide his pills. And that was *my* investigation. I searched that flat, and never thought to look.'

Sarah was silent for a minute, stepping carefully around a cluster of crocuses. 'There was no sign of rohypnol in Shelley's blood, was there?'

'No. Not according to the pathologist, Tuchman. But he's an old man, you know ...'

'He missed it, you mean? If so, he ought to retire.'

'Yes. Could be. Anyway, that may explain it but it's not much of an excuse. I mean, all along we were wondering how Kidd persuaded Shelley to make love to him and get into that bath, when the only reason she was in his flat was to dump him for good and pick up her stuff. If only I'd found those pills as I should, I'd have taken them to Tuchman, he'd have checked, and everything would have been clear. She couldn't possibly have killed herself, she was too doped to know what was going on. Instead, her sister finds them, and look what's happened to her now. It's my job to charge her with murder, for Christ's sake!'

He found another stick and flung it as far as he could, out into the muddy swirling water, then stood and watched it borne swiftly away to the sea.

If he'd been expecting sympathy from Sarah he was disappointed. 'You should have seen her mother, Terry.' Sarah strolled to a little paved observation area above an old watergate. She turned and leaned with her back to the railing, the collar of her coat turned up against the fresh spring breeze. 'The woman was devastated. She's lost both daughters now.'

'I know.' Terry leaned on the railing beside her, looking out across the river. 'Miranda talked about that, too. How her mother meant to sacrifice herself. But in the end she couldn't let it happen, she said. *What sort of daughter would I be, letting my mother go to prison, for a crime I committed myself?'*

'I might have got the mother off,' Sarah said. 'There was still a chance. Not a big one. But with Churchill planting those hairs ...'

'If he did.'

'What?'

Terry shook his head grimly. 'That's another thing. Miranda admits she wears her mother's clothes sometimes. Like when she went to the woods a few days before, to check things out and loosen the fence, she was wearing her mum's wax jacket. She might have dropped something then.'

'So your boss might even be innocent?' Their eyes met, Sarah's shocked and angry. 'Christ, Terry! After all the things I said about him! Do you believe that?'

'Not really. But it adds a doubt.'

'My God!' She pushed herself away from the railing, and walked away along the path. 'What a murky world we work in.'

'Murky?'

'Mucky. Foul. Confused. One stupid mistake by you and all this happens.'

For a while they walked on in silence. The vehemence in her tone surprised him, and yet the pain, he thought, was deserved. Most of it anyway. After a while she stopped and turned towards him.

'I trusted you, Terry, damn it! After you saved Simon last time I thought you'd get everything right. I should have known better.'

'I'm not superman, you know.' As he stared into those intense, hazel eyes, Terry wondered if he saw the hint of tears? Surely not. She wasn't the type. And yet ...

'Clearly not. Very far from it, in fact. It's just that sometimes, Terry ...'

'What?'

'I could wish that you - that any man, really - but if it isn't Bob any more then you would have done ... I'm sorry, I'm not making sense.' She walked briskly off the path to the riverbank and stood hunched for a moment, staring at the muddy water. Then she turned and came back. 'Look, what I'm trying to say is, just like you I spend my life dealing with human inadequacy. Clients who lie, cheat, get smashed out of their heads and beat their wives and children. Policemen who lie on oath, plant drugs in kids' pockets and even rise to high rank, like your boss, whether he did it this time or not. And I try to stand up against this on my own, making sure that what I do in this sink of swirling iniquity is somehow straight and honest, while all around me people are casually wrecking each other's lives and lying through their teeth. I'm used to it, but just sometimes, Terry, I think it would be nice to meet someone as competent and reliable as ... as I try to be, anyway. And just for a moment - a moment back there - I thought that might be you.' She smiled and shook her head bitterly. 'Stupid of me, I know. It doesn't work like that.'

She turned and began to walk away down river, her hands thrust deep into the pockets of her long coat. Terry ran after her, turned her to face him.

'That was ... your idea of a compliment, was it?'

'No it wasn't. It was the opposite. We're part of the system, Terry, we make mistakes, we get things wrong, we wreck people's lives. The criminal justice system. It chews people up and spits them out in small bits.'

Terry nodded. He took his hand off her shoulder and for a while they walked side by side.

'It's not just you,' she said, relenting. 'It's me too, I should have asked more questions before I agreed to prosecute Kidd in the first place. I should have been tougher on the psychiatrist. That sodding pathologist Tuchman should have done his job. And as for Will Churchill ... well, that man should be put down.'

Terry laughed. 'He will be, one day. If he doesn't do for us first.' They walked slowly on. 'What this adds up to,' he said at last. 'Is that we should do better.'

'Exactly,' she said passionately. 'Much, much better - always and all the time. That's it, Terry - that's what these two cases have made me think. Justice means getting it right - or else why are we here?'

'All right,' he said wryly. 'If a lawyer can talk like that, the world must be changing. Where you boldly go, I'll follow. Stumbling with feet of clay.'

She smiled, the tension partly released. 'All right, I know it sounds pompous, but that doesn't stop it being true, for all that. You do that for me, will you? Get it right, let me believe in justice, for a change.'

'I know it exists,' said Terry. 'We just don't see enough of it, that's all.'

'Next time, we'd better look harder.'

They turned back towards town, strolling through the dappled sunlight under the trees. When they passed under Skeldergate bridge they stood for a moment, a man and a woman quietly talking. Behind them, the elegant stone buildings of the city's Crown Court. In front, the muddy swirling river rushing swiftly to the sea.

Companions, but still apart.

Printed in Great Britain
by Amazon